sharp and dangerous virtues

sharp and dangerous virtues

A NOVEL

martha moody

SWALLOW PRESS
Ohio University Press, Athens, Ohio

Swallow Press
An imprint of Ohio University Press, Athens, Ohio 45701
www.ohioswallow.com

Printed in the United States of America
Swallow Press / Ohio University Press books are printed on
acid-free paper ⊗ ™

20 19 18 17 16 15 14 13 12   5 4 3 2 1

Library of Congress Cataloging-in-Publication Data
Moody, Martha.
 Sharp and dangerous virtues : a novel / Martha Moody.
    p. cm.
 ISBN 978-0-8040-1141-9 (hc : alk. paper) — ISBN 978-0-8040-4051-8
(electronic)
1. Food supply—Government policy—Fiction. 2. United States—Foreign
relations—Fiction. 3. Dayton (Ohio)—Fiction. I. Title.
 PS3563.O553S53 2012
 813'.54—dc23
                               2012016940

For my sons

contents

2047

2048

2071

a family and a place

HOWARD, AGE TEN, was doing a report on America's two great-est natural wonders, the Heartland Grid and the Grand Canyon.

"The Heartland Grid's not natural, son," Chad said.

Howard gave his father an incredulous look. "It's *plants*," he said. "It's how America feeds the world."

North of Dayton, Ohio, where Chad and Sharis ("It rhymes with Paris," she said) Gribble and their sons, Howard and Leon, lived, there was a polymer fence close to twenty feet high, a fence that went *forever*, surrounding a dedicated ag-ricultural area of over fifty thousand square miles. The Grid was roughly the shape of a nine-by-twelve casserole. Inten-tional villages dotted its landscape, roads crisscrossing it at ten-mile intervals.

"We never fed the world," Chad said. "We feed ourselves."

"I have pictures of the Grid," Howard said, undeterred. "Miss Bishop says her father went there. He was driving a truck and he picked up lettuces. Only one time, but he got to eat there. He said they had delicious coleslaw."

"I'm sure all their food's delicious. It couldn't be fresher."

"They won't let you spend the night. They say they have too much work."

Chad gave a noncommittal grunt. He didn't believe that too-much-work line, not for one minute. He said, "The Gridians have always been clannish."

Howard shot Chad a questioning look. "They stick together," Chad said. "They live in special towns the government built for them. They don't have visitors or talk with other people. They don't even mo-com with people who aren't them." He searched his mind for an example. "Kind of like the Johnsons"—their next-door neighbors, an older couple with a grown son.

"They're gone," Howard said.

"What do you mean they're gone?"

"The Johnsons moved out. Their house is empty. There's furniture in there, but no car, and no more Johnsons! The Gilberts are gone, too." Neighbors down the hill. "Atunde told me and Leon they were leaving. His mom said Atunde wasn't supposed to tell anyone, but he knew we'd come by wanting to play."

"When did this happen?"

"I don't know. A few days ago. The Johnsons went first."

Good Lord, Chad thought. He had heard of people leaving the city itself, but not suburban neighborhoods like theirs. He felt ill. He thought of the party at their neighbors George and Gentia's a few weeks before. George had said they were sniggering idiots to stay, and Sharis, Chad's own wife, had spoken up to say she wasn't going to teach her kids to flee. "Dayton is our home, and we're staying," she had said.

"Have they told you much about the war in school?" Chad asked Howard now.

Howard looked confused. "You mean the trouble up north? Miss Bishop says it's really far away."

Chad had had, between the ages of about six and nine, a terrible fear of earthworms, not of the worms themselves but what they did. He imagined them writhing and burrowing underground, riddling the soil with tiny tunnels. A footstep in the wrong place might end up with Chad swallowed by the earth. His relatives would never know what happened.

"I mean the conflict. I mean . . ." Chad was filled with the prickling dread he used to feel when he was sent into his yard to fetch the paper. Parks and the schoolyard were okay—every square inch had been tested—but how could Chad trust his own lawn? "Want me to draw it for you?"

"Sure!"

"Good," Chad said, relieved. Calm them both down. "Where's Leon? Leon should hear this." Leon was seven and had a personality as spiky as his hair. "What do you mean put my head on my pillow? I put my feet on my pillow!" And that was indeed how Leon slept.

"Leon!" Howard screamed. "Daddy wants you!"

Chad went to the kitchen desk drawer for a piece of paper and an old-fashioned pencil. "What's up, Daddy-o?" said Leon. He lit up when he saw the paper and pencil in Chad's hand.

Chad sat down at the big blue kitchen table and pulled out chairs for Howard on one side and Leon on the other. He drew a rounded rectangle wider than it was tall and decorated with appendages—Florida, Maine, Texas. "Okay," he said. "So here we are"—he put an X denoting Dayton below the protuberance that was Michigan (the one entity he'd drawn accurately, he thought, because it looked like a mitten.) "And this whole country, all the U.S., used to be rich and happy and basically the center of the world." To the right of his map, Chad drew a stick figure with a big head and smiling face. Not enough. He put a crown on top.

Chad's father had been an upright, even boring, man, an auditor for American National Bank. But every morning before he went to work he waited with Chad and his brother at the school bus stop and a weird merriment exuded from him. It was only then that Chad's father used The Voice.

"Oh, oh, you boys you are zee terror."

Or: "Your boos driver, she look like a beeg potato."

What Chad remembered most fondly of his father was The Voice. Chad hoped his own boys remembered him by his drawings.

"So that was then," Chad said, waving at the stick man with the crown. "But then the U.S. got into wars, and then the economy went bad, and then the weather got all crazy—for example, you didn't have hurricanes come inland like we do now—and there were new pests that ate crops, and before you knew it, it was the Short Times." He drew an arrow from the figure with the crown to another figure below it, this one slumped and mournful. He sprinkled some tears down the page and put an upside-down crown at the figure's feet. Howard and Leon laughed in delight.

Chad felt a pang at making jokes about these things. "But it was really bad, the Short Times," he said. "It went on for years. People didn't have enough food, and they got tickets for gas and electricity, and the health system got overwhelmed, and . . . Up in what used to be your mom's old town there was an outbreak of rabies. You know about rabies?" Leon shook his head. "It's a disease," Chad said.

"From raccoons?" Howard asked, sounding pleased.

"Exactly." To brighten the mood Chad started drawing a raccoon. "People were looking in the dump for food, and the raccoons that lived there bit them."

Leon said, "That looks like a cat."

"I made the legs too long."

"Give him big teeth for biting."

Chad did. Leon giggled.

"But it wasn't funny, really," Chad said. "It was terrible. I mean, I was a kid and I wasn't worried, it was normal life, and then my parents died." He immediately regretted mentioning this, but Leon seemed unperturbed.

"From raccoons?" Howard asked, his voice anxious.

"No, not from *raccoons*," Chad said. "From pneumonia. Infections in their lungs. Don't worry, that wouldn't happen now. We have better antibiotics."

Chad's father, in fact, had died over thirteen years before, in February, two months before the announcement of the Grid. Chad's mother died a month later. They were both fifty-four. People died then, during the Short Times. Doctors saw diseases they'd only read about: tuberculosis, measles, cholera. For people with only National Health Care, like Chad's parents, there were shortages of antibiotics. Chad felt a certain gratitude for the timing of his parents' deaths. Most people who'd had friends and relatives die during the Short Times found comfort in their loved ones' unknowing. A death before the Grid was an innocent death.

"At any rate, it was bad," Chad said, putting a big X over the raccoon. "People were desperate. This was the early thirties, and there were all sorts of ideas about how to get more food— that's when people stopped eating meat, for one thing—and then the government destroyed a couple towns in Oregon"— he went back to his map of the U.S., drew a star near the left upper corner—"to set up this enormous farm and, well, that farm was terrifically productive, so the government looked for place to make a humongous farm."

"And we have the best land right here in Ohio!" Howard cried. Chad wondered if he'd heard this from Miss Bishop.

"Can I go?" Leon said. "This is not what I'd call interesting."

"No, Leon, you should hear this." Chad turned to Howard. "Yes, Ohio has great land, flat and fertile and all that, but also this part of the country . . . The towns were dying and a lot of the land was owned by foreign companies, and the U.S. wanted to kick them out." He drew a quick stick finger with one leg up, kicking. "See, Leon? See the man kicking? At any rate, parts of Ohio and Indiana and Illinois were what they picked for the big farm. And a little bit of Michigan." Chad shaded the area. "So they moved all the people out of the towns, and the air force came in with these new disappearance bombs, bombs that basically turned things into dust . . ."

"What kind of things?" Leon asked. "People?"

"No, not people."

"Raccoons?"

"No, Leon, nothing living, bombs that turned buildings into dust, okay? Just buildings. At any rate, then the government brought in soil people and irrigation people and road people and they built the Grid. A little over a year later we had food. It was amazing, really. You had to admire the technology." He drew another stick figure, this one beaming. "That's the woman who was president then. Brandee Cooper from Colorado, woman of action." He added some hair.

"Char," Howard said, using the latest complimentary term. Leon had lost interest. He had scooted his chair back and was bent over picking at a scab on his knee.

"Your mother was from a town up there," Chad said. "Where the Grid is now. She grew up in one of the towns that was destroyed. They don't say destroyed, they say reclaimed."

"Is that why she doesn't have parents?"

"Everyone has parents," Chad said. "Even clones have parents. Well, at least one parent. But yes, that's why your mom doesn't have parents. They died during the Gridding. They weren't killed, nothing like that." He glanced quickly at Leon, the boy still engrossed in his injury: he had managed to free all but the very central portion of his scab. "It was their choice," Chad said firmly, as if there were no reason to question it. He didn't want Howard asking more questions. Sharis, years before, had said they should never tell the boys. "And, okay, so now we're now and the Grid is great, it works, we eat, so everybody wants it." Under the map, Chad drew a circle and divided it with several diagonals. "That's a pie, see? The rest of the world wants a piece of that pie. Because they have their own Short Times now."

Leon briefly examined the scab sitting on his finger, then popped it in his mouth. Chad decided to ignore this.

Howard said, "Atunde said the rest of the world is against us."

"Not the whole world. Mexico's on our side. And lots of countries are neutral. Europe, China, Australia. Look." Chad turned the paper over and drew a big circle. He made some shapes for North and South America on the left and Europe and Africa on the right, letting Asia and Australia disappear over the globe's right edge. These places are against us." He made big scowling faces out of South America and Africa. "They call themselves the Alliance."

"Bye," Leon said, jumping from his chair and heading out the back door.

The previous week, Chad and Sharis had attended a party at their neighbors'. People had been drinking and there was lots of loud conversation.

—For graduation! Sending them to Alabama for graduation! Like it's just a trip.

—And normally she's very organized, but after her office closed she . . .

—And the Calmadol! Ten doses a day at least, and now that you can't get it on your health card, he . . ."

Sharis's voice, in Chad's mind, had been the only clear one. "I'm not going to teach my kids to flee. Dayton is our home and we're staying."

—You should hear our neighbor who's in air force intelligence. There's a lot of dissention in the Alliance we don't hear about. He says the Africans hate the Suds.

—You want to be ruled by fear? Wumba Bumba to that African music!

"They aren't *Africans*," Sharis had said. "They're regular Americans."

Walking home with Chad, Sharis had spoken again about the Melano custodian in the church in downtown Dayton where she'd stayed the night after the Gridding. "Are you the light man?" she'd asked, and she saw again the worried concern on his face.

The door slammed behind Leon. Chad tried not to wince. "And then," Chad said to Howard, "and this really, *really* upset people, Canada went against us. Canada, our neighbor to the north. "Here's us"—Chad made a rough rectangle—"and here's Canada." He filled this in with angry crosshatches. "So that's how the Alliance can get into Cleveland and threaten to capture the Grid. There's Lake Erie up here"—this part of the drawing was getting crowded, so Chad did no more than tap the area—"and Cleveland's on the south side of the lake and Canada is right across the water. So it's handy for the Alliance to have Canada helping them. You know if our enemies got the Grid it would really change things." Chad hesitated. "People can't believe it about Canada," he said.

Now Howard was looking bored, so Chad sketched another animal to the right of the globe.

"Is that a cow?" Howard said.

"No, no, no," Chad said. He added a stick figure in a big hat to the back of his animal. "That's a Canadian Mountie. A policeman on a horse. When I was a kid, my favorite movie was about Mounties."

"Okay." Howard bent over and pulled on his shoes, his broad back and wide buttocks facing Chad. Howard's weight was a comfort to Chad: it would take Howard a long time to starve.

"The Alliance won't capture the Grid, though, don't worry," Chad said. "It's really well defended. Bristling with missiles." To the left of the globe, Chad drew some fat arrows pointing upward. He considered these a moment, then found himself doodling wiggly curls all over the paper. What in the world was he drawing? Worms.

Howard stood. "I'm going outside now? I've got to help Leon with his fort." Leon was the brother with ideas. He was also way too skinny.

"Sure." Chad crumpled the paper. "You'll need to pick something else, though. As a natural wonder. There's a reason they call the Grid communities *intentional* villages. Because the Grid's not . . . "

"I'll ask Miss Bishop," Howard said, disappearing out the door.

tuuro and the boy

AT WESTMINSTER PRESBYTERIAN, the church in downtown Dayton where Tuuro worked, the new (five years) pastor liked to call him Our Director, using a hearty, booming voice that made Tuuro squirm inside. Tuuro was in maintenance. Aunt Stella, not Tuuro's real relative but his godmother or whatever she was, liked to say people could have all the automation and lifestyle control they wanted, but somebody had to sweep the floors. Tuuro swept the floors. He liked his job, the piles of crumbs and lint and plastic children's rings and bits of straw (straw! where did that come from?) he accumulated at the end of a Sunday. The detritus of the world consoled him with its humble dailiness, and Tuuro enjoyed disposing of it handily, lifting a burden and tossing it away. Once he wrote a ditty about it:

> The dust is flying in the air
> the lint is going too.
> If you think clean is Godly I
> sure have the church for you.

Irreverent, really. Maybe slightly hostile. Not a poem he would have recited to the pastor. Tuuro knew what he could say to people or not. He had a daughter, Lanita, who lived with her mother outside Chattanooga. Tuuro had lived with Lanita's mother, Naomi, for almost seven years, and the relationship had split up, not, Tuuro had come to realize, over his lack of ambition, as Naomi had told him at the time, but because of the way Naomi had come to picture Tuuro. He knew how he looked: tall, darker than mahogany, dignified, with a face something like a cat's, high cheekbones and alert eyes. On the street mothers jabbed their daughters to take a look. But the Tuuro Naomi saw looked nothing like this man: her Tuuro was smaller, and he was cringing. He looked to Naomi, Tuuro realized, the way he looked to himself.

Not that he wasn't a good man, as Naomi liked to say, but Naomi wanted something more. No, she wanted something *other:* lust, scenes in front of the neighbors, a man who would twist her against the wall and say, Shut up, woman. She found that man. She and the wild man fled Ohio, landing in Chattanooga when a wire burned out in their car. Then something happened, Tuuro was never clear what. The original wild man was now in prison, and a new, slightly less wild man lived with Naomi. Tuuro was under no obligation to do so—the court had sided with him—but he deposited money in Naomi's account monthly to help cover Lanita's expenses. He lived for the rare days he saw his daughter. She was six.

"Can't she stay with me when you're back in Ohio?"

Naomi's sigh seared through the phone. Naomi was coming to visit her sister in Columbus.

"I send you money every month, Naomi," Tuuro said. "What more do you want?"

"Oh, I know, Tuuro. You're so *good.*"

Tuuro bit his lip. "Why can't Lanita stay here with me while you're at your sister's?"

"Is it safe?"

"Of course it's safe. It's fine here. It's normal." Safer than Columbus, he was thinking. The quickest way from Dayton to Columbus was driving through the Grid, on one of the walled-off interstates.

"It is not normal."

"Naomi. Cleveland is far away."

Naomi gave another heavy sigh. "All right, she can stay with you. I'll bring her by Thursday late and pick her up Sunday. But don't you be feeding her a lot of sweets. I've got her off sweets."

"Did the sweets hurt her? Is she fat?"

"Sweets always hurt," Naomi said. "Always. Nothing hurts like sweets."

"WHAT DO YOU want for breakfast? Cereal? Eggs?" Tuuro's apartment was the entire second story of a small frame house. His kitchen and living room stretched across the back, and the two bedrooms took up the front. His landlady lived downstairs. The house was two houses away from the house in which Paul Laurence Dunbar, the great African American (although people didn't use that term now; the preferred word now was Melano) poet, had been born. The Dunbar house was a historical site that had never gotten much traffic, and since the Short Times its windows had been boarded up and its grass rarely mowed.

Lanita, Tuuro's daughter, sat in an old wooden chair at the kitchen table, her feet swinging. Tuuro had sweet rolls in the breadbox, but thinking of Naomi he didn't dare offer them.

"I want an egg that's scrambled."

It took Tuuro a moment of rummaging in his refrigerator to realize he had no butter. "I can't cook that, Muffin. I don't have the butter to cook it in."

Lanita regarded him solemnly, and he saw her mother's contempt in the wrinkling of her forehead.

"I'm disappointing you," he said. She didn't deny it. "How about a three-minute egg?" Tuuro asked, inspired. "You don't need butter for that."

"A three-*minute* egg?" Her voice was skeptical.

"You boil it three minutes. It's good. You'll see."

Maybe six minutes later the egg was on her plate, chopped up and runny, and Lanita was eating it with a large spoon, eyes down and face serious, concentrating on every drip, and Tuuro, watching her, felt not swept, not washed, but swamped with love for her, so sloshily heavy he could barely stand.

She pushed the empty plate away and looked up with her luminous eyes. "Another one."

She ate three, one by one, which Tuuro told her was nine-minute eggs, and when he picked her plate up from beside the sink he almost asked her, "Did you wash this?" before he realized the plate had been truly licked clean.

"You liked it," he said. "You liked what I made for you." The gratitude in his voice almost embarrassed him. To cover himself he made one of his silly rhymes:

> *Three-minute eggs*
> *Three-minute eggs*
> *My baby begs*
> *For three-minute eggs*

"Nine-minute eggs!" Lanita complained, smiling. She came over to him and wrapped her arms around his waist, and then she stood beside him, hand hanging on the back of his belt, a silent companion as he washed the dishes.

AND THEN LANITA was gone, back to Chattanooga, and the pastor was standing behind the desk in his office saying, "Tuuro, how are you?" and stretching out his hand. Tuuro reached out warily to shake it. Once the pastor's hand had held a tiny pillow that made a fart, once a device that snapped Tuuro's fingers, once a live toad. The pastor didn't play these tricks on his parishioners. "Don't worry," the pastor chuckled now. "Vera cut off my access to the Magic Source."

"Good," Tuuro said—a remark as close to rebellion as he dared go.

The pastor waved Tuuro to a chair, then sat behind his desk and absentmindedly tugged at his ear. "Tell me, did you have any bread left over from the Palm Sunday potluck?"

It was almost July, and Palm Sunday had been in April. Did the pastor think Tuuro's memory was that good? It had been a cold spring, with several late snows. The weather experiments of the early thirties had, as an unexpected side effect, resulted in "old"-style winters and hot summers: it often snowed by Thanksgiving. "If I did I fed it to the birds."

"That's Christian, I suppose. Our brethren birds. How about after the Easter reception? Tequila Huntington said there was a whole sponge cake and half a loaf of lemon bread in the cupboard by the fridge."

Maybe it was his race, or his temperament, or some forgotten trauma of his childhood, but Tuuro was always steeling himself for news of what he had done wrong. It made him cringe to think of himself cringing, but there it was. And he did do things wrong, didn't he? He wasn't perfect, although there were moments, turning to inspect the Sunday school classrooms before he flicked off the light, he felt he was. "Are you the janitor did the bathrooms?" someone would ask, and Tuuro would freeze, wondering what he had missed. "That's the cleanest bathroom I ever seen!" the person might say, and Tuuro would be flooded with gratitude and relief and, yes, surprise; his face would light up in what he knew was a rewarding way. He got hundreds of compliments. He was a kind and conscientious man and he did his work well. But he could never quite believe that people would praise him and not find the fault.

So when someone found a fault, Tuuro accepted it. Hearing his mistakes was almost a relief. "I didn't see any extra food at Easter," he said now. "Maybe I should have."

"There are some things missing," The pastor said. "A sterling silver plate, and Jip Cooper brought a cut-glass server."

Tuuro shook his head. "I'd remember those, I think. I'm pretty sure I didn't . . ."

"Well, that's too bad. No one hanging around that night? No intrusive interlopers?"

The pastor used phrases like that in sermons: fair-weather Philistines; complacent Christians; reductive religionists. He would never dream that Tuuro, listening from his station in the supply room behind the pulpit, would think of them as vacant phrases. "No," Tuuro said.

"Too bad." The pastor waved his dismissal and Tuuro was already to the door when the next question came: "Have you checked the narthex lately?"

The narthex was the anteroom at the back of the sanctuary where people stood and gathered before and after the service. Tuuro remembered starting this job and not knowing what a narthex was. Now his chest tightened and his tongue felt too big for his mouth: what else had he done wrong? "I cleaned it Sunday after services."

"All of it? I was in there to pick up some hymnals for the Chorale Society, and I noticed some brownish streaks on the cupboard beside the front door. Low down. Isn't that strange, I thought, Tuuro doesn't usually miss things. See? You have us spoiled."

In the narthex the late afternoon sunlight patched the hot and humid air with pinks and greens. The narthex was separated by a wall of stained glass from the sanctuary. At one end of the narthex, where Tuuro entered, a hall led to the church classrooms, social hall, and offices. Once upon a time, the whole sanctuary/narthex complex was air-conditioned all week, but those days of excess were long gone. Now the only steady air-conditioning was in the pastor's office. Tuuro opened the big front doors to get some air, glancing at the lower cabinets as he passed them. Brown streaks. The pastor was right.

Tuuro flipped the overhead light on in the narthex and walked down the side aisle of the sanctuary to the maintenance closet, where he filled his wheeled bucket with water and soap and rags. "Fastidious boy," his Aunt Stella used to call him.

Back in the narthex, Tuuro squatted. A whole wall of oak cupboards flanked the front door, their shelves filled with hymnals and prayer books, a ledge separating the cupboards into lower and upper sections. The hymnals kept in the bottom cupboards were the old ones, rarely used. And it was on the doors of these cupboards, inches from the floor and running horizontally, that Tuuro examined the series of brown streaks. He swiped at one with a wet rag. Naomi, his ex, had had terrible periods, dripping out of her and onto the bathroom floor. The reddish brown on Tuuro's rag looked familiar. Blood.

Not dripped, as if it had spilled from someone. Not beside a doorknob as if someone had scraped a hand. But low on a cupboard, a thing a person shouldn't brush against at that level. And going on for inches, no feet, maybe three feet, as if a bloody something had been dragged alongside the wood, although there were (Tuuro checked now) no spots of blood on the floor.

Tuuro stood and shut the big front doors.

Tuuro knew what he expected when he opened the cupboard. So much violence since the Gridding, so many refugees, people stripped from their surroundings and turned casteless and angry, unfettered by grandmothers and neighborhood policemen and people who knew their names. The troublemakers were largely young males. The other day a woman's body had been found wedged behind a door at the public library. Instinctively, Tuuro pinched his nostrils as he opened the cupboard door.

It was a boy. A small Melano boy, not more than five years old, curled up in the cupboard facing out as if he were simply hiding, his nappy head tucked down to his chest. Tuuro touched his shoulder, cold and stiff. He wrapped his arms around the small chest and unwedged the body from the cupboard, slipped it on its side onto the floor. The boy's face had a pleading, confused look. Tuuro felt for a second as if he were looking at himself.

Tuuro's clearest memory of his mother was her shoes. A blue pair with suede appliquéd sea-stars, an olive-green pair with seams stitched in a yellow zigzag. His mother liked to scoop Tuuro up so his legs dangled. A lilac smell. After she was shot by the man Tuuro called Uncle, Tuuro was raised not by his father (no one was raised by a father) but by his great-aunt and his grandmother Tati, who lived together in a welfare apartment that was actually Tati's, where Tuuro had to scoop his toys and himself under the bed when the caseworker arrived, because children were not allowed. The great-aunt had an ex-sister-in-law Tuuro was told to call Aunt Stella, who lived in an apartment down the hall. "To whence are you headed, little man?" she might ask. "To whom are you carrying that candy?" A stickler for grammar. She had what Tuuro later learned was an erect carriage: she always stood high with her neck extended, like an African queen, like a Zulu, she said. Tuuro could be Zulu, she liked to point out, that height and those high, wide cheekbones and almond-shaped eyes. Really, a remarkable-looking people.

People who adopted Melano boys got subsidies from the state of Ohio, because people didn't want to adopt Melano boys. "That adopting you should require a bribery is a tragedy and a crime," Aunt Stella said. "I couldn't be sure which it is more." But she and Tuuro would live better if she adopted him. They could leave this ill-kempt building with its slovenly occupants and rent a house with a yard and honeysuckles edging the back fence. A back door as well as a front one, three steps up from the yard to the kitchen. They would be a family. Tuuro could call her Mom. Would he mind calling her Mom? Or would that be sad for him?

"I could call you Mom," Tuuro said.

In his dream of how it was, she indeed adopted him. They moved to their little house in Englewood. Tuuro went to a good school and wore a uniform; when he got off the bus each afternoon, Aunt Stella was waiting by the fire hydrant. They had a dog. They barbequed in summer. Tuuro spoke correctly. No one stomped on anybody's heart.

It had been, in its way, a terrible childhood, not because he was unwanted but because after his mother's death he was wanted too much, by three aging, angry women who each had their own purposes and plans. Tuuro remembered sitting on the brown plaid couch at Tati's, eyes darting from face to face as he tried to figure out what they wanted, to whom he should acquiesce, to whom he should say "to whom." Now Tuuro saw in the dead boy's face the same confused pain that he had felt, and all Tuuro wanted was to make it end.

He picked up the body and carried it to his supply closet behind the pulpit, which no person but Tuuro ever entered, cleared a space on the bench against the wall there, and set the boy down. He could not get the boy uncurled. There was a wound in the left chest, a complicated thing with congealed blood mixed with torn fabric, an area he would have to clean, Tuuro knew, but for now something he chose to ignore. There was a streak of dried blood coming out of the right ear. Tuuro turned the light off in the supply closet, stood outside it praying the Lord's Prayer for himself more than the boy, then closed and locked the door.

He took a ten-minute bus ride home. He left his apartment to return to the church with a duffel bag full of supplies, remembering even the hat to cover the wounded ear.

He took off the boy's clothes and, starting with his face, washed him with a washcloth scented with cologne, cleaning off every part of him, even the bits of blood next to his wounds—which must be knife wounds—in his chest. As he worked he dried the boy with his fluffiest towel. Under the boy's blue shorts there was a surprise, dried stains on his white underpants, urine and stool and blood, which wasn't right, which hurt Tuuro in his soul. He said the Lord's Prayer again, left the body on the bench, the towel carefully draped over it, locked the door, and took a bus to K-Bob's East to buy clean underpants, carrying the soiled underwear in a paper bag that he dumped in a bin outside the store. He bought the best children's underwear they had, boxer shorts in red silk with a black waistband. He returned to the church, finished his washing, oiled the body especially over the knees and elbows, where the skin was ashy, dressed the boy in the boxer shorts, and wrapped him in a red-and-green-and-black scarf Naomi had once given him for Christmas. Tuuro then shut the door to the closet again and walked to the social hall to get wood for the coffin.

Tuuro went through the planks of wood stored at the back of the stage. No one would miss a few boards. It was evening now, but still light out, and Tuuro checked the parking lot through the window to be sure the pastor's car was gone. Making a coffin would involve banging. Tuuro knew his boss's habits: unless there was a committee meeting—unlikely in the summer—the pastor would not be back during the evening.

By the time the boy was nestled on his side in his coffin, his lips over his broad white teeth oiled, a drop of cologne placed in the indentation below his nostrils, the city was almost dark. These days there were fewer and fewer lights at night, and Tuuro wanted the burial finished before he had to use a light to see. "Good-bye, my son," he said, kissing the boy's forehead, and then he hammered the board onto the coffin's top. It was sad to no longer see or touch him: Tuuro thought of the boy's puzzled face, his long fingers and slender wrists.

He dug a hole in a bare patch behind a prickly shrub in the church garden, a place Tuuro had never liked much (the volunteer gardeners were lazy) but one that would have to do. The hole was maybe a bit sloppy, not quite deep enough, but every minute it was darker and Tuuro wanted to be done. Beads of sweat dripped from his nose. He laid the coffin in the hole and shoveled dirt over it. The hollow thuds echoed like cannon shots, the worst sound in the world.

Another prayer.

But where was the service? The boy deserved the service.

Why am I creeping? Tuuro thought. Why don't I put the lights on? But he was creeping, without the lights on, through the narthex and past the social hall and the classrooms and into the pastor's office, a place which, for the sake of cleaning, Tuuro had a key.

There, Tuuro closed the curtains and put the light on. He went through the pastor's computer index, then his bookshelves. *The Book of Presbyterian Liturgy. Seasons of Life. Today's Rituals for Today's Times.* He finally found the service he wanted ("ashes to ashes, dust to dust") in a book with a broken spine that made him sneeze as he leafed through it. He took the book outside and, with a flashlight, read the entire service over the grave. He replaced the book in the pastor's office. Then, because it was too late for the buses to be running, Tuuro walked the three miles home.

TUURO BOLTED awake in the middle of the night: *But he has a mother.*

A cold sweat washed over him. He got up and stood over the toilet, wanting to vomit.

So what if Tuuro didn't have a mother, so what if other women, not his mother, fought over him? Why in the world did he assume the same about the boy? The boy who was just a boy, maybe four, maybe five, who lay now in the dark, warm ground. Of course the boy's mother, his only mother, his true and real mother, was frantic now, looking for him.

Tuuro dressed and ran back to the church, his left little toe sore, a blister rubbed open, the air still hot and sticky even as the dawn made a pink stain in the sky. He would unearth the coffin, go into the church, call the police to tell them what he'd found. The police would say oh yes, thank you for calling, we have the mother right here. They would bring the mother over in their car, her eyes like draining holes in her broad face, but when Tuuro prized the coffin open (he hadn't used that many nails), she would understand. As terrible as her son's fate had been, Tuuro had, in his small way, eased the pain of it. He pictured the boy's mother kissing her son's face, running her hand over the boy's thin shoulders, touching the scarf with which Tuuro had dressed him, turning her eyes to meet Tuuro's, acknowledging in that gaze their mutual love for the boy.

By now it was light out. If he was lucky, if he kept running, this could all be over before the pastor showed up to his office.

Two blocks from the church a big dog ran down the center of the street, a twist of red and black and green trailing from his mouth. Tuuro broke into a cry, understanding. He had forgotten about the dogs.

There were scores of dogs, newly feral, that had been abandoned to the streets when people left Dayton. During the Short Times abandoned dogs had been a problem, too, but now the situation was worse, because most members of the Containment Squad were volunteers from the southern—the wealthier—suburbs, and a disproportionate number of those people had found a way out of town. Tuuro had heard that the Containment people now simply shot dogs in the street. As Tuuro ran now he cursed himself for not making the coffin stronger, for not burying it deeper, and he begged God again and again to let the boy's body be intact. He was so worried about the dogs he never imagined police cars and a van outside the church. He didn't notice the horde of people, some in uniform, in the garden.

Who is this? Why are they here? Tuuro thought when an arm stopped him. Then, even worse, he spotted the pastor. "Tuuro!" the pastor cried, lifting his hands in the air. "Do you know anything *about* this?

THE LAWYER'S NAME was Brandon English. He was the color of a peeled potato, stocky, probably fifty, wearing a rumpled shirt and pants it looked like he'd slept in. For Tuuro, who kept himself neat, the attorney's disdain for his own appearance was puzzling. It might be alcohol, it might be a runaway wife, it might be so much power that looks didn't matter.

"Mr. Tuuro," the lawyer said. "Don't tell me if they roughed you up." He removed his perc from his pocket, set it on the table between them, then slumped over its tiny holographic screen. He did have power, Tuuro thought: those holo-screens were expensive. After some minutes he looked at Tuuro with an unvarnished weariness and said, "First off, you need to know something: this boy of yours is Nenonene's grandson."

Nay-no-nay-nay. The name was somehow familiar. Tuuro ran through his list of neighbors. No. Tuuro said, "Does the boy have a mother?"

"Of course he has a mother!" Mr. English closed his eyes; when he opened them he looked, if possible, even wearier. "Even in our crazy modern world, a child has a mother. But it's Nenonene's *son* that is the father. I don't know who the mother is. Some woman. The wife of Nenonene's son."

Tuuro stared. The boy did have a mother.

"Nenonene!" English repeated. "The general. The African. The one who runs the Alliance from that hotel basement up in Cleveland."

Tuuro tried to shift his mind from the mother to a famous grandfather, but it was an ungainly process, like an old machine slipping laboriously into gear. Of course Tuuro knew Nenonene! Everyone knew Nenonene. But as a name, a concept, not as a real person.

"My God," Tuuro said after a moment. "Nenonene is the enemy. What was this boy doing in Dayton?"

English shook his head impatiently. "His parents live here. Nenonene's son is an American citizen. He has a PhD from somewhere south. International finance or global economics, something like that. He teaches at Wright State. He didn't keep his father's name. The son's name is Norris. Ken Norris."

Tuuro nodded blankly, trying to take it in. Still, the boy had a mother. "And this little boy, what was his name?"

"Cubby Norris." A very American name. Not a name you'd expect for Nenonene's grandson. Maybe the mother had picked it.

"Does Cubby"—Tuuro paused on the name; you could say the boy had been hidden in a cubbyhole; how savage, to make a name into a place of death—"have brothers or sisters?"

"Not currently. The wife is pregnant. Very pregnant." English hesitated. "I saw her as I came in. She'd just seen the body."

"The boy was young."

"Four and a half. He was tall."

"How is the mother?"

"Devastated!" A look of incredulity; a quick glance around the room. "What do you think?"

"I wanted to talk to her. I wanted to tell her I cared."

English's voice turned cold. "How long had you cared?"

"Since I found him! I never knew him alive. I told the policeman everything, don't you have . . . ?" And Tuuro waved at English's holographic screen.

At this, English made the holo-screen disappear. He sat for a moment, considering Tuuro, the sides of his cheeks moving as if he were chewing at their insides. "Let me ask you this straight out: Are you a homosexual?"

"Oh no," Tuuro smiled. "Never."

"Why are you smiling?"

Tuuro straightened his face. "It's ridiculous. It's something I never considered."

"You speak well. How far did you go in school?"

"I finished my first year at Sinclair." The local community college.

"Why didn't you go on?"

Tuuro shrugged helplessly. "Money."

"Reasonable. Are you political?"

"Political?" Tuuro laughed awkwardly. "I've never voted. I know it's a duty, but . . ."

"You didn't know about the boy's connection to Nenonene?"

"How could I know? I come across this, this"—Tuuro saw again the boy's tucked head—"tragedy, this small boy dead in my church, and I picked him up and . . ." "My" church, he'd said: not something he would say in front of the pastor.

"I'm your lawyer," English interrupted. "Don't tell me things I shouldn't know." He leaned into the table. "Now," he said, "it would be absurd to think you hurt this boy to send a message to Nenonene, am I correct?"

Tuuro stared.

"Or to his son. You might be sending a message to his son. But it would be absurd to think that. It was a simple crime of passion, right?"

"A crime? I never hurt this boy. I came upon him, I saw the . . ."

"You didn't do it."

"He was a boy! A little child."

"No conspiracy. Absolutely no political motive."

"I went home to get him a blanket, I took a hat for him."

A light had appeared in English's eye; he sat up a straighter. "This wasn't a molest-y thing."

"It was like he was me!"

"You didn't do it," English repeated, wonderment in his voice. "Well, the genetics will take care of that."

"It's terrible to find the body of a child," Tuuro said. "I have a child."

"Okay, okay, I believe you." English sighed. His shoulders sank, the spark that had seized him suddenly extinguished. "But damn, you managed to do right by the wrong body."

lila wakes up (1)

SEYMOUR, LILA'S ASSISTANT, appeared in her office. "There's a Federal wants to talk to you."

"You mean State." The State people were pests. The loss of Cleveland had thrown them into a tizzy. By June 2047, the cavernous lakefront edifice that had been built as the Rock and Roll Hall of Fame was a tracking station receiving information from Canada and Alliance ships in the Atlantic. The BP tower was a pile of rubble called Strike One, the Federal Building was the Centro de Gobierno (the Alliance had let the South American forces name this one), and the former Terminal Tower was a military headquarters, with General Nenonene's quarters taking up the basement of what used to be the Ritz-Carlton Hotel. It was all confusing. Many people had left Cleveland, but many more people hadn't. Why couldn't they? Their houses. Their businesses. The schools for their children. Their elderly relatives who didn't understand. All of it made sense, and yet it didn't make sense. With the Grid already knocking out a good third of the state and Cleveland occupied, there wasn't much State of Ohio left. The people in the state capital in Columbus reminded Lila of befuddled bees circling a destroyed hive.

"No, darling. I mean Federal."

"Federal?" Lila sighed. Federal people rarely bothered her, but when they did it was never pleasant. What environmental edict were they obsessing about now? "Okay." She turned to face her screen. "Put 'em on."

"I mean they're here," Seymour said. "A youngie-girl."

"In *person*?" Lila swiveled in her chair. She tried to remember the last time anyone had made a call on her in person. What made Federal think she had the time for in person? More ominously, what did Federal need that they sent a real person?

Seymour brought in the Federal, a tall woman—good Lord, did they take them straight out of college these days?—with an eager, open face and an athlete's stride. The youngie sat.

"What a surprise!" said Lila. "You're really a Federal? Who do you represent, exactly?"

"I'm from Agriculture," the youngie said, dipping her head. The Department of Agriculture had planned and now controlled the Grid. Since the Gridding, Agriculture had become a shameful part of the government. People had been known to pretend they worked in other parts of the government. It took, Lila suspected, an act of will and faith to half-stand and extend her hand across Lila's desk. "Michelle Everly."

"Michelle," Lila said. "Lila de Becqueville." A lovely face, Lila realized, sculpted and high-cheekboned. The lashes at the corners of Michelle's eyes tangled in a wanton way. A slight scent of lemon to her, probably perfume.

"I've heard about you," Michelle said, settling herself back in the chair. "I've heard you have an excellent system. Best treatment system of any city your size. Superior flood protection, aquifer maintenance, nice leach fields, reliable sewage . . ."

"Thank you." Everything she'd said was true. The Water Queen, Lila called herself. Not that she told anyone this.

"My mother remembers you coming to her school," Michelle said, reddening slightly. Michelle's mother! Lila was shocked at how this dated her, and she made it into a curse: *tu madre.* "You used to give talks on the history of water in Ohio."

Michelle's face was eager and imploring. Inside herself, Lila felt something shifting. "Your mother remembers me?" she said. It was true: early in Lila's career, twenty, twenty-five years before, she had given talks. This was during New Dawn Dayton, the halcyon period before the Short Times when all sorts of industry—including Prestige Polymer, Armitage Steel, even Consort and its premier nuclear plant—had come to Dayton because of the city's abundance of water. Lila thought how little she remembered of Ohio's water history now, although somewhere she still had the data chips.

"You talked about the Great Black Swamp. And malaria."

"Lima, Ohio, was named after Lima, Peru," Lila said. "They imported quinine from Peru as a malaria medicine." Malaria in Ohio: people used to be incredulous when she told them. *The drainage tile used to dry northwest Ohio could be stretched from the earth to the moon.* The diversion of water from the Great Black Swamp had created lakes that were still, over a century and a half later, among Ohio's largest. Now the lakes were recreational areas, but in their early years after their formation they were notorious for mosquitoes and disease, places a sensible person avoided.

Lila said, "You know they used to call Cincinnati Porkopolis. That was because of water, too."

Michelle gave Lila a thrilling sidelong glance.

"They built a canal south from Middletown to the Ohio River," Lila said. "Once the canal was built, farmers could move their pigs to Cincinnati, and from there the pigs could be shipped by boat east to Pennsylvania or west to the Mississippi. People don't think about it, but water opens markets." Lila was surprised at the fervor in her voice; she *did* remember. She glanced at Michelle. A young youngie, Lila thought with a wave of fatigue. Then she relaxed: if Federal really wanted something from her, they wouldn't send a girl like this. "So what are you here for?" Lila said brightly. "Training? Advice? Employees?" Michelle's lips were parted, her dark hair swept down her back. God, that long hair. Lila could brush that hair across Michelle's mouth and kiss her lips through the curtain of it. She could lift it off her neck and nuzzle the pale spot behind her ear. Lila's voice came out surprisingly husky. "You running a little dry up on the Grid?"

A spot at the end of Michelle's nose turned suddenly red. A flaw, there was always a flaw. Even in her glory days Lila had had one. The flaw had been Lila's profile, her slightly bulging stomach. Now her belly lay across her thighs like a sleeping cat. Suddenly Lila felt angry at Michelle's bosses. A little training mission here, get out and talk up the old folks, the powers-that-be of this or that inconsequential city. The jerks that would send a young woman to do this. "Am I a little too close for comfort here?" Lila asked, her voice quickening. "You *are* running dry on the Grid? I'll tell you what: you get me a steady power supply for my treatment plant and I'll give you all the water you Agros want."

For a second the youngie looked confused, then she drew herself up and pulled on an invisible jacket of authority. "We don't have any influence over electricity. That's Consort." Lila was old enough to remember the days before Consort, the aggregation of utility companies that had grown up in the early twenties. It had seemed so logical then, Consortium, with states shipping electricity and gas and wind and solar power back and forth, but then Consortium got bigger and bigger, the nickname "Consort" used first by the more intelligent, referring—ha, ha!—to its relation to the government, then taken up and somehow euphemized by the company itself, making it a cheerful name, a name implying convenience and compatibility and even a gleeful communion. "Consort with us," the top of each bill used to read.

"But you're a Fed," Lila said.

"Of course." Michelle leaned forward eagerly. "Consort is a business. Who are we to interfere with business?" This was a slogan: when the Alliance leaders pointed out how America forgot the poor, Americans responded with a truism about business.

God, Lila hated these rote answers. "Then why are you here?" She demanded. "You seem to want to interfere with my business."

"You're water. You're still regulated. Water is local."

"But you want to make my water not local." Lila leaned forward. She decided to mention the rumor she kept hearing. "You want to transport it, just like those farmers who sent their pigs to St. Louis. You need it to irrigate the Grid."

Michelle's face had become shiny, more blotches joining the red spot at the end of her nose. "No. Not the Grid. Definitely not the Grid."

"Then where do you want to send it?"

Michelle leaned forward into Lila's desk and pushed up her sleeves, as if Lila were finally asking a grown-up question. "People at Federal are smart. You'd be surprised: Federal is very realistic."

Lila was quiet, waiting.

Michelle, silent, propped her chin on her hand and stared at the wall behind Lila's head. What was back there? Lila thought suddenly, wanting to turn and look.

"Extremely realistic," Michelle said, lifting a hand to smooth her hair.

A hand-drawn picture of a fanciful fish, flowing in a blue stream. A photomontage of a turbine and the outflow over a dam. An old poster—Lila's favorite—from the *We Save Wawa* series, featuring a priest and a transvestite. The transvestite was actually (no one but Lila knew this) her assistant Seymour in his younger days. The *We Save Wawa* campaign had been a huge hit. Not that individual conservation really made a difference—industrial water use, in New Dawn Dayton, had dwarfed any use of water for baths or yards—but the campaign gave ordinary people a goal, and promoted the image nationwide of Dayton as a water capital.

"And that means . . . ?" Lila said now. She'd never get to bury her nose in Michelle's hair, never. Might as well give up lusting. Lila thought with regret of Janet, whose hair had always smelled of chlorine. How long ago was that, twenty years? Janet could never resist her. Lila intimidated people terribly, in her day. Lila had hammered them with questions they could neither answer nor forget. And she'd used her influence not just for seduction but also for public service. *Lila de Becqueville,* the governor of Ohio had introduced her, *community asset.* She wondered if she was too old to use her influence now. Not that it mattered. She was having no effect on Michelle.

And suddenly Michelle, looking much older, less ingenuous, was patting her cheek with her fingertips, little quick pats, as if she were dabbing it with powder, and indeed her little blotches were fading. "Not the Grid," she repeated. "Definitely not the Grid." Her eyes wandered, in an aimlessness Lila was sure was feigned, until they met Lila's wide ones. "I know about you," Michelle said, and Lila felt a buzzing thrill in her chest. "My mother doesn't just remember your water talks. She remembers you later. She told me all about your leadership during the Short Times. I know about the ads, the time restrictions, everything. You know what my mom says? You made sacrifice fun."

Was there a personal connection? Was that why this youngie was here? "Do I know your mother?" Lila asked.

"You should hear her talk about you. She was at the Needmore Rally."

"Need less," Lila mumbled, meaning to be dismissive, surprised by the wistfulness in her tone. RALLY ON NEEDMORE: NEED LESS! "Did I know your mother"—Lila hesitated—"personally?"

"She knew you. I mean, you were a public person." Lila sighed in relief. Sometimes she could hardly believe the hussy she had been. On the other hand, she'd been a force: just last week a man in a weather-beaten coat had come running across the street to shake her hand: "Is it you? Is it really you?"

"You were wonderful," Michelle said in a puzzled way, her lovely face clouding, and what Lila felt most keenly was the "were." Lila was, once. "That's why I wanted to come talk with you." Michelle was sitting up straighter now, her crisp tone returned. "But I don't have much direct information now. I'm here solely to prepare the soil. Don't be surprised if you hear more from us. Be prepared."

"Us? Who's us?" Stupid thing to say. The old Lila could do better than that. *Prepare the soil:* Michelle must be an Agro to her bones.

"We'll call you," Michelle said. "When we need you, we'll call." Lila felt a flicker of unease, a brief pause and thump of her heart, a sensation she was having more often these days. Michelle unaccountably winked. "You could have fun."

An up-and-comer. Federal had sent Lila an up-and-comer. "Are you staying here?" Lila heard herself asking. "Are you going to be in Dayton a while?"

"I live in Pittsburgh, but I'll be in and out." Pittsburgh, east up the Ohio River.

What did that mean? What did that *mean*? And Lila knew, as Michelle rose and walked out the door, that Lila would have difficulty resting that evening, that she'd be up with her discarded laptops flicking through old and potent images, Ohio water history, herself in the old days, her lovers in the old days, periodically squirting honey in her mouth and sucking on a piece of lemon. Tonight she'd probably go through two lemons, maybe three, putting off the moment that she placed her head on her pillow and pulled up her covers, nestling her hands, which always needed warming, between her thighs. Tonight the rituals of her solitary sleeping wouldn't console her, because when the lights went out she would be troubled relentlessly, wondering her old worries about where she'd gone wrong, and on top of that, what were the Feds thinking, who was behind it, and why had they had sent to Lila, a woman who made no secret of her proclivities, such a young and creamy up-and-coming girl?

"WANT A BUZZ?" Kennedy, her hand trembling, lifted the bottle from the table.

"No thanks, just straight coffee. I'm cutting back." A relief to sit in this familiar seat, across from a familiar face, after the events of her morning. Lila felt the memory of Michelle whirl away, the simple sight of orange-and-blue cushions washing her morning clean. Coffee-bar decor, like the national mood or skirt lengths, tended to cycle: bright and garish to cozy and dark. The latest incarnation was bright.

"Self-denial." Kennedy rolled her eyes. "Are we getting old or what? I got up in the middle of the night to pee and caught a glimpse of myself in the mirror. Oh my God, talk about an uto." This was a private joke, their own acronym: uto, pronounced oo-toe, meaning ugly, tired, old. Lila wasn't sure anymore which one of them had made it up. Kennedy's belly was as vast as Lila's; she had a problem—freely discussed—with recurring yeast under her breasts. "So what have you been up to?" Kennedy said. "They still working you hard at water?"

Lila shrugged. She had nothing to hide from Kennedy. Back in the late twenties, when Kennedy was executive director of the Metro Library, she and Lila had shared a difficult lover named Leesa. Over time and multiple conversations, Kennedy and Lila had become allies. Leesa threw over both of them to marry an African male, and was now stuck in Cleveland in an enclave of traitors and Alliance functionaries. Lila and Kennedy both enjoyed the thought of Leesa growing old with a devious man. "A lot of undercurrents these days," Lila said, shaking her head. In her old days she was delighted how many metaphors referred to water and liquids. Now she barely noticed.

Kennedy nodded. "In the library too."

"Agriculture sent a youngie-girl to talk with me."

"To talk with you? In person? A youngie-girl in your office?" Not surprising that Kennedy focused on the youngie: Kennedy had never been interested in politics. Agriculture to her was probably no more suspect than Education. She shook her head in wonderment. "Why?"

"You tell me. Her manner was oblique. Referred to my being a hero to her mother." Lila and Kennedy exchanged a rueful look. "Said they'd be contacting me. Then she left."

"Was she sexing you?"

"Maybe. Can you believe it? Nothing direct"—Lila paused—"damn it."

Kennedy shook her head in appreciation. "I'm surprised anyone from Agro could be subtle."

Lila bit her fingernail consideringly: maybe Kennedy did understand about Agro. "She seemed apologetic about it." Lila eyed Kennedy. "That might be subtle."

Kennedy frowned. "Maybe they told her to act apologetic."

"Subtler yet." Lila shook her head, dislodging the image: the girl's wanton eyelashes, her dim scent of lemon . . . "You read anything good lately?"

Kennedy smiled. "Believe it or not, yes. I read Nenonene's autobiography. I can see why they want to suppress it. It's inspirational."

"Poor beginnings and a rise to consciousness and power?" Nay-no-nay-nay, Lila thought, accenting the third syllable slightly. Quite a melodious name for a despot.

"Exactly! He was one of fourteen children. And his father died of HIV, even though the vaccine was out. Did you know he taught himself English using a typewriter?"

"I hadn't heard that."

"He did! Tremendous discipline. He doesn't believe in waste, so he drinks only water from the faucet, never uses a cup. He has a special chef he trusts, but he eats right out of the pan. He sleeps in a single bed. And every morning he wakes up and walks around the basement of the old Cleveland Ritz-Carlton thirty times. Thirty times."

"For exercise? Why not take a walk outside?"

"People might shoot him, that's why. Lila. Don't be naive."

"He's pure." Lila smiled, remembering a photo of Nenonene standing on the hood of a parked car, wearing a white suit with a high collar and a fez-like cap with horizontal stripes, holding up his right arm in a benediction to the hundreds of people around him. A brilliant move, that outfit: a get-up like a priest's when he was actually a general. "That's why people like him."

"Pure, right. Some people think he's pure Antichrist."

Lila smiled. "Someone called me the Antichrist once. You come home and rub lotion on your hands and think, are these Antichrist hands?"

"I wouldn't think anyone would call you that, you being a woman."

"Ah, but not a real woman."

The coffee-bar door opened, and a man of maybe twenty-five entered, a small boy with curls at his nape holding his hand.

"Have they invited you up to the Grid yet?" Kennedy said. "I hear a whole brigade from Consort's going."

As the young man waited at the counter, the boy beside him sagged to his knees. "Daddy!" the boy said.

"*On* to the Grid? A tour?" Lila asked, Kennedy's words just sinking in. No one went on the Grid. When the Gridding occurred the adults of the area had all been classified into Farming, Manufacturing, or Professional, and the farm people alone—the effs—were given the option to stay. Now the effs who worked the Grid were so cloistered the government paid the state of Florida to arrange a private Grid getaway two weeks every February.

"Stand up!" the father snapped.

"Apparently. It's a business thing, I'm sure. No one really thinks they're going for free."

"You can't stand up?" The father jerked up the boy by his arm until his feet barely grazed the floor. "Three years old and you can't stand up?"

Lila said, "Why would they be wooing Consort?" But her eyes were on the father and son.

"You should call Agriculture. Demand a tour yourself. They think they can buy you with a pretty girl?"

But Lila was no longer listening to Kennedy. The father had thrust the boy into a chair and returned to the counter; behind Lila the boy was whimpering, snuffling squeaks that reminded Lila of a pet rat she'd had as a child. "I can't stand it," Lila said.

Kennedy shrugged. "We're not parents."

"He's tired. Can't his father hear he's tired?"

"We're all tired, Lila." Kennedy reached for her handbag.

The man came back to the table with a drink and some bread. The boy quieted as he sat down. "Pood?" he asked hopefully.

"Daddy doesn't buy pood for whiners." The "p" of "pood" exploded on his lips.

"You go ahead," Lila said to Kennedy. "I'll stay and finish my coffee." When Kennedy was gone, Lila went to the counter and ordered bread and apple juice, and as she left she placed these on the table in front of the boy. "If you eat, he eats," she said to the father.

The little boy looked terrified. "Daddy, can I eat it?" The father's eyes went shifty; Lila waited a moment to watch the boy pick up the bread and hunch away from his father. "He gets every bite, okay?" She hissed, pleased when the father cowered.

I still have it, Lila thought as she walked out the door, not sure why she hadn't wanted Kennedy to witness what she'd done.

LILA COULDN'T SLEEP. The oldest trick in the book. A younger person, a sexually attractive person, and they walk in and drape you with flattery and when you're practically licking their fingers they ask you for something. Was Lila supposed to fall for that? Was she that transparently weak? Did the Agros (or someone beyond the Agros, someone in the Defense Department or Environment or God knows where) really think she'd jump for their bait like some widemouthed fish? Had they pegged her as that desperate, that lonely?

She was desperate, she was lonely. She'd wasted her life. In interviews, in discussions, what did people say made their lives worth living? The small things: family, friends. For years, Lila had thought the small things didn't matter. Her successful gestures were all public. Her father had left the family, dying years later in a residential hotel. Her mother had passed away in a nursing home four months after Lila last saw her. Her siblings were like strangers. And then there were all those lovers, come and gone.

Lila got up, flicked on the bathroom light, and inspected herself in the mirror. Salt-and-pepper hair in a pageboy, bangs chopped across her forehead, a sagging chin, gray teeth, breasts lying almost flat against her chest. The mole beneath her left eye, once a beauty mark, now drooped on its stalk like a wilted flower. An uto, just like Kennedy. Ugly, tired, old. It wasn't the ugly that offended her; it was the tired. Years ago she'd loved being alive. She wanted love, she wanted fame, she wanted a child. What had happened to all that energy? Was there anything she yearned for now? Even something simple like eating ice cream or feeling a breeze? Sitting on the edge of the bathroom cabinet, surprised and almost grateful for such emotion, Lila started to cry. The youngie, the youngie had woken her up.

what sharis knew

SHE MAY NOT have gone to college, but Sharis knew things. Here was knowledge she kept to herself: deprivation and the threat of danger made her feel alive. Weeding, stirring, chopping, always planning. Every day was not the same. Basic things mattered.

Food mattered. Food mattered tremendously, and Sharis's parents each summer, as part of their survivalist ethos, had planted an enormous garden. Sharis knew how to start lettuces, the best way to post tomatoes, the mixture of soap and water to spray on Swiss chard. All her married life (which was all her adult life) she had not planted anything, but this spring, with Cleveland being taken over and the whole world, it seemed, turned against America, she'd said to Chad, her husband, *Sweetness, we should plant things this year.* Chad had tilled a large rectangle in the sunniest and flattest portion of their yard. This happened to be in their front yard, which a year ago would not have been acceptable, but neighborhood standards had changed.

Now, by mid-July, they had . . . Well, anyone could guess what they had, because Sharis was an industrious woman and the weather was good and even the Grid, which critics said raped the soil, exhausted resources, used too many chemicals, etc, was projected to have a record year.

Chad and Sharis lived south of Dayton in the suburbs, on a private lane off Far Hills, the main road from downtown. Chad and Sharis's street wound down a hill through trees and then curled up a hill to a sunnier area. Chad's drawing of their street would make it a snake. Its tail would touch the main road, the cul-de-sac where Chad's and Sharis's house sat would show up as the snake's open mouth.

Chad and Sharis lived in a nineties home built with a two-story great room. Like most of those homes, theirs had been modified during the Short Times with new, lowered ceilings. Sharis liked the puddles of light that formed below the ceiling cans. She liked the overstuffed chair in the corner, the beautifully grained wooden bowl, the hanging clock decorated with hand-painted flowers. Sharis had grown up in a dark house; for her father, closed curtains were a moral imperative. In contrast, now Sharis had drapes only in the bedrooms. Sometimes, lying on the couch in the great room, looking out the wide front window, Sharis imagined the empty space above the ceiling as a hidden room: if the troops swept down from Cleveland, she and Chad and the boys would have a place to hide. What an adventure that would be, something for the boys to remember forever—the aim of an adventure, always, being the exhilaration of survival.

There was one cabbage in her garden that Sharis had watched for a month, getting bigger and bigger and not precisely rounder but *vaster*. When the cabbage was as big as it reasonably could get, Sharis cut it and carried it into the house. She and Chad made a sort of party of it.

"Ten pounds," Sharis guessed. She set the cabbage on the bathroom floor and peered at her weight on the scale. "Hand it to me, honey." If she was editing their family, this was a moment she'd leave in. Of course, she took on only respectable clients, not people with cameras in their bathrooms or even bedrooms. Chad picked up the cabbage, its dark outer leaves studded with slugs and wormholes, and handed it to his wife. "Eleven," Sharis said firmly. Her voice rose in its girlish way: "Char, as Howard would say."

"What's char?" Howard asked breathlessly, arriving at the top of the stairs. Even a trip up the stairs made him pant.

"The average war lasts seven months," Derk said from the blue table in the kitchen. Derk had been a history minor and, after Dayton: The Roots of Midwestern, one of Chad's most enthusiastic students. He worked at American Motors running a paint machine for tanks. Derk lived with his parents. He'd tried to enlist in the military, but a childhood infection had left him with a bad heart. "Your husband taught me that," Derk added.

"I did?" Chad said.

Derk's shirt was off because of the heat, and the thumping of his defective heart twitched the few hairs on his chest. Chad hoped that Sharis didn't notice this; it was the sort of thing she might comment on.

It was fun then, it really was. Sharis was slicing her huge cabbage in the kitchen: a quarter for cabbage rolls, a quarter for coleslaw, and a half for sweet-and-sour soup. Her massive knife flashed and gleamed. She thought of a cabbage seed, sun, water, something-from-nothing. How could anyone doubt the existence of God in a world with eleven-pound cabbages? She wasn't a religious maniac like her parents (never), or a dopey optimist like Chad, but a cabbage like this gave you hope.

"How you doing with the Calmadol, Derk?" she asked.

His wife didn't realize, Chad thought, that she intimidated people. She was small—"petite," people said, "like a little ballet dancer." When she turned, her dark brown hair spread out shining over her shoulders, and when she was busy or impatient, she would grab the whole great hank of it, twist it around her hand and drop it to the left of her neck. Her lips were full and pink; her brown eyes heavily lashed and often narrowed.

Derk's mouth jerked, and Chad, thinking of his friend's wispy father, his impossible mother, gave Derk a smile and a roll of his eyes. Chad was six foot four and two hundred eighty pounds, but he scared no one. "Make yourself small,"

Chad's mother used to say, marshalling her sons through the crowded aisles of the grocery.

"I'm fine. I'm on the lowest dose," Derk said, his eyes fixed on the blue table.

"They passed it out up north the day they did the Gridding," Chad said in a companionable way. "Didn't give people a choice. Just woke people up, lined them up in the streets, and squirted it in their mouths." He glanced at Sharis as he spoke, invoking her complicity. She had watched this from a stand of trees twenty feet from her parents' house, a fact known only to herself and Chad.

"What was wrong with those people?" Derk said. "Why'd they stand there like sheep and take it?"

"Maybe they were stunned, Derk," Sharis said, her voice rising. "Maybe it was like a dream for them." Chad shifted in his seat, wondering how much she was going to give away. "Plus, if you wouldn't open your mouth for the Calmadol, they gave you a shot. Those shots knocked people out."

"Gridding was the stupidest thing the government ever did," Derk said. "They wouldn't be dropping bombs on Shaker Heights if the government hadn't done that."

"No one's dropping bombs on Shaker Heights," Chad soothed, relieved Derk hadn't noticed the immediacy of Sharis's words. "From what I've heard, the Cleveland takeover's been remarkably peaceable. I think the Alliance will be sorry they did it."

"You may think the Grid's stupid, but we're eating," Sharis said. "For thirteen years we've been eating. We're still eating." She was parroting Chad's words, and Chad felt suddenly— uncomfortably—as if she were his child, spouting his ideas in a speech contest.

"Those Africans and the Suds, they don't eat hardly anything," Derk said, his animation returning. "That's how they can run such a big military. I mean, they practically feed all their troops off what they draw from Canada."

"Canada has a rich agricultural heritage," Chad agreed. "No one's going to starve when they've got Canada."

"I hate Canada," Sharis burst out. "Don't talk to me about Canada."

Chad smiled apologetically at Derk. Whenever he and Sharis had visitors, Chad found himself missing his mother. His mother who kept a pot of soup on the stovetop, who believed, forty-plus years too late, in counterculture, who forbade video games and even resisted a computer in the house until Chad reached middle school and the gifted program made it a requirement. Chad's brother had it easier, being younger: he even got a cell phone.

It wasn't until college that Chad had recognized how sparely his family lived. At his parents' house the plates didn't match the bowls, guests drank from decorated plastic cups passed out at ballgames, and the bathroom off their kitchen was a tiled cube with no fan and a door that incompletely closed. Any of these things could have been changed—money was not, was never, the issue—and it struck Chad as he reached adulthood that his mother was indeed a resister. The unmatched dishes were a choice. And Chad's clothes from Meijer's and Walmart: a choice again.

Chad's mother was a tall blonde with watery eyes. In contrast to Chad's father, who called himself a "nothing," she called herself a tikkun olam—a heal-the-world—Jew, and drove Chad and his brother to Hebrew school twice a week and made sure they got through their Bar Mitzvahs. Unlike all the other women in their synagogue, even the fat ones, she had very protuberant teeth. "Didn't they have braces when you were young?" Chad's little brother had asked.

"My teeth work fine," Chad's mother said, baring them and chomping. "Like a horse's."

No other Jewish mother Chad knew would compare her own teeth to a horse's; no other Jewish mother would call the Torah "just a bunch of stories about rescues"; no other mother of any stripe wore shoes patched together with duct tape. His own mother, Chad supposed, had prepared him for the oddness that was Sharis.

"Zucchini brownie?" Chad said, holding out a plate to Derk. His mother's recipe, Sharis's garden.

HERE WERE SOME Ohio casualties of the Grid:

Wapakoneta, birthplace of the first man on the moon, where General Theodore Marshall, on the day of the flattening, was observed outside the former Neil Armstrong Heritage Museum lifting his sleeve repeatedly to his eyes.

West Liberty, with its downtown restaurant famous for pies and potato salad, although the family-owned cave outside town with the white (calcite) formations, Ohio Caverns, was left unbombed and was outfitted, according to rumor, as a shelter for the Gridians in case of armed invasion.

St. Henry's, once noted for turkeys shipped as far away as Tel Aviv, Saint Petersburg, and Damascus, was replaced by soybean fields that would be rotated (as were the majority of the Grid fields) with wheat and corn. No one knew what had happened to the turkeys. There were stories of a lavish dinner held in the army tents, the scent of roasting meat overpowering the odor of bombs and burning, although everyone in the battalion denied it.

Tipp City was leveled, as was Lima (pronounced like the bean, despite the town being named for the city in Peru), Versailles (rhymed with fur tails), and Milan (long *i*, accent on the first syllable).

Three people had shot themselves during the reclamation of Utica, leading to a brief (it lasted minutes) armed rebellion and the composition of a song:

> *The ghosts of Utica*
> *Just wanted to be free*
> *To live their simple lives*
> *The way it used to be.*

The towns of northern Indiana and Illinois and southern Michigan all had similar stories; the big cities—Cleveland, Toledo, Detroit, Fort Wayne, and Chicago—were spared.

The Ohio Historical Society had a goal of interviewing every person from Ohio who'd been Gridded. They were making a database. They were proving someone cared.

IF YOU TOOK a five-pointed star and tilted it slightly to the right, as if it were racing, and centered it over the shield shape of Ohio, the star's center would be the city of Columbus, the state capital, and Cleveland would sit at the star's uppermost tip. Dayton would be in the star's bottom left arm. Dayton's origin was similarly modest: it had been founded as an investment. At the University of Dayton, where Chad as a tenured history professor taught every third year a two-semester course on Dayton history, the investment angle was always the first thing that he mentioned.

It was true that in 1749 the French declared, by means of mounted plaques, possession of the Ohio River and "all streams that fall into it." The land that later become Dayton was on one of those contributing streams, so technically one could say that the French first claimed the land that would be Dayton. But the French were hunters and fur trappers, not settlers. No one threatened the natives or the wilderness until transplants from Pennsylvania, baby citizens of a baby country, started canoeing up the Miami River from the Ohio, looking for places to land and stay.

A number of Indian raids and settler counterraids resulted, culminating in a famous battle where white men's scalped heads dotted a field like pumpkins. Then a military man known as Mad Anthony Wayne brought up a punishing brigade from Louisville, stunning twelve Indian tribes into submission. The 1795 Greenville Treaty between the Indians and the United States of America effectively ended Native American life in the area. A generation before, few Indians had seen a white man.

The tribes scattered. Seventeen days after the Greenville Treaty, the parcel of land on which Dayton was built was sold to four investors. The seller was a man named John Symmes, who by some wishful connivance had declared himself the land's owner. The buyers knew a village would drive up the value of their investment, and announced that their land was available for settlement. A hypothetical village was named Dayton after one of the four investors, General Jonathan Dayton, who never set foot in the area but who had been, nineteen years earlier, one of the signers of the Declaration of Independence. Maybe his name carried some status. The other three investors gave their names to three blazed trees.

North to south, the Stillwater River empties into the Miami River. Then the Mad River comes in, the three rivers together forming the Great Miami, a river which takes a meandering course to the Ohio River fifty miles south. The Miami River was named for a tribe of Indians; the Stillwater and the Mad, for the qualities of their flow. The surveyors who worked for Dayton and his partners marked their trees at the confluence of the Miami and the Mad. It was a rare settlement that didn't owe its existence to water.

Dayton's first settlers used poles to push their low-sided boats upriver from the Ohio. Rivers then were uncontrolled, wide in places and narrow in others. They had whirlpools and shallows and enough shoreline trees to sometimes meet and make a tunnel. The nineteen men and assorted women and children who made the journey to Dayton were dismayed to find, instead of the rough buildings they expected, nothing but three marked trees.

"What do you think?" Chad would bellow, his big-man tie swinging. He always wore a tie for this course, sensing that it added to the drama. He rehearsed his speeches, filling them with unexpected or irreverent facts that woke students up; his colleague Ramsey had acidly suggested Chad re-name the course "Dayton: A Celebration." But Chad couldn't help himself. "Would you have obeyed those three spots of paint? Would you have left your boat? What do you think of the people who did—were they determined? Docile?" Slight pause. "Where they desperate?"

You shouldn't stay here, said the local Indians. Maybe the settlers didn't want to believe this; maybe they thought that the Indians were up to their usual tricks. In fact, the Indians told the truth. *This place won't be good for you. It floods.*

GENTIA, ONE OF the Gribbles' neighbors, was telling Sharis about a day years before when she had met her husband's boss. George was his own boss now: he owned a business that installed and serviced home alarm systems containing small generators. In case Consort crapped out—in case, say, the Dayton nuclear plant was bombed—not only would George's alarm still function, but people's electricity would function, too. A perfect product for uncertain times, Gentia said.

Gentia and Sharis were in the kitchen of Sharis's house; Gentia sat, like Derk had, in the guest seat at the end of the blue table. Their kitchen was like an airport, Sharis often thought, visitors passing through.

"And I was so nervous," Gentia said breathlessly, "because I'd never met anyone important, and I was hurrying along in my high-heeled shoes, and you know what George said to me? 'You're walking like a fat cow.'"

"You're kidding," Sharis said. George was not small himself.

"That's what he said. And that was years ago, when I had a figure."

Fat cow. Sharis would never repeat that line. But Gentia, Sharis noticed, repeated it gleefully, a fresh salvo of shots aimed at her husband. Gentia and George had been married for thirty years (Chad and Sharis had been at the anniversary party); they had two grown children, both unmarried.

"And you wonder why I want to put cyanide in his coffee. I bet Chad's never like that, is he? Oh no." Gentia's voice was suddenly mocking, "Chad's a gentleman. But you work. You bring in some cash. And back then I was nothing but a frau. I said to him once: 'George, you've got to treat me with respect.' You know what he said? 'Gentia, respect is something you *earn.*'" Gentia smirked. "So now I'm earning it."

Sharis sighed. Thirty years. She looked at George in the backyard helping Leon tie his shoelaces, and tried to imagine him saying such horrible things. Squatting as he was, George was the shape of an egg. Of course, you didn't know what Gentia had said back, or said before. You never really knew what went on in a family. Belatedly, Gentia's last comment sunk in. "You're earning it?" Sharis asked.

"I'm bringing in the big bucks, baby. I'm selling alarms! You know me, aren't I a natural salesperson? Everybody wants a system. You know who thought up that antibomb guarantee?" Gentia pointed elaborately to herself. "I know what people want. I do."

Sharis nodded. There was something spookily compelling about Gentia, with her sureness and big jewelry and her happy wallowing in the muddy puddle of her marriage. She threw lots of parties, inviting Sharis and Chad as the young people.

"Listen, it's an ill wind that blows nobody good. This conflict is a gold mine for us. I tell George every night: I love the threat of war."

CHAD WAS SCHEDULED for his Dayton course again this fall. He was adding some information on geography: explaining the three glaciations that, pushing down from Ohio's northwest corner, had moved like snowplows across the state, flattening the ground and pushing ahead ridges of gravel and stone. The final glaciation, the Wisconsin, occurred some fourteen thousand years ago. The ridges of stone that had been the glaciers' leading edge were now western Ohio's modest version of hills. The northwest corner of Ohio had been pressed flat. The glacial melt on its surface formed an ur–Great Lake that stretched a hundred miles west of Lake Erie's current border, and remains of this lake lived on for thousands of years as the Great Black Swamp. The Great Black Swamp was drained in the late 1800s to provide land for farming. The glacial melt that sank into the earth became the aquifer. Thanks to the glaciers' heavy scraping, no caves of significance opened to the surface of western Ohio; there were, however, huge caverns filled with water far underground.

Chad toyed with the idea, that year, of having Dayton speak in the first person. If Dayton could talk—if any loke could talk—what would it say? A novel point of view to pique his students' interest. *Hi, I'm Dayton. I'm glad you're studying me this year!*

Maybe not. Ramsey would have a field day.

But words came to Chad unbidden, late one night when he was standing in the kitchen eating ice cream straight from the container. Later he couldn't fall asleep for hours, because he'd thought he was a Grid supporter. I'll test it on Sharis, he thought. Because she was from one of the reclaimed towns. Because she'd been there at the Gridding. But for years she hadn't spoken about that time, and Chad wavered, worried that his words would stir up some silt or sludge inside her.

Still, he needed her opinion. Sharis didn't have Chad's education (Chad had earned his doctorate), but he never doubted that Sharis was as smart as he was. Maybe smarter. Everything she saw or heard, she remembered. The next day he presented his class in the basement, Sharis sitting in the big red leather chair Chad had moved from his parents' house, Chad pacing in front of her. They'd done tests of Chad's lectures before. Almost always, Sharis said "Very good!" or "I get it, but . . ." and produced some minor suggestion.

Chad said: "I can't tell you how the Grid has affected me. All my fellow lokes just north of me—Piqua, St. Mary's, Troy— they went away. I heard about them all the time, their fairs, their factories, their nature centers, their disasters, and then they were simply gone. They were, then they were not. I never dreamed such a thing. It's as if my celebrated aquifer were shrinking, as if every day, no matter how clear and luminous, runs the risk of cold and clouds. It's as if a new wide vein has been slipped under my ground, a vein not of chalk or limestone, but of fear. Any day now, people will poke in the ground and hit it. For a loke, what one dreads isn't change or age or even decrepitude. A loke is like a person: it fears death."

Chad raised his eyebrows and looked hopefully at Sharis. She shook her head and blinked and looked away. *It works,* Chad thought, delighted.

wanted

NO ONE CAME anymore. No families appeared in the parking lot, children tumbling from the cars and screaming; no solitary birdwatchers worshipped in the Church of the Woods; no school buses disgorged their loads and waited, their drivers lingering at their vehicles like coachmen near their steeds. Charles and Diana, Aullwood Audubon Nature Center's two full-time paid employees, had spent the summer almost totally alone. Charles hadn't escorted a morning nature walk for days, although in the past he had guided groups of up to thirty. The two interns, fresh out of college, had been yanked by their families to safer jobs in Virginia and Wisconsin. The hyper-oldie guide who liked to dither about watching Prince Charles marry the *real* Princess Diana had transported herself to Florida. The gift shop volunteers hadn't shown up for weeks, and even Edna, the only volunteer who dusted, no longer bothered to message that she wasn't coming. Charles suspected that Aullwood's peculiar position—just south of the watchtowers and electrical fencing of the Grid, just west of the old Dayton airport (which saw a lot of military use these days), just north of I-70—gave it a sinister air. If it lay five miles in any direction but south, the nature center would be inside the Grid.

Charles had an apartment on the property, above the turtle exhibit in the Education Building, but where Diana spent her nights he wasn't quite sure. For several days, he was certain, she hadn't left the nature center grounds. She had told him she hated going back to her apartment, on the electric robo-tram that was always empty, past the closed houses and the unmowed lawns of northern Dayton. It was the middle of a heat wave, the planes droning over them, and Diana, the titular nature center director (chosen over Charles, and he was bitter about this), who had a categorical if not particularly scientific mind, was much better than Charles at identifying the aircraft. Several afternoons they lay on the flat rocks of the amphitheater and watched the planes pass overhead. There's a C-16, she'd say. That's an F-24, or a Scorpion (a new sort of bomber), or a Turkish Delight. "My," Charles might say, shaking his head, lifting his shirt to scratch his belly, "a woman who knows her machinery." He knew most males would at least pretend an interest in the planes, but he knew by chirp and feather and flight pattern every bird that cut the nature center's airy way. Birders thought he was a wonder; he didn't care what other people thought.

One afternoon—a Thursday? He'd lost track of the days—Charles fell asleep on a bed of moss under a tree, and when he woke up and staggered along the creek bed toward the Education Building, he happened upon Diana by the stream, pulling her cotton shirt over her head with a single hand, her back twisting in a disturbingly erotic way. He said, "What are you doing?"

Diana didn't seem surprised to hear him. She unlatched her bra and dropped it on the ground. "It's a *nature* center," she said, coyly yet firmly, dropping her shorts and unpeeling her underpants, "and I'm hot." Smiling and totally naked, she turned to face him.

Charles felt his penis swell. "What could be more natural?" he said.

"Exactly." Diana nodded approvingly, like a teacher. She brushed a dried leaf out of Charles's beard. She'd been a teacher, Charles knew. She'd been a teacher, then some sort of counselor for people considering cloning (he didn't understand this, exactly; she'd worked for a doctor), then she'd had a bad experience and returned to college for a Masters in business. When they first met, five years before, she'd been hired on as the coordinator of investments. Her being a businesswoman repelled him. Despite her wild head of hair he'd thought of her as asexual; no sparks had ever flown. But now he saw her delicately upturned breasts and pink nipples, her modest tuft of pubic hair (reminding him of the hopeful crest of the pileated woodpecker, one of his favorite birds, not, unfortunately, spotted at Aullwood since 2024—the Grid had had some devastating effects on birds), and her overabundant hips, really quite triangular, spreading from a small waist. She smiled, turned, and slowly approached the creek, bending over to splash her face with water, displaying herself just as a female wolf would, her buttocks dappled with leaf-shadow, her pink cleft beckoning him in that animal way, and it was no surprise to either of them when he stripped off his clothes and came behind her, slipping into her right there on the stream bank as she moaned and maneuvered herself to lean against the log which had, in the old days, been the forest's lure to adventurous children to cross the stream and come inside.

Afterwards they faced each other, strands of her curly bangs plastered to her forehead, her pubic hair clumped and dripping. She cupped in her two hands his penis, now sadly shriveled, looking down as if its power still amazed her. "We should do that every hour," she breathed.

Charles felt something like panic.

She lifted her eyes to his, turquoise-blue irises flecked with orange-brown, the coloring of a bluebird. "We're Adam and Eve," she said.

Trouble. She had a boyfriend, Charles knew. A man who also lived at the far end of the electric tramline. "I don't think I'd make a very good Adam," Charles said. "I think of myself more as a male wolf." For several months now, Charles realized, she hadn't mentioned the boyfriend: it was possible he'd left.

She glanced at him from beneath her eyelashes, behaving Charles recognized as classic courtship. What a relief that he could see it for what it was. "That's biologically predetermined, you know," Charles said. "That little look up."

"Excuse me?"

"That look." He mimicked it for her. She made a quick gasp and released his penis. "I just want to be fair," he said. "I want you to understand the sort of behaviors instincts will drive you to. It's very common for the urge for sexual intercourse to be magnified in times of danger."

Her look had hardened; Charles noticed a flush across her chest. "Thank you, Professor."

"I don't mean to discourage you," he said, glancing down at her nipples. Deep in the fold of his mind there was a fact about erect nipples that eluded him. "I mean, I enjoy instincts."

"You seemed to, briefly." She folded her arms across her chest, blocking his view. Her voice rose. "But I guess this is no Eden!"

"I've never said it was Eden," Charles said, surprised that, in the course of the hundreds of tours he'd led, that word had never come up. "*Eden* is not in my vocabulary."

"No. Of course not." Diana looked around her and found a flat rock the size of a large maple leaf that she held with her left hand in front of her groin. She then uprooted a fan of honeysuckle to hold over her chest. She took a few steps backward away from Charles, turned her back on him, and reoriented her honeysuckle behind her to cover her buttocks. With a dignity as comical as it was unassailable, she stalked to retrieve her clothes.

LANSING PETTIGREW WAS sitting across from Lila. Another messenger from Agro, several notches higher than the luscious Michelle. Lila had known Pettigrew for years. An officious, superior man. Once, in the midthirties, in the middle of a meeting with the county commissioners, Lansing had had to clear his throat and tap his finger on the table to get Lila's attention. For that, he had never forgiven her.

"So far we've supplied everyone," she heard herself saying. "It's a good solid system."

"A solid system? Perhaps you forget you're discussing a liquid."

Lila shifted in her seat. I hate this man, she thought.

"We've done studies," Lansing said. "We think you could easily give up the northern aquifer."

"No."

Lansing Pettigrew smiled. "Let me use your keyboard a moment." He reached across her desk and tapped in a code so quickly Lila wasn't sure if it was numbers or letters. "There," he said. "Drag up Wonderwater." Lila opened the file.

"You see you're losing population," Lansing said, nodding at a graph on the screen, "and there's no reason to assume the trend won't continue. Dayton's not a lure these days. And you already have a very water-conscious populace. Your legacy." He smiled more broadly. "So holding on to all your water is optional." His eyes met hers. "You could even say it's selfish."

> *Don't be selfish*
> *Don't make our city pay*
> *Shower for ninety seconds*
> *Every other day!*

A jingle from Lila's "We Save Wawa" glory days, accompanied, during the Web and television spots, by marimbas and guitars. "I don't know how we got so *Latin*," Seymour-the-transvestite-assistant had complained one day, a comment that still made Lila smile.

Old times. Happy times.

Now Lila was forced to defend herself. "I'm not selfish. I'm looking out for my population."

"You could look out for your country."

"Why do you need more water for the Grid? I thought you people were swimming in water. You have some kind of water defense plan? You planning to blast planes out of the sky with water cannons?"

Lansing snorted. "I warned Michelle you were a character."

The night before, while Lila was masturbating thinking about Michelle the youngie, who'd never reappeared in her office, Lila thought her labia seemed smaller. Was that possible? She checked herself in a mirror. It was possible. Her ripest parts were dry and wrinkled, the skin dull and the hairs half gray.

What was a person, traveling through life? What did one person matter? Once Lila had mattered. For the last six months, on her office computer, Lila could get into Watersystems Dayton and Waterhouse and H2O-ville, but Wonderwater was closed to her. It had never been closed before. She wondered what it meant that Lansing Pettigrew had opened the site for her now. Was it a threat? A promise? An invitation?

"I heard some people from Consort got invited to the Grid," Lila said. "If you want my water, why don't you let me visit there? Don't I get to see how my water would be used?" Idle curiosity, she'd think later, was all that had fueled this request. Everyone wanted to visit the Grid. Everyone wanted to tell people they'd been there.

"Lila, Lila. It's not easy to get permission to visit the Grid. Even I couldn't get in there."

Things were happening, she realized. Water was changing, and she was being purposely left out. Years before, after the Gridding, Lila had quit her Water Queen job. At the time, she felt ashamed to be in government, and guilty and confused that the Gridding had happened at all. Her quitting generated wrath and tearful, earnest moments in the Water Department, as if her leaving was a death. A year later she had calmed down, early crops from the Grid were being distributed, and Lila asked to be hired back. She was, but it wasn't the same. People who had stayed in the Water Department didn't know what to think of her; they couldn't trust her; they had learned they didn't need her. Power, Lila realized then, wasn't just a matter of position. Power was a matter of *seizing* it. Now Lila wondered, almost idly, if she had the energy to grab at power again.

"I was an Official Witness!" Lila said, her voice ringing with righteousness. "I was there at the beginning. Doesn't all I've done count for anything?"

"Lila," Lansing said, shaking his head.

A week later Lila was in her car driving east on I-70 to Columbus. I-70 ran all the way across the country, from San Francisco to Philadelphia. The media liked to say it "bisected" the Grid, but in reality it divided the Grid into an upper three-fourths and a lower quarter. When the Grid was conceived (this came out later, in the Waye Report), it was expected to lie only north of I-70, sparing such southern towns as New Lebanon and Yellow Springs. But the fertility statistics on the land south of I-70 were compelling, and the long ribbon of Grid land below the highway—a ribbon that stretched from Columbus, Ohio, across Indiana and Illinois all the way to the Mississippi River, interrupted only by the cities of Dayton and Indianapolis—was known as the AUL, an acronym for Area Under the Line, the phrase itself a joke, because among the engineers who planned the Grid was a cadre of mathematicians who remembered with fondness "Area Under the Curve" (AUC) from their calculus days.

The highway was four lanes in each direction and heavily traveled. There were sections of road further east with magnets embedded in the asphalt to control traffic flow, but on this section of road a vehicle had the freedom to pass. America was much less mobile these days than during Lila's childhood, when her family's thoughtless drives to Montana and

Colorado bespoke a reckless freedom. Amazing that people had lived for years with no sense of the world's limitations. All they'd cared about was the price of gas.

The Grid was hidden from the highway on either side by a high partition made of recycled tires and polymers and decorated with painted murals of agricultural themes. During the Grid construction the partitions were put up within days of the evacuations, before the towns were leveled. Guard towers topped the walls every five miles or so, and between the towers the wall was topped with electric fencing and surveillance equipment. No one got onto the Grid without permission. Everyone knew people who knew people who had a friend who'd tried to sneak onto the Grid and been rebuffed, who even—who knew if these stories were true?—had disappeared.

Boring drive. Straight road, flat, and dominated by trucks. The partitions on each side gave Lila the sensation of shooting down a river through a canyon. Lila clicked her car into a maintain-speed mode and bit her lip. If the Feds truly wanted her water, they'd better give her something in return.

"You're security clearance P-3," the youngie-girl in Columbus said. Lila wondered why she wasn't higher. "Lucky I'm in a good mood," the youngie said.

IT STARTED INNOCENTLY, because Chad had an eye for errors. He was sitting in his bedroom chair reading on his holo-screen an article about Sharis, "the first gigastar," and her "almost twenty-five years in show business, starting with her big break in 2023 playing Keela Ward in *Dakota Blues*."

"*Dakota Blues* didn't really come out in '23, did it?" Chad asked his wife.

"Wait a minute, Chad. Let me finish this."

Chad's Sharis was at her editon at a desk in the corner, trying to fit in the Schneiders before dinner. Sharis was a life-editor: she went through hours of footage and found for a family the few minutes a week they would want to view over and over. She had fallen into her work, really. She had artistically compiled footage of a neighbor's wedding; people liked it and passed it around, and then a family living in Louisville asked if she'd edit scenes of them at home. After that the whole thing just took off. Sharis was hardly the only life-editor around, but she thought she had a special touch. Her editon was bulky, almost as big as an old laptop, but for Sharis the visual resolution was worth it. The Schneiders had been her clients for almost ten years, from couplehood through the births of their three children. They lived a happy life, with a house on the water in Houston and a vacation house in Mexico, yet they always worried. Sharis could edit a week of theirs in forty-five minutes. She rarely had to flow their clips on real time to hear the words.

Chad said, "You were named for Sharis the actress, right? Your parents didn't just dream up the name."

"I guess so."

The Schneiders—speeded up—were in their dining room at some sort of party. Sharis knew the grandparents from both sides. Suddenly everyone threw their heads back, mouths flying open.

"Uh-oh," Sharis said, reversing the clip and flipping on the audio. "Cute kid comment."

"Because if *Dakota Blues* came out in '23 and you were named for her, the oldest you could be is twenty-four." Sharis was thirty-two. "I'd've married you when you were ten." Chad laughed. "What would my mother say?"

When Chad and Sharis were married, in a judge's office in downtown Dayton, Chad's little brother had been the only person from either of their families at the wedding. Both of Chad's parents and all Sharis's family were dead. At that time Chad had had a fantasy that his Sharis would change her name, because a name as famous as hers could never be her own. Now, years later, it seemed to Chad that the only real Sharis was his wife.

Chad read some more about Sharis the gigastar. "I can't trust a thing in this article," he said, shutting off his holoscreen and setting his perc on the table next to the chair. He stood and stretched his arms over his head, touching the ceiling. "How can I, when they can't get a simple date right?"

"Got it," Sharis said. She was proud of her life-editing, because she gave every week a shape. She considered clients only on referral, and in the last two years her client list was full. She made twice what Chad did as a professor. "Now," she said turning, "what's this about my age?"

Chad walked toward her, bent over and kissed the part at the top of her head. "Are you lying to me about your age?"

Sharis sighed. "Okay. You're right, I'm not thirty-two. I'm twenty-seven. I didn't really finish high school. I added five years after the Gridding because if I said I'd just turned fourteen I'd've ended up adopted or something. It doesn't matter. I've always been very mature."

The bones in Chad's legs turned to water. He sank onto the bed. "So when I met and married you, you were . . . fourteen?"

Sharis nodded impatiently, raked her fingers through her hair. "My birthday's right, I just moved the year back." She punched another button, and the Schneiders resumed.

Impossible. Chad saw Sharis's legs swinging against the bleachers. The day Chad met her he went home and looked on the Internet for the distinction between "haughty" and "insolent." She was part of a group of young women, all refugees from the Grid, clustered on the fourth row of a stack of bleachers at a city park, yet she—with her hooded eyes, high cheekbones, her swinging legs and sweep of hair—was the only one he thought of as above him, although all of them were above him, on their perch. He interviewed them looking up, an odd sensation for a man so tall. Chad was a roving reporter then for the UD television station, working on his doctorate on weekends.

"Your name?" Chad had asked, his microphoned hand stretched in the air.

"Sharis Sunbury."

"Can you tell us about your most frightening moment?"

Sharis said, "I wondered when I'd get to wash my hair."

That night in bed, Chad couldn't keep Sharis Sunbury out of his mind. Was she shallow as a puddle, or was she impossibly deep? The other girls had been unsurprising. One had seen an old man "pass out cold"; another kept talking about her family's dog. Those girls went on TV.

Three months later, Chad and Sharis were married. She didn't have her identity papers, but she had signed an affidavit. The notion that Chad had married a nineteen-year-old still surprised him (and yes, maybe titillated him, too). But . . . a fourteen-year-old?

"What difference does it make how old I was?" Sharis asked now, flicking a paper clip across her desk.

"Is it love or lust?" Chad had liked to say, rolling her on top of him. She had a way of arching her back and lifting her pelvis, sliding herself down onto what she called his maypole.

"Love," she'd say. "Lust. I don't know."

"Good God," Chad said, standing again and walking toward the window. "I could have been arrested."

"And as long as we're being all truthful, I'm really Cheryl May Smith. I mean, that was the name I was born with. But when the army people dropped me off at that church, I decided to change my name to Sharis Sunbury."

Of course she had changed her name. Chad turned and moved closer to her, aware that he was using his size to make himself a presence in the room.

Sharis said. "How boring is Smith? They didn't have any ID on me. I could be anyone."

"But your parents had just . . ." Chad lifted his hand to his forehead. "I could have changed my name to Gamble," he said, not sure why this seemed important. His father had offered once, very seriously, to change the family name from Gribble to Gamble, and his mother had just laughed.

Sharis said: "After what my parents did, why should I want their name?"

Chad felt as if the floor beneath him had suddenly gone soft. He didn't know if he'd be able to stay upright, if he could walk properly, if to cross the room he'd have to grip the edge of the chest of drawers. He had thought he was his wife's protector, but for years she'd been protecting him. What kind of fourteen-year-old could do that? Who was this woman, really? How much tougher was she than he was?

"I see your point," Chad said, sounding calmer than he felt. "You've been through a lot." *A lot*—he started to laugh almost hysterically at that description.

"It's not that big a deal," Sharis said.

Chad bit the inside of his lips to stop himself from sounding giddily deranged.

"I promise you," Sharis said. "I'm exactly the same person."

TUURO'S JAIL CELL was painted white and always cold. The air-conditioning never stopped. The bail was high, and no one Tuuro knew could afford it. He thought sometimes the pastor would show up with bail money, but the pastor never came. There were other prisoners in the jail—Tuuro heard them through the walls—but Tuuro was kept apart. He was in a center cell of a row of five cells facing five other cells; in this pod, Tuuro was the sole prisoner. Tuuro lay on his cot under the blanket with both his shirts on and his arms wrapped around himself and dreamed about his daughter, Lanita, and making her nine-minute eggs. Rare thing at age thirty-three for a Melano man from Dayton never to have been in jail. Well, now he was normal.

The lawyer English visited. He came into the common room and spoke through the bars into Tuuro's cell. "Good news," English said. "The genetics cleared you of the rape."

Tuuro didn't move under his blanket.

"You could thank me," English said, and Tuuro remembered cradling the boy's buttocks and rubbing them with oil.

The anti-rape, Tuuro thought, and yet at that time the boy had been dead. When he was raped he was alive. My God. Who would do such a thing? That must be sin, Tuuro thought. A thing a person would give anything to erase.

Tuuro sat up on his cot, pulled the blanket around him like a cape. "Will they let me out, then?" There was a whomping noise, and a fresh blast of cold air shot out from the vent above the door. Outside Tuuro's cell, Kelso the guard stood at the door to the pod and stared at the seam between the wall and the ceiling.

"There is a charge." English looked embarrassed. "Not murder, they don't have the evidence. Desecration of a corpse. I know"—English took in Tuuro's stare—"it's a crazy charge. No one at the office believes it either. You had nothing to do with the dogs! All we can figure is that they're wanting to flush out Nenonene." English glanced toward Kelso and gestured to Tuuro to stand and come to the bars. "He was very attached to this grandson," English whispered. "Supposedly he wants to visit the boy's grave."

"The general, Nenonene? He wants to visit Dayton?"

English smiled tightly, his eyes searching the cell behind Tuuro. Is he looking for a camera? Tuuro thought. But when English spoke his voice resonated with the wistful admiration Tuuro had heard before—but not from a white man—when people mentioned the Alliance general. "He's not your average person, Nenonene."

When English left, Tuuro curled back on his side again, his hands rubbing his arms. The cold air was still blasting. Before English's visit he'd felt as if he'd been tossed into a big forgotten hole. Now it seemed this hole wasn't forgotten at all. He glanced up at the vent, wondering whether the cold air was reward or punishment.

Years ago he had been wanted. He'd been fought over.

—Darling little boy, that little boy's not growing up to be a stucko addict like some people.

—*Look at you, all scrawny. Those ribs stick out like corrugation. Why don't you play outside, boy? Build up some meat on those bones.*

—*Reading already! I'll bring him some good books for him to read.*

—*Tuuro, look what Tati found. Almost full!*

—*I hate to see a child of intelligence living in a house without words.*

He had never seen it as bliss, his childhood. Quite the opposite. But now he understood the comfort of being wanted.

some tales of sanity

AMONG THE MANY rescue stories of the Torah, Chad's mother's particular favorite was the tale of Joseph, the boy with the coat-of-many-colors that his father had given him, the youngest son so hated by his brothers that they planned to kill him.

Of course that wasn't the good part. That was the nasty part.

The good part was that the oldest son, Benjamin, persuaded his brothers not to kill Joseph but to abandon him in a pit, then take Joseph's coat and stain it with animal blood and take it home to their father to show him that Joseph was dead.

The best part was that Benjamin planned to rescue Joseph from the pit, although when Benjamin went to do this he ran into traders traveling to Egypt who bought Joseph from Benjamin as a slave—a twist of fate that worked out well for everyone in Joseph and Benjamin's family, because it led to Joseph being accepted in the royal Egyptian court as an interpreter of dreams, which led, over time, to a position of authority for Joseph in the Egyptian government, which led to Joseph eventually identifying, testing, and helping the brothers who had abandoned him years before.

Benjamin, in Chad's mother's opinion, was the stealth hero of the Joseph story. Not that Benjamin was perfect, not that he did everything he hoped for, but he was the brother with a good heart and a plan, and those two things together could lead to greatness.

IT'S WELL KNOWN—as Chad said in his Dayton course— that in 1913 John Patterson saved Dayton. John was born in the town, and he grew up to head National Cash Register, known locally as NCR or "the Cash." He started the company in 1885, and was its CEO until he died. By 1890 National Cash Register was the biggest employer in Dayton, and by 1911 it had sold a million cash registers, a huge volume at the time. They were *the* cash register company. Their products showed up in the paintings of Edward Hopper. In building his company Patterson made innovations that transformed business: clean and well-lit factories, the whole idea of a sales force with "territories," international sales. For Cash employees he set up night schools, gardens, group exercises, and a credit union. In exchange for this attention to his workers, John Patterson had certain expectations. He could, and did, fire a room full of people in one outburst. An executive who'd disappointed him came back from a trip abroad to find his desk and chair in flames on the company lawn. (That last story was apocryphal, but Chad always used it, admitting its unlikelihood only after the class reacted.)

Patterson was—no surprise—insanely competitive, and he saw no reason for cash register companies other than his to exist. He condoned certain shenanigans. A defective register might be affixed with a competitor's name. A merchant who mentioned purchasing another company's product could be threatened. NCR lawsuits for libel and patent infringement cluttered the courts. All this resulted, in 1913, in an antitrust conviction for John Patterson and the sentence of a year in jail.

Notice my words, Chad would say: the *sentence*. Patterson appealed, and five weeks later it started raining. You could almost say that the resultant disaster was the answer to Patterson's prayers.

LYING CURLED UP in his cellblock bed, Tuuro thought of Nenonene. Everyone knew the stories. What Nenonene had done, originally, was what most of the world thought impossible: he unified Africa. Oh, not totally, and not without grief and murder, but Africa was now a different place. It was a threat. After all those years of Muslims versus Christians, of famines and epidemics and tribal warfare (and it wasn't just Africans who noticed that word "tribal," as if African hatreds were primitive and inescapable), now the African Union was a player on the world's stage. Of all the African countries, only Egypt was not part of the AU—a reflection of the U.S.-Egypt alliance forged in the early twenties.

It helped his rise that Nenonene was from Gambia, an out-of-the-way country that threatened no one; that he was educated, the son of a doctor and trained as a doctor himself, although he never practiced; that he was an unevangelizing Christian as likely to quote Mohammed as Jesus or John Wesley; that he was, in the peculiarly un-self-conscious way of some people of faith, comfortable with his own power. It also helped that he rose to leadership under the wing of Mamawe, whose cheesy corruptibility (he had once sold mineral rights to two provinces for American cash, two thousand pounds of pornography, 720 German rifles, and a case of Cointreau) made Nenonene appear all the more virtuous, at the same time Mamawe's unvarnished power gave Nenonene protection and clout. And Nenonene made his mark. He saw himself, during the siege of Rabat (known by some as the Massacre of Rabat, or the Forty Days), as the embodiment of Pinchas, the priest in Numbers who ensured his place at the top of the rabbinical line by impaling an Israelite and his heathen bride together in their private parts.

When a colonel had betrayed him, Nenonene had shot the man in the heart himself, Nenonene standing right in front of him, his jaw set and a video camera running. He was from an older time; a warrior, a man as capable of violence as of self-restraint.

I could talk to him, Tuuro thought. He would understand me. Tuuro saw them in two wingback chairs, half facing each other, coffee in china cups on the table between them. Tuuro would wear his gray suit, Nenonene his full uniform with medals. Tuuro would tell the general about the brown streaks, the cupboard, his grandson who reminded Tuuro of himself.

"I am lucky you came upon him," Nenonene would say, in his deep, British-accented voice. "Thank you."

An audience, that's what they called it. An audience with the pope, or with the president. All Tuuro wanted from Nenonene was an audience.

He spent hours thinking about Cubby, going over all the steps he'd taken with his body; he thought about Nenonene, what it must have been to be the smartest child in a small town in Africa, sensing you were born to a great destiny; he thought about Lanita eating his nine-minute eggs. When he jerked off he closed his eyes and remembered Naomi. Kelso, the guard who brought him his meals and sat reading magazines in the common room, had become a companion: a squat man with bushy eyebrows and a bad back and a wife he described as "not 100 percent."

"What do you do in here?" English the lawyer had asked, pulling at the neck of his shirt with his index finger. There was an old-fashioned TV in the common room, but it was broken. "Aren't you going crazy?"

Tuuro said nothing. He was supposed to go insane? Insanity was the expected state for a Melano man in jail with no entertainment? His own mind couldn't be enough? In the middle of a morning on his twenty-fourth day in jail, Tuuro spat at the wall. In five minutes the spit was dried and vanished.

Tuuro remembered Dakwon, his aunt's downstairs neighbor in the apartment building, a man in his twenties who could walk everywhere on his hands. Down steps, along ledges, on top of a log. Dakwon's shirt fell around his shoulders, the twitches of skin and muscle in his chest and belly exposed. Tuuro thought of Dakwon's hands, their sudden grips and accommodations. When someone tossed a ball at him or placed a brick in his path, Dakwon turned his body into a line of concentration. That must be sanity, Tuuro thought: keeping yourself, by attention and adjustments, upside down yet upright in the world. Insanity was nowhere near as compelling. Insanity was the fall.

Tuuro regretted the explosion of spit that had escaped his mouth. He thought of God and Nelson Mandela. He watched a spider in a corner build its web. He got Kelso to talk about his family. He smiled.

CHARLES AND DIANA managed to avoid each other for days, despite their being the only two people in the Audubon Center. Diana wandered in the woods, Charles at the edges of the fields. Diana got her water from the pump in the old garden, while Charles got his from the stream and chemically disinfected it. It wasn't apparent to either of them why the city water had disappeared, but it had, about three weeks before.

He'd forgotten the spring, Charles realized. The spring wasn't technically on Audubon land, but it was close, bubbling out of the ground in a grassy cleared concavity at the top of a wooded hill. Charles hadn't been there since winter. A tiny pool filled with running water and native watercress, feeding a stream that ran off down the hill. The spring was less than two miles away, and Charles could take thermoses to fill. He was sick of chemicals.

The trail to the spring was overgrown but trampled. Deer path, probably. The day was hot with thousands of mosquitoes, and Charles hurried through the woods up the hill. By the time he reached the clearing he was breathless and sweaty. There, in the center of the pool, sat a naked Diana.

She had to have heard him. Charles was filled with fury. That Diana had stayed on in his nature center. That she had found his spring. That she had the audacity to sit in it. He stood on the ledge above the pool and waved his thermoses. "Not very sanitary for drinking water now!"

She didn't answer, just shook her head and crossed her arms over her breasts and glanced behind her to her clothes, maybe ten feet away on the grass.

Charles pictured throwing her clothes into a tree. "I thought you got your water from the spigot in the garden."

"It's a peaceful spot here. Was a peaceful spot."

Charles banged his thermoses together. "Until you spread your human juices all over it."

"My what?"

Suddenly Charles knew just how he looked and sounded. He thought of the loincloth he had worn during the last three Indian summer celebrations, how he'd imagined it had made him look earthy and appealing. "Getting a little ventilation?" one of the elderly volunteers had asked, making him jump as she flicked the leather with her finger.

"I'll just go back," he said now, backing away. "I'm sorry I disturbed you."

Diana looked up, startled. "Didn't you come here to get water? I'll get out."

"Oh, no. This is your spring."

"I can't say it's my spring." Diana stood, one arm across her breasts, the other guarding her crotch. She looked like Venus. "That's like saying it's your sun, or my summer." She backed up to her clothes and, after a second's hesitation, pulled on her shirt first. "It's the world's spring, bubbling out like this," she went on. "I mean, who can own water?"

"Artesian," Charles said. "Pushed out of the top of the aquifer." Using, as he often did, a bit of knowledge as conversation.

They made love on the grass, and when they were done Charles too took his clothes off, and then they stretched out on their bellies and lay—as Charles pointed out—like two happy turtles basking on a shore.

CHAD BURROWED THROUGH the clothes in his chest of drawers. He had no hope of wearing his old pants, but there was a shirt from high school he could still button, barely. He turned to the side and pulled his gut in and looked at himself in the mirror. Not bad. His hair was thinning but not gray. The creases his father had had around his mouth were only fine lines on him.

"What are you doing?" Sharis was standing at the bedroom door. "I thought we could look up my family," she said, waving something in her hand. Chad turned toward her, confused and embarrassed, then realized what she was holding.

The Triple-A maps of old Ohio had taken on the glow of artifacts, kept in drawers to be carefully unfolded, or preserved between sheets of plastic and hung on walls. Plain City, Van Wert, Bellevue: erased, eradicated, absent. The new maps had no town names at all in the Grid section, only a vast green space, crossed only by the superhighways, labeled "The Heartland Grid." Some of the maps bore agricultural symbols—ears of corn, sheaves of wheat. There was such a sameness to the maps these days, Chad thought, as if even their designers had become cautious. Yet perhaps in every era there was sameness, so ubiquitous that no one even noticed.

"Be careful," Chad said, because Sharis's unfolding the map seemed dangerously quick and young to him.

Sharis sighed and spread the map out on the bed. "There," she said, pointing. "My mother's parents were from Greenville. Lloyd and Jessica Henson."

There was a museum in Indianapolis called the Heartland Heritage Museum. It was filled with school board notes and scenic postcards and sections of gates from large houses and other flotsam that had been, in the confusion and intensity of Grid Day, retrieved. The museum, privately funded, had a warehouse in Indiana close to the Ohio River. Few people were aware of this, but there had been a fire at the warehouse, and the artifacts of northwest Indiana were gone.

Sharis had never mentioned her mother's parents. Since the boys had been born it was as if her life before had never existed. Chad said, "Are your mother's parents still living?"

"Dead. But my mother had a big sister. Her name was Aunt Margie and she lived . . ." Sharis bent over the map, brow wrinkling ". . . here. Defiance."

He said, "You think your aunt could still be alive?"

"It's possible."

"Was she married? Did she have children?"

"I had a cousin. Rachel. She was two years older than me. They lived in town. I don't think they're effs now."

What was Rachel like? Chad wanted to ask. Did you like her? Did you spend Christmases together? But all those questions seemed too intimate. He blinked. "What about your dad's side?"

"His parents were divorced. I don't think I ever met his dad. His mom used to live with us. Meemaw."

Chad's mouth went dry. "Your grandmother lived with you? Was she with you when . . . ?" He couldn't bring himself to finish.

There had been a fairly concerted effort by the government to promote the Grid transplants to the general U.S. public as heroes (giving up their homes for the common good), but the more vocal transplants tried to grab the microphone with complaints, and after a few years the government's attitude became benignly forgetful.

"Oh, no," Sharis said, her eyes still roving the map. "She had another son besides my father, and he got killed in a motorcycle crash, and she had his photo of him beside her bed with a cross next to it, and when my father got all crazy-religious he said his brother's photo was Meemaw's idol. He wanted her to burn it. So she left."

Chad swallowed. "Could your grandmother still be alive?"

"I doubt it. She was already an oldie." Sharis's gaze returned to the map. "And I don't see where she lived. It wasn't far from us. In Beulah."

But they couldn't find a Beulah. "Belle Center?" Chad suggested. "Botkins?"

There were only two and half million transplants, a drop in the American bucket. The Ohio transplants (that was the word that was used, not "refugees") were settled largely in the Dayton/Cincinnati area (population over six million) or in southeastern Ohio, which was technically part of Appalachia and too hilly and rocky for farming. The Indiana transplants had a new city built for them in the karst country between Indianapolis and the Ohio River. All the transplants got government pensions and housing allowances. "Maria Stein?" Chad, still searching the map, asked Sharis. "Ada?"

Arguing during a meal: there was a weighted moment. Didn't so-and-so remember fourteen, fifteen years ago before the Grid, when breakfast cereal cost three times what it did now and there was a shortage of corn syrup to make candy? Even Sharis, who was young and healthy, had been too underweight to have periods when they first married. Conceiving Howard had taken some time. But conceiving Leon was effortless. Effortless! It was fun! The way it should be. How could someone disagree with food? Right there on people's plates was Chad's argument.

"Bellefontaine," Chad said. "That sounds like Beulah." He waited a moment, thinking maybe Sharis hadn't heard him. "Bellefontaine?" he said again.

She was crying. Chad scooped her up and sat them both down on the bed. He stroked her hair and said that he was sorry. In an odd way, he thought, these were his happiest moments.

"WHAT ARE YOU trying to do, exactly?" Kelso the guard asked, looking at Tuuro wedged upside down in his cell.

Tuuro told him about Dakwon walking on his hands.

"I could stand on my head once," Kelso said. "When I was about twelve. Come on, I'll unlock you and you can practice out here."

They shoved the chairs and table and TV aside in the common room, leaving a bare patch of wall against which Tuuro could lean.

"I'll hold your ankles," Kelso said.

Fortunately, Kelso caught Tuuro before he crashed. "Try it again," Kelso said.

DAYTON'S MARCH 1913 flood was also known as the "Great Flood." There were earlier floods, but this one changed things. Dayton made the front page of the *New York Times*. Dayton's downtown lay just south of the confluence of rivers where the first settlers landed. There was a levee to protect it, but the levee was too low.

The Indians had warned them.

Twenty feet of cold and coursing water. Horses swimming frantically in the current. Houses and railroad cars washed away. People scurrying to their second floors, to their attics, to their roofs. Gas lines breaking; explosions; fires.

Before the water overtopped the levee, before dawn, John Patterson—the corporate paterfamilias/maniac who ran National Cash Register, his jail time postponed by an appeal—walked the south levee of the Miami and saw trouble. He summoned his executives to an emergency meeting at 6:45 a.m. The name of their company, he said, was to be temporarily changed from National Cash Register to Dayton Citizens' Relief Association. The mission of this new company was to help out people who would soon be driven from their homes. His executives (you can imagine, Chad said) were startled. Glances around the table, bitten lips, a timid Sir, is that really our job? Isn't the levee still holding? Patterson said, "This meeting was not called to discuss the issue." He ordered his company to start making bread and soup in the company kitchens, to tap the company wells for drinking water, to send employees out to buy up clothing and staples, to build rowboats big enough to transport six people. "Start turning out the boats within an hour," John Patterson said. He designated a company building to be the flood relief headquarters, with floors for a hospital, a maternity center, a dormitory, and a laundry.

By 7 a.m., when the water first came over the levee, John Patterson's meeting was over. Evacuation, food, and shelter: the man had planned it all. And it worked.

"SON," CHAD SAID. Howard looked back at him over the top of Chad's car. "Tuck your shirt in."

Howard scowled and tucked. Fourteen, Chad thought. Three years older than this clown, and I married her.

He didn't lock his car (he never locked his car), but for a fraction of a second he visualized a clear shield flowing around it—radiant, protective—which Chad always thought of as *bondad*. Why he thought of a Spanish word instead of "goodwill" he didn't know, but *bondad* was what he thought. He had never had a thing he owned stolen, not from his house or his car, and Chad believed this was because of bondad. He wished ill of no one, and in consequence no one hurt him.

A good heart and a plan.

Bondad, his old apartment mate in college had said. Sounds more like bonehead.

There weren't that many cars at today's game. There weren't that many cars in Dayton, period. Consort's unreliability had made recharging cars a problem. And selling a car to ship to a more stable part of the country was a handy source of cash.

"Maybe I'll bring Leon to the next game," Chad said as Howard trudged behind him.

"Yeah, right," Howard said. They both knew Howard's brother had no interest.

Chad had been coming to watch the Dragons play baseball all his life, dating back to Fifth-Third Field and a friendly dragon mascot named Heater. His parents had hired Heater for one of Chad's birthday parties. Chad and his father had been part of the steady fan base that transformed the Dragons from Single A to Triple A baseball. Chad had had Dragon seats he called his own in three different stadiums, all in downtown Dayton.

It was a hot evening, and there were empty seats around them. Chad scored the game on his perc. "You want to do this?" he suggested. "Picks up your interest in the game." Howard shrugged. "Here," Chad urged, passing his perc to his son, but Howard let the thing almost drop from his hand. Chad made an exasperated face and checked Howard's response: his little eyes (Sharis's eyes) glared back from under a thatch of hair. Howard's hair didn't so much grow from his head as sprout, reaching a critical height and then toppling over. The rest of his face was doughy and unformed, but his eyes gave some hope of intelligence.

Chad didn't know how he'd ended up with two such different sons. Howard was as lumpy as Leon was spiky. Chad fretted about both of them. He could imagine Howard spending his life oozing from one chair to the next, and Leon having to be grabbed by someone to sit down for a moment.

"Look at the arm on that catcher," Chad whistled.

Maybe he should talk to Howard about his weight, set up a schedule of exercises for the two of them together.

Howard said, "Can I get a hotdog?"

He was much too big. Little Leon's body was ropy, while Howard's body didn't have a single muscle visible. I wasn't that big as a child, Chad thought.

"If you're truly hungry," Chad said.

The hotdog did make Howard happier. "Leon can't eat hotdogs," he said in satisfaction, because Leon's front two teeth were missing. Howard scored two innings himself, noting that the Dragons' pitcher always seemed to get behind on the counts. "I'm impressed you noticed that, Howard," Chad said. "Now, let's see if you can tell me what he's throwing."

Chad was concentrating so hard on the pitches he didn't notice the faint throbbing from the sky. Shadows were darkening the field before Chad looked up. "What the . . ." he said, and there they were, maybe twelve helicopters, painted shiny white and nearly silent, a dense formation over the field. Hot air stirred by the rotors, the smell of exhaust. A small American flag on each fender, like a tattooed side of a buttock. Chad glanced at the crowd around him: everyone was staring, mesmerized, into the air.

Chad would think later: the shadow of a dark wing over the field.

The pitcher stopped. He dropped his arms to his sides and craned his neck and looked up like everyone else. The baseball dribbled from his hand onto the mound, and although Chad thought fleetingly that the runners on second and third could legally break for home, no one on the field moved.

Not again, Chad thought, thinking of Sharis's stories of the Gridding.

"Poison?" Chad had said. Sharis (fourteen-year-old Sharis!) was seated across the picnic table from him, one hand shielding her eyes from the sun, telling him about the Gridding. Chad's brain had been blank, besotted, and then it was clicking as madly as a Geiger counter. "Your father mixed up *poison* for you?" Chad repeated, thinking he'd misheard.

"Char!" Howard was whispering. "Oh man, char! This is the charrest thing I've ever seen!"

"They're army helicopters. Hopi Hellions," Chad said.

"He always said the government was going to come for us," Sharis told Chad. "That was his guaranteed way out."

"Where are they going?" said a man in front of them, turning around. "The Base?"

The old air force base, which used to be a research facility, now housed troops from both the air force and the army. But the base was east, and these helicopters were pointed north. Chad said, "Maybe they're headed up to the Grid?"

"It's the soldiers, honey. Just like Daddy said." Her mother woke her up by leaning over her bed and blowing a strand of hair off her daughter's forehead.

"Am I dreaming?" Sharis (Cheryl) asked, but she knew she wasn't because she was hungry. Except when she was sound asleep, she was always hungry.

"It's the middle of the night. Just like Daddy said." Her mother's uncombed hair stuck up from the back of her head.

Sharis's mother touched her cheek. "Just remember, honey, there's never hunger in heaven."

"Is Howie up?"

"Your father's with him. Come on"—her mother coaxed Sharis to her feet.

"Let me get my shoes."

"Cheryl Mae! You don't need your shoes."

"But she let you get them, right?" Chad said. "And your robe?"

Sharis walked into her closet, slipped on her shoes. She took her robe off the hanger. "They're going house to house? The soldiers?"

"Just like he said."

They would all sit on the sofa in the living room. They each would have a wineglass, although the parents in the family didn't drink. A festive occasion. The best glasses.

The helicopters passed and still the pitcher stood frozen, the ball rolled to the edge of the pitching mound. The catcher walked up and talked to him, handed him the ball. The pitcher nodded. His next pitch hit the batter in the elbow. The batter fell to the ground writhing, holding up his elbow for the umpire. A lot of that was dramatics, but still.

Howie, small and blinking, was huddled against the arm of the sofa. Sharis's father was still standing, waiting for his wife and daughter. He held out his arms. Bastard, Chad always called him in his mind. Murderer.

Through the chinks in the living room curtains Sharis could see lights; outside she heard the murmur of motors and voices. She'd imagined it noisier.

"Let's sit down," her mother said.

Her father sat next to Howie, then Sharis, then her mother. Her mother reached around and touched Howie's hair with her fingers. "I love you, little buddy," she said.

"I don't want to drink it," Howie said.

"Come on, Howie. It's your favorite. Look at this"—the father sloshed the liquid—"grape." The father stuck a finger in the liquid and held it out. "Lick it off my finger."

Chad looked to the bullpen and made out the Dragons' manager pointing at a scrawny kid. Apparently this guy was supposed to take over on the pitcher's mound. "Who's that, Daddy?" Howard asked.

Hard knocks at the front door. Sharis's parents exchanged glances. "Hold him down," her father said. Her mother lifted Howie from the cushion and placed him in her lap, her arms tight around him. Her father made a hole of Howie's mouth and poured the purple liquid in.

Chad couldn't find the new pitcher's number on the roster. That was the minors: players came and went. "Good God," he said, looking closer at the kid. "He looks like he's about fourteen."

"Come on, people," a man's voice said from the door. "All your neighbors are out here. We can't wait forever."

Her mother swallowed the last of her own drink and gave Sharis an anguished glance. "Pick up your glass, honey."

"She didn't say 'Swallow it,' did she?" Chad said to Sharis. "She planned for you to live."

"Come on, people. You won't be hurt."

"Give me liberty or give me death," her father whispered, downing his drink in one gulp—a line that made Sharis giggle because it was so corny.

"Unto you, Lord, I commend my spirit!" That was her mother, surprisingly loud.

"Come on, people!" There was a low babble of voices, then the buzz of a drill. Sharis stood, dropping her glass onto the table. She ran out through the kitchen to the back door, glancing back at her heap of family. Her glass had toppled, purple liquid spreading on the wood.

"I know she wanted you to run away," Chad told Sharis. "She had a plan for you."

"*I* wanted to live," Sharis said. "I'm not insane."

"Koogie," Howard said. That was a new word to Chad, but from Howard's tone he took it as an affirmation.

"Jesus," Chad said after a few moments watching the new pitcher. "He can throw."

Everyone who attended that game remembered it, not just for the helicopters but for its other phenomenon: Joe Mateus pitching for the first time. Later, Mateus said the helicopters were an inspiration. He wanted to throw hard enough the pilots couldn't see the ball. The attendance that evening was just over a thousand, although later maybe a hundred thousand people said they'd been there. Chad remembered it as the day he started locking his car, the night he realized *bondad* was not enough.

true believers

JOHN PATTERSON, DAYTON'S flood-time hero, made his fortune in cash registers. Cash registers are—think about it, Chad said—an open admission that money is a temptation and people steal. The early National Cash Register sales literature stated this fact quite freely. Why should a merchant spend big money on a machine to tally sales and issue receipts? So an employee couldn't charge nothing. So an employee couldn't slip a friend two dollars of change instead of one, or pocket a customer's payment, or miscalculate a sale. So a customer couldn't return a sales item and say he'd paid full price. The cash register business was founded on the propositions that employer and employee have inherently different interests, that transactions benefit from daylight, that money is a powerful lure. None of the cash register's suppositions about human behavior is positive. It is, in its essence, a surveillance machine.

The other invention associated with Dayton—Chad went on—is more uplifting. Wilbur and Orville Wright were the bottom half of four brothers; their father, with whom they lived his entire life, was a United Brethren bishop known for his devotion to his family and his obstinate, often divisive, theological convictions. Their mother died of TB before Wilbur and Orville reached adulthood, and Wilbur nursed her in her final days. Their sister, Katharine, who also lived with their father, was the rare woman of that time who sought and obtained a college degree. The Wright brothers were not college-educated; in fact, neither of them finished high school. They were bright enough—the family had hopes of sending Wilbur to Yale, and Orville in seventh grade won an award as the best math student in the city—but for years they bounced around, the sort of young people that in a higher social stratum might be labeled dilettantes. When Orville tried to date a young woman from a prominent local family, her mother said, "You stay away from that boy. He's crazy." As a youth, Wilbur, after a hockey injury, was laid up for years with heart palpitations, writing later, with some passion, of how a man can become "blue." He worked as a clerk in a grocery store, as a printer, and briefly published a local newspaper. Eventually he and Orville opened (Chad winked at this moment, said, "this is the famous part") a bicycle shop, where they built the bicycles they sold. The Wright Brothers were slight, neat, slim-hipped men—birdlike, you might say. They always wore business suits, Orville's much nattier than his brother's. Shy and awkward, they never courted or married. Wilbur wrote to a relative: "I entirely agree that the boys of the Wright family are lacking in determination and push."

And yet. "For some years," Wilbur wrote in 1900, "I have been afflicted with the belief that flight is possible to man."

"Afflicted," Chad said. "Isn't that an interesting word?"

"EDUARDO, MI HOMBRE," the man in the booth said. "You guiding the woman's tour today?" Lila was the sole passenger in a truck entering the Grid, her car left behind in an underground garage. She had been iris-scanned, beamed by a materials detector, and patted down. She would be spending the night in a Grid guesthouse. She had been told to bring a change of clothes and toiletries, but no percs or phones were allowed. Her driver, Eduardo, had driven right up to the Grid barrier and through an archway that led to a checkpoint. Behind the checkpoint was a slightly shorter wall that was curved to block any outsiders' view. There were soldiers with rifles on either side of the road; on the left, beside the checkpoint, a woman soldier seemed to be making time with the man in the booth.

Eduardo had a definite accent, and Lila wondered where he'd come from. He was taking her, he said, to the guesthouse at Village 42. Other than that he'd said little. Perhaps his English was a problem.

"Shut your mouth!" the female soldier cried to the man in the booth. She leaned into Eduardo's truck and spoke directly at Lila. "Don't let these mariachis give you a bad first impression." Lila nodded awkwardly. "You been on the Grid before, darling?" the female soldier asked. Her hair beneath her hat was poufy and clearly took effort.

Lila, stiffening, shook her head. She didn't expect another woman, especially one younger than her, to call her darling.

"You'll love it," the woman said. "Everyone loves it. Best place in the world."

This surprised Lila speechless, and suddenly the checkpoint man was handing back her pass card, the gate was raising, the female soldier was waving, and Eduardo steered them right then left and there they were, two people in a truck with a wall behind them, looking out under a heat-hazed sky over 25 million agricultural acres that used to be part of Ohio.

It was less flat than Lila expected. Oh, it was flat: flat and huge and green (although the acres of wheat had their golden look) but flat less like a plain than like a beach, with small rises and hillocks and ridges. There was a road straight in front of them going north and a crossroad that extended east and west, and Lila knew from her reading that ten miles north there'd be another crossroad, with another crossroad ten miles beyond that: not for nothing was the transformed landscape called the Grid.

"We go north first," Eduardo said. And suddenly, with the fields falling from the road around her, it wasn't enough for Lila to be here, on the ground: she wanted to be in a plane above the landscape. She wondered at her own greediness, reminded herself she was lucky to be here at all. She sneaked a glance at the speedometer: eighty. Eduardo's hand was relaxed on the steering wheel; he looked around the Grid with possessive nonchalance. "Corn's good this year," he said. And indeed, the corn plants were erupting from the ground like thousands of green fountains. Thousands? No, millions, and Lila, who in water was used to big numbers, felt almost humbled by the thought.

"Wait a minute," she said after fifteen or twenty silent minutes. "Can we stop and look?"

He glanced at her, then halted the truck in the middle of the road. Lila almost objected, but of course no one else was coming, and if they did Eduardo's truck could be spotted from miles away. "Look," he said, waving his hand, and Lila got out and stood in the road.

So this was the Grid. It was broad and not quite flat, and it was alive. Vegetatively, not humanly, alive. Lila's forehead was slick with sweat. The Ohio sky had been transformed into a Big Sky. Every few miles there was a row of ten or twelve trees. She pointed at one of them and called out to Eduardo, "What?" "Windbreaks," Eduardo called back from the truck, and this was understandable, although today was hot and still. In front of Lila and behind her, in fields as thick and lush as a giant's carpet, was soy, the new American mainstay, usually processed into fake meat. Northeast, miles away, beyond acres of corn, buildings of a village shimmered on the horizon. They looked wavery and insubstantial in the heat. No cars.

All the intentional villages had numbers. Village 28 people had heard about: it was the processing center for perch and walleye from Lake Erie. "What number's that?" she called to Eduardo, pointing to the buildings.

Eduardo frowned and turned off the engine. The whine of an insect became audible. "Oh," he nodded when she repeated her question. "Village 104. They got a school there. We're going to 42." He pointed east.

In the middle distance a reaper crossed a field of wheat, shooting out a spray of chaff. If Lila strained her ears she could possibly hear it. Other than that there was no human sound or motion. The fields of wheat had a teeming look. A fly landed on Lila's shoulder.

"How many kids in the school?" Lila called, unwilling to leave her spot in the road. A bead of sweat ran down her forehead and stopped at her eyebrow.

Eduardo climbed out of the truck and approached her. "Thirty? They got two teachers, I know that."

How did they get teachers? Lila wondered if they advertised on the media. No one really had contact with the effs: rumors said they were clannish, suspicious. They married only each other. They rejected embryonic preselection. The Grid had its own message and info system, and data from outside were blocked. Family members that had been removed during the Gridding could send perc messages to the family members who stayed to become Gridians, but in return the outsiders got rare, sporadic answers, usually around holidays. The religion of the Gridians might have changed. There were stories of churches with stalks of wheat on the altar and roasted soybeans in place of communion wafers. "What are they like?" A friend of Lila's had asked a waitress once in Florida, where the effs took their group vacation. "They're people," the waitress had answered. Then, unburdening herself (and the Florida workers, Lila's friend pointed out, surely signed confidentiality agreements and were monitored): "They dress like bumpkins, and they don't tip diddly."

"Where do you live?" Lila asked Eduardo, glancing at his clothes. A buttoned shirt, jeans, work boots: he looked well-dressed enough to her, but she'd never had much sense of fashion

"Twenty-nine. Nice place. Good people. We call it Gayville."

It surprised Lila enough to hear Eduardo's town had an actual name and surprised her more to hear what the name was. She wondered what things about her the youngie in Columbus had read on the computer, what information had been passed on. Suddenly she wondered why Eduardo had been sent to guide her, if he . . . "Why Gayville?" she burst out, regretting her question right off. She shouldn't ask questions. They might kick her out.

Eduardo shrugged. "It's always been called that."

As if the origins of the name had been lost in time. The Grid was only thirteen years old, and it had taken a good year, Lila had heard, for the villages to be established. Until they were built, the effs lived in clusters of trailers.

"Do you have a mayor?"

Eduardo laughed. "There're only three hundred and six of us. We don't need a boss."

"Are you married to a woman?"

"Tamara."

"Kids?"

"We have three." He reached for his pocket. "Want to see them?"

"Cute," Lila said, inspecting the photo. *Like normal kids,* she thought. Everyone in the country distrusted, even feared, the effs: people who'd agreed to stay when towns they'd lived in or near were destroyed; people who seemed to thrive in communal isolation; people who apparently had no desire to escape the life their government had planned for them. Their staying on the Grid was like a collective back turned upon what people had taken to calling Free America.

She got back in the truck and Eduardo drove on, a series of small hillocks breaking the cornfields around them, surrounding a very round hill that reminded Lila of something. She twisted her neck to look back at it, a mound like a dromedary hump against the sky, and then she remembered the Indian mound near Lancaster, her hometown. That was when it hit her: this hill, like the Indian mound, was a burial hill of sorts: in it lay the remains of a town.

Bombed, then bulldozed. A new style of B-and-B.

Lila had never really liked this part of Ohio. Too flat, boring, windy. Yet suddenly she was overwhelmed with recollections of things that were gone: the stands of trees lofty as mesas, dark entrances like caverns at their base. Propane tanks tethered like dogs beside small houses. Farmhouses with green-black roofs and a baffling array of vents: square pillows, spouts, chef's hats. Cows nosing their way across the fields. Gone, all gone. And that was forgetting the towns.

She turned her face to the window, and Eduardo must have picked up some distress in her posture, because he seemed to be driving faster. The fields around them went to wheat and wheat, then corn on one side and wheat on the other, then corn and corn and corn. Lila found to her surprise that she was blinking back tears.

"Mile per mile, America's most wanted," Eduardo announced, repeating a slogan. He slammed on his brakes and Lila was thrown forward. "Almost missed the turn. Sorry." They squealed to the right, onto a road that looked exactly like their first one.

And, a few miles later, he stole a look her way: "Were you from around here?"

"From Ohio, but not Grid Ohio. I was born in Lancaster." A town that still existed.

Eduardo twisted his mouth in a considering way. "Southeast of Columbus?"

Lila was surprised he knew.

"Pretty down there. Hilly," Eduardo said. He hesitated, then hazarded a confession: "I like hills."

"Me too." Lila thought of the mounds behind them. "But not your kind of hills." She glanced at Eduardo to see if he realized she knew. *Best place on earth. Everyone loves it.* Like hell.

His eyes stayed on the road. New hillocks appeared to the north, far away. "It's good here," Eduardo said after a pause. "Wait until night."

They rode for an hour, skirting distant villages, and far away Lila spotted a farmhouse, which as they got closer looked exactly the way it should—two stories, painted white wood, wrap-around front porch, side door with a concrete stoop. A vision from her childhood, the old Ohio back in the nineties and aughts. A free-standing garage stood in the back. The mailbox was spotted like a Jersey cow. All that was missing was the barn with peeling red paint.

"Home, home on the Grid," Eduardo said, half-singing. He was from the hill country of Texas, he told her, and grew up speaking Spanish. He was one of the rare people accepted on the Grid as a volunteer. They pulled into the crushed stone driveway. "This is the guesthouse," Eduardo said. He pointed at an upstairs window. "You'll sleep there."

White curtains tied open with sashes marked the room that was surely the kitchen. A gray striped cat sat on the stoop in front of the side door. He eyed them warily, then streaked off as Eduardo opened his truck door. This is spooky, Lila thought. This is worse than Disney Universe.

A woman was already coming out the side screen door as Eduardo and Lila approached. She was forty or forty-five, wiry, short haired, wearing a simple white shirt and khaki slacks and a bangle on her arm. She wasn't unattractive, but her facial features and expressions seemed, like her body, pared down, as if she'd been constructed for efficiency. "Allyssa Banks," she said, holding out her hand to Lila. "Welcome to the Grid."

Allyssa and Eduardo chatted in the driveway for a few minutes—about weather and some new storage system for grain—and Eduardo got back in his truck and drove off. Lila realized it had been years since she'd heard the sound of pebbles under tires.

"Come on in," Allyssa said.

The kitchen floor was linoleum patterned to look like bricks. The lighting fixture was a frosted square of glass tucked up at the corners like a hankie. The refrigerator was a large white rectangle that hummed. "Incredible," Lila said. "Just like I remember."

"Wait until you see one of the villages," Allyssa said. "They're real, too. Tomorrow we'll go over to 88 for breakfast and a tour. I'll orient you this evening. Your room's upstairs."

They passed through a small dining room, its table covered with a white plastic lace overlay on top of a green tablecloth. In the living room sat a long curved sofa, an old-fashioned glass-screened TV, a Stratolounger, and two plastic deck chairs. A lamp with shells pressed into its base stood on an oak coffee table. Upstairs there were three bedrooms, all with double beds, and one narrow bathroom. Electric fans were fitted in the front two windows.

"Your choice," the woman said. "If you pick the room without the fan I'll move it."

Lila picked the room at the back, farthest from the road.

"My room's off the kitchen," Allyssa said. "You can clean up and I'll meet you downstairs."

"Best food in the world," Allyssa said at dinner, setting Lila's plate in front of her. People certainly are prideful here, Lila thought, but as she ate she thought Allyssa might be right. Soy loaf, mashed potatoes, fresh green beans with mushrooms, and lettuce and tomato with Thousand Island dressing. "We grow the green beans and potatoes at Plant City," Allyssa said. Where's Plant City? Lila wanted to ask, but something about Allyssa discouraged questions. She did request seconds on her food, thinking Allyssa could only take this as a compliment. She wondered how Allyssa stayed so thin. Knowing Lila was in water, Allyssa spent the dinner talking with clear knowledge about the Grid's average rainfall, irrigation system, and drainage, sounding, Lila thought, like some educational tape.

"I've never seen so much corn," Lila said at one point.

"That's just around here," Allyssa said. "Wheat and soy are the major Grid crops."

"How long have you been here?" Lila asked during dessert, peaches on soy ice cream, a treat Allyssa didn't partake of.

"Me? Personally? Almost fourteen years."

"Since the beginning?" Lila said in surprise, and this question seemed to release a switch inside Allyssa, because suddenly she started to talk like a real person.

There were no other Grid visitors tonight—a relief, Allyssa said. The Consort people had been here three weeks ago and refused to share beds: they needed cots in all three bedrooms. Nothing was right for them. They wanted peas instead of cabbage, decaf coffee, air-conditioning. As if this was a hotel instead of someone's home. "So you do all the cooking?" Lila asked. "Clean people's rooms?" She was having a hard time figuring his woman out.

"I do everything," Allyssa said, her low-pitched voice almost purring.

Lila felt a tug of wistfulness. Lila had said things like that, once. She asked, "If you've been here fourteen years, were you in on the planning stage?"

"Of the Grid?" Allyssa gave Lila a respectful look. People didn't wonder about her, Lila realized. They took her as a simple hostess. "I was at an experimental farm in Australia called Lindisfarne." Not only Allyssa's voice, but her whole body was relaxing; she reached with her bangled arm to scratch the cat under the table. When Lila caught her breath, Allyssa looked up sharply. "You've heard of it?"

"Vaguely," Lila said. "Didn't they develop a good desalination system?" Allyssa nodded vigorously, and Lila had the sensation she had just avoided a landmine. She knew the desalination system had been renowned, but that wasn't why Lila remembered the farm's name. Something odd had happened at Lindisfarne, some scandal or crime, but Lila couldn't quite remember what.

"The government people who were interested in maximal production came to us—it was during the Short Times—and asked us to help plan an agro area. It only took us six weeks to scout possible locations, and another six months to plan. We worked day and night, studying data from all over the U.S., picking the site, planning the crops. I came over here in '32 with the study group. Basically, we thought it up, and then the government took care of the logistics."

Bigger than the Hoover Dam, people said. A more ambitious project than the Yangtze flooding. As world-changing as the Panama Canal, as the A-bomb, as the Weather Station. And here Lila sat in the center of it with one of its founders, in a farmhouse designed to look innocuous. The enormity of it made Lila dizzy. Back in Dayton she was being marginalized; she might never sit talking to power again.

"Are there other people here from Lindisfarne?"

Allyssa frowned and counted mentally a moment. "Six others." Very serious, Lila thought. And, oddly, all one color: her eyebrows and skin and hair were medium beige, broken only by a sprinkling of freckles on her nose. Born in Washington State, she'd said, although her mother was originally from Ireland. "I met my husband at Lindisfarne," Allyssa said.

"He's one of the six?"

"No. He lives in Paris."

"France?" Allyssa flashed a rare smile, and Lila shook her head in surprise. Almost impossible to imagine a man in Paris married to a woman living here. Outside, the crickets had started. "Is he French?"

"American," Allyssa said. "He visits every couple of months."

"Do you have children?"

A tiny wince, then Allyssa waved her hand toward the window. "This is a magical place. How could a child compete?"

Lila felt a chill. She was sitting with a true believer. She saw in her what Lila had once possessed: excitement, faith, fervor. Yet Lila had never been selfless. She'd wanted game tickets, messages from the vice president, children. She'd never spoken of Dayton as magical. In the spectrum of social believing, this woman was way beyond her.

IMAGINE (THIS IS Chad's example) you are sitting with a friend on a hillside, watching the buzzards. "Look at the way the tips of their wings bend," your friend says.

You watch a minute. "So?"

"It helps steady them in the air." Your friend gets out a paper and pencil.

"Interesting," you say, not really meaning it.

Your friend (his name is Wilbur) is frowning, drawing.

Afflicted. It is not too strong a word.

LILA SAT IN the Stratolounger, Allyssa in the deck chair. They talked for hours.

A social structure modeled on the Amish, leavened by some of Janet Hailey's ideas about pioneer family resilience and data from the long-term space flights.

An Israeli-German defense system at the northern border.

Town architecture done by Kyoto Masuki, based on photographs of farmhouses and towns from the American 1950s, a famously stable era.

Old-time computers and phones in centralized, communal locations. No percs.

Two-parent families.

Grandparent-centered, communal child care.

Persuasion, not coercion.

The likelihood of a "farmer's gene."

Small schools with low teacher-student ratios and specially trained teachers.

A theologian of sorts, Richard Osbourne, living in Village 57.

Pride in their products, their lifestyle, their Gridian way of life.

Gridian sports.

Lila suddenly remembered why Lindisfarne was famous. They'd had a zero population growth policy, and their leader (Germant? Germantz? he was a home-schooled product from somewhere in the Midwest, patchily brilliant, charismatic, handsome, the usual commune-leader combination) developed a policy of forced abortions. There'd been a video, Lila remembered—a screaming and thrashing woman being carried through a clinic's doors.

"What about birth control?" She blurted.

Allyssa hesitated. "We have excellent medical care. Everything's up-to-date. There's a nurse-doctor at Village 88, where we're having breakfast. I'll introduce you."

"But what about population size? Do you try to limit that at all?"

"Gridians are very responsible," Allyssa said. "This life is paradise to them. I really think part of the Grid's genius was its self-selection, and Gridians have farming in their blood. To be able to do it, year after year, to see and eat the fruits of their labors . . . They have no desire to change."

"But what about accidents? Don't people ever have accidents?"

"Accidental children? Unlikely." Allyssa rapped the arm of her deck chair. "Come on. Let's go outside."

They walked silently across the grass into the fields, the cat darting between them, the moon glowing and elliptical like a slightly worn coin. Eduardo was right, it was a different thing at night, with the crickets and the rustling corn, water trickling from the irrigation tubes at their feet and the whole sensible world a wide and seemingly endless expanse of fertile earth. Lila felt the dome of heaven above her, like the first person in centuries to believe in a flat earth. But everyone who lived on the Grid must feel this. In the kitchen of the guesthouse hung the famous satellite picture of '35: the United States a patchwork of brown, green-brown, gray, and beige, the Grid in its right center glowing like a great rectangular emerald. Grid green. That green was a declaration: an inarguable abundance, a wet slap in the face to those who said it couldn't—or shouldn't—be done. It was done. It worked. People ate, people lived. The Gridians lived their insular, useful life, so content you never heard of anyone escaping it. And now the rest of the world—Lila thought of the occupiers of Cleveland, the gray- and mud-faced soldiers with their shabby uniforms and ill-fitting hats—wanted the Grid too. She couldn't blame them.

Lila turned back toward the guesthouse, her heart suddenly hard. The Suds and the Afros and the Euros would never get this. Never.

"See?" Allyssa smiled.

always a story

THERE'S ALWAYS A STORY, Chad liked to tell his students: that's how the news media work. And a proper story has a beginning, middle, and end. There may be epilogues and prologues (there usually are); someone in the future may pop up with a reinterpretation; one story may segue into another. But there's always a story. In essence the news media couldn't be more conservative. Their thought is highly traditional, like human thought, and it hasn't changed in the two hundred and fifty-plus years of Dayton's history.

In 1913 the story started with catastrophe. The Great Flood death toll was in the three hundreds, much smaller, thanks largely to the efforts of John Patterson and his company, than it could have been. Still, property damage was tremendous. On top of that the city was faced with a new enemy—anxiety. Shortly after the waters receded, a local businessman named Adam Schantz made the rounds with an "audacious" proposal: the private fundraising of a million dollars for flood prevention for Dayton. The campaign started immediately. John Patterson spearheaded the effort. A slogan—"Remember the Promise You Made in the Attic"—was introduced and the fundraising goal more than doubled. The story of Dayton's

1913 flood ended in triumph with the construction of the five dry dams above the city. The epilogue was public praise and the city's survival.

That summer, 2047, the story was the Alliance and its threat to the Grid. The story started with the invasion of Cleveland, and it was in its expository phase now, with Nenonene and his cronies hanging on to Cleveland by their fingernails, talking up its orchestra, its art museum, arranging payments to its politicians. Why was Nenonene there, if an assault on the Grid wasn't expected? And if the Grid went, what would happen to Dayton? It had its air force / army base (northeast), its factories (north and west), its nuclear power plant, a stable aquifer and flood protection. What invader wouldn't want it? And if Dayton's people kept leaving, at what point would an invader need only to show up? Could Dayton end up as farmland, too?

CHARLES AND DIANA moved in together at the center. They positioned their bed—a mattress they carried in from the interns' house—under the flying owl, next to the exhibit of stuffed turtles. They spent hours talking. Charles thought he really hadn't lived compared to Diana, with her romances and failed marriage and fertility clinic job. Every incident she recounted emphasized to him his lack of worldly experience. What could he talk about with her? Mostly he asked questions.

"Most clone-parent relationships are normal," Diana said at one point, not wanting to discuss it more, but Charles had heard stories: mothers who, obsessed with their cloned daughters, tried to erase all the grievances of their own childhoods.

"Some people think it's not normal," Charles said. "You can love your clone too much."

Diana rolled her head in Charles's direction and smiled. Of course he would think of self-love: he was that sort of man. You could tell by looking at him his mother had adored him beyond reason. But Diana knew that self-love wasn't the problem, the problem was self-hate. She had a terrible memory of the clinic, the woman with blue eyes and a tangle of dark hair screaming, "Get rid of it! Just get rid of it!" and all the commotion and fear it had taken to do just that, with the pregnancy being so far along. But the specialist had done it, the fetus lying in pieces on the surgical tray, its disarticulated arm as big around as a hotdog, because, as the specialist said, this was the woman's decision completely, being that the fetus was her clone. Like brushing your teeth, he said, or defecating: in so many of your daily acts your own cells are destroyed. The specialist was a pleasant man. He parted the sea of children at the yearly fertility picnic like a guardian angel, but there was the mad scientist in him, too. *Let's try this; no, let's try that! What if we . . . ? Oh dear, we'll do it differently the next time.*

Diana was a counselor at the clinic. Why did the blue-eyed woman not want her clone anymore? Why, at this late date? And would she consider carrying it to term, putting it up for adoption?

"Just get rid of it!" the woman shrieked. Something she had shoplifted, Diana gleaned, a filthy man she'd slept with. No crimes Diana would consider capital. *I hate myself and want to die.*

"Get rid of it!" the woman screamed, so loudly they had to shut the fire door.

"Oh, I don't know," Diana sighed to Charles now, turning her gaze to the stuffed owl in suspended flight above them. Charles had a comforting armpit: cozy, with a yeasty scent. "People aren't livestock, you know. They're complicated." Charles nodded, respecting her superior knowledge. And to Diana *this* seemed simple, lying nestled into Charles. Part of her wished the war would never end.

"GEORGE AND I have been thinking"—Gentia moved herself heavily through Sharis's front door—"and we want you to do us."

"Edit you?"

Gentia nodded. "We have a security setup in every room. All we'd have to add is the cameras."

"You don't want every room," Sharis said quickly.

"What do we have to hide?" Gentia laughed harshly. "Seriously, though. We want a history for our children."

"I'm not really taking new clients." George and Gentia never talked about their children, both of whom lived far away.

"Chad's tenure that lofty, hunh? I thought you could use the business."

Clearly Gentia had no idea the level at which Sharis worked. "I have nine clients," Sharis said. "Including a family in Houston and a couple in Norway. I have a Spanish family, too. Translation modules," she added in explanation.

"Consorting with the enemy."

"Their lives are like ours." This was not quite true. The Spaniards had a whole flowchart of relatives, and the Norwegians, surprising for a northern climate, often walked around their house nearly nude. "I'm expensive."

"I guess you would be, with clients like that. How much do you think you could get out of us in a week? Two hours? Three hours?"

"Maybe ten minutes. That doesn't sound like much, but you've got to keep things moving." How can I refuse business? she thought. And yet . . . "I've never had a client I actually know," she said.

"Do you know us?" Gentia said.

TUURO WALKED UP the outside steps to his apartment, the brightness of the sun a relief after his days shut inside. "Mr. Simpkins, you're free," his lawyer, Mr. English, had said. "They dropped the charges. You can go home."

About 4 p.m. The door off the deck was locked, and it took a moment to remember the key in his pocket. Eight weeks of keys in someone else's pocket. Tuuro felt a sudden lightness of heart. He waved to the sheriff's car waiting in the alley, and it pulled away.

His apartment was as stuffy as an attic. His landlady downstairs must have closed his windows. He went around opening things up. At his bedroom, he leaned on the doorframe and smiled. His wide bed had never looked so welcome.

He went to the refrigerator to get a pop, and when he opened the door he felt a surge of betrayal. Dried and fissured cheese, crusted milk, a cut sandwich with mold blossoming from its seams. His landlady could have emptied out the fridge. Tuuro grabbed a garbage bag and starting tossing.

Ashamed of him, maybe. Angry at him. *My best tenant and you ended up in jail!* But Kevious Welty had been arrested for armed robbery, and he still sat on the landlady's porch and watched the street. She had a whole cadre of Brown Street tenants in and out for drunk and disorderly. This rotten food: as if she were calling him guilty.

But then Tuuro's cringing kicked in. Good-hearted woman, nothing wrong with her, and she had closed his windows. His fridge probably never crossed her mind. And if she had decided not to empty it, maybe that was something he deserved. He wasn't friendly. He sat out front with the guys who played checkers and watched the traffic and drank just one beer. "The Deacon" they sometimes called him, knowing he worked in a church. Tuuro realized he was behind on his rent. His landlady could have tossed all his things out.

Judging. There he'd been—judging, something the Lord warned against. He picked up a cantaloupe, his hand sinking in the rot of it. He wondered if his days in jail had changed him, made him not exactly bitter but less generous in thought.

He wondered about his bank account, if the church had deposited his last paycheck. He could call the church and ask. But he didn't want to talk to the pastor. The pastor was a merry man, jokes and asides and teasing conversation, but when you came right down to it: where was the person? The pastor was a meticulous construction of a person, lifelike from every angle but hollow at the core. Tuuro remembered him backing away from Cubby's ravaged grave. How could a man like that sustain you?

Tuuro could sustain you. He stood up, washed his hands, twisted shut his bag of rotten food. He opened his only outside door, the door at the back of the house—what a pleasure it was to open your own door—and descended the steps to his landlady's garbage pails. Something hit his left jaw.

A thump which was his body hitting the stairs. The pain was tremendous. A shout, footsteps, a flash of navy blue. The garbage bag dropped from his fingers and bounced down the steps. Shot, Tuuro thought, surprised he hadn't heard it, but when he touched his face he didn't feel blood. On all fours he pulled himself up the few steps to his deck, then rolled himself through his door. After a few seconds he willed himself to roll backwards to push the door closed. He tried to open his mouth, but the pain in his jaw crescendoed into actual noise.

In the bathroom he pulled himself up on the cabinet, facing the mirror. The side of his face was deformed and purplish; he touched it gently with his fingers, surprised it had swelled so quickly. He hadn't been shot, certainly. A rock? Why? What had the voice been shouting?

Loud steps on his outside staircase and a banging. There was a straight view from the hall outside the bathroom to the door, and Tuuro stood a moment, wondering if he should risk exposure. Another set of knocks, more insistent. "Tuuro, are you there? Tuuro, it's me."

Kelso was still in his uniform. "Jesus," he said as Tuuro let him in. "How'd they know you were out?" He hesitated, then answered his own question: "Must have someone inside." He looked at Tuuro's face. "What hit you?"

Tuuro explained, ending with the obvious question.

Kelso's woolly eyebrows met. "Listen, some people think Nenonene wants you killed. He gave a speech in Cleveland . . ."

Tuuro almost couldn't grasp it, after his fantasies about Nenonene talking with him, thanking him, and sitting in an armchair next to him talking about the boy.

"He said vengeance was the Lord's, but man could be its agent, and that's why . . ."

Tuuro led Kelso down the hall to his bedroom, closing the door behind them. The safest room. The room no one could see into. "But the genetics!"

Kelso shifted uncomfortably. "Not everyone trusts the genetics. And even if they did, they might not trust the people announcing the results." Kelso angled himself over to the bedroom window, peered out toward the street. "This a pretty safe neighborhood?"

"I always thought so."

"Can I message my wife?" Kelso asked. "I left my perc in the car. I need to keep in touch with her. She's not . . ."

"One hundred percent," Tuuro finished, pointed Kelso to the antique PC in the corner of the room. When Kelso tried to log on the thing was dead. "Does this happen?" Kelso asked.

For a split second, peeking out the window, Tuuro thought that he was seeing things: the phone and cable lines to his house had been cut. A bristling handful.

Kelso breathed in quickly, almost a whimper.

"I have friends I can stay with," Tuuro lied. "You should leave now when it's light out, and everyone will know you're not me."

They both chuckled.

"I don't feel safe leaving you," Kelso said.

"The door to the deck is the only egress," Tuuro said a moment later. They were crouched side by side now, leaning on the inside wall of Tuuro's bedroom.

Kelso smiled. "I always wanted to talk pretty like you."

"Thank you. My"—and here Tuuro hesitated an instant, wondering what to call Aunt Stella—"foster mother insisted on proper speech." She had never become his mother. She had found an elderly widowed doctor and forgotten about Tuuro totally.

"I can tell. Your mother died sometime?"

"When I was six." He didn't tell Kelso she'd been shot.

"Me too. Nine. Cancer. Your dad okay?"

"I've never known my father."

"Oh." Kelso glanced quickly in Tuuro's direction. "My father was okay. Then I have that sister lives in Oklahoma." He fell silent for a moment. "You had that brother."

They had talked about this when Tuuro was in jail. His brother had been killed. Drugs.

"Your life," Kelso said now, and he seemed to be struggling with how to phrase this: "I wouldn't want your life."

"Thank you," Tuuro said.

"Geez," Kelso said a few minutes later, squirming against the wall, "I've gotta sit down." He dropped to the floor and stretched out his legs in front of him. Tuuro followed and looked at their four legs, a hairy bit of Kelso's left calf exposed.

Kelso fanned himself. "Lucky it's cooler. If you'd gotten out a week ago we'd be melting now."

The sentence made no sense, but it was perfect. And suddenly Tuuro was suffused with a floating sensation he could only call happiness, that here he was back home and talking with a friend. They talked about Kelso's current and past houses; about the high cost of remodeling; about Sharis, who, amid much fanfare, had renounced her U.S. citizenship and was moving to Australia; about ex-President Cooper's debilitating illness, which was not quite Parkinson's; about different brands of spaghetti sauce; about razors; about how Kelso's wife had days so suffused with fear she couldn't bring herself to open the oven door. During all this conversation, it was peaceful. A beam of light shot onto the bedroom floor. Sunset.

"Tuuro, listen to me," Kelso said. "It's been almost two hours and we haven't heard nothing. I want you to walk out that door with me and lay down in the backseat of my car. I'll take you to my house. There's nobody big on Nenonene in my neighborhood."

"But your wife . . ."

"She can't live wrapped in cotton." Laboriously, Kelso got to his feet. "I've been thinking about this. We'll just walk right out. You let me hold your arm it'll look like I'm arresting you."

They left by the only door, walking quickly outside and down the steps, and just past the bottom of the steps a man (a kid, really, and very light-skinned, not like Tuuro imagined) burst from the side of the house and fired two shots, one pinging into a garbage can, the other piercing Kelso's hairy calf.

"I'm a police officer!" Kelso croaked as he went down. "You got hell to pay!"

Kelso's face went so white his eyebrows looked like something from a disguise kit. "Take my sock off and wrap me up, okay?" Kelso said, his hands tight around his calf, blood seeping through his pants and between his fingers. "Don't worry, I'll be fine." Tuuro's trembling fingers tied the sock. "Here, take the keys out of my pocket. Tuuro, you get going."

"But where should I go?" Tuuro was appalled at his own voice. The English was perfect, but the words came out as ragged as a string of curse words or a howl of pain.

"Somewhere south. Go south, Tuuro; it's safer down there. Hurry. See my car there?" Kelso nodded down the street. "Blue."

Tuuro bent over to grip Kelso under his arms.

"Are you crazy? I'm too big for you! Just go. Call the cops right away from my car. They know this neighborhood. They'll be here in two seconds."

He was right. Tuuro nodded and ran for the car. Hurled like a stone, he thought. He screeched down his own street in Kelso's car, turned on Third, turned on Philadelphia, passed two police cars already headed Kelso's way. At the corner of Philadelphia and Ludlow dark figures appeared beside the car and pounded, yelling, on the passenger window. Tuuro gunned the car and headed off for I-75, the highway south to Cincinnati, filled less with fear than a sick realization—part relief, part embarrassment on Nenonene's behalf—that the allies of Nenonene were easy to shake off.

IN A SMALL, detached brick rental in a suburb of Dayton, an interview was going on. The interviewee had a wobbly chin and the wide-eyed, dazzled look of a baby, as if he had jumped directly from infancy to adulthood. Fat Boy, the interviewer thought. *Can you tell me the names and ages of all your family members at the time of Gridding? What was most distinctive about [name of town]? How would you describe [name of town] to someone who'd never been there?* The interviewer was thankful, as always, for the Historical Society checklist.

Fat Boy was from Port Clinton, west of Cleveland on Lake Erie. He'd been ten. When friends visited from New York City, they couldn't believe Lake Erie wasn't an ocean. Mayflies hatched from the lake in June, blew out of the water, and stuck wherever they landed. Fences, cars, sides of houses covered with mayfly fur. A smell to them, a lake smell.

The interviewer paused over his perc. "Where were you resettled?"

"Near Middletown. Oak Creek Estates. Three-bedroom detached house. Prefab." Fat Boy looked at his knees.

"School?"

"Shitty school. They brought in teachers from Puerto Rico, I could hardly understand them."

"What did you do for fun?"

"Fun? You know. Games."

"You weren't living near any of your old friends?"

"They didn't do that for us. They didn't keep our town together." The interviewer already knew this. For some communities, there had been breakdowns in their plans for relocation. Political issues, economic issues. "I tried to meet some people," Fat Boy continued, "but I got in with this crowd that stole, and my mother found out and she got rid of them. Then it was like, why bother? I moved to Dayton because I might as well. My big sister was here." Fat Boy worked his mouth. "I think they're lucky, the Gridians. They got a life, up there."

The Historical Society interviewer had heard a hundred variations of this line. He wondered if Fat Boy recognized what he was saying. Probably not. It was the Historical Society's job to make the connections.

"Do you ever think"—the interviewer bent close, his breath almost touching Fat Boy's shoe—"of what they took away from you?" Fat Boy blinked, looked up. The interviewer's voice got softer. "What gave them the right to dismantle your whole life? Think about it: don't you wonder how they *dared*?"

"WHAT DID THE Gridians look like?" Kennedy asked.

Average white people, Lila said. Except for Eduardo and a few Melanos in the dining hall, almost everyone was white. Old-fashioned. They dressed casually, really no differently than any other non-city Ohioan. Several of the adolescents had the pierced web between the thumb and first finger that was the latest style. They ate breakfast at long communal tables, but Lila and Allyssa sat apart, and the people who came up to speak to them (to Allyssa, really) had the look and sound of show people playing a part. "Did you taste those tomatoes from Village 6?" "We got almost two inches the other night; Leon in 28 said they measured two point six." Only the young children had the tiniest interest in Lila. They peered around and through their mothers' panted legs, and one boy asked her, in an accusatory tone, "Are you really from a *metro*?"

"It was like eating with Amish people," Lila told Kennedy.

Lila used to sit in the backseat as her mother drove northeast of Columbus to Holmes County to visit the Amish. It wasn't visiting, really; it was gawking. "Look, look, there's a horse and buggy!" Lila's mother would say. Or: "See how that little girl's dress doesn't have any buttons?" As exciting as spotting deer. The modern people who were the Amish's neighbors ("the English," the Amish called them) were less transfixed. But to Lila and her mother the Amish were more than people. You glimpsed them in gaggles, tipping their heads to one another, shy and glorious creatures you would never have the chance to know.

"Am I going to get to talk to anyone?" Lila had asked Allyssa.

"You're talking to me!" Allyssa said.

People drove around the countryside looking for Amish bake sales and fruit stands, and it wasn't that their produce and cakes were especially tasty, it was that the purchase bought the presence of *them*. Maybe you could glimpse their lives, their hopes; maybe they'd follow you, talking, to your car. Useless. The Amish were never lured away. Within their own families and community there were surely arguments and love affairs, grudges and rebellions. These an outsider could only imagine. The Amish, like the Gridians, betrayed themselves only to each other.

Kennedy said, "I always thought the Amish were boring. I hate the Amish."

Kennedy said, "Lila, all it is is a great big piece of farmland."

a dose of yearning with the mashed potatoes

"TERLESKI MESSAGED US," Sharis said. "There's going to be a meeting about Cub Scouts." It was late August. School was starting in a week.

Chad sighed. "Cub Scouts?" Chad would be starting classes, too. Two people from his department had left—an assistant professor and an instructor—and virtually none of the East Coast students were returning. Chad would be teaching classrooms of Catholic Ohioans. Other than his Dayton course, always enjoyable, the year already sounded dull.

"There aren't going to be many boys," Sharis pointed out. "Maybe six. Seven if they let in Bruce Hawthorne. He should be going on to Boy Scouts, but there is no Boy Scouts. So he wants to redo Webelo."

"How can there not be Boy Scouts? Didn't they learn anything earning their survival badges?" Chad had never liked the Boy Scouts. From the moment they threw him in a pool and asked him to remove his jeans and blow them up as a flotation device, he was convinced the whole organization was loony.

"They don't have a leader. Terleski's a leader!" Sharis was startled at the fervor in her voice. What did she care about

Cub Scouts? But she admired, she realized, Terleski's dogged-ness in keeping his den going. Everyone was giving up, hiding inside, talking about not sending their children to school. Terleski, like Sharis, like Chad, was holding out for normal life. President Baxter, in his daily messages, was endlessly reassuring. The Euros, rumor had it, didn't think the U.S. was winnable; they might persuade the Suds and Afros to pull out from Cleveland as a first step to an Alliance-U.S. truce. "It's only Bruce who's switching from Boy Scouts," Sharis pointed out. "And he's not very tall."

The house next to them had been abandoned. "Hi, doll-face!" its elderly owner, Mr. Hofmeister, used to call to Sharis. "How are my little devils?" He had talked to Sharis on a Thursday, and the next day he and Mrs. Hofmeister waved as they backed out of their driveway. That was the end of them, so far as Chad or Sharis knew. Chad kept mowing the Hofmeister lawn, and Sharis cut their flowers for her own house. She couldn't help feeling resentful that the Hofmeisters, for all their purported realism in leaving, hadn't planted vegetables instead of flowers.

"You think Leon doing Cub Scouts is a good idea?" Chad said now to Sharis. Because how could he dispute her opinion, she who had a life experience doctorate in survival?

"Of course," Sharis said. "Keep him busy."

In the summer, Sharis missed her little brother's dirty fingernails. She could forgive her parents everything but him. At night she pressed her ear into Chad's chest to hear his heartbeat. His arms wrapped around her felt like a warm stockade.

"WHAT DO YOU think," Chad would ask in his class this year (and he hoped he got a Dayton class, without a Dayton class he didn't think he could keep going), "are typically midwestern virtues?" There was always silence after this question, and then a few tentatively raised hands. The answers were predictable: perseverance, diligence, politeness (suggested politely), modesty ("people aren't too full of themselves here? they don't think they're too char and all?"), orderliness, thrift. One thing, politely, was never mentioned: ambition. And this omission gave Chad his opening.

The glider designers of the Wrights' time had been concentrating on building a machine that was "inherently stable," that would steer through the air like a car rolling down a road. But Wilbur and Orville were bicycle builders, and what makes a bicycle stable? Not the machine itself, but its rider. Orville, the little brother, thought the key to a successful heavier-than-air machine would be to give the human flying it more control. "I like Orville," Wilbur said. "He likes a good scrap."

The buzzards, Wilbur noticed, when buffeted by a gust of wind, "regain their lateral balance . . . by the torsion of the tips of their wings." He was standing in his bicycle shop talking with a customer, idly twisting a long thin box in his hands, when he noticed how the ends of the box could be angled while the center of it stayed steady. He pictured the broad sides of the box as the upper and lower wings of a biplane. He discussed his idea with Orville, and they built a model, a biplane kite with a five-foot wingspan and double sets of strings secured to the tips of each wing. They kept the kite level in the air by adjusting, with the strings, the relationship between the wings. They called this "wing warping."

It should be possible, Wilbur and Orville both believed, to build a machine to make man fly. At first their goal was to build a pilot-controlled glider, so a human could steadily ride the currents of the air. Later—in 1903—they decided to add an engine and propellers, aiming for a machine that could get into the air and stay aloft by its own power. Accomplishing their goals required an orderly approach, the sequential solving of various problems—many of which they could anticipate—and the completion of certain tasks. Their family thought they could do it. They thought they could do it.

You don't think that was ambitious? You don't think that was audacious?

This is where Chad raised his hand and shook his finger "They were as ambitious as Napoleon," he said. "As ambitious as Adolf Hitler, as Bin Laden, as Nenonene now. Even more ambitious! More audacious! They didn't care about conquering land. They wanted the sky."

HOW HAD THIS happened? Lila had gone up to the Grid out of simple curiosity, her first impression was shock at the burial mounds of towns, she'd spent a night in a farmhouse calculated to be Essence of Farmhouse, and now she wanted to live there, she dreamed about cornfields, their mice and rustling invading every crevice in her mind. But how could she stand living there, realistically? Where were the trees? Where were the theaters, the plazas, the restaurants? She wasn't a farmer. She couldn't tell a soybean from a lima bean. And those Gridian families, those luminous children—would they tolerate a lonely lesbo like herself?

She didn't care. The practicalities weren't the issue. It was as if Allyssa had fed her a dose of yearning with the mashed potatoes. Home, the Grid seemed like home. A real home, with creaky stairs and drawers with missing knobs, a place where she would always feel safe. Her own condo seemed suddenly foreign to her. Her snobbish sofa looked like it had never been sat on. The children of the Grid could be her children, she could be their auntie, the one they ran to with small injuries and treasures.

A small house on the edge of one of the villages, a bouillon cube of a house with its own cool basement.

—*We're having problems with the irrigation system down by 33. Low pressure and what's coming out looks cloudy.*

—*Go talk to Lila. She knows everything about water.*

Like falling in love, when every cavern of your mind is suffused with one person. And it had hit her just as love often did, unexpectedly, as if a doorbell rang in the middle of a dull afternoon and on her porch sat a huge gift. *What is this? It's . . . my God! It's everything I've always wanted. It's perfect. I didn't realize how incomplete I was.*

A meaning to her life.

CHAD WAS PICKING tomatoes in his garden when the impulse first came over him. His neck was hot, the tomatoes were hot to the touch, and suddenly he wondered if this was the last time he'd be picking hot tomatoes in his yard in Dayton. So many variables. If they'd have a garden next year, if they'd have a home next year. If Dayton would exist, if Chad would still exist.

He laid his bowl of tomatoes on the porch and headed out to memorize his yard.

The drainage ditch, incompletely mowed. The peculiar patch where grass had never thrived. The tiny rise where the boys, as toddlers, sledded. The flat and sunny area Sharis had turned into her amazing garden. The ivy vining up the gray trunk of the maple.

There were things he was missing. He looked more. A white squirrel bounding through the grass, alleged a descendant of some odd variety imported by John Patterson. A woodpecker rattling the tulip poplar. What kind of woodpecker? He didn't know. Was this a sin, to not know his own fauna? In the patch of pachysandra beside the house, any shovelful of dirt would turn up worms. Happy worms. Harmless worms.

My yard, Chad thought. Mine.

"MOMMY?" LEON SAID. "Can we go to the troll bridge?" Leon lately was much less intrepid. Two months before he would have gone off to the troll bridge without her. His front teeth had grown in, and there was a gap between them; Sharis wondered if this notch would make him look boyish all his life.

The troll bridge was in the woods beside an abandoned elementary school about a mile from Sharis and Chad's house.

The boys and Sharis used to play a game there, Sharis hiding under the bridge like a troll (the creek was almost always dry) and grabbing at the boys' ankles as they ran across.

"Why not?" Sharis said. They hadn't been to the troll bridge for ages. Chad had gone to UD to do some planning for his courses, and the boys' school didn't start for two more days.

They walked a fairly straight line south, down streets without sidewalks past brick and frame one-story houses. Another hot, sunny morning. No one was out, but some windows were open, and Sharis heard an occasional child's whine, and at the corner of Grantland and Jenny a man's loud voice came from a corner window: "I'm not a machine, you know?" Sharis hurried the boys past.

We've been too cooped up, Sharis thought. The uncertainty of the summer had kept them in their own yard. But the south suburbs were perfectly safe. You heard about wild dogs in Dayton proper, and that little boy had been murdered in the city back in June, but even the people who'd left admitted the south suburbs were secure. It was their fear of the future that drove people away.

Some of the yards they passed were filled with not just grass and weeds but garbage and debris. Sharis glanced at Leon and wondered if he'd wandered this far before. Now he was walking ahead with his chest stuck out and his arms swinging. *I allow that,* Sharis thought, and she worried that Leon needed her behind him to display his bravado.

One pale brick ranch looked as if the house's entire contents had been dumped on its front lawn. "Looks like the house just vomited," Howard observed.

"Hey, look at the owl!" Leon said, turning, pointing at a figurine in the grass. "Can we keep it, Mommy?"

"I don't think anyone lives here now," Sharis said to Howard. "Leon, you can keep it if you carry it." She moved herself across the road to stand under the shade of a tree as her sons inspected the pile.

"Why would anyone throw all their stuff on their front yard?" Howard said, heading her way empty-handed. "Do you think their neighbors got mad and threw all their stuff out?"

Sharis felt nauseated from the sun and heat. "I have no idea, Howie." Between her eyebrows she felt the twinge of an incipient headache. Howie was her brother's name.

"Hey," Leon said, running up to her, "this owl has a broken foot. Can you fix it when we get home, Mommy?"

"I don't have extra owl feet at home, I'm sorry."

To her astonishment Leon started sobbing. "I want my whole owl! I don't want my owl broken!"

"Leon." Sharis knelt and pulled him to her, wrapping her arms around his shoulders, wishing that he weren't too big to carry.

She saw, over Leon's shoulder, a shadow crossing Howard's face. "Do you think maybe the people died and a ghost tossed out their stuff?"

Leon stiffened in her hug. "No," Sharis said. "Absolutely not. That I don't think."

"Mommy," said Howard, "are you and Daddy going to die?"

Sharis hesitated.

"Uncle Howie died," Howard said.

Sharis had an idea that raising children was like weeding. The big weeds you needed to pull right out. The little weeds you could take your time with. Worrying about death was a Big Weed.

"I'm going to stand up now," Sharis said to Leon. "You okay if I stand up?" Leon nodded, Sharis stood, and they continued on their walk. "Listen, boys, everybody dies. That's just what people do. Every person we see or know is going to die. But you guys and Daddy and I won't die for a long, long time. And what happened to Uncle Howie will never, ever happen to either of you. I promise that."

"How did Uncle Howie die?"

"It was an accident. He drank poison. He didn't know."

"How would I know if something was poison?"

"You need to ask Daddy or me first."

The stoplight at the corner of Waterloo and Whipp wasn't working. The patch of glass at the corner was a foot high and seeding. Leon was still fretting about his owl, stroking the chipped leg with his thumb. "Shut up about that stupid owl!" Howard yelled. "It's not even yours. It's a dead person's."

"Howard, stop being mean to your brother. Leon, we will work on fixing it when we get home." A twig and some glue might help mend the owl, she thought. "In the meantime you need to be strong, Leon. If you can't stop sniveling we will not go to the troll bridge. Do you understand?"

Leon wiped his nose on his hand and quieted himself. They crossed the street.

"See?" Sharis said. "It's not the end of the world."

The old school looked as decrepit and creepy as ever, but the woods beside it were deep and cool and appealing. The trees here—as on Custard Lane—truly towered. It was possible in this place to imagine a Dayton before people. Well. Before white people.

They entered the woods and followed the trail down the small hill to the streambed, across a log, and along the other bank to the troll bridge. As they walked Sharis had to push back honeysuckle branches. She had never noticed rubbish here before, but now the stream was littered with cans and rags and even a bicycle frame.

"I go first!" Leon cried, handing Sharis the owl before he took off. Howard followed, yelling for Leon to slow down.

Then: "Mommy," Howard's voice, odd and flat, came from the path in front of her. For once Sharis, running toward him, didn't wonder why at age ten he still said "Mommy" and not "Mom." "It's Abba."

Abba was Chad's impossible great-aunt who lived in Cleveland. It couldn't be Abba. And, no, it wasn't Abba, but it was a woman, surrounded by trash, sitting ahead of them on a rock beside the troll bridge. She had wispy hair and wore a ragged T-shirt and shorts, and Sharis thought she must be crazy, someone who'd run out of her medicine or a gene therapy failure, but the woman looked up and said "Hello," in a tired but resolute way, like any woman sorting through a mess. She was probably not much older than Sharis.

"It's not Abba," Sharis whispered to Howard. "It's someone else."

Sharis walked onto the footbridge, the boys following her slowly. "There's a house on Jenny with all kinds of stuff in front," she said to the woman.

"Oh, I've been there. Crap." The woman nodded at a bundle behind her in the dry bed of the creek; Sharis was startled to see that this was a sleeping baby, wrapped in a thin blanket and wedged on a corduroy pillow between two rocks. "What I really need is food. I'm nursing. Sometimes you can find wood chairs at those houses," the woman said, picking up a cereal box and peering into it. "I keep those for fuel. But the chairs at that Jenny dump were plastic." She glanced up. "I live just south of here, on Siena."

Sharis knew Siena. The houses and lots there were closer in size to Custard Lane's, where the minimum lot size was an acre, than the area they'd just walked through. My God: a woman in this state lived on Siena?

"Mommy," Leon edged up onto the bridge and poked at Sharis's back, "is she a real troll?"

"Leon! She's a regular person."

"I'd say I'm an irregular person," the woman said, "at this point."

We have food, Sharis thought, thinking of her garden, and she almost offered it, but then she stopped herself, the mere presence of this woman hinting at all Sharis and her family had to lose. "Let's go, boys," she said.

"Mommy!" Leon stamped his foot. "I want to do the troll!"

"Not today. We'll leave this"—she almost said "poor," but she stopped herself—"woman in peace. Come on! Here—" She held the owl out for Leon.

Leon crossed his arms. "I'm not going to carry it. That's your choice: play troll or you carry the owl."

"I'm leaving it here then," Sharis said firmly, setting the owl down on a plank of the bridge. Leon screamed so loudly that the baby stirred and starting shrieking. "Leon, damn it, I . . ." Sharis grabbed Leon's wrist and yanked. The woman bent over to pick up her baby. "See that plant with the heart-shaped leaves?" Sharis said to the woman. Leon was crying, tears as big as M&M's streaming down his face. "That's wild ginger. You can dig it up and chop it and use it for flavoring."

"Flavor," the woman nodded, furiously patting her baby's back. "Yum, yum."

"Leon, let's go." Sharis pulled him again. "Are you leaving your owl here?"

"I hate the owl!" Leon said, picking it up and hurling it over the bridge railing toward the woman. She jerked backward, but the owl landed far beyond her.

"You killed it," Howard said, because the owl was now dust and pieces. "You said you loved it and then you killed it."

"Let's go home, boys," Sharis said. She felt as hollow as one of those painted wood Russian mother dolls stripped of all the smaller dolls inside it. They got home. Sharis made creamed soy-bacon on toast for supper.

"How was your day?" Chad said. He had gone down to UD.

Sharis said that it was fine, they had walked to the troll bridge.

"The troll bridge still the same?" Chad said. Sharis said not exactly, now there was trash in the streambed. She didn't mention the woman, because Chad would probably want to go help her, and their little group of Gribbles didn't need more stress.

"Probably all the park people got laid off," Chad said.

"It's still a pleasant park," Sharis said. Howard and Leon eyed her with flat curiosity, not adding to her story. She smiled at them queasily, hoping that the two of them would keep quiet. Because nothing was certain. Because you could think about fairness and generosity all you wanted, but in the end survival was what mattered.

TWO WEEKS LATER Lila was gripping the rung of the ladder, toes curled in her shoes, telling herself not to look down. Five more rungs and she could see over the barrier. Sunday afternoon and she was visible, so she had to steel herself against someone yelling. She wore a jacket with the water department logo. The Vandalia water tower, in a northeast suburb of Dayton. Climb up and she could see the Grid. She'd rehearsed in her mind all manner of scenarios.

—*Hey, what are you, crazy?*

—*I'm with the water department. Checking the tower.*

For the Gridding, Lila heard later, everyone on the Homeland Security as-needed call list was called. No one was told why. They were sent to a bevy of small towns in special government cars equipped with computers and video cameras, and at 1 a.m. (midnight in Illinois and Indiana) they received information about what was to happen. An official witness in Paxton, Illinois, distressed at what he surmised was about to take place, drove his car to the local police station and tried to run inside, but the town's other witness, a woman who'd worked with the FBI, used the government's right to privacy as justification and shot him with a Calmadol fledget. Troops moved into Paxton without problems. By 3 a.m. the female Paxton witness was being touted on the witness network as a hero.

Lila was sent to Upper Sandusky, Ohio. On the dashboard between the two front seats of her government vehicle the computer screen printed a country map, her car a moving red point on its surface. Other government cars were moving blue points, and even in this relatively unpopulated county there were maybe forty other cars. It was a bad time for the country. Dayton with its water-hungry industries was relatively spared, and the northwest part of Ohio was stable, being former and current farmland where people were at least aware of hunting and canning and the production of eggs, but parts of the central cities had been decimated, and blue-collar suburbs were hard-hit, too. In Albuquerque and Atlanta there were reports of cannibalism.

Lila reached Upper Sandusky. The map on her screen changed to a city map. When she pressed a button, facts about the town appeared. Founded 1805. Named Upper Sandusky for its position on the upper portion of the Sandusky River, which flowed north to empty into Lake Erie. Former canal site. Famous for its Hand Corn Husking Festival, which had recently been revived.

It was after midnight. Behind a restroom in a park Lila saw tips of burning cigarettes. A young woman with long blonde hair ran down a side street. She stopped and turned as if she recognized Lila's car, but at the sight of Lila's face she darted down an alley. Some houses had upstairs lights on. A man in a windbreaker carried a child's bike through a door in a wooden fence.

Stop now, the screen in her car said.

What's happening? Lila thought. Why was I called? To prevent abuses, the summons had said. To keep a record.

Trucks approached in Lila's rearview mirror. Troops got out, marched two by two to people's doors. Huddled families, children crying, the Calmadol truck like an ice-cream van, shouted threats, buses walling the troops from view, medics with syringes approaching the pinned resisters.

Later, Lila and the three other Upper Sandusky witnesses celebrated in a restaurant in Dayton, ordering steaks on the government all around (and no one ate steak then). Well, that's over, Lila had thought. I'll never be back there. She remembered feeling calm and useful, certain that the Gridding would work out. Social planning was a lot like water conservation, she'd thought, only on a bigger scale.

Now, she could see over the barrier. The green fields were as bright as malachite; the wheat a rustling golden beige. *I belong there,* Lila thought. *I need there.*

ONLY FIVE CHILDREN in Leon's first-grade class showed up. By the end of the week the principal had bundled the three first-grade classes together and moved Leon's original teacher to gym and art. Howard was starting fifth grade, the last grade in the school: only ten students in his class appeared. Howard's teacher was distraught and threatened to move to Wisconsin to join her brother and his wife.

There was an evening open house the second Tuesday after school started. Howard's teacher never arrived, so Sharis and Chad went to Leon's classroom. Leon's teacher wanted the children to draw happy pictures! She wanted them to read hard words like *idea* and *surprise*! She wanted them to love numbers! It was a relief to leave her classroom and butt into, on chairs in the multipurpose room, the laconic pragmatism of the principal.

"We'll be here every school day teaching your children," she said. "That's the law."

"Your kids don't show up, this school may shut down."

And: "The threat of war is not an excuse for bad behavior."

"She's a wonder," Chad said as they walked home. "We could use her at UD."

Sharis had a sudden feeling that praising things was dangerous, that a compliment might function as a hex. Sharis said, "She's okay."

"MICHELLE?" THE VISUAL feed stuttered and restarted—Lila's office computer was so damn old—but then Lila saw her, the same long hair and wanton eyelashes. "Thanks for talking to me," Lila said to the youngie. She'd visited the Grid,

Lila told her. And afterwards she remembered how Michelle from Agro had come to visit her office, how Michelle had said that Federal could use her help. "And I was impressed by the Grid, Michelle. I thought it was miraculous"—Lila winced at her own words—"so I thought I'd call you, see if there was anything I could do for you regarding that." God, she'd ended in awkward splutter. Her rehearsals had sounded better.

Michelle looked blank. "It wasn't exactly Grid stuff," she said. "What I came to you about. And I gathered you weren't interested."

"Did you find someone else?"

"Not exactly."

A surge of impatience and hope. "Is there some way I can help you now?"

Michelle was frowning, her eyes darting to something—someone?—off the screen. "You want the Grid?"

"Ideally." Lila struggled to keep her voice and visage light. It was easier to talk when the visual feed wasn't working—as it often wasn't on the antique county computers. "I do want the Grid!" Lila said brightly. "I *like* it." What a sight she must be: an uto grinning. Michelle was as lovely as ever.

"Okay." Michelle's eyes darted again. "Let me work on it a few days. I'll see."

The young rule the world, Lila thought.

CHAD SAID, "LEON said the woman had a baby."

"A toddler," Sharis said.

"Does she have other children?"

"I don't think so. I didn't ask."

"Does she have a husband?"

"We didn't have a big conversation, Chad. We just came upon her. I was surprised, to be honest. She looked a little creepy. Leon thought she was Abba."

"Thank you," Chad said.

"Oh, you know what I mean."

"Look at our garden. What are you planning to do with all our tomatoes? We have thousands of tomatoes."

"I'm in the kitchen every day, Chad. I'm making tomato sauce, I'm canning."

"That's my point! We have plenty of food to share with a hungry neighbor."

"She's not a neighbor, Chad. She lives a mile away."

"Spare me," Chad said, turning from his wife in disgust.

"It's not realistic, Chad. I don't have containers. I don't even know where she lives!"

"Okay," Chad said. "Okay." He left the bedroom, headed downstairs and sat in the sofa looking out the front window. He tried to set aside the horrible thought that he was lucky to have a wife like Sharis.

CINCINNATI, FOR TUURO, was not a bad place. He could disappear. He worked for weeks unloading produce in a garage behind an abandoned office park. The knot on the side of his face turned colors, shrank, and faded; it was only a small lump now, and he could open his mouth freely. No one asked him about it, or asked him more than his first name. He was paid in cash by a severe-looking woman whose heels clicked on the floor. The origin of the trucks from which Tuuro unloaded grain and vegetables was never mentioned, but Tuuro believed the cargo came from the Grid. Once the trucks were empty, another crew reloaded them with wooden crates so heavy they required a forklift. When Tuuro asked one of the workers about these crates the answer—"You dunno nothin,' you dun see nothin','" a quote from a movie called *Troubletown*—was enough to convince Tuuro the crates held something suspicious, maybe guns. Tuuro slept at night nestled in a doorway of the abandoned office park, a big stick at his side. There were men who slept inside the garage, but they were territorial and drank. This job paid too well, Tuuro thought. It scared him.

On a drizzly day with a touch of fall in it, Tuuro left the office park. He had some money now, enough to establish himself in a new home far from Ohio. He didn't know exactly where he was going, fate, he was certain, would guide him. He was walking south beside a road through the suburbs, taking care not to slip on the grass. A car pulled up beside him and an attractive blonde female passenger poked out her head to ask where he was going.

The car was warm and dry. Tuuro sat in the back next to two daughters. "Scoot over for the man," the mother said. "Come on, Gertrude. Move over, Edna."

"What's your name?" the father asked Tuuro.

"Tom," Tuuro said, cringing as the name left his lips.

The family was headed for Tennessee to visit relatives. They wanted their children to meet all kinds of people.

"I have a daughter in Tennessee," Tuuro said, and he thought fleetingly of showing up at Naomi's door and asking to see Lanita. He imagined his daughter running down the stairs to him, the way she'd spread her long thin arms. He knew he'd never live this. It was still possible people were after him in Nenonene's name, and he couldn't risk exposing Lanita.

"See?" said the mother of Gertrude and Edna. "He has a little girl, just like you."

Tuuro shifted toward the door, careful not to brush against the child.

"What's your line of work, Tom?" the father said.

"Maintenance."

"Oh, that's steady, isn't it? What doesn't need maintenance? What's your ultimate destination, Tom? We'll take you as far as we can."

"Into Kentucky. Maybe just . . ."—Tuuro tried to remember the name of the town across the Ohio River from Cincinnati, a place he'd visited with Aunt Stella years before—"Covington."

"Covington's so built up now!" the woman cried. "You should see the soccer stadium. And the . . ."

But Tuuro had drifted off in his mind, down those narrow Covington streets with the brick shotgun houses, to the railing overlooking the Ohio River, the river slaves had swum across to reach their freedom. "That Ohio shore," Aunt Stella had said. "That was freedom, on that shore . . ." They were nearing the river via the highway now, their course slightly downhill, the skyscrapers of Cincinnati to their left, to their right old office buildings that had been converted into apartments for the people displaced from the Grid, as well as the edifice that was Consort Tower. "You look pretty squished back there," the man was saying. "We'll get to Kentucky right over the bridge and set you free." And it was those words, partly, with their unfortunate echo, and partly Tuuro's shock in noticing, on the opposite shore, what had become of Covington, and partly Tuuro's sense that he was heading *the wrong way* across the Ohio River: it was all these things, and something else, that opened his mouth. "I changed my mind," Tuuro said. "Let me out here."

"Here?" the man swiveled his head anxiously. "There's no exit here. We'll let you out across the . . ."

Tuuro put his hand on the door handle. "Oh my *God*," the woman said, her hands flying into the backseat. "Edna. Gertrude!"

The pavement was racing past, and Tuuro dropped himself out gingerly, as if he were rolling onto his own sweet mattress, and the next thing he knew he was curled on his side at the edge of the road, cars swooshing past him hurling pebbles in his direction. His face was wet with what he thought was rain, although later he found it was blood. He struggled to his feet and pointed himself north, away from the river. Kelso said south, but Kelso didn't know. Tuuro knew. With each step he became more upright. He was heading back to Dayton, across the Grid, all the way to Cleveland. Like his ancestors, all he wanted was his freedom, and Tuuro's only chance of freedom was Nenonene.

"AND PERSISTENCE," CHAD would say. "Don't forget persistence. Laura, you mentioned persistence."

In 1900, Orville and Wilbur built a biplane glider with an eighteen-foot wingspan, large enough to carry a man. Wires ran from the tips of the lower wings to a cradle in the center of the glider's body. By sliding the cradle from side to side, the astute pilot could warp the wings and keep the glider steady in the air.

In September, they took this glider to Kitty Hawk, North Carolina, and a strip of coastline where there were reliable winds. The Wrights planned to test and perfect wing-warping by flying the glider tethered to a derrick like a giant manned kite. The brothers, basing their calculations on German glider pioneer Otto Lilienthal's tables of lift, determined that an eighteen-mile-per-hour wind would take the glider and Wilbur aloft. It didn't. The most weight the glider lifted was fifty pounds of metal chains or the local postmaster's nine-year-old nephew.

The Wright brothers came home to Dayton frustrated, wondering why their glider wouldn't fly. Maybe the fabric on the wings was leaky. They tested sealed versus unsealed fabric: no difference. Other glider experimenters had preferred wings more curved than theirs. For their next year's testing, the brothers constructed a machine with highly curved wings. In 1901, they transported it in boxes back to Kitty Hawk. This glider, Wilbur said, was "state of the art."

Their new glider didn't work either. It had even less lift than the previous year's model, and on top of that the wing warping was lousy. The brothers came home mosquito-bitten and unhappy. They weren't getting younger: Wilbur was thirty-four, Orville thirty-one. They'd heard of their twin siblings—Otis and Ida—who'd died in infancy before either Wilbur or Orville was born, they'd seen their mother die of tuberculosis, and Otto Lilienthal, one of their heroes, had been killed in a glider crash. In that time, death was real even to young people. Wilbur predicted that man would someday fly, but "not within our lifetime."

SHARIS WAS USING wild ginger in everything, because dried spices had gotten too expensive. She peeled the hairy, dirty roots before chopping them to toss into soups and omelets or mix them into her salads. At first the wild ginger tasted strange, then familiar and even tasty, then so ubiquitous and overpowering it was almost an insult, and Sharis one day picked up a plastic plate of scrambled eggs—their dinner—and threw it against the wall. "Do we have to have wild ginger in everything?" she shrieked.

The boys fell silent, staring.

"You're the one who puts it in, Mommy," Howard said.

"It's going to freeze soon, anyway," she said, calmer already. "The plants will die off."

"We should get out," she said to Chad that evening.

"My job is here," Chad said.

Sharis was silent.

"I'm teaching my Dayton course. I'm not going to leave town when I'm teaching my Dayton course." Only ten students were taking it, but all of them seemed eager.

"Are you insane?" Sharis said. "Does your Dayton course matter more to you than your own children?"

Chad didn't answer. The two of them didn't speak the rest of the evening. "Other people are people, too," Chad said as Sharis rolled away from him in bed.

"What a wise old man you are," she said. He left and slept on the sofa downstairs.

TUURO WALKED INTO downtown Cincinnati. He found a message center and typed a message to Kelso's perc, waited half an hour for a response. He was just about to leave when the stylish man (he was clearly wearing lipstick, a new fashion) behind the counter called him. "Your contact's answered," the man said in a pleasantly deep voice, nodding at an old-fashioned phone receiver on the wall. The message center was empty except for the clerk and Tuuro: business was always slow, the clerk said, the days before the checks came in.

Kelso's voice was hearty. In the hospital they'd found out he had diabetes and put him on a special diet. He'd lost weight and felt a hundred times better. It was lucky he'd been shot, really. The police had found his car in Cincinnati and had it driven home to Dayton. How was Tuuro?

"I realized what I need," Tuuro told Kelso. "I need to talk with"—and he turned his face away from the man behind the counter, whispered into the phone—"Nenonene."

A pause. Tuuro could visualize the shock in Kelso's face. "He's in Cleveland!" Then: "What if he thinks you did it?"

What Nenonene had done to the colonel—the shot into the heart—hung like a banner behind any conversation.

"He won't think that, not after I talk with him."

"He might! He's the enemy. Nobody sent him the genetics."

"It won't matter." Tuuro doubted Kelso would understand this. What Tuuro wanted from Nenonene was a resolution, a judgment of himself and his motives, and his faith in Nenonene told him it had to be fair.

Kelso said, "I wouldn't come back through Dayton."

A ragged man walked into the message center, bringing with him a blast of damp air and a white cardboard box wrapped with string. "What do you mean you got no message?" he said. "My sister promised me a message."

On the phone, Kelso's voice had dropped. "Go north to Lebanon, cut northeast from there, and slide up along the bottom of the Grid into Columbus. You get there you can look into transportation."

The man behind the counter said something in a firm tone. Not taking his eyes off the angry customer, he slid open a drawer.

"I heard a fellow lives in Mount Vernon ships goats to Cleveland every week." Kelso's voice had dropped; Tuuro could picture his hand cupped over the phone. "The Alliance people eat them. You should try Mount Vernon. That's only, like, twenty miles from the Grid border."

"I need my message! How many times I have to tell you I need my message?"

The clerk's hand hovered over the top of the drawer. "Don't threaten me, sir. You don't want to threaten me, sir."

Tuuro saw at that moment what was going to happen. "I'm hanging up now," Tuuro said to Kelso, his voice rising over the ragged man's curses. "I thank you." He was outside in the rain before the shot was fired. Tuuro was certain that the aim, just like the clerk's lipstick, had been precise. Self-defense, the clerk would say. Tuuro would have to agree.

Tuuro stopped and asked a woman the way to the bus station, then waited outside an hour for the Lebanon bus. He listened, but he never heard sirens. Five years ago, even one year ago, a shot and a dead body would have gotten some response.

Order, he thought. Peace. Nenonene. He was gazing at the decorative edging on a building across the street when he realized that a group of men had surrounded him, and were moving him toward the open back door of a large car.

flying

"NOW WHAT VIRTUE kicks in?" Chad said, resuming his pacing. "They're discouraged, they're disheartened, they don't believe in themselves they way they used to."

Thrift, someone suggested. The Wright Brothers recycled their glider.

No. Although they did recycle their equipment, always. They were conservers.

Determination?

"More specific," Chad said. "We know they were determined."

Modesty? someone ventured, to scattered titters.

"How about the opposite of modesty?" Chad asked, cocking his head. "How about something that doesn't say to someone else: *You're right, oh you're right?* How about the virtue that says: *You could be wrong?*

Skepticism. Yes, that virtue. It hit the Wright brothers that Lilienthal's tables of lift, the basis of all their calculations, could be wrong. No, I'm sorry, Lilienthal's tables *must be* wrong.

How audacious! What a thought! Lilienthal, a German, was the father of modern gliding. In the ten years before his postflight death, in 1896, of a broken spine, he had launched himself on more than two thousand flights, in a variety of gliders he designed and built himself. He studied birds. He launched himself from a hill he'd constructed into which he'd built a cave to store his equipment. He was a passionate hobbyist like the Wrights themselves, as well as the brothers' hero, and it must have cost the Wrights a small chunk of their own self-confidence and happiness to doubt him.

Still, they dared to doubt him, and to that end constructed, in the back room of their bicycle shop, their own wind tunnel. It was six feet long and sixteen inches per side, with a viewing window in its top and a fan mounted on its end. "We spent nearly a month getting a straight wind," Wilbur wrote. They made all sorts of miniature wings and tested them for lift at different angles, confirming to themselves that they were right, that Lilienthal's lift tables were indeed inaccurate. The brothers then designed and built, based on their experiments, the ideal wing. They cut the fabric for this item on their living room floor.

"Nothing earthshaking," Chad said. "Steady forward progress. Open minds. One task, then the next, at various points amending things they'd done before. It's a way to live life, isn't it? It's a way to dream."

OCTOBER. SHARIS PUNCHED the button for real time and again watched the back view of Lars the Norwegian walking down the hall. All the times she'd watched him—and sometimes seen him and Clara, his wife, naked and communal in the living room—and she'd never had this reaction. Something about the curve of his hip, the play of light and dark on the towel over his ass. Half the size of Chad, sleek and muscled. He flicked his shoulders back and she almost moaned. He was probably older than Chad, but his hair made him look young to her. She imagined the droplets of water at its tips. The living room camera picked him up now. He was alone. He pulled the towel from his hips and swung it to his tilted head, rubbing his hair—almost as long as hers—dry. His legs were slightly apart and his equipment swung. Then he disappeared into the bathroom. When he came out he was tucking in his shirt.

She ran it again, and again.

AUTUMN WAS THE PERFECT time to be in love, with the migratory birds coming through. Charles had realized that Diana knew little about the natural world. Her nature center interests until now had extended little beyond donations, trusts, and bills. She had read all the tags in the museum, but she hadn't spent much time outside. But now, in their splendid isolation (they were ridiculously well-provisioned, thanks to a solar generator and a paranoid volunteer who'd insisted, years before, on stocking up for the coming attack by China), Charles was delighting Diana with the cornucopia of the natural world. "Look," he might say, "loco weed," splitting a pod to empty out a handful of jimson seeds. "Hear that?" he'd ask, testing to see if she recognized the "Q" call of a flicker. The pond still as glass; the meadow grasses higher than their heads; the crunch of the morning frost. At night, as they huddled in the center, they left one window open so the cool air made their bodies feel even warmer. Outside they heard the owls' hooting, the rustle of their wings, the alarmed chirps and thrashing of their prey.

"We'll look for owl pellets in the morning," Charles said. "You can dissect them to analyze an owl's diet." Poison ivy berries, he had told her, were a favorite food of warblers. There is nothing in nature without a purpose.

"Amazing," Diana said. "You know everything!" She smiled and nestled her head into his armpit. He was a respite to her— they both knew this. She thought that in a way he knew nothing about the modern world. This afternoon, just before they crossed the bridge that led to the pond, Charles had heard a sound that thrilled him. "Cup your hands," he'd said, and Diana had stopped beside him with her hands cupped behind her ears, her eyes intently unfocused, lips pursed. "Three high notes"—Charles whistled them softly—"and then the song."

They waited. That beautiful ball at the end of Diana's nose: Charles could almost see it trembling.

She'd leave him. Women always left Charles—and Diana knew perfectly well why—but for this moment she was his completely.

They heard it. Diana's mouth flew open in delight, her eyes searching for Charles's.

"Ruby-throated kinglet," Charles whispered. "Very tiny, very rare." And they crept forward, binoculars ready, to search for it in the trees.

"YOUR FRIEND'S HERE," Seymour said at the door of Lila's office. Lila swiveled in her chair expecting her fellow uto Kennedy but there was Michelle, tall beautiful Michelle, the youngie from Agriculture.

"Oh!" Lila struggled to stand. "I'd given up on you." This was a generous statement. Lila had been to the water tower weekly, watching the harvest and the gleaning, the fields now stubbled and bare, and at each step in that glorious sequence the thought of Michelle had been trampled beneath Lila's feet. Stupid, unreliable youngie. Youngie without power. Betraying youngie.

"My boss and I thought I should come talk to you in person," Michelle said. "Fill you in a bit." She lifted her left hand and swept it toward the door; Lila was once again struck by the length of her eyelashes. "Let's take a walk," Michelle said.

It was a damp and misty fall day, although the day before had been brilliant. They took the walkway along the river, read the sign where the first settlers in Dayton had landed, then crossed the pedestrian bridge to Sawyer's Point, the triangle of land formed as the Mad River joined the Great Miami. "This park was beautiful when I was a kid," Lila said, stuffing a discarded pop can into a full wastebasket. "They used to have fountains that shot out across the river." She pointed.

"Is that how you got started in water?"

"Who knows?" Lila sat on a bench facing downriver, Michelle beside her. Facts from her old water talks flooded back to her. The 1913 flood. The five dams,

Look," Michelle said. "No one understands this. Why are you looking for a job outside of Dayton? On the Grid of all places? Most Ohioans resent the Grid."

"Not me. I was there. I saw it."

"You saw it as an outsider. We get a lot of information—it's really Agriculture that runs it, or that started running it—and . . ."

"I was there overnight. I ate their food."

"It's a very closed society. They're not like you and me. They've become . . ." Michelle hesitated, then went on: "Have you heard about their churches?" Lila snorted to herself: religion was the least of her worries. "The people used to be regular. Now no one outside understands what they are. It's like they have this agricultural religion. You know, feasts and blessing seeds and burying totems in the planting season. They've got some festival going on now—they build huts outside covered with cornstalks and eat in them for a week. That's not Christian. My boss says they've gone pagan."

Ridiculous, the fear people had. As if the Gridians after fourteen years on their own could be that different from anyone else in the country. Next time she climbed the tower, Lila would have to look for the huts. "What," Lila asked sardonically, "they sacrifice babies to the harvest or something?"

"They have very strict population control," Michelle said, and Lila thought fleetingly of Lindisfarne. But Lila approved of abortion. "Very strict. When the Grid was established, my boss said, Agro was worried that the Gridians would rebel against outside control. But their lives are more controlled now than ever, and they don't even listen to outside. You know they don't let anyone under twenty-one use computers? And the adults' use is monitored."

"I know people have all this fear of them, but it must be a decent society. No one seems to want to leave."

"Would we hear if they did?" Michelle shot a glance at Lila. "Listen, Agriculture has very little control over the Grid these days. Maybe no control. That's a secret, Lila. The Grid always meets its crop quotas, its energy costs are always acceptable, so people there feel justified in telling us to stay out." Michelle's voice dropped. "The Agriculture Secretary went there and got put up in a trailer. They wouldn't even show him a school." The brown water moved in front of them, steady and slow, both the rivers having crossed the Grid to reach here. In the one hundred and fifty years since the Great Flood, the water level in the Greater Miami had varied only seven feet. The dams protecting Dayton had held. "My mother says you saved Dayton," Michelle said, a quiver to her voice.

An exaggeration, Lila knew, a misconception, but still a thrill to hear. *You saved Dayton.* Hardly. Maybe. She'd helped draw in certain industries, which had a positive effect on the region. She'd promoted individual conservation of water. It didn't take reality to make a public hero. "If you go to the Grid you'd be moving backwards," Michelle said. "You'd be, I don't know, not evolving but devolving."

"You think too much of me," Lila said. "I'm tired and I want something simple, and the Grid sounds simple."

"They've sacrificed personal freedom for security. That's what my boss says."

"People must feel useful," Lila said. "They must feel a connection with nature." She struggled to make her voice sound gentler. "And with each other. Don't you think it scares them the Alliance is right next to them in Cleveland?"

"They say they'll chop up the Alliance soldiers for fertilizer." Lila shifted on the bench, wishing Michelle hadn't said this. "*No harvest like an Alliance harvest.* That's their slogan. They don't trust American troops to protect them, they say, because they'd be too merciful. You know what they call the

Alliance occupation? *The world's biggest concentration of organic matter.*"

"Sloganeering," Lila said quickly, trying to keep the shock out of her voice.

"I think they mean it. And they probably have slogans like that about Americans, too."

Lila swallowed, her mouth gone abruptly dry. "Well, they are dealing in essentials. Food and land and death. In a way you have to admire them."

"Do you?" Michelle was looking at the river, her face clouded, and Lila wondered why she herself felt so vulnerable to the appeal of a Gridian life, a life of loyalties and enmities so ingrained they seemed instinctual. A life, in a way, without thought.

"You know I was there at the beginning," Lila said. "I was a witness."

"They're like ants," Michelle said, not seeming to hear her. "Ants in a colony."

Lila shifted her eyes in Michelle's direction. "Is that what your boss says?"

"They cull out their problem children, put them in their own towns, and let them go wild. Sometimes they even kill each other."

"At least they're not killing their parents!"

Michelle drew herself up straighter, tucked in her chin. "All right," she said with a quick nod, as if she had reached some resolution. "Let me tell you what we need. It's not water for the Grid, it's water for the Ohio."

"The Ohio River?" Fifty miles south, in Cincinnati, the river at their feet emptied into the Ohio. The Ohio was tightly controlled and locked, and even so the river towns occasionally flooded. Hard to imagine anyone wanting its water level higher.

"We're moving water toward the Mississippi. It's a defense project; I can't tell you more." Michelle glanced at Lila, who must—she realized—look stunned. "It's very responsible,"

Michelle added hurriedly. "The best water minds around are in on it."

Wonderwater, Lila thought. *The best water minds around.* Ah, where that left her. "Why Dayton's water?" she asked.

"You can spare it. Thanks to you, you know."

"Not really. It's a water-rich system." Lila spoke almost automatically, trying to gather her thoughts behind her words. "Are you building some big reservoir on the Mississippi? Do you want to increase its depth overall? Are there big attack boats you want to run?"

But Michelle ignored her questions. "Look, you're not the only system we're asking. All across southern Ohio and Indiana and Illinois, we need help. Those are Grid states, and Defense thought if Agriculture did the asking the assumption would be we wanted water for the Grid."

"Then why are you telling everyone the water's for Defense?"

"I'm not telling everyone. I'm telling you. Think of it: water can be a barrier. You can blow a bridge or you can flood the bridges out."

Lila gazed at the youngie. "This is too deep for me," she said. A water metaphor.

Michelle laughed. "Don't be silly. You're as deep as they come."

"No. I'm not political." Lila frowned. "Couldn't you just commandeer the water? Not tell me?" A wondrous dark blue coat Michelle had on, full of soft folds at the shoulders half hidden by her curtain of hair. Why was Lila just noticing this?

"You'd notice. We'd be laying new pipe."

"Can I say no to this?"

Michelle sighed. "My boss could help you. She could get you onto the Grid."

"To live?"

"If that's what you want."

"I want a home."

"What are you doing for Thanksgiving?"

flying

Lila sat and looked over the water. A line of rocks broke the surface of the Mad, stranding the river like a comb. Lila would do for Thanksgiving what she always did, a dinner at Kennedy's with a mixture of friends, most of whom stopped by on their way somewhere else. "Friends," Lila said.

"I'm going to my parents.'"

"Lucky you. My parents are dead." What had she been lacking all these years? How had she not recognized it? An uto sitting on a park bench, yearning for home. She realized Michelle was gazing at her. An up-and-comer; a youngie with a future; someone who could help her out. "Okay," Lila said, turning toward her, "you can have our water. I'll cover for you with the commissioners."

"That's great." Michelle seemed suddenly flustered. "That's wonderful." She was nodding. "I'll talk to my boss about some tit for tat." She suddenly blushed, the red spot on her nose flaring. "I mean, quid pro quo."

Lila stared open-mouthed at Michelle.

So long since she'd done a seduction. She was almost frightened to attempt it.

But then she was doing it. "Tit for tat is good," Lila said earnestly, the ferocity of her old stirrings a surprise. She looked at Michelle's face; the youngie was blushing so fervently Lila had no hesitancy in moving on. Soft, wet words; words like a probing tongue. "I mean, tit is always good, and tat can be delicious." To a good girl like Michelle, Lila realized, Lila was the bad girl who thought sexy thoughts, who shrugged at Michelle's horror over the Gridians.

Michelle seemed to have stopped breathing. Lila laid her left arm on the bench behind her. She stroked the wondrous coat. "You think your boss would let you give me some tit for tat?"

"I don't know," Michelle breathed, "oh, I don't know." They kissed. "But I have a boyfriend!" Michelle cried.

Lila felt like she was caught up in a whirlpool, twirling down. This is like a rape, she thought. I'm *using* her. But it felt so good that Lila didn't care.

"HAVE YOU PICKED a name?" Chad asked. Derk was back, sitting at Chad and Sharis's big blue table. He hadn't visited for months, since he'd lost his job when the plant closed and his parents insisted he sell his car. Sharis was at the counter chopping. They had thirty-six pumpkins, and Sharis was consumed with making use of every one. Derk's girlfriend was pregnant.

"Enola Gay," Derk said.

Chad started. "Where'd you get that name?"

"We just thought of it. Don't you think it's pretty?"

"Unusual," Sharis said. "Cheerful."

Chad's colleague Prem taught the world wars. Chad would have to check Derk's records to see if he'd taken that course. "Enola Gay was the name of the plane that dropped the atomic bomb on Hiroshima," Chad said. "You can't name a child Enola Gay."

"Chad!" Sharis objected. "Nobody remembers! Derk was a history minor, and even he doesn't remember."

"What do your parents think?"

"They like it. They might not have liked the name Gay twenty years ago, but so long as queers stay queers, it's fine."

"It's a terrible name." Chad's shoulders slumped; his very cells seemed to be sagging. "What's your next daughter's name going to be? Holocaustia? Stalinette?"

Derk and Sharis stared at him with their bold, affronted faces.

"DID YOU FINISH the basement pantry?" Allyssa asked.

"It is finished," Tuuro said.

"I don't know what else you're going to do. I thought this place was clean before you got here." Allyssa tapped the kitchen table with her fingernails. She was, Tuuro thought, remarkably beige. Even her lips and nails were that color. "I wish I could send you into the village. You must hate this waiting."

Tuuro had awakened weeks before in a double bed in an upstairs room, under flowered sheets and a pink waffle blanket. The last thing he remembered was a car door being opened, and being pushed inside. A shot of Calmadol, maybe. When Tuuro awoke it was daytime, but the shades were drawn. He crept out of bed and peeked outside, the earth around him so vast and brown he felt like an ant in the center of a sandbox.

He knew where he was. What he didn't know was why.

The bedroom door had opened, and the beige woman had walked in. "Hello, Mr. Simpkins," she said, extending her hand. "Glad you've awakened." She strode to the window and released the shade. "Have you figured out where you are?"

Tuuro nodded.

The beige woman smiled and spoke slowly, as if she were announcing a great prize. "There's someone close to us who wants to see you. Have you heard of General Nenonene?"

SHARIS SAT IN her groundcover planting bulbs. For the last three years she'd sprinkled daffodils and tulips through the groundcover in the side and back of their house, and every spring the yard was prettier. She could bury the daffodil bulbs herself, because squirrels didn't like them, but the tulips had to go in about a foot deep, which required Chad and his shovel. "How many holes do you want?" he'd said, and asked her where to put them. He was more accommodating, really, than he'd ever been, which made Sharis feel a surge of love for him. Ridiculous to lust after Lars, a man three thousand miles away who didn't even speak her language. She had a feeling he swore: the translation module had been developed by missionaries and was quite prim, and there seemed to be words missing.

The bulbs had been deeply discounted. Sharis bought over two hundred. "Act of faith," the clerk said as she rang them up, her tone not admiring but sardonic. There were other gardeners shopping. One woman pulled a wagon heaped with amaryllis bulbs. "Indoor forcing!" she said. "Won't they be beautiful at Christmas?"

"Mommy?" Leon asked. "How can a squirrel go straight up a tree without falling off?" He was dropping the bulbs into the holes, after Howard had put in the bone meal and water and stirred up the soil.

"I don't know, honey, that's just what squirrels do."

"But how?"

"Leon," Howard said, "how do people walk on two legs without falling over? A squirrel can't do that, can he? Squirrels probably think we're amazing."

"Doesn't Howard have a good point, Leon?" Sharis asked. She was quick to praise Howard these days. Howard's teacher seemed to have abdicated from teaching almost totally; Howard said that most days his class sat and watched films on their own percs. Spelling lists? Sharis would ask. Reading assignments? Homework? No, no, no.

"And think about this, boys," Sharis said. "We're putting this lump in the ground that's going to be a beautiful flower in the spring. Isn't that amazing? It's an everyday miracle."

"If we're alive in the spring," Howard said.

"Howard, you're a big stupid fuckface!" Leon shouted.

"I would never have said that word in front of my parents," Sharis scolded, still reeling from Howard's comment. "Never." Bad language was a little weed; obsession with death was a big one. But she didn't have the strength to yank at the big weed now. "You know who's really stupid?" Sharis's voice rose. "The people who don't rake their leaves! I hate them. They are the stupidest people on earth." Hacking at the weed of fear instead of trying to pull it out.

"Like the Hofmeisters?" Howard asked, making Sharis grin.

"Like the Hofmeisters." Sharis threw a handful of dirt over a bulb.

"And the Perrettis?"

The Perrettis hadn't been around for weeks, and they'd left tomatoes rotting on their vines. "I hate the Perrettis."

"I do, too!" Leon said, jumping up and down. "I hate them!"

"You little animal," Sharis said. Leon was a continual relief to her. His wiriness, his spikiness, his lack of concern about others: he seemed to be geared to survival.

She and Chad had raked and then mowed all their immediate neighbors' yards, piling the leaves on the edge of the street, where the leaf-sucking truck—just like every year—had come and taken them away. See? Life went on. All over Dayton there were yards thick with leaves and fallen limbs, footballs weathering and deflating, lawn chairs blown into hedges and spiderwebs on railings and doorframes. All over Dayton. But not here. From the air their neighborhood would look normal, the best place in town to come home to.

NOTHING EARTHSHAKING. STEADY forward progress. Open minds.

"So what do you think?" Chad said. "You think they came back to Dayton at the end of 1903, after they'd made man's first powered flight, and their hometown had a tickertape parade?"

A shy collusion of half-smiles and looks, with the braver students shaking their heads no.

"No!" Chad said. "A thousand times, no! First off, tickertape parades weren't invented until the twenties, and they're a New York City phenomenon, because the tickertapes were stock market byproducts, and second, no one even realized what the Wright brothers had done. Even the article in the Dayton paper was confusing, because the writer thought that what the brothers had done was a variant of hot-air ballooning."

In the fall of 1902, the glider worked almost perfectly at Kitty Hawk, except for an occasional tailspin. Orville suggested making their machine's fixed rear rudder movable, like a ship's rudder. Wilbur thought of linking the rear rudder's movement to the wing warp controls. It worked. They had lift, they had control—the only thing they needed was propulsion. Over the next year they designed and built a propeller and an engine. Neither task was easy. Books in the Dayton Public Library were not particularly helpful. Imagine, one of the brothers said, the propeller as a wing traveling in a spiral course. This was a useful idea, and by June they had two propellers. The design and production of the engine they farmed out to Charlie Taylor, their mechanic and bicycle shop helper.

The first Wright Flyer, as it came to be named, was never fully assembled in Dayton. The bicycle shop couldn't hold it. The central portion of the machine blocked the passage between the front and back rooms of the shop. To wait on their bicycle customers the brothers had go out the shop's back door and come in from the front.

The brothers shipped the pieces of their 1903 contraption to Kitty Hawk in September. The weather that year was terrible, windy and rainy. It took three weeks to put their craft together, in a hangar they had built the year before. Once the thing was constructed, they played with it as a glider. A much-heralded rival flying machine, the Aerodrome, the creation of the head of the Smithsonian, started and ended its inaugural flight by sliding into the Potomac River. To protect their craft from such a fate, the Wrights added landing skids to it. They mounted its engine. A propeller shaft was broken, and a friend of the Wrights took it back to Dayton to Charlie Taylor for repair. Charlie fixed it, but upon its return to Kitty Hawk the shaft broke again. This time Orville himself took the propeller back to Dayton, returning with steel shafts December 11.

"This story holds no suspense for you, does it?" Chad asked his students. "You know how it will end. Guess what: Wilbur and Orville did, too." On December 16, two days before the fifty-nine-second flight that is in all the history books, the flight that would introduce the modern era of air travel,

Orville cabled his father. "Success assured," he told him. "Keep quiet."

The Wright brothers came back home to Dayton. Beyond their family and few trusted friends, no one knew what they had done and no one would know for almost five years.

Between 1903 and 1908 Wilbur and Orville made hundreds of flights at Huffman's Prairie, an area just northeast of Dayton. This prairie would later become an airport (Wright Field) and then an air force base (Wright-Patterson AFB: the uplifting and the pragmatic aspects of Dayton combined in its name). The Wright brothers picked this area to test their crafts for practical reasons: it was a flat area with good winds, and it was at the end of a tram line. Mr. Huffman let them use his land for free, asking only that they not disturb his cows. Over that prairie Wilbur and Orville figured out how to fly in circles, how to take off without wind or elevation, how not to stall.

In August 1908, the brothers at last went public. Wilbur spent two minutes aloft over a field in France, observed by a crowd of airman wannabes. Orville, outside Washington in September, performed for government officials and stayed in the air sixty-two minutes. Men wept, and this was not a weepy time. *Imagine,* people said—the royalty and the commoners, the scientists and the daredevils, all the thousands of people who flocked to see their flights—*two bicycle builders from Dayton, Ohio.*

"As if they were handy fellows," Chad said. "As if they were"—he nodded at the classroom door—"a couple of Mr. Jenkses." (Mr. Jenks was the building custodian; this line was guaranteed a laugh.) "Do you think that pretending that the Wrights were simply bike builders helped make their achievement palatable? Like taking to the air was a big cake you could cut up and pass around the world? Think of those brothers. They were daring, they were wildly inventive, they were careful, they were *afflicted*. Listen to me"—and here Chad got emotional: his voice cracked and his eyes filled every time—"those brothers were extraordinary. Those brothers were not like any mechanics you or I will ever know. And this city supported them. Orville was standoffish, people used to say. Wilbur had his head in the clouds. Then someone else would laugh and say Oh yes, Wilbur did have his head in the clouds! I submit to you that that is typical Dayton: a gloss of disapproval overlying a wall of tolerance. That's not true everywhere, folks. Dayton was a good hiding place for them. Dayton let them experiment, crash, rebuild; it ignored them until the world said not to; it let them be unknown. Think of the gift those brothers gave the world: not only did they show man how to fly, they made it look easy."

waiting for winter

PREM LEFT. PREM had a sick cousin, suddenly, back in Cambodia, and before the dean had reassigned his classes, Prem was gone. He left his glasses in the drawer of his desk, photos of his daughters hanging on the wall. He rolled up his degrees and piled their disassembled frames on the floor. Seventy-five years before, his mother at age sixteen had fled the Khmer Rouge, the address and telephone number of a cousin in America hidden inside a Bic pen. When she arrived in Ohio in December, she thought all the bare trees were dead. Terrible country, she thought. Within three years she was back in Cambodia. She married and had children, Prem among them. Prem had come to the U.S. for graduate studies—his expertise was the world wars—and stayed when he got the UD job. Chad couldn't remember if he'd been a U.S. citizen.

Chad stood at the door of Prem's office, taking in the disarray, unable to walk in. "I'm not really blaming him," the department secretary, KayLynn, said, "but it makes me furious, you know? How're we supposed to keep going if everyone leaves?" She waved at the frames on the floor. "He could have left it neat!"

"I'll take them," Chad said suddenly. Wood, paper, posterboard: these could be fuel. Prem's whole desk, come to think of it, could turned into fuel. "Why don't you leave?" Chad asked KayLynn, because as a single woman she easily could.

Her eyes widened. "This is my home." Chad knew Kay-Lynn's house, a battered frame two-story flanked by frat houses, where she had lived all her forty years. "What about you?" KayLynn asked Chad. "You've got your kids and all."

"I don't know," Chad said. It struck him he had never been less sure. He'd had a naive view, he could see, that history would swirl through them yet leave them curiously untouched, like a house swept off its foundation and deposited intact downstream. Their house might just as well be crushed. Prem was a supremely practical man; his leaving was a statement. He didn't care for himself, Prem had said once, but war was tough on families.

"What's going to happen?" KayLynn wailed suddenly. "I'm here with a bunch of historians: can't you tell me what's going to happen?" The light through Prem's old window drove her back into the hall. "Ramsey'll stay," KayLynn said, shaking out the plackets of her sweater as if she were straightening her mind, "just out of stubbornness, and Montford doesn't have anywhere to go. I figure if you're not going the next one will be Hanning." Lisa Hanning, the medievalist, had a young child. KayLynn frowned. "We've got a pool, you know. Johnny Riley in student housing started it. Name the date Frost resigns." Frost was the university president.

"He won't resign. He'll leave. Run the university from his place in Tallahassee."

KayLynn snorted. "We're lucky if there's a third of the student body here."

"My Nixon seminar is down to two students."

"Montford had to cancel Luther and the Reformation."

"Catholic school," Chad observed.

KayLynn leaned against the wall and laughed. "You're incorrigible, you know that? Incorrigible." Chad smiled happily down at her, wishing that Sharis thought that he was witty.

MICHELLE WAS ASLEEP beside her, vertebrae curled like a winding staircase, late-afternoon light made golden by the autumn leaves. It should be beautiful, it should be plenty, but sex wasn't like it used to be for Lila. It no longer pressed her with its old ferocity, and Michelle's enthusiasm—her screams, her moans, her digging her separated fingers into Lila's scalp—seemed oddly pointless and self-centered. Lila used all her tricks on her, and Michelle responded, so vigorously Lila heard herself thinking, more than once: Did I ever act like that? And then she felt a distance from her own past, maybe her own body, because her lovemaking in the past had involved almost no thought, and certainly no judgment.

It wasn't rape, not really, Lila thought. More like prostituting herself for the chance of the Grid.

In the meantime, her customer was smitten. "I won't need a boyfriend if I have you." Within days there were ten, twelve daily messages on Lila's perc, one of them showing Michelle lying on a sofa naked, moving her hand over herself and singing, "How Do I Feel?"

What's wrong with me? Lila thought as she garbaged the images. She was using this young woman to get at something obviously crazy. Lila wanted to be a different person, to normalize herself and her desires, turn her yearning back towards a woman the way lesbians a hundred years ago—for the sake of family peace, propriety, children—had tried to fix their yearnings on a man. But she couldn't do it.

Skeins of wool she'd knit into afghans and children's sweaters. A pet, maybe a golden retriever. They'd send her to South America to learn dousing. Oh, Lila—the Gridians would shake their heads—what a miracle that she found her way here!

"WHAT'S THERE TO be nervous about? The camp's perfectly safe. They'll do crafts and campfires. They don't even let them take percs. Howard begged me, he **begged** me. And Terleski says he can take Leon, too."

Chad lifted his eyes from the blue table. Howard did almost nothing lately. He got home from school and sat. "How many nights?"

"Two nights, Friday and Saturday. They'll use your tent."

"It'll be freezing."

"So they'll wear extra clothes!" Sharis burst out. "I don't understand you. Who cares if Prem left? Did you ever agree about anything with Prem? Cub Scouts is normal life. You wanted normal life." Lars this morning had danced around the kitchen entertaining his nephew, tossing a pancake so high in the air it went off the screen

"I did." Chad noticed his past tense. "I do."

She wasn't going to get panicky—that wasn't her way—but if Chad got any more gloomy Sharis could leave and take the boys. It would be no problem: all her clients, even George and Gentia, exclaimed about the quality of her work. She had a fantasy about showing up at Lars's Norwegian door.

"SEE THAT BARE patch in the leaves, with the marks in the dirt? That's a deer scrape."

"Where a deer fell?" Diana asked.

She knew nothing. "Mating season," Charles said. "The rut."

"Rotten when mating's a rut."

What was the word for that sense of humor? Brittle. Charles chose to ignore it. "The male deer, the buck, scrapes aside leaves with his hooves and then he urinates—sniff it, smell that musky odor?—and then he marks a tree nearby by rubbing his antlers on it."

"All the tricks to drive a girl deer crazy!"

"It works," Charles said. "Lots of Bambis."

They walked further down the path and into the prairie. Beads of dew hung on the grasses. Spider webs were scattered through the grasses like miniature clouds. "Look at those beautiful webs," Charles said. "They're called . . ."

"Bowl and doily webs," Diana said. "You've told me about fifty times."

"YOU AGAIN!" ALLYSSA stood, extending her hand.

"See how you affected me?" Lila tried to laugh. They sat down across from each other at the walnut table. Lila had hoped for a meeting at Allyssa's farmhouse, surrounded by clipped and flat fields, but Allyssa had arranged instead to come to Dayton.

Allyssa was dressed elegantly, in a green suit with a high collar, and the brown line around her eyes was surely evidence of makeup. Lila wondered if it was a treat for her to be outside the Grid, sitting in a tenth floor of a downtown bank building wearing fancy clothes. "So," Allyssa said, glancing at the holo-screen of her perc. *She* doesn't have to go to a central computer like the average Gridian, Lila thought. "I understand you're interested in a Grid position."

Lila felt a lurch of dread: Allyssa was too smooth, too polished, as if her fancy clothing were a sort of armor. "Yes," Lila said.

Allyssa's eyes turned to her holo-screen again. "Give me a few minutes to run your résumé."

The résumé was a risk, Lila knew, but when she messaged it she'd had hope. But watching Allyssa watch it was excruciating. Lila talking at the viewer, segments of Lila's old shower campaign including the jingles, old footage of Lila's speech at the Needmore/Needless rally. It was even more desperate than the messages Michelle had sent her.

Allyssa tapped her fingernail on the table. "Your specialty appears to be water conservation. I assure you we don't have problems with that."

"I didn't think you would, I . . ."

"I understand how you made your reputation," Allyssa went on, not seeming to hear her. She nodded at the holo-screen. "You advertised."

"You mean during the New Dawn Dayton days? Of course I advertised. I used the means available. I got the word out. That's efficiency. I changed people's minds."

"We're not interested in changing people's minds. Our people have made up their minds."

For a moment Lila was stymied. Then she said what she believed: "I would love the Grid, I know. I'd be devoted to it."

Allyssa looked up in surprise, her gaze softening. "*Devotion*, that's an interesting word. Did you know its root means 'to vow or pledge'? *Vote* and *devout* are word cousins. Jeff Germantz loved *devote*. He was interested in the origins of language because language and agriculture are the two oldest intentional human activities in the world. Have you seen pictures of Jeff? He had the most incredible eyes. Green as emeralds, green as the Grid. Photographs never did him justice. You couldn't say a sentence without his talking about some word root. Do you know where the word *word* comes from?"

"Pardon?" Lila, transfixed, was hardly listening. Allyssa had taken on the aspect of a queen, her green suit falling like royal raiment from her shoulders.

"I'll look it up for you," Allyssa said, and in few taps she had it. "*Word*," she read from her holo-screen. "It's from a very old root, W-E-R. Jeff called *wer* a tree with huge and numerous branches. One of its definitions is 'to speak,' of course, so that's *word*, *verb*, *proverb*, but there's another definition that's 'to turn,' and that's *verse* and *vice versa* and *introvert* and *universe*, and then there's the definition 'to cover,' which gives you *warranty* and *garment* and . . ." Allyssa looked up. "My husband wrote this program."

Lila was startled. "You were married to Germantz?"

"Oh, no." Pink flared on Allyssa's beige face. "No, my husband just worked with Jeff. Jeff was older. Jeff never married. My husband's name is Lincoln Hawley." Allyssa smiled confidingly and dropped her voice. "I don't usually tell anybody he wrote *Origins of English*."

"Where is he now?"

"He's in Paris."

"No, no, you told me that before, when I was visiting. I mean Germantz. The one who headed up the Grid." He was dead, Lila was sure, but where had he been buried?

"He founded it. He didn't head it. That would be very un-Jeff, to head something. In his way, he's still alive. He's on the Grid. He's part of the Grid." Allyssa's face changed, slipped into a dreamy look. "People don't realize there are a million aspects to changing people's thought."

A dim sensation moved through Lila's mind, that there was something strange that she was missing, but the sensation was so vague—a shadow of an elephant, not an elephant—and so incongruous (the shadow of an elephant lumbering across a cornfield) that Lila dismissed it almost without realizing she'd done so. "Is there something else I could do besides water?" Lila asked. "Help with cooking? Serve drinks?"

Allyssa stared at her, and Lila felt hopefulness surge inside her like a bounding dog.

"I appreciate your enthusiasm, and I told Agro I'd do what I could, but it's a very difficult time to bring someone on the Grid," Allyssa said. "It's not you in particular, it's anyone. At this time."

"I'm adaptable, Allyssa."

"I'm sure you are."

"I'm tough."

"Tough's not the issue."

"I feel like I've been called there, Allyssa. I've never felt this way. Do you think Nenonene will attack? Is that why you don't want new people?"

"We're watched all the time, you know. Not by the Alliance. By the U.S." Allyssa's voice went hard. "By *your* people. They send up Hopi Hellions. Big white flying cockroaches."

"Allyssa"—and here Lila dropped her voice, thinking there could be a listening device planted somewhere—"I could fight. I'm a woman without children. I don't have to worry about protecting anyone." Lila could hardly believe she was saying this. "I could be useful," she whispered.

"I wish you could be," Allyssa said out loud.

"God, I'm sorry you have to worry at all," Lila said. All the passion missing from her lovemaking had settled in her voice. "I know you set the thing up with such faith."

Allyssa frowned and clicked her holo-screen off. "I'll tell the Agro people we spoke. You're interesting, Lila de Becqueville. Don't let anyone tell you you're not interesting."

Lila felt like a twenty-year-old again, a grievously young and rejected suitor. She barely made it to the elevator without crying. It was no consolation at all that the next week Michelle was returning for a visit.

DIANA REMEMBERED OPENING the specialist's private round freezer, waving away the billow of frosty air, peering down at the trays of frozen embryos stored in concentric circles on the shelves, each labeled with sex and race and hair color and three admirable characteristics—intelligent, tractable, outgoing—along with a price code. It bothered the specialist there weren't more customers for his designer products. He had patented a gene obsession sequence derived from himself and placed it in each of the intentional embryos. "Athlete, scholar, parent—who doesn't need a bit of obsession?" But the intentionals didn't have the market appeal he'd expected. "People always want part of *themselves*," he'd cluck, his mouth curling as it did when he discussed prematurely aged wine. "Even when their selves aren't very interesting. Look at our patients: mediocrities making mediocrities." With this, the specialist's face was transformed by his beneficent, old-man smile, the smile that his patients talked about, that he posed with. If he'd been really smart, Diana thought, the specialist would have patented the genes for his own smile.

She'd met an intentional once, accompanying a woman who came in for a consultation. The girl was three years old and beautiful, and as Diana talked to her mother the girl removed the hairs from her hairbrush and laid them one by one on the exam table. "I don't want another one of these," the mother said. "I mean, she's great and all, but I want a kid that's more ordinary. Maybe my own eggs with a little touch-up."

"Twelve, thirteen fourteen . . ." The little girl was counting the hairs,

"Okay," Diana said, clicking the box by "egg improvement."
"Will we be using your husband's sperm?"

The specialist almost convinced her that for humans to survive there must be improvement. But here, in the deep disarray of the woods, there was order, there was interdependence, there was survival. The seasons wheeled around independent of man; the vast weather experiments had failed— that is, they had been too successful, turning an already overwarming climate into a wildly cycling one with highs and lows well past historic baselines. "Why don't we have a baby?" Charles had asked one night, nuzzling her in the bed under the stuffed owl. That he should want a child with her shocked her; she actually leapt from their bed and stood naked in the cold. "No!" She said. "Don't you know the risks of an unimproved child?" They spent the rest of the night two inches from each other but miles distant, as if Diana were atop one mountain and Charles another, and since then they hadn't had sex once. They still shared the mattress, but only for warmth.

Charles told her, several days later, his theory of souls. Only a lonely, damaged soul, in his opinion, would pick a custom embryo, while the strongest souls would go where they could take their chances. The strange thing was, she knew exactly what he meant. Maybe this was why she laughed out loud when he told her his theory, why she made fun of the whole idea of souls, making reference to the souls of bugs and stones and trees. "It's a soulfest out here!" she said, throwing her hands up around her. Charles left to fill the bird feeders, disappointment in his padding walk.

She shouldn't be mean to him. He was a kind man, and it was totally her choice (she still had her apartment in town)

that they were stuck here together, with every night a little colder, the frost each morning thicker on the red leaves of the poison ivy. But at times Charles's staggering array of wildlife facts felt like a net thrown over her head. She almost yearned for her old boyfriend, who made a point of being ignorant and mean. There were trees she didn't know the names of, ones she wouldn't mention to Charles. Her ignorance about them was the pocket of air inside the upturned boat. She didn't go so far as to pull up the putty root lilies, but she made a point of stomping on their leaves.

Why am I so cruel? Diana thought. What genes are bad in me? Which soul—unlucky or stupid—got stuck inside me? Get rid of it! the woman at the clinic had screamed, meaning: I hate me! Kill me! What had happened to the soul of that destroyed clone? That poor lost soul.

Without their leaves the maples were very beautiful, their limbs like roots that reached into the sky.

INTERESTING: MIDDLE ENGLISH from Norman French from Latin *interesse*: "to be in between," to matter, to be of concern. From Indo-European *es-*, "to be."

"I'LL TELL YOU what started it," Allyssa said to Tuuro as she paced. She was back and changed from her errand in Dayton, and Tuuro was at the stovetop sautéing onions, still bubbling with satisfaction that she'd trusted him alone. He had scrubbed out the bathtubs, cleaned the floors behind the toilets, changed and washed the sheets on both their beds. "We asked for three weeks of vacation for our people instead of two. It went all the way to President Baxter, and that moron turned it down. That was '43. Can you imagine? He said the Gridians got to rest all January. Said another week of vacation would be"—Allyssa made quotation marks with her fingers—"'disruptive.' He thinks we're nothing? He thinks we don't matter? You watch. A month from now the Grid will be the most important place on earth. There won't be a goatherd in Peru who doesn't know us."

NELSON AND SOLGANIK, *Computer Genies*, their card read (a card! what an antiquated custom), and Lila wasn't sure what was most intimidating, their bubble bottoms beneath their matching pink crop tops or their taut (tucked?) faces and enhanced eyelashes or their manicured nails. Whatever forces had pushed Lila into uto-hood must meet strenuous, daily resistance in Nelson and Solganik. They had to be, from what Kennedy had told her, at least twenty years older than Lila. Legendary broads from Cincinnati, Kennedy said.

Sue Nelson was running through programs, images and pages flashing across Lila's office computer screen, as her partner, Leslie Solganik, leaned over the back of her chair and watched. "Not bragging, but we're the only people in Ohio could do this job for you," Nelson said. "These kids, they don't know the furniture. They know what's on the tabletop, sure, but they forget about the table. Leslie and I know the insides of the drawers. We know where the glue dries up and shrivels. We were born before the mainframe!"

Since her visit with Allyssa, Lila had been up the water tower two more times. The last time there'd been a slight movement—someone watching her?—at the top of the barrier on the Grid side, far right in her field of vision. Possible that she'd imagined this. She hadn't mentioned it to Michelle, who seemed to no longer be serious about getting Lila onto the Grid. "When would I see you?" Michelle asked. "How could I visit?"

"People nowadays can't even get rid of things," Solganik said in a irritated tone. "Think you can just sweep the tabletop. Ha! You heard of Kinsey Concrete? Makes those big pipes you can walk through? We cleared out a whole account for them. Made it disappear. Guy there didn't believe you could do such a thing. You got any programs you want rid of? We could be trouble. Got a map of the whole water system? It's gone."

Lila said, "No, it's not. It's in my head."

"Then you're a valuable woman. Voila." Nelson leaned back from the screen. "Wonderwater. I'll write out the door so you can get in again. Memorize and eat." She grinned. "Do the debit to Nelson and Solganik. Did I say debit? No way. We're the girls you pay in cash."

Seymour appeared in the door to Lila's office. This morning the doughnut shop Seymour frequented had been locked, its lights off and cabinets empty, and Seymour had been so distraught that Lila walked back with him to the shop to confirm what he'd seen. Seymour was worried about the clerk there, the one who called him Mister See.

"Seymour, guess what," Lila said, "Nelson and Solganik got us Wonderwater."

His mouth dropped open, his eyes taking in the beaming women. "Char," he said. "Charmegaly." He always knew the latest slang.

"THAT BUSINESS WITH the colonel," Allyssa admitted, "that was a nasty business." She and Tuuro talked often at night, seated at the kitchen table—or rather, Allyssa talked and Tuuro listened, rubbing along together almost like little brother and big sister. Allyssa was sick of General Nenonene being so damn busy, but in the meantime what could they do? Tuuro shouldn't leave the house. It wasn't that anyone Gridian would see him, Allyssa said; she was hiding him from the good old U.S. of A.

Allyssa had heard that the video was edited to show only the second shot, the gush of blood diminished, to make sure the whole scene was acceptable to be run on every channel. They didn't show the colonel begging or the grazing of his ear. Afterwards Nenonene went to a sink and washed his hands. The rest of his workday went normally, and that evening he attended a state dinner in a room with chandeliers. The women wore beaded gowns and tiaras, the men tuxedos; Nenonene wore his same bloody uniform. People were afraid to look at him, even more afraid not to. By the time he went to bed he was a legend.

A madman, a brute. A man whose instincts were tribal ("I mean that in a good way," Allyssa said.) A military man who believed in military justice, who gave his betrayer the chance to die an honorable death. A clever politician who had the courage—the guts—for a single brutal act, knowing blood spilled then meant less blood later on. A master publicist. He could be all these things—Allyssa thought he was—and yet the Gridians were willing to sign on with him, because even if the General was imperfect, he was still a man of hope. "He respects the Grid," Allyssa said, her eyes narrowing. "The whole of it and each of us as individuals. And you don't need to worry, Tuuro. He respects you."

She was totally colorless, Tuuro thought, in that she was all one color. He thought of her like a lump of clay, something you could slice right through and find the inside and the outside just the same. She worked hard. She cleaned and answered messages and cooked dinners and made trips to this and that village. He had spotted, one evening, the sliver of pink just inside her lower lip, and the vision was so unsettling he'd gone directly to his room. Desire in this situation would mean nothing but disaster, and, for Nenonene, Tuuro understood, he must stay pure.

"My husband heard him speak once," Allyssa said. She recounted how the General extended his finger and scratched at the back of his scalp. "A little bald spot there," her husband told her. "He's worried it away."

Late at night, in her downstairs bedroom, Allyssa turned on her perc. *General Nenonene,* she messaged, *I am finding Tuuro Simpkins to be an honorable man.* She sat a moment looking at her words. *He admires you greatly,* she added.

WONDERWATER CONFUSED LILA. There were the usual rain reports for every American county, the aquifer levels, usage tables. But there was a whole new section, too, with rain data for the rest of the world, data that must have taken considerable time and connections to obtain. There was also, at the end of these tables, tucked into a corner, as it were, a long article about world water resource management that read almost like a treatise, that had no author listed, that used words Lila had never heard in a water context. Water farming, water wickets, aqualimbo. Lila knew—at least by reputation, and she'd met two of them at conferences—the original minds behind Wonderwater, but their names weren't on the site now. No one's name was on the site. At the end of the article were a series of icons unaffected by clicking. That was wrong: an icon should open into something. Maybe these weren't icons, but designs. Could they be hieroglyphs, designs with meaning? A message to those in the know? Lila copied them down and slipped them into her desk's center drawer, thinking she would recheck the site later, see if the icons had in any way changed.

SHARIS ATE THE last bite of Leon's soyburger and went outside to clean the grill. They grilled through the winter on an apron of brick that jutted out from the back of their house.

"You killed Chubby!" Leon's voice rang out from inside. "You killed our pet!" As if Howard had finally done a worthy, manly thing.

"I didn't mean to!" Howard cried. "I was just holding him!" Sharis next heard blows and crying. Chubby was Howard's hamster. Too much passion in this house, Sharis thought wearily. Let Chad take care of it.

A beautiful night, the stars looking hurled across the sky. With the neighbors' houses dark, the night sky was much easier to see. Sharis used a wire brush, enjoying its sound. When they went to sleep now she let Chad hold her, imagining his arms were Lars's arms. She had made a private movie of Lars's best moments. Sitting at the kitchen table smoking, wearing a brooding look. Dancing around the kitchen with his shirt off, his toddler granddaughter on his shoulders. She didn't always like the things he said, so she turned off the translation feature. Something about him, every time, that stirred her. His wrists. The way he narrowed his eyes. It was booming hard to edit him. Not that she put in more of him: if anything she put in less. But the scenes she put in of his wife were less flattering, and she overdid it with his grandchildren, presuming they were the family members he'd like to see.

"Look at the little homemaker!" said a mocking voice out of the darkness. Gentia appeared in the pool of light from Sharis's window, George beside her. "Nice to see someone else in this neighborhood has the guts to stick around. Does Chad have any students left in his classes?"

"A few. How're the security systems?"

"Great!" Gentia said. "We're not selling as much lately, but we're monitoring a lot of the empty houses."

"Any trouble?"

"Not like Detroit, thank God," George said. "Michi-gone," people called it.

"You know who's our biggest market now?" Gentia asked. "Those Melano neighborhoods the west side of I-75. We've had people pawning their media centers. They sit there in perfect peace and silence, waiting for the bombs."

George shifted on his heels. "Chad inside?" he asked. When Sharis nodded, he disappeared.

Without George, Gentia seemed suddenly diminished. She walked in a circle around the patio, looking at her feet. "I'm getting sick of this, I'll tell you," Gentia said. "Are they going to attack the Grid or not? If they get the Grid, will they get Dayton? What would they do with the Base and the Consort plant? It's getting on my nerves, and I can't stand it."

"I'm sorry." Sharis knew from her loops that Gentia spent most of her time in her living room messaging on her perc and making sales, while George sat in the family room in front of the TV. Sharis was grateful for the times the living room camera inexplicably was turned off. George and Gentia were incredibly boring. At Sharis's suggestion they had cut their weekly program to five minutes. Sharis suspected that she could hit the high spots in fifteen seconds.

"Why are you sorry?" Gentia said. "What do you have to do with it? It's going to drop to zero degrees and what are we going to eat? Why are you staying here, anyway?"

Maybe ten seconds. Maybe five. Sharis said, "Chad feels loyal to Dayton." A simplistic way to put it—and it didn't account for her not fighting him—but Gentia didn't deserve more.

"Right. Here's a question for when the lights go off: does Dayton feel loyal to him?"

CHARLES STUDIED THE birds circling a big maple. "Something's coming in."

"Why don't you check your perc?" Diana asked.

Days since they had opened any link to the outside world. They lived like people of sixty, seventy years before, when all people had was radio and TV. Except they hardly used those, either.

There was a storm front moving in from Canada, across the upper plains and into Ohio. Up to a foot of snow was predicted for Chicago, as the storm moved east and south in its stately and merciless way.

"We've got all that food," Diana said.

Charles shrugged. "If the power goes, we have firewood. Might not hurt to bottle up some water, in case the pipes freeze."

The pipes wouldn't freeze. They were new pipes, with thermal protection; several years ago Diana had paid the bill that brought them. "Even if we're living like a hundred years ago, we're still not living like a hundred years ago," Diana said. "We have modern materials!"

"Great." Charles often felt he had been born in the wrong era. He mistrusted synthetics, hybrids, genetic engineering, clones. Standing in bird blinds wearing rubber boots and wool. Fucking to make a baby. Those were the days.

He was ashamed of how he ratcheted things up for her. Making a fuss over the fruits children knew as monkeybrains, taking her on a special walk to look at puffballs big as human heads. He remembered, a mere two months before, the two of them pursuing birdsong. Delicate, transcendent, a twig of song inscribing itself on the sky. Now they were reduced to giant puffballs.

But Diana made no mention of leaving, and for that he was grateful. He liked being alone, but when the ground froze and the snow came, it would be lovely to have someone to hold. He hadn't had that luxury in the past. The frogs hid at the bottom of the pond, the ants burrowed into the ground, and even the gophers, in their tunnels, nestled together. That was what creatures did in winter, retreated and huddled and survived. You couldn't get more basic than that. And Diana was a person he could huddle with.

GRADY WAS A Gamma Force pilot who liked to say he was his own United Nations. In his blood there mingled Scandinavians, Jews, Blacks, Italians, a Polynesian, Native Americans, Poles, and a Japanese woman who claimed descent from the royal family. The only thing Grady could imagine his ancestors had in common was a ferocious urge for sex. He could make sense of his ancestry no other way.

"He sits there looking at her, like he's totally dazzled by her presence, like he's just a dull guy in the middle of his boring day and now he's walked in and spotted this ball of lusciousness and he can't believe it, he's afraid if he takes his eyes off her she'll disappear, he's almost afraid to speak to her because clearly she's an angel—but he's got to speak because how can he go on living if he doesn't?"

Grady smiled, stared down into his drink.

"It's astonishing," his copilot went on. "It's like their clothes have dissolving seams. They just fall right off! And look at him!" The copilot waved his hand, indicating Grady's drooping and lashless eyelid, the indentation in his forehead, the scar that carved a canyon from his ear to the side of his mouth. "It's not the looks, obviously," the copilot confided to the group around the table. "It's the look."

"Freaks have no shame." Grady winked his hairless eyelid. "Professional secret." Everyone laughed, as Grady knew they would. Every once in a while he wouldn't mind being surprised.

"God gave you your good looks," Grady's mother once said, "but that bike crash made you interesting."

"MR. QUARIN?" CHAD looked up, started counting. Ten students. Other years he'd had thirty. But today there were only nine.

"He went home," said another student.

"Home home?"

"His parents pulled him out."

"Where is home?"

"Here. Dayton."

"He's from Dayton and he's leaving? He'll miss Paul Laurence Dunbar and his poetry. Charles Kettering and the self-starting engine. The Dayton Peace Accords. He'll miss the whole damn twentieth century."

The students were looking at one another. "I think his parents just wanted him safe, sir," said a young woman.

"Where would we be if everyone stayed safe?" Chad's right arm, unbidden, jerked up and down like some demented doll's. "That's your highest aspiration, to be safe? You think George Newcom thought he was safe?" Newcom's tavern had been the first public tavern in the region; periodically his corncrib served as a jail. "You think John Patterson felt safe exporting cash registers to India? You think Orville felt safe in the air above two hundred cows? Cows he'd promised not to hit? What the hell kind of virtue is safe?"

All nine students stared back at him. Jesus, Chad thought, they'll fucking fire me. But he had tenure.

"A midwestern virtue, sir," someone said, and the students tittered.

Chad's arm dropped. "Okay," he said. He took three cleansing breaths. "We'll do the Dayton newspapers today," he said. He'd planned to fit in Paul Laurence Dunbar, the Melano poet who'd died of TB, the man who knew why the caged bird sang, but that was a story so sad he didn't have the heart to tell it.

"I don't want another hamster," Howard had said as Chad dug a hole for Chubby. "You can't buy a new best friend."

LILA WOKE UP at 3 a.m. and couldn't fall back to sleep. She opened up Wonderwater and rechecked the mystery icons: no change. She collected the dried lemon rinds from around her bedroom and put them in her wastebasket. She went to the bathroom, switched the light on. A woman of power. A valuable woman. An interesting woman. Yet in her mirror she saw nothing but an uto. The horrible mole on her cheek seemed to be growing: she wished she had the guts to snip it off. Michelle had a pair of glasses she wore for reading, and on her recent visit she had grabbed them from the bedside table. "So I can see you better," she said. As she bent over Lila, the corner of the eyeglass frame stuck out through her curtain of hair. Lila had never felt so exposed.

Outside there was rattling and howling, a cold wind blowing in; not removing her gaze from the mirror, Lila used one hand to push the cracked window closed.

the monitor station

IT SLEETED FOR three days in mid-December, turning to wet snow at night. Ice was everywhere. The trees were spectacularly and weightily encrusted, twigs and branches snapping in the breeze. A mitten Leon had left outside turned as stiff as plaster.

Sharis and Chad had turned their thermostat down to fifty, because who knew, with winters starting early now, what they'd pay for fuel. At some point the university would have to cut professors as well as staff. Some of the untenured professors had cut themselves, but Chad and his history colleagues stayed around, restless and vaguely guilty, discussing Prem and joking in the halls about the point at which a job became a sinecure. Chad worried he had no right to a continued salary. But in another way he felt he did: by continuing his teaching, he was maintaining a Dayton institution.

These days, with the ice, Chad didn't attempt to go to campus. The semester was over, and all he had to do was grading. He wondered if the university would reopen after Christmas break. The last few days of elementary school before Christmas break had been canceled as snow days, the frozen roads too risky for buses.

In the family room, Sharis had strung popcorn and dried cranberries around the mantel, and sat a tinsel tree on a chest of drawers. Chad tolerated these Christmas decorations because they seemed so sad. Sharis's family growing up had been no more interested in a garish Christmas than Chad's father.

On cold nights, they slept downstairs. They had a fireplace and plenty of wood (their own, and there was nothing to stop them from invading the woodpiles of their absent neighbors), Sharis spread blankets and sofa cushions on the floor in front of the fire, and the whole family slept huddled together in their clothes, under bedspreads, afghans, and old coats. "Like one of your campouts!" Sharis exclaimed to the boys. Terleski's Cub Scout Den was going strong, although Leon had been banished from the latest sleepover after a "Mr. Wag-Wag Penis" escapade at a campfire. "I'm the den leader!" Terleski had said. "I have morals to uphold!"

On the fourth day of bad weather—December 20—it warmed up enough for the sleet to turn to rain.

"I want to keep sleeping downstairs," Leon said. "I like our cozy nest." Both Sharis and Chad found this odd: Leon, their spiky child, enjoyed sleeping nestled between his parents, while Howard, whom they thought of as the needier child, slept behind Sharis to avoid being touched.

That night they were all warm and asleep when a thump shook the house. Everyone woke up, their fear a charged nimbus around their bodies. No one breathed. Deathly quiet except the raindrops on the roof. This is it, thought Sharis. This is what we've been pretending couldn't happen. Her mouth filled with acid and regret.

Leon's head popped up. "Was that thunder, Mommy?"

"Thunder," Sharis agreed, her eyes searching the dark. Thunder in December? In the orange glow from their log she made out Chad, ten inches away from her across Leon's head. Her arm was under Leon's neck, and she wondered if she drew him closer if a watcher would see the movement, if a man at their front window wearing night vision goggles had Leon in his crosshairs at this instant. Her heart was beating like a running deer's, its white tail flashing surrender.

"Bomb," Chad breathed, angling his mouth toward her ear. She shivered at the warm puff of his exhalation. Her eyes roved, looking for a movement or a light. Nothing.

"You stay here. I'll look." Chad astonished her by raising himself on his hands and knees and crawling away.

The space in front of the fire, which had seemed so cozy, now seemed enormous and exposed. The log on the fire was glowing, and Sharis saw them all tossed into the hearth; saw herself rolling the log into the feet of an intruder; heard Leon's screams as his hand was held to the flame. Dear God, let it be quick. She slid her hand behind her toward Howard, and he gripped it so tightly his nails hurt her palm. The tinsel tree gleamed like a mockery of happiness. The smell of shit filled the room: one of the boys, Sharis thought.

We were fools. We will be punished by the death of our children. *No! No!* Sharis almost cried. *Take me instead!* Why hadn't her mother cried that? Although maybe Chad was right, and she had. "Get over me," Sharis hissed at Howard, and Howard after a second's hesitation scrambled over her hip, his elbow hitting her chin. "Lie down next to Leon," Sharis said, pushing herself onto all fours and straddling her children. She imagined herself as a monstrous spider, hairy and ferocious.

Chad was crouched at the door to the kitchen, looking around. Sharis lifted her head and followed his gaze. There was no chink in the front curtains; she couldn't believe that anyone was aiming at them from there. If another person was in the house, there'd be breathing. She heard nothing.

Chad stood and picked up a flashlight from the kitchen counter. He left Sharis and the boys frozen in position, their breathing so fast and shallow it seemed as though a sigh might crack their chests.

"Don't move now," Sharis whispered to her boys, "but if I say run, you leave the house and run. Don't worry about Daddy and me, just go."

"Down to the troll bridge?" Leon asked, too loudly.

Sharis nodded. "Anywhere," she said. "But someplace protected. Break into an empty house and go to the kitchen."

Chad looked through the crack in the curtains out the front window: no one. He crept to the front door, his back against the wall. No one there. The noise had come like a blow from somewhere above. But nothing suggested their house had been damaged. No wind blowing through a window, no drips or outdoor scent. Chad slipped up the stairs, and with each increase in elevation he was more sure that their house was intact and they were alone inside it: their husk, their cave, their sanctuary. He stood at the door of the boys' room and looked in, the beds like dark boats setting out to sea. Calm swept over him: after all these months of uncertainty, their home was still their home. He pictured his family downstairs on the floor, their fear suddenly sweet, almost pathetic. Everything was intact. He glanced into his and Sharis's bedroom and the guest room: peaceful and dark, the windows secure. He walked into the hall, opening his lips to call down the stairs: Sharis! Boys! Everything's fine!

Another blow. The house shook, and Chad hurled himself to the floor of the hallway, in case something—what?—flew in through a bedroom window.

He listened for a whimper from downstairs: nothing. Whatever was hitting was hitting upstairs.

He crept on his hands and knees from bedroom to bedroom. Everything as peaceful as before, everything unchanged. Someone's mocking us, Chad thought wildly. Teasing us. We're prey to them.

Sharis and the boys appeared upstairs and crouched huddled in the hall. "Jesus!" Chad whispered. "Why'd you come up here?"

"What is it?" Sharis whispered back.

He knelt in front of them. "It's only someone trying to scare us. I don't think it's a bomb. There's no damage."

"A grenade?"

"A grenade would have exploded."

"It felt like an explosion."

"But there's no damage! Get back downstairs, if there're bombs out you should be in the basement." Commandos trained to creep and hide. Men under the beds, inside the closets.

Leon whimpered. "Daddy, I'm scared of the basement."

Chad could handle Howard crying, but this was Leon. Chad struggled to keep his voice steady. "Sharis, take the boys to the basement." The words came out too loud, echoing in the hallway like another blast.

"No," Sharis said.

Howard had separated from his mother and was sitting with his back against the wall, staring straight ahead. "Daddy, can I die with you?"

"Sharis . . ."—be calm, Chad told himself—"get —the—boys—to—the—basement."

"You take them! If you want a die in a cold wet place, you take them."

Howard did start crying now, big terrified sobs. "I want Chubby back."

"Chubby was an old hamster, Howard," Chad said. He moved to Howard and tried to get an arm around his son's shoulder, but Howard pressed his back into the wall in resistance. "He had a good life." The smell of shit was awful. Had Howard pooped on himself? Chad wrestled an arm behind his son. The wings of his shoulders were almost unfindable under his layers of flesh.

"Chubby was stupid," Leon said, his voice choked at first, then rising. "All he did was sleep and run around in that stupid wheel."

Leon is angry, Chad thought. Good. Good. He left the hall and started crawling toward the boys' room, aiming his beam of light under the bed.

"He was not stupid," Howard said. "He knew me! He liked me!"

"Be quiet!" Chad hissed. "Do I have to hear arguing in the middle of an air raid?"

"It's not an air raid," Sharis said. "If it's an air raid, where's the damage?"

"That's what I said! That's exactly what I said! And a minute ago you were argu—"

Another crash, very close, toward the back of the house, outside the boys' bedroom. Howard dropped to the floor and gripped Sharis's leg. For a moment it felt as if the air itself was pressurized around them.

"Wait a minute," Sharis said. "I'm thinking something." She stood up. "Give me the flashlight," she told Chad, and the three males watched her creep into the boys' room and flash her beam of light onto the roof above the kitchen. They heard a low laugh. "I was right," Sharis called. "It's ice."

Under the beds was empty. The closet was empty.

"Ice?" Chad pushed himself to standing and walked to Sharis.

"The ice hanging from the gutters." Sharis spoke in a normal voice, shocking Chad with her volume. She must be sure, he thought. "It's raining and the ice is melting, and what we hear is when a big chunk falls. I'll shine the flashlight for you. Look."

Across the upper third of the roof were chunks of ice the size of cinder blocks. "Wow," Chad said. "Amazing." As they watched another chunk fell, the sound no more ominous than the clang of a cymbal.

Leon had appeared beside them. "Mommy? I think my tongue is bleeding."

"I bit my tongue, too." Sharis switched on the bedroom light. "Why don't we make popcorn? We'll all get cleaned up and go downstairs and use our cozy fire to make popcorn."

Chad couldn't sleep. He sat in the lounge chair in the family room, watching his pile of family. When Sharis opened her eyes in the morning, he had two words for her. "We're leaving."

She nodded and sat up. "Okay. I'll get the suitcases."

"In a few days. I've got to finish this semester's grades, I have to get money, and I want to check out the Internet to decide where we should go. Plus we should drain our pipes and all. We can leave Friday, after Christmas. It's not an emergency, really. We might as well be prepared."

"You Boy Scout, you."

"I was never a Boy Scout." Chad looked at Sharis, thinking that she couldn't understand him. In her mind, he was sure, she was already packing suitcases. The night of the Gridding had made her, truly, a refugee: unencumbered, suspicious, ready to leave anywhere at the slightest provocation, equating—when it came right down to it—survival with flight. While for Chad leaving Dayton was like giving up his childhood religion. Dayton might not survive. *Bondad* was not enough. Prem had left. To think of such things was terrifying. Persistence. Reliability. Modesty. Any one of those midwestern virtues—he saw this— could work against him. Perhaps already had.

"A night like that makes you think," Sharis said, pushing herself off the floor, still wrapped in her blanket. "You": Chad noticed that word. Sharis sat down in the armchair across the table from his. The boys were still asleep. Chad looked at Sharis's profile, her eyes half closed, head sunk in the upholstery, and that they were a married couple side by side in a pair of armchairs seemed almost comical—it was reality, yes, but the sort of external reality that mocked understanding. In reality, they were a couple with a chasm between them, into which either of them—or both of them, or their children—could easily slip and fall.

Dear God, Chad thought. Dear God. It irritated him that he was thinking of praying, and in such a beseeching way. He had never wanted to be one of those people who turned to religion only when they were in trouble. After all, he didn't lead any kind of steady religious life. His mother had. His mother, for example, would have torn off searching for that woman and her toddler.

Chad thought: Shma Israel, Adonai Eloheinu, Adonai Echad. Which meant only "Hear, oh Israel, the Lord is your God, the Lord is one." Which comforted him by not asking for anything, and by being a prayer that other Jews had recited for thousands of years.

"WE USED TO talk about Jeff Germantz all the time. He was our standard. 'What would Jeff do?' Sort of a joke for us." Allyssa stood and walked to the kitchen window, and for a second Tuuro almost thought she would burst right through it; the kitchen seemed too small and fragile to enclose her.

"What was wrong with it, Tuuro? Did you hear about excessive force? Loss of life? Disrespect? I know there were some pets that disappeared, but . . . What else was there, anywhere, except a few suicides and heart attacks? The Gridding was clean, Tuuro. Perfectly clean." Tuuro grieved at the emotion in Allyssa's voice. "No one remembers that. The U.S. has held a grudge against us from the beginning. We give them grain, we give them food, and what do they give us? Not even respect."

Food for Life, Tuuro thought, recalling the post-Grid slogans. *Remember that Well-Fed Feeling? It's ba-a-ack.*

"People forget how bad it was. My husband had a neighbor who got brucellosis. That's supposed to be from dead animals." Allyssa passed her hand in front of her eyes. "My husband worked in Washington, he knew what was coming. People say we destroyed people's lives. People got new lives, Tuuro. They got houses, they got compensation. And they lived. They and the rest of the four hundred million, they lived. A little relocation and property reassignment isn't a big price for people's lives."

She was arguing with herself, Tuuro realized. He didn't even have to nod.

"You want to talk about victims, talk about the military. It destroyed Callahan, and Jeff thought he was the best general the air force ever had. All those Grid-shocked grunts . . . They didn't get federal bonuses like the transplants, did they? They didn't get new two-stories with swimming pools and media hookups.

"What else could we have done, Tuuro? The Historical Society's talking to people like it was some evil plot, like President Cooper and her henchman said hey, let's take out the towns. And it wasn't. I mean, sure, it was a plot, but it was a desperation plot. I heard about it from my husband. People were crying in cabinet meetings. People back then—serious people, government people—were saying it was the end of our country as we knew it. And it was, Tuuro, okay? It was. Citizens were helpless. You may not have seen it so much in Ohio, but my husband was standing in line behind this woman in Washington to collect his ten pounds of potatoes, and this woman turned around and said: So I just slice these up and put them in the oven and they're potato chips?"

> *Up here where the land is flat*
> *The Grid is King and that is that*
> *But why does sweet Allyssa feel*
> *In fear about her own next meal?*

"And the Oregon Project worked! People forget: that hare-brained utopian project was on everyone's mind. It only got done because Senator Goebbels wanted it for his state and not California. But it worked! No one expected all that wheat. Two loaves of bread for everyone in the country. I have to tell you, Tuuro, that made an impression. We even heard about it at Lindisfarne."

"You could have just moved people off the farmlands," Tuuro said, voicing an argument he had heard. "You didn't have to destroy the towns."

"And make the effs second-class citizens? Destroy their houses and not the houses in the county seats? I'll tell you the truth, Tuuro, keeping the towns was a consideration. That's what President Cooper wanted at first, and the Agro secretary. But Jeff Germantz was adamant the towns would have to go."

"Why?"

"Jeff had vision, Tuuro." Allyssa's brown eyes brimmed with sincerity; Tuuro wanted, more than anything, his own eyes to look believingly back. "He wanted the Grid not just set apart but uniform; he didn't want town people and country people. There'd be sabotage from the townspeople if the towns weren't destroyed. Plus, leveling the cities opened up more acreage, and after Oregon we knew every acre mattered. And it was kind of a lollipop for the air force, gave them something to take out." Allyssa smiled ruefully. "Callahan was thrilled, at first."

Tuuro shook his head and looked toward his window; behind the clouds there was the slightest hint of sunshine.

"You understand it, don't you?" Allyssa asked. Her eyes were imploring and her lips slightly open; Tuuro looked away. "You're a good man, Tuuro, and I want you to understand. Jeff used to quote Chairman Mao: *A revolution is not a dinner party.* It's kind of silly, but you see the point."

Tuuro thought:

> *What you say may not be true*
> *But I'll believe what comes from you*

WONDERWATER HAD MAPS—it had always had maps— and one day Lila noticed a tiny mark, almost a star, near a blank area north of Dayton, in the suburb of Vandalia. Vandalia of the old Dayton airport, of the Trapshooting Hall of Fame; Vandalia one mile from her water tower. Lila perused maps on other websites: no marks like this.

"Have we got numbers on output up there?" Lila asked Seymour. "No one could be bleeding us, could they?"

"Consort?" Seymour said, sitting down. The cooling tower at the nuclear plant used an ungodly amount of water, and the head honchos there were always complaining about their water bills.

"They wish," Lila said. "But their plant's ten miles south."

"That's why they'd bleed up north. Harder to trace." Even sitting down, Seymour towered over Lila. He hunched down to look at her monitor and knitted his plucked yet earnest eyebrows.

"Or the Grid could bleed us." Not the Defense Department, Michelle had said, not yet: they were having problems getting funding. "See, Seymour?" Lila pointed at the mark. "There's a main right through this field."

"You wouldn't hide something right out on the tabletop," Seymour said. "Doesn't make sense."

"Unless you thought it was a secure tabletop. And it was, until we got in." Lila slapped at her cheeks with her hands as she stared. "We should go up there. Physically, I mean. Poke around the monitoring station."

"Great!" Seymour headed for his coat.

"I can't go like this." Lila gestured at her clothes. In truth, she wanted to be prepared with a change of clothes and tooth-brush in her bag, in case—by some magic she half believed in—a visit to a place marked on a Wonderwater map ended with her being swept onto the Grid. *She came here?* she imagined some Gridian saying. *She got into Wonderwater? Wow, we might as well move her in with us.*

Lila had said to Seymour: "Wear some boots tomorrow and we'll go. Okay?"

Now Lila and Seymour were in her car driving north. The day was cloudy and gray. Clots of ice were melting on the sidewalk. "I haven't been so excited since Naiesha Van came here with her diamond show," Seymour said. "And that was two years ago."

"Did you buy anything?"

"That's when I had the half carat put on my tooth," Seymour said, pulling down his lower lip. "If anything happens to me, you take it."

"Oh, Seymour!" Lila made a face.

"I'm serious. You can just use pliers and pull out the whole tooth."

Taking the street north from downtown Vandalia, they passed through a chicken-wire fence with an empty gatehouse. Seymour rolled down his window and peered out. "Yoo-hoo!" he called.

In the distance in front of them, the Grid barrier loomed like a great sea cliff. Seymour hopped out and peered through the gatehouse windows. "Nobody." He tested the door. "Locked."

"Strange," Lila said, looking beyond the gatehouse to a street lined with simple one-story frame houses. "This gated community does not look very posh."

"Neighborhood watch gone crazy," Seymour suggested, getting back in the car. They drove ahead. A pickup sat in the driveway of one house; another yard held a windmill painted like a man with swinging blades for arms. On the near side of the chicken wire there had been signs of life: two children pulling a wagon, a hand pushing open a curtain. Here there was nobody. Lila was filled with unease. There was a woman from Consort whose head had been found in the stairwell of an apartment building near Generator B. Very few people knew about that. Lila had heard about it at the Lesbian Holiday Potluck, where a woman who worked for Consort's CEO had pulled her aside. "Didn't you know her?" she'd said. "Weren't you on some county committee together?"

The water main ran under a field just next to the Grid barrier. It wasn't really a no-man's-land, but it had that look. The street they were driving on simply ended, the pavement stretching fifteen feet into the grass, then stopping. Lila parked the car at the edge of the asphalt and got out.

She had no idea what they were looking for, what the mark might indicate. There were no paths in the grass, although in the summer it had clearly been mowed. Lila tried to remember who had jurisdiction over this patch of land. The county park service? In the distance, to their left and close to the Grid barrier, sat the typical water department monitoring shack, a wooden structure maybe four feet high, a padlocked door in its top. "Let's start there," Lila said, pointing to the shack, and they were halfway to it, Seymour in front of her, their boot toes wet and their treads filled up with slush, when the world changed.

"TOUCH UP THE dining room," Allyssa said. "I finally heard. It'll be soon."

THERE WERE PEOPLE, including his brother, Chad used to message on his perc almost every other day, but about a year before he'd found he was wearying of his correspondents' jokes, their gabbing about work and family. His friends weren't the right e-friends, he realized: he needed someone in Cleveland, or Detroit, another of the lost or threatened areas. He still played chess—in silence except for the moves—with a woman in Tampa. She was the e-friend he felt closest to. He saw them as an old pair hunched over the game board, occasionally grunting in pleasure or consternation at the other's move.

He hadn't perc-ed anyone in so long he felt guilty doing it, and he hated to be asking a favor right off, but what choice did he have? Someone might point them in the proper direction, give them the serendipitous tip that would change their lives. He sent messages to forty-three people. Most of them didn't respond, and the ones who did were helplessly sympathetic—"I might know someone who . . ."; "outside of town there's a mobile home park where . . ."; "if there's anything I . . ." His chess friend didn't message back a move.

His parents had been right. They never believed computers would change the world. In Chad's adolescence he'd hurled words at them: "reactionary," "Luddite," "troglodyte." But now Chad decided the new world was the old world after all, a place made ungenerous by fear. In every concerned message he saw versions of his old misguided self. As if prayers and hopeful wishes were enough. Good God. His mother at least had made and delivered casseroles.

Sure, you can come to Omaha, his brother finally answered. If Lily won't move her stuff out of her room, we'll give you guys the garage. *If.* Stupid princess. Chad wasn't even sure he wanted to see his brother, considering that he'd raised a child like Lily.

Chad consolidated his money and got a guaranteed cash card, cleaned out his office, carried furniture into the basement. Every physical task was a relief to him, a chance to do something real.

Sharis was already packed and ready. She sat at her editon, foot jiggling. She had moved her work downstairs to the living room, and she found having the boys nearby made her editing faster. The editon was heavy but portable. She could edit from Bangkok, she said.

Sharis had noticed something about Bebe, the mother of her Texas family. Bebe's attention to her children was intermittent and intense. She spent hours ignoring them, talking on her perc or reading, but suddenly something would hit her and she would tease or play with them extravagantly, like the mother in a park who makes the other mothers feel dull. Sharis had for years put these happy scenes in her life-edits, which probably explained Bebe's enthusiasm for Sharis's work. But these scenes were in essence a lie. The Schneider kids must realize this, too: Sharis noticed that the boy sometimes cringed when his mother approached him, that the girl was spending more time at her friends'. That's not me, Sharis thought as she watched Bebe. Sharis saw her own attention to her children as running at a steady hum. Of course, she thought, it's easy to use someone else's behavior to make your own look better.

Still, she wondered if Mr. Schneider realized. She could edit a bit differently, show him how things really were. A service to him, really. Sharis's father used to take her into the basement and lay a bullet on her tongue. "See?" he'd say. "Nothing to be afraid of."

If Sharis had told this to her mother, it might have changed things.

"I don't know where we'll go exactly," Chad said. "Omaha if we have to. We'll just go."

nenonene's voice

"YOU DIDN'T PUT out a cup for him," General Nenonene said. Such an innocuous phrase, and so mildly uttered, but something in it—Tuuro heard it—suggested a moral judgment. The words sent the four men who accompanied the General, as well as Allyssa, all scurrying back to the kitchen.

Not what Tuuro had expected. Not the Tuesday evening, not the helicopter in the crushed stone driveway, not the puddles of ice melting on the kitchen floor, not Nenonene. The General, wearing gray trousers and a white shirt with buttons and a collar, was the shortest man present. When he shook Tuuro's hand he gave a quick nod. He did look like his pictures. But those pictures made him larger and more prepossessing, less like an ordinary man. Like a movie star they film on boxes, Tuuro thought. Tuuro glanced back into the dining room: six chairs with high laddered backs and needlepoint floral cushions, placed just so around the circular wooden table. "Thank you," the General said, plucking the cup and saucer from Allyssa's hand and turning back to the dining room, the men jostling behind him. Tuuro followed. "Some coffee?" the General asked Tuuro. His voice was very British, and not loud. The media did not do justice to his voice. On the media, his voice could be bargained with. "Yes, sir, please," Tuuro said. The General turned to the large round metal coffeepot sitting at one end of the sideboard.

The General pushed the lever on the coffeepot, filled up Tuuro's cup. His right hand hovered over a small pitcher. "Cream?" Above the sideboard was a painting of a wheat field, the frame of which had shed a ribbon of dust when Tuuro cleaned.

"Black, please, sir." Aunt Stella had told him to say *sir* and *ma'am*. As a way to elevate the discourse.

The General handed Tuuro his saucer and cup of coffee, indicated a seat at the table, and sat down just as Tuuro did. The other four men sat down a second later. Allyssa, from the kitchen, shut the door.

The General sat up very straight, his back off the back of the chair, his bland, smiling face replaced by a prideful self-possession, like the ruler of some obscure country who had made it through Cambridge with honors. "So, Mr. Simpkins," he said, "we meet at last." Tuuro hid a smile, because this sentence sounded so much like an actor. But he *is* an actor, Tuuro realized.

The General glanced around the table. "Gentlemen, this is Tuuro Simpkins, who found and buried my grandchild." A heavyset man with jowls and skin like rawhide gave a nod, as did a dark man in a military uniform with medals. A white man with nervous eyes and a blue shirt spotted with some foodstuff reached a hand across the table to Tuuro and said, "Matt Kellogg." The fourth man, another white man, looked like a grizzled farmer; he wore a loosely knit sweater and eyed Tuuro without any acknowledgment, and it was in reproach for this, Tuuro realized, that General Nenonene dropped his head and said to Tuuro in a confidential voice, "Our sullen guest is Mr. Rafferty, of the Ohio Historical Society."

Allyssa had mentioned the Historical Society. Tuuro's eyes slid over the General to Mr. Rafferty and back. The rawhide man smiled. The air was thick with promises and collusions.

Tuuro eyed the arm of Mr. Rafferty's sloppily knit sweater. Could Nenonene trust a man like that? Then he caught himself: who was he to second-guess the General?

"Now, Mr. Simpkins—may I call you Tuuro?"—Tuuro nodded—"Tuuro, I'm sure you wonder why we brought you here."

It took Tuuro, still wondering about Mr. Rafferty, a second to answer. What good would the Historical Society be to Nenonene? In a practical sense, what could the Historical Society do? "You wish to speak to me about your grandson."

A muscle in the General's jaw leapt. "I know about my grandson," he said. "My daughter-in-law's brother, Cubby's uncle, he killed my grandson. I know this. I understood this when I first heard of Cubby's disappearance. This brother was what they call a pederast. I had warned my children, but they disbelieved me. Cubby's murderer has been taken care of. Privately done, in a doctor's office. I am sure he understood just what was happening. I have my people everywhere, even in Dayton, Ohio."

Tuuro nodded numbly, not certain he was understanding. Mr. Rafferty scratched his nose. A chair creaked, and Matt Kellogg looked quickly down. The General's eyes traveled to Mr. Kellogg, then slowly back to Tuuro. "Mr. Kellogg is our liberal," he said. "There are certain things a liberal won't permit himself to understand."

Silence. Tuuro ran his tongue along the inside of his teeth. The wheat field painting had been grimy with a sticky substance; Tuuro had used mineral spirits and toothpicks on the corners.

"Your grandson was a beautiful boy," Tuuro said. "I tried to honor him."

A spasm crossed Nenonene's face. He sighed. "Mr. Simpkins, we must move on to other issues." He hesitated. "His skin was well oiled. Here," the General pointed at the indentation above his upper lip. "I appreciate that."

"You're welcome."

"Mr. Simpkins, Tuuro, I would like to enlist you in our cause. As a helper, not a soldier. You know what we desire.

We desire peace and prosperity for the entire world. Respect for all. An equal distribution of assets. An end to nationalistic wars and bickering and the beginning of a government that is truly equitable to all."

Tuuro nodded.

"We also desire an end to genetic manipulation. If the children of the rich are created to be advantaged even beyond their parents' wealth, surely the gap between the lucky and unlucky will grow." Tuuro nodded, surprised. He had never before heard this expressed as a policy of the Alliance. "The next step, if we allow this genetic tinkering to proceed, will be the production of a tractable, subintelligent working class." The men around the table seemed to be relaxing, as if Nenonene were turning down a road that they knew well. "A slave class, if you will." The General looked Tuuro in the eye. "Do you remember your Declaration of Independence? *We hold these truths to be self-evident, that all men are created equal.* That statement was indeed a revolution, Mr. Simpkins. A change in the idea of what is human. A king was held no higher than a farmer. In those words, I assure you, the destruction of slavery was foretold. Yet over the last thirty years we have had a backward change." Nenonene was talking faster now, and some of the precision of his consonants had rubbed away; he was looking in the air, not at Tuuro. "And that change must be stopped. Because people will never have the chance to be equal if they are created . . ."

"But it doesn't really work," Tuuro interrupted. "They try to make children perfect, but . . ."

Nenonene smiled indulgently. "It doesn't work yet, Mr. Simpkins. But the scientists are busy, and someday, I am sure, they will perfect a human strain. Not a perfect human, you understand. But a human perfect for someone's purposes."

"Like a robot," Tuuro said, his mind filling with comprehension. "Like a human tool."

"Perhaps like a very good dog. Hard-working, good-tempered, loyal."

Tuuro blinked. *Allyssa,* he thought. *Me.*

"In our world," General Nenonene said, "every man will indeed be created equal. In our world, a baby will be born into an infinite future. In our world . . ." But Tuuro was no longer listening. The speech was gathering velocity and volume, reminding Tuuro of the sermons of his former boss the pastor—sermons rife with repetition, with pauses and headlong rushes. Sound without sense. Or: sound with some sense, but not as much as you first thought. Like a herd of buffalo, Tuuro thought. But that wasn't right for Nenonene. Like a herd of impala. But that could be wrong, too, because who knew what animals lived in Gambia? Tuuro realized in shame that he knew no more about Africa than its general outline on a map. He didn't know where on the continent his Zulu forebears—if they were his forebears—lived. "But to help us prevent this," the General was saying, "to help us *win,* we want to use you, Mr. Simpkins. I put it baldly because I'm a simple man."

"Me? Why me?" Tuuro eyed the men around the table; Matt Kellogg smiled at him almost tenderly.

"We use what's at our disposal because it is at our disposal. Do you understand? We use it because we can. Cubby's death was useless, a tragedy. I find as I get older, I hate wastefulness. My Protestant upbringing. You'll go on the media. You'll speak clearly; we will tell you what to say. Do you understand me?"

Yes, Tuuro thought. No. Not in your particulars. "I do," he said.

"Good." General Nenonene nodded. "We will make a life for you in Cleveland. Do you need a woman?"

"Now?" Surely he wasn't talking about Allyssa.

"A wife," the rawhide man said, surprising Tuuro by speaking. "Do you need a wife?"

A wife picked out for him like an item off a store shelf? A Cleveland wife? An African wife?

Matt Kellogg cleared his throat. "What Mr. Colon means, Tuuro, is that there are many lovely ladies in Cleveland. We could introduce you to some of them."

"No," Tuuro said, suddenly embarrassed, glad the door to the kitchen was closed. "No, thank you."

Mr. Colon checked his watch. General Nenonene was like President Baxter, Tuuro thought, a man so important his time was parsed into five-minute intervals. Tuuro's own life was measured in rougher blocks—afternoons, mornings, days, weeks. Perhaps his life was indeed of less value than Nenonene's. *Created equal.* Did Nenonene really believe that? For a moment Tuuro had the urge to kiss the General's hand.

"You'll help me," Nenonene nodded, his face as composed and beneficent as a priest's. What storms he goes through! Tuuro thought. It seemed to him that in minutes the General had galloped through a month's worth of emotions. Perhaps that was what a public life demanded.

"I'll help you," Tuuro promised, and the General stood. They all stood. On the way out through the kitchen, Tuuro again noticed the mess of footprints by the door. "Excuse me," he said to Allyssa, reaching behind her to the utility closet, for the mop still damp from his cleaning that afternoon.

"Conscientious," the General said, watching Tuuro as he swiped the floor. "Admirable."

"I made it better," Tuuro thought when the door closed behind the men: his usual contented sensation after working on a room. And it was a wonder to have the simple square of clean brick-pattern linoleum to hold on to, amidst his squall of impressions and feelings. Outside, the bubble of the helicopter's interior glowed, the shapes of the men climbing into it like shadows on a lamp.

"What does he want from you?" Allyssa asked, her nose pressed to the window in the door. "When is he taking you?"

LILA WAS AWARE of grass smushed against her face, making her itch, a scent of wet dirt, and a trickle of something down her leg. She was alive. She remembered a huge noise and the earth moving. Then she was asleep again, but asleep aware of her aliveness, and it dawned on her she needed to get up, that lying prone like this she could be a target. But where was here? Lila couldn't remember, but when she lifted her head she saw a body with its legs peculiarly splayed, and after considering whether or not it could be *her* body—but no, because the legs she was looking at were right beside her head, and her legs she could feel in their usual place—she forced her head to turn and her eyes to travel to the body's head. My God, was that Seymour? She only knew him from his hair. Such a high head he had had, so far from the ground. She thought of the diamond in his tooth. Oh, Seymour . . . Her eyes moved back quickly to his feet. His boots: for some reason people removed dead men's boots. She laid her cheek back on the grass—she had a face, her face was intact—and the coldness of the ground made her moan; she felt a trickle down her leg again, and that sensation reminded her that she was the Water Queen. The Water Queen had to be worth something. The water map of the county flashed before her, the pumping stations and the mains and the reservoirs and on top of these—superimposed—the tiny mark, which was here, which was *where she was*.

Her face was pressed into the grass, she was drooling, and around her right thigh the sensation of something square pressed into her leg. Michelle? No one ever touched her but Michelle. "No bones broken, but you're bleeding," a man's voice said. "Hold still and I'll put some sealer on that wound."

She thrashed her head around but couldn't quite see him, and then she sensed him crouching next to her, fishing in something—a knapsack that hung from his shoulder.

"You're okay," the man said. "I'm going to roll you onto your back." He did this, quickly, and then she was gazing down her body at his profile: short brown hair, full lips, and a hoop earring, a face like a handsome pirate's. "Don't worry, I'm army. I crashed my copter over there"—he nodded in the direction of a line of trees—"but I ejected."

"I'm water," Lila said. It came out *Oh wanna.*

"Sorry." The man unhooked a canteen from his belt. "Take all you want. I've got a tank back in the cow. It was supposed to self-destruct ten seconds after I beeped the all-clear, but I think it missed that day's lesson. See it?" He pointed across the field. "Or maybe suicide's against its religion."

The man supported her head, and Lila took a sip from the canteen. She understood why she couldn't speak: her teeth were sticking to her cheeks. How ironic: the Water Queen thirsty and she didn't know it. She gazed down her own body. Her thigh was bleeding and her pants torn. She saw some yellow globules that must be fat, but the man put her head down before she had a chance to be frightened.

"That your friend?" The man, squirting sealer in the hole in her leg, nodding toward Seymour's body.

Lila nodded. "What happened?" The words were clear enough, although she still had an awful taste in her mouth.

"Looks like you were shot, to me. From that direction." The man indicated the Grid barrier. He turned his face to her, and she was startled by the scar on his cheek, a white gash like a crescent moon. He was a pirate. "How many shots did you hear?"

"Let me think," she said, but there was nothing to think about, she'd been walking across a field with Seymour, and now Seymour was dead and a man was squirting sealer in her wounds. So this was war. She was exhausted. She drifted off.

She woke up thinking Michelle was doing that irritating thing again, reaching between her legs when Lila was trying to sleep. She moaned and pressed her legs together, and when she opened her eyes the pirate was crouched beside her. Had he ever left? How long had she been sleeping? She didn't like his looks even though he was smiling, fine lines erupting from the corners of his mouth up to his nose. "I'm the Water Queen," Lila heard herself saying. "I know everything about the water supply in this county."

"That's why you were up here? Something to do with water? This is a restricted area, you know." I'm a government official, Lila thought in confusion, dimly aware of an injustice. The pirate patted her leg, sat back on his heels. "I'm from Gamma Force myself," he said. "My copilot's checking out the houses."

Gamma Force? Gamma Force and its equipment were famous. Gamma Force was the one part of the military that was still closed to women. *Real American Heroes, Real American Men,* read the posters. There were Gamma Force dolls for boys. Gamma Force, it was said, answered directly to the president. They did whatever they were asked to do. They must be protecting the border, Lila thought. She strained over the top of grass to see what the pilot had called a cow. It was a bulbous helicopter, gleaming and white. As she looked at it she realized that Seymour was no longer beside her. "Where's my friend?" she asked.

"I buried him."

"Did you take his boots?" That was a thing, Lila thought. She'd seen it in movies.

"No. We have Gamma Force boots."

"Can I see your ID?"

"Sure." He held it out, with its holographic photo, and she must have seen his name then, she had to have, but it was something she could never later remember. "Can I see yours?"

Lila reached into the left cup of her bra and held out her card. Susannah Shore was the woman from Consort whose head had turned up in a stairwell. No body had been found. Lila knew Susannah, vaguely, from government meetings. A mother, always frazzled and sloppily dressed. A future fellow uto. Her ears had been cut off, someone said. Trophies, someone else said. Men did that. Something else she'd heard of.

"That wound's looking fine," the pirate said. He reached into his knapsack and took out a wrapped pill. "Antibiotic. You're not allergic, are you?"

The antibiotic tasted like wintergreen. He got her upright, but she couldn't walk. "Here. Drape your arm around my shoulders." Up close he smelled as cologned as a man at a party.

"Are you a pirate?" Lila said.

"Pilot, right."

"I'm really useful," Lila said. "I know water." Right foot, right foot. With his holding her, she didn't have to use her injured leg at all. It was weird, the pilot seemed to be palming her breast, but maybe she was imagining it, the air cold and getting blacker, and when she next awoke it was dark and she was alone. Where's Seymour? she thought, remembering his delight about the diamond in his tooth, and tears slipped from her eyes.

And then Michelle was bothering her again—*Get out of here, let me rest!*—and when she woke up again the pirate was sitting beside her, staring down at her face. She squinted as she looked up at him, not against the light—it was barely light out, dawn? dusk?—but because she wanted better to see him. Odd face, with that scar: half handsome, half deformed. But his eyes (this was the strangest part) were looking at her caressingly, as if, in her sleep, she had turned into someone else. "You have a strong nose," he said.

"I'm a lesbian."

Asleep, awake. At least she guessed she was awake, since she was trying to figure out if she could move her injured leg and leave. Wait a second, was her leg injured? Yes, it was her leg. But she could move her toes on both feet, and rotate her ankles, and she realized to her surprise that her legs were warm, in contrast to her cold nose and ears, and when she managed to crack her eyes open she saw that it was daytime and somehow she was in an open-air bed, on a mattress, under what must be an insulating blanket, a pillow of some sort beneath her head. When she looked directly up she saw the shiny belly of the helicopter. The cow, Lila remembered.

The pirate was ten feet away from her on a fold-up stool, reading something on his perc. "Hey," she said, "did you set me up like this?"

He turned to face her, and the corner of his right eye fanned out in happy wrinkles, although his left eye, scarred, stayed flat. "We fly prepared. My copilot'll be back soon. We've been checking out the area."

"Isn't someone coming to rescue you?"

The pilot smiled. "They know we're okay." He stood up, reached inside the helicopter for the canteen. "Here." He dribbled a stream of water into her mouth.

"Beautiful nose," he said, and she realized he was stroking it. She couldn't keep her eyes open, she was that warm and tired.

"Where's Seymour?" she mumbled.

"I told you. He's all tucked in."

A woman of power. A valuable woman. An interesting woman. He was stroking her cheekbone now, his fingers making a detour around her mole. Beauty mark, ha! At a certain age a mole becomes a mole.

"When my copilot gets back, we'll get you to the hospital."

His hand was on her collarbone, her breast. It moved down across her belly, ferreting, warm. But he's a man! Lila thought.

"Can you open your eyes?" His voice was very gentle. "I don't want to keep going unless I know you're cool with it."

She opened her eyes. His head above her was a featureless shadow. Cool? His hand was so very warm. "Okay," she said, not sure what she was agreeing to.

"I'll have to arrange your leg so I don't hurt you."

All she wanted was to sleep. She knew she needed to survive, but survival seemed like too much work. *If I let him do what he wants, he'll let me sleep.*

"I won't hurt you."

How very peculiar. Something was burrowing between her legs, something fatter and somehow warmer than a finger; there was a weight against her pelvis and a smell.

The pirate moaned.

Oh! His penis was inside her. This had never happened. But the sensation was inoffensive, a thing bouncing up and down like a sewing machine needle. Lila decided to ignore it. Because this was rape, wasn't it? Men did this. And she was almost half asleep.

"YOU CAN'T LEAVE." The soldier leaned into Chad's window, the sky behind him gray and spitting snow. Enough of a shock to see Far Hills Avenue blocked off with military vehicles, soldiers walking around with rifles, but these words hit Chad like a shot. He should have realized, Sharis said later. She had suspected half a mile away, when she spotted the dark forms of the parked trucks across the road. But Chad hadn't noticed the trucks. He'd been thinking about Omaha, wondering just how monstrous his niece Lily really was. She would undoubtedly be nicer to Chad and his family than to her parents.

"What are you talking about?" Chad said to the soldier.

"Presidential orders. No one can leave greater Dayton."

"Why? What happened?" A sensation of scrambling, Sharis now lying across Chad and looking up at the soldier.

"Of course I can leave Dayton." Chad pushed Sharis back into her seat. The soldier looked jumpy, unformed, the rifle over his shoulder too big for him. "I'm an American. People have been leaving Dayton for years." His voice raised. "Since 1796 they've been leaving Dayton!"

"Not since six this morning, sir."

Chad glanced at the dashboard clock. Nine twenty-three. He looked into the backseat, where Leon and Howard sat surrounded by blankets and clothes. He could get on the freeway and go south. He could cut across 725 and go south on 741. "I'll go another way."

"The whole area is surrounded, sir. All the routes out are blocked. If you're spotted at three separate checkpoints, they'll impound your car."

"Is this martial law? We don't live in a country with a history of martial law."

Sharis laid a restraining hand on Chad's knee.

A mad dash in the car across a field. A walk through the Sugarcreek Reserve and keep on going.

"Don't you watch TV?" the soldier said.

"What does that have to do with anything?" Chad said. "Sometimes we watch. But we don't make a habit of . . ." Chad trailed off, seeing the soldier's face.

"The Grid succeeded, sir," the soldier said. "That's what happened, the Grid succeeded."

Nothing made sense. "What do you mean, succeeded? You mean the Alliance finally attacked it and . . . ?"

The soldier's voice took on a new tone, part pity and part triumph. "The Grid pulled out. It says it's not part of the United States."

"You mean seceded," Chad said. "S-E-C- . . ."

Sharis leaned over him again. "When did this happen?"

"Last night at midnight. They sent their lady senator to the president with a Declaration of Independence. She's in jail."

"Have we declared war?" Sharis asked.

The soldier's expression contorted. "It's not like *declared* declared, it's like they want to declare it but if they do it's like admitting the Grid's separate, and the Grid doesn't say it's part of the Alliance yet, at least, and . . . everything's all bungy. See?" He addressed the boys in the backseat. "This is a serious day. You'll remember this day. Look"—he turned back to Chad, addressing him, Sharis realized, as if Chad were mentally defective—"you've got to go back to your house. Don't you have a perc? Turn on your perc. President Baxter is speaking to everyone at noon." He pointed helpfully. "You can turn around in the dry cleaner's."

"Fuck you!" Chad screamed, lurching the car forward. They turned around in the dry cleaner's and screeched onto the road toward home. Chad could imagine exactly what Sharis was thinking. *We should have left days ago. If you hadn't been so slow getting . . .* He was ready to erupt with any provocation, but as the blocks passed in silence his anger ebbed. He had underestimated her, he realized.

He supposed he should turn on the car radio, but all he wanted now was silence.

Chad turned left on Custard, their own lane. "I don't know why you started to spell for him," Sharis said.

"How could we have left earlier?" Chad screamed. "I had to get the cash! I had papers to grade! I had a whole house to pull together! Was I supposed to know the Grid was going to secede? Did I know today we'd end up with martial law?" *We should have left yesterday,* he was thinking. *Why didn't we leave yesterday?*

"In my experience," Sharis said after a pause, "shooting off your mouth is rarely helpful."

"Piss on your experience," Chad said, and Leon, in the backseat, giggled. But Chad had envisioned the night of the Gridding so often—the heap of family on the sofa, Sharis slipping out the back door—that the thought of what she'd been through did calm him, returned him to his bigger, better self.

Chad let the car roll down the Custard Lane hill without his foot on the gas. He looked into the backseat. "Tree or not?" Their little ritual.

"Not," the boys chorused. The car made it about a quarter up the hill—just shy of the big tree—before Chad needed to press the gas pedal again. "Phooey," Chad said. "You boys were right." The boys bumped their fists in celebration.

"What's there to be afraid of, more ice?" Chad asked as the car climbed the hill. And to Sharis: "We're lucky you did all that canning."

They had bled the pipes, turned off the heat, boarded up the windows with limbs and firewood. All that could be undone. Most of their food and some of their clothes they'd brought with them. "We'll survive," Sharis said as their car pulled in the driveway. "We will. I guarantee it."

"She guarantees it," Chad echoed, grinning back at the boys. Persistence. Optimism. My God, he thought, we are insane.

A stooped woman was standing at their front door, her head topped by a bowl of straight white hair. No one spoke. Chad's heart pounded in his ears: one thing to meet a scrawny soldier two miles away, another to see a strange person in your doorstep.

Chad thought: it's a man in disguise, come to kill us.

Sharis thought: it's the woman from the troll bridge, come to kill us.

Harold said, "Mommy, is that Abba?"

"Oh, my God," Chad said. "It is Abba." His mother's aunt from Cleveland.

"Remember Abba?" Howard said to Leon. "Did you know a woman can go bald?"

"Hi, kids!" Abba turned and walked toward them, waving both hands and smiling. She wore a green coat with missing buttons, and knit gloves thinning at their fingertips. Behind her on the doorstep were a suitcase and a string bag full of canned food.

Abba was barely taller than Leon. "Now don't start worrying, I'm not a big eater," she said as they got out of their car. "I got into Dayton at two this morning, can you imagine? The bus drove us down I-75 from Cleveland to Columbus and then I-70 from Columbus to here. Right through the Grid. I've never been there—have you been there? But on the highway they have these blockades and you can't see . . ."

She's even worse than my spoiled niece Lily, Chad thought. For a second he envied Sharis's lack of family.

" . . . and when we got here some people were going to hotels or calling their families and I said, I'll just sleep here on this bench, use this as a pillow." She pointed to her suit-case. "And I did, I slept very well, I didn't wake up till almost nine." Her voice went up and down, up and down like a child's roller coaster. "Don't I get a hug?" she said to Howard and Leon.

"Why come here?" Sharis said, aiming Abba toward their front door. "Why now?"

"I came in by bus, honey. Like I told you."

"We were just trying to leave," Chad said.

"Don't you know? You must know. Well, I didn't know exactly but I got a message from the very highest levels. They said I should get out of Cleveland if I could, and I knew I could because I . . ."

Chad was busy calculating Abba's age. She must be over ninety. When Chad was a child she'd already been an oldie. *Oldies get funny,* his mother used to say. *She's got a good heart.* He'd come upon his father and Abba in the living room once, his father asleep and Abba talking on. "The word count on that woman!" Chad's father said.

"Here you go, Leon. One for you, too, Howard." Abba handed each boy a hard candy. "I wish they were made with honey, because the man who drove me to the bus last night used to keep bees, but . . ."

"Are you planning to stay here?" Sharis said, her eyes meeting Chad's over Abba's head. "Have you left Cleveland for good?"

"I'm not a Nervous Nellie, but when someone from the very highest level calls and . . ."

Abba had worked for a man whose brother was a Cleve-land official. "It's fine," Chad said. "We have plenty of room." Thinking *bondad, bonehead.* Thinking of Prem, who noted that in his country all the generations lived together, even though some of them were not the easiest people. Before Sharis had gotten the door unlocked, Abba had mentioned her old boss, the other passengers on the bus she'd come in on, Sharis's shoes, the boys' haircuts, how rotten Dayton looked compared to Cleveland.

She had asked that the date of Chad's high school graduation party be changed, because that Sunday was not a good day for her. She had shown up at every family gathering with a can of peas for her personal consumption. "I wanted to get married," she used to say, "but the man God meant for me got killed in Desert Storm."

Yes, she was old, she was family, but did that give her the right to take over their life? Her presence in her long dark coat in their living room was like a smudge on their domesticity. Beyond her lay the pile of blankets and pillows they spread out on the floor to make their nest, and as Abba appraised the room and offered her thoughts on their sofa, their lighting system, and the temperature of the house, Chad kept thinking, over and over: *there's a war on and I'm stuck with Abba?*

2048

tuuro's confession

TUURO WAS EXPECTED to memorize his confession. There was nothing for him to take home and study because nothing should be leaked out. The confession was extremely explicit, because—Mrs. Calder said—people were idiots and needed things spelled out. *Something came over me. I took out my swollen penis and I forced . . .*

He couldn't read it.

"What do you mean you can't read it? You can read, can't you?" Mrs. Calder tugged her cross out of her cleavage. She had worked for twenty-eight years for a man she called the crown prince of Cleveland newscasters. He had retired to California, so now she worked for Nenonene. "Everyone trusts me," she'd told Tuuro. "I'm what you call impeccable." She was certainly not what Tuuro would call impeccable, her feet up on her desk, boots dripping melted snow.

Tuuro read the speech again. The only way he could get through it was to say each word alone, as if he were reading a list.

"You don't sound real," Mrs. Calder said. "You're worse every time." She bit her thumb. "Haven't you ever totally lost control? Think of a night you got drunk and hit somebody."

Tuuro looked at the floor. He had been moved from Allyssa's two weeks before to a Cleveland apartment—the first floor of a frame house—by a woman named Akira who referred to herself as the General's henchwoman. Another henchwoman brought him groceries. He understood from the beginning that Nenonene had plans for him, but plans like these had never crossed his mind.

"Are you perfect?" Mrs. Calder said. "Are you one of the chosen few who've never done anything wrong?"

He thought of his feelings about the pastor; of the girls he looked at late at night on his computer back in Dayton; how he'd walked off from the message center in Cincinnati, knowing that the lipsticked man was about to shoot the customer. He said, "No."

"Then can we have a little passion? A little remorse?" Mrs. Calder's eyes narrowed. "Your daughter's how old, six? They say a kid can only remember one month back for each year of their age. She's probably forgotten you by now."

She will want to forget me, Tuuro thought. Nenonene, he thought, almost choking. The conversation he'd imagined them having—what a joke. Instead Tuuro had been prepared as an object of use, brought to Mrs. Calder's office to practice a script about his performing acts worse than any he'd ever imagined, all at the will of a man who would use anything, even his own grandson, to consolidate his power. The monstrous thought filled Tuuro that Nenonene could have arranged Cubby's death himself. He had certainly arranged for the demise of Tuuro. Tuuro saw again Allyssa at the end of the stone driveway, waving after him until he couldn't see her from the back window of Akira's car. Would Allyssa, at least, understand that he was mouthing a lie?

Tuuro tried to speak, but his emotions were too much for him. "Just keep reading the thing, okay? We've got a timeline here." Mrs. Calder said. "Jesus, I told Neno it'd be easier with a pro."

IT WAS THE Audubon calendar arriving in the mail that made them think to turn on Diana's perc. They hadn't had mail for weeks. The road to the Center over the Englewood Dam (one of the famous Dayton saving dry dams—a giant earthen wall with an opening at its base for the Stillwater River) was less than a mile away, and the electric mail carts were as solid and reliable as any vehicle. But Charles suspected the mail carrier let their letters accumulate until he could no longer postpone the trip.

They didn't look like people worth visiting. Charles had stopped shaving, and the hairs of his lower beard caught on the upper buttons of his shirts. Diana, who had only summer clothing, had taken to raiding the lost-and-found boxes, and often felt so cheerfully motley she'd rush into the bathroom to gape at herself in the mirror. The women's lost clothing was decorated with flowers and squirrels and pine trees, as if a visit to a nature center required a sartorial nod to nature. The men's clothing was at least practical.

She and Charles were once again happy. It had struck Diana that she wasn't all that nice, or all that stable. Charles, in contrast, was both. She starting liking him again the day in December the trees were encrusted with ice, and Charles chipped away at the frozen limbs that had pushed the bird feeders to the ground. He used his breath to melt the openings to the finch feeders, and refilled each container with seeds. "Rough time of year for birds," he said, his eyebrows bristling with frost.

"Napkin," she might say, handing it to him, waving her hand under her chin.

"Is that supposed to be a *bluebird*?" he might ask, peering at her shirt.

It was January 7 before the calendar arrived, and they used Diana's perc to tune into media, which told them that the Grid had announced its succession ten days before. Dayton, Indianapolis, and Columbus had all been quarantined and were allowed no exits or entrances other than trucks and planes containing supplies deemed "vital to local living" (VLL). All the Grid borders were surrounded by American troops—a naval fleet sat in Lake Erie north of Cleveland—and, although there had been some tense moments, stray threats, and gunshots, no actual fighting had occurred. The U.S. had not officially declared war. Negotiations were in process, talks termed "sensitive" and "high-level." The Grid wanted recognition by the U.S. of their own president and government, control of their own production, and the ability to market their commodities to entities other than the United States. Their provisional constitution was loosely based on the U.S. Constitution. The Alliance countries, with the exception of the EU, which was stalling, had officially recognized the Grid as a nation. There were rumors of a Grid-Alliance pact, although both sides claimed no more than friendship. President Baxter had "every confidence" that food from the Grid wasn't needed for the U.S. Grain supplies, even subtracting the Grid's output, were forecast to be more than adequate through the summer.

"Let's run away," Diana said, eyes fixed to the screen. They had noticed more planes overhead recently—they'd even commented on it—but since they were near the old airport they often heard planes.

"We are away," Charles said. "Look." And he turned off Diana's perc.

"I HAD A dream." Sharis told Abba.

The boys were at school, and Chad was outside chopping wood. Sharis was scrubbing wild onions in the sink. Chad had dug a hole in their backyard to store their extra vegetables. "You know where our root cellar is?" Sharis had asked the boys, stamping her foot on the dirt. "Here!" Abba very much approved of the winter cellar. She hadn't realized Chad had married such a practical girl.

"All of us," Sharis said—by this she meant her immediate family not including Abba, but that would have been cruel to mention—"were walking down a road lined with trees—it was beautiful, it was like France— and suddenly things were shooting up from all around and we were screaming but it was nothing, it was fireworks, it was a show for us because we were walking down that road."

"Good attitude," Abba said. "That's a dream with a can-do spirit. Have you been to France, Sharis?" She went on, not waiting for Sharis's answer. "I like the French, I don't care what people say. And they do have a beautiful country."

Sharis opened the utensil drawer. She knew Chad found Abba difficult, and she did talk almost constantly, but she gave off the reassuring hum—the refrigerator hum, Sharis thought—of an appreciative life, a noise that transmitted itself through all her stories: her friend's children went bad, but the grandchildren turned out to be wonderful; her friends (they were all women) lived with impossible husbands, but got nice houses and went on cruises when the men died. Sharis had come to anticipate the final line of these tales: "Things worked out."

Abba slept on the sofa. Their communal bed on the floor wasn't right for her—the surface was too hard and no one really wanted to touch her—and the upstairs bedrooms were too far away, but the sofa, like Mama Bear's bed, Abba said, was *just right*. And she'd agreed (after Chad, to Sharis's embarrassment, threw a fit that first night) to use the dining room to listen to her bedtime music.

Chad was ungenerous with Abba. If Abba said she was cold, Chad would turn up the thermostat one degree. She complained again, not quite directly ("Golly, it was warmer than this in Siberia! Did I tell you about that trip? We . . ."), and Chad found her a sweater. When five degrees would have made her toasty, would have made everyone happy.

"We're headed for a war!" Chad had bellowed the night before at dinner. "Haven't you heard of 'gathering storm clouds'?"

Abba said, "Don't pop a hernia over it." Sharis and boys couldn't stop laughing. Chad got up and started on the dishes.

Honestly, the quarantine had changed their daily life more than Abba had. Cook, clean, sleep, cook, clean, sleep. Daily life was as stubborn as time.

A SHORT WOMAN with pulled-back hair and the pinched face of someone who didn't wear her dentures was banging at Tuuro's back door. Tuuro recognized her as his upstairs neighbor. "You got something for me?" she said.

Tuuro patted his pockets, confused. Possible, more than possible, that she was a spy. The woman glared. In her hand she clutched an empty string bag. No one in Cleveland looked happy. She said, "I don't got what you got, okay? White women don't bring me groceries."

"Here," Tuuro said, hurriedly pulling things out of his fridge for her.

"And some crackers?" she suggested, peering past Tuuro's shoulder.

Her parting gaze was shrewd. "We all got to look after each other, these days," she said. Tuuro sighed, remembering the minister and his *munificent ministrations,* the *gifts of soul and body* that could *heal the fractious world.* There was ice on Tuuro's steps, and the woman gripped his railing with both hands.

"YOU THINK IT'S right to let them go where we can't see them?" Chad asked from beside the window.

Outside it was almost fifty, a January thaw, the ground a mixture of melting snow and mud. Chad ran the media on his perc all the time these days. The situation was terrifically unstable. The Gridians had—as Herbert Daniels, Chad's favorite newsman, said—"the fire of revolution in their eyes." Plus, they were well armed. On top of that the Grid was peppered with defensive missiles, installed at its creation to protect it from the rest of the world. Who controlled these devices now was a matter of intense conjecture. Chad was sure there were U.S. government employees busily calculating the military cost and political ramifications of blowing the Grid to smithereens.

"Chad and Sharis, stay calm and alert," President Baxter's latest personalized perc message had said. "It's always safe to stay inside."

"They're right behind the Hofmeisters," Sharis said. "I saw them three minutes ago." Chad was home all the time now, because UD had been closed—"mothballed," the administration called it—with its employees placed on skeleton pay. The boys' school had been shortened to five hours four days a week, and grade levels had been consolidated. This was in the suburbs. In Dayton proper school had been canceled.

Chad, his hand on the doorknob, glanced at Sharis. She was measuring flour, a look of intense concentration on her face. "I'm going to find them," he said.

"Go right ahead."

"I care about my children."

"Really?" She dumped the cup of flour in the bowl, releasing a white spray.

Chad stopped, turned to stare at her. "I don't know why you want to make things worse. Why can't we pull together, be a family again?" Damn Abba. Their only moments of peace now were when she was asleep.

Leon came streaking across the lawn, something striped in green and yellow across his shoulders.

"Leon, where's Howard?" Chad shouted out the door. "Leon, what is that?"

Leon lifted his arms like a bird and came hurtling toward the house. "I'm a Hopi Hellion!" he yelled. "I have the power to swoop and save! Howard's coming," he added at the door.

"Wipe your feet." There was Howard, a striped thing across his shoulders, also, ambling toward the house.

"Is that one of the Hofmeisters' awnings?" Sharis asked.

Leon twisted to look at his shoulders. "Is an awning the thing that hangs over a window?"

Their laughter was like an umbrella, pulling them in. They laughed so hard they woke Abba up.

EARLY IN JANUARY, during a thaw, Lila, still on crutches, returned to her office to work. The ragged strip of wound in her leg was filling in from its bottom and sides; she had been in the hospital for Christmas, and later Kennedy brought her meals and stayed up late with her watching old movies on New Year's Eve. News of the Grid's secession had been almost a relief to Lila, because now she understood what was going on. Wonderwater was a Grid site, its tiny star as well as the mysterious icons betokening something only Gridians should know. It was likely Seymour had been shot by someone atop the Grid barrier. It was likely the Grid was water-bleeding Dayton.

"Not bad," the nurse in the emergency room had said, glancing at Lila's leg. She looked again at the substance the pilot had sprayed in Lila's thigh. Her voice changed. "Where'd you get the Gelfoam?"

"An army pilot fixed me up. His helicopter crashed near where we were"—Lila faltered, not sure exactly what had happened—"shot."

The nurse gave her a quick glance. "Lucky girl. A helicopter right there, Gelfoam . . ."

It hit Lila for the first time that the pilot's presence had perhaps not been random, that he could have been watching the border, or her. The nurse peeled the Gelfoam off Lila's wound, and Lila was surprised that the only sensation was a tugging. "It's impregnated with anesthetic," the nurse explained. "What happened to your Sir Galahad?"

Impregnated, ha! Thank God she was too old to worry about that.

Sir Galahad, right.

In the emergency room, Lila pushed up on her elbows and shifted her bottom. She didn't think she was imagining the sensation of Sir Galahad's semen still leaking out of her, a disconcerting sensation. It *had* happened. She wanted to tell someone, but in the light and brightness of the emergency room she didn't know how to bring it up. And she was alive. Perhaps that was worth whatever price she'd had to pay.

Lila said, "He flew away when the ambulance arrived. He and his copilot."

"His helicopter crashed, and he flew it away?"

Lila felt—with a sort of whooshing thud—a large dark curtain fall over part of her mind, and she was relieved to see that it completely blocked her view of the pilot, the field, Seymour's body, all the events she had started to think of as *that day.*

"You'll need to stay here a while," the nurse said crisply. "Dressing changes, antibiotics, rehab. I'll call the coroner's office, find out about your coworker's body." Her voice dropped. "How far were you, exactly, from the Grid barrier?"

Lila frowned. She had never been good at distances; surveyors used to laugh at her estimates. "Length of a football field?"

"One hundred yards," the nurse said, nodding. "That's plausible."

"Are you seeing many wounds like this?"

"No. We're seeing these wounds, mostly." The nurse tapped her head. "A wound like yours is almost refreshing: it tells us what we're dealing with."

"What are we dealing with?" Lila said. Even as the thought of knowing more alarmed her (did she really want to lift up a corner of the curtain?) she wanted the nurse to take the question in the largest possible sense.

"Oh, just a physical wound." The nurse smiled. "A basic, limb-sparing wound."

"Good," Lila said.

The nurse lifted her hand to signal an orderly, and Lila was wheeled upstairs.

DIANA PICKED THROUGH the discard pile of clothes, looking for mittens. Did Charles have a dry pair? She wanted to walk outside. If he didn't have a pair, she'd use her pockets. She was hankering for some water from the spring.

Charles was shut up in his office, as he was for an hour or so each day. He kept a perc journal of the weather and the birds he'd seen and various natural phenomena, complete with photos and rudimentary drawings and graphs of temperature and precipitation. She'd never barged in on him before, but they were getting along so well it didn't seem like barging.

Charles was sitting at his desk with the holo-screen open in front of him, and he startled and twitched and made the screen disappear the second she walked in.

"Whatcha doing?" It was so clear she'd caught him at something, she kept her tone light. "Dirty pictures?"

"You caught me."

"Charlie," Diana chided, sidling up to him, "aren't I dirty enough for you?"

"Oh," he said, his voice suddenly thick, "are you *dirty*." But he didn't have an erection, and Diana was sure whatever he'd been viewing had no sexual content at all.

A TALL, FRECKLE-FACED woman with Seymour's delicate features appeared in Lila's office. It was Cora, Seymour's older sister. Lila had a soft spot for Cora. Neither Cora nor her mother approved of Seymour's proclivities, but Cora was the one who made sure that Seymour was invited to family events. "I'd like to hate her for being pious," Seymour used to say about his sister, "but no one can hate her."

Cora said, " . . . what Mom and I really want are the personal details. We know he was hit in the abdomen, but did he suffer?"

"Who talked to you about him?" Lila asked, startled. Seymour, hit in the abdomen? His face was gone.

"Mr. Wilder," Cora said. "The man from the government. The man you talked to."

"But I never . ," Lila started, then stopped.

"Did he suffer?" Cora asked again.

"No," Lila said. "It was instant." She'd been wondering whom she should talk with about the Grid stealing Dayton's water. Agro? The air force? The mysterious Mr. Wilder? The Dayton mayor was at his vacation house in Florida, Lila was sure. The city commissioners hadn't held a public meeting in months. The city manager ran things, but he was shut up in his office and never answered messages. Lila felt a rush of nostalgia for Gerald Ferrescu, the city manager during the New Dawn Dayton times. Yes, Ferrescu had been ridiculously corrupt, but protecting his own interests made him as alert as a guard dog. His ears were up and his eyes open all the time.

"I'm wondering if you saw his face. Did he look at peace?"

Maybe Lila was wrong, maybe an entity other than the Grid was bleeding her. "He looked surprised," Lila said, surprising herself. "But not bad surprised. He looked"—she searched for something—"surprised by joy."

Cora's small face lit up. Lila felt a strange sensation in her chest, as if two torn halves of sweater were being knitted together. She had given Cora a gift. The gift might be a lie—and where had it come from? how in the world had she found those words?—but still, it was a proper gift, gratefully received.

Long tears and worn spots had appeared in the occluding curtain in Lila's mind. The moths were going at it, and soon *that day* would be revealed. Who the hell was Mr. Wilder? If the shot had indeed come from the Grid, why hadn't the story made it into the media? How had a pilot in a crippled helicopter flown away? If Lila had indeed found herself in the middle of something, was there any way to guarantee her safety? She couldn't call anyone, she realized. There was nobody to trust.

As Cora reminisced about her brother—his size eighteen shoes, his hopelessness at piano—Lila was hardly listening. Seymour's death she could survive. The things the pilot had done she could survive. What she might not survive was treachery.

There was something people always equated with power. "*Blank* is power." Something basic. Knowledge, she thought suddenly. Knowledge is power. Well, she knew the water map. She plotted the steps to make herself indispensable, composing in her mind what she'd tell Nelson and Solganik, the computer genies who could clean under the tabletop.

"VERY GOOD," GENERAL Nenonene said. "Convincing."

Tuuro nodded. He had kept his eyes closed through the viewing of the tape.

"A splendid performance!" the General said, his voice rising. "You could be the next Manning Lennon!" The General smiled broadly, then seemed to notice Tuuro's face and silence. He waved the men accompanying him aside, then closed the door to the room. "You're performing a great service," he said to Tuuro. "You may not understand this now, but you will later."

Tuuro shrugged. These cheap compliments were worse than silence. *Performance.* Oh yes, Tuuro was performing. The General, too.

The General touched his shoulder. "No harm will come to you or anyone in your family, I assure you." He hesitated, made a considering face. "People need a story, Tuuro. Something to bridge the barriers between them. And you are helping me make that story."

Tuuro nodded, but only because he had to. The scene wouldn't end—he understood this—until the General had wrested from him this nod.

"DID YOU WATCH his confession? Oh, God." Gentia shivered.

"The worst was that he looked like a normal person. When he started I felt sorry for him, but the more he went on . . ."

"Sick, sick, sick. That little boy could have been Leon."

Sharis closed her eyes. "Maybe I shouldn't let them play outside. But I hate to keep them cooped up, they're normal kids . . ."

"Honey, these are abnormal times. Don't talk to me about it, you know what I think. I'm in security. George would probably forgive him." Gentia drew out the "forgive" in a mocking way. "Did I tell you he's turned into a religious fanatic? Every time he doesn't answer me, he's praying. At least that's what he says. Did you hear about the truck?"

"What truck?"

"A Dorothy Lane Market delivery truck, full of gourmet food. It was headed to some Consort party, and it went over the Salem Street bridge and guys jumped out at it and starting firing. They got the truck. Yesterday. Aren't you getting any media? It's all over. Lots of questions about where the police were, I'll tell you that."

Sharis nodded, but she wasn't really listening. "I wonder what Nenonene will do to him."

"I have to say the General has a sense of justice," Gentia said. "What would you do to Tuuro Simpkins, castrate him? Stick his balls in his mouth and let him hang?"

"Gentia!"

"Okay, time to go home." Gentia pushed herself upright. She stood for a moment getting her balance, the tip of her tongue protruding like a strawberry. Only fifty-two—Sharis knew that from the tapes—but she seemed a decade older. Chad was looking ragged lately, yes, but still it seemed impossible that he was closer to Gentia's age than to Sharis's. "Okay, the Sunday after this we'll get the verdict," Gentia said. "He said it took twelve days, right? Some African thing." She lumbered to the door. "I can't wait. I've already got his confession on a chip, and I'm going to record the verdict for my grandkids. Honey, I love what you do, but this is what we call *history*."

"THANKS FOR COMING here. I'm worried. Our department computers have been sabotaged."

Nelson and Solganik, the legendary computer broads from Cincinnati, exchanged glances. Today their matching tops were pale yellow and their fingernails gold. How they'd gotten past the barriers into Dayton Lila didn't know, but neither of them looked the worse for wear.

"I think it's the Gridians," Lila said. "I'm sure they've been bleeding our system, and now I'm looking at our maps and they're not accurate, they're showing flows and variances we've never had, and I think that they think they can use the computer to keep covering their tracks. So all we want is the local water maps eradicated. At every level. You know, the way you said you could."

Nelson extended an admonitory finger. "But your system is a government system. We can get in deep doo-doo messing with a government system." Her thick eyelashes twitched.

"Don't you already mess with government systems?" Lila said. "I mean, you made it into quarantined Dayton."

A pause. "We don't want to mess with systems that will mess with our systems," Solganik said. "If you catch my drift."

"You ladies remember my assistant, Seymour? He was here when you got us into Wonderwater."

Solganik frowned. "Long fingers? Had to bend down to get in the door?" Lila nodded; Solganik looked at Nelson for confirmation. "Sure, we remember him."

"He's dead," Lila said. "He and I went up north to look where they were bleeding us and the Gridians blew his face off."

"But I didn't, they never . . ."

"It's never been made public," Lila said. "The media ran his obituary, no cause of death or anything, but other than that there was no publicity."

The genies' mouths were gaping; for the first time, to Lila, they looked old.

"They used our maps to lure us up there, okay?" Lila said. "On the maps, they dropped the flows so low it didn't make sense to us, so Seymour and I had to go up there, and that was when they struck. They must have shot at us from over the Grid barrier." All of this except the last sentence was a complete invention; the last sentence, I then realized, could well be an invention, too. "So I hate our map, okay? I don't trust it, I don't like it, I don't want to move it elsewhere. I just want it gone."

Nelson and Solganik exchanged glances.

"Who else is going to help us? Look." Lila stood and rolled up the leg of her pants; her leg wound, under its clear covering, still gaped like a slashed piece of steak. "That's where I got hit."

Lila sat back down. Nelson had gone pasty, and Solganik looked as if she were about to retch. "I'll pay you, of course," Lila added.

"No." Solganik said. Her face had become ferocious. "We'll do it for free."

"WE WERE LUCKY to get it." Gentia held the tray propped on her belly and moved through the crowd in her living room. "Don't ask." Sausages wrapped in puff pastry, a bowl of mustard dipping sauce perched in the center. An impromptu party, she'd said when she'd messaged Chad and Sharis. A celebration of three weeks barricaded in Dayton. Show old President Baxter he could coop them up like chickens and they'd still have a good time.

"Gosh, and these shrimp! Where did you find shrimp, Gentia? I'm so sick of fake meat I could scream."

"You sell alarms, you meet people," Gentia said. "We know everyone worth knowing. And some people not worth knowing!"

Chad was talking to a UD anthropologist he recognized from faculty meetings—an older man with a permanently surprised expression and full tenure—and an engineer who did something with optics at the air force base. "Is it tomorrow already?" Chad said.

The engineer nodded. "Twelve days. That's an African thing."

"Building suspense," the anthropologist said in his unfortunate haughty tone.

"Oh, sure," the engineer grinned. "But that's the African custom, twelve days."

"I've studied African society for over thirty-five years, and I've never heard of a prescribed time between confession and judgment," the anthropologist said. "I think Nenonene simply . . ."

"Are you an African?" the engineer interrupted sharply.

"You know I visited Africa once"—Chad heard Abba's voice behind him. "Such a large place! I remember I was sitting in our boat and I thought: Here I am eating a doughnut in the center of the Congo."

"All right, everyone!" Gentia was standing in the center of the carpet, cheeks flushed. She clapped her hands high in the air. "Tin roof sundaes in the kitchen!"

Leaving the kitchen with his sundae, Chad felt a pang of sadness for Sharis, so proud of flavoring her cabbage soup with frozen chives and dried tomatoes from their garden. He would have sat with her this moment, but she was sitting with Abba. "Oh, she's adorable!" Gentia had said. "How old is she again?" Facing out the window, Chad found a seat on an ottoman in the family room, away from the other guests. Vanilla ice cream, chocolate sauce, peanuts, maraschino cherries: everything was delicious. Months since he'd been this full. As he ate, the reflection of Gentia wandered past in the window, and outside a large van pulled into George and Gentia's drive. The driver got out, opened the back of the van and struggled to unload an upholstered chair. His feet cracked the snow. Who had the money or will to buy furniture these days? The doorbell rang. "Oh, look!" Gentia said. "My wonderful chair!"

Into Chad's mind, unbidden, inarguable, swam the picture of the hijacked grocery truck, the dead driver pinned behind the door. The more he ate, the more he recognized the taint of the food, the salty wash of blood coating even the luminous cherries. But he ate everything.

esslandia

TUURO'S TWELFTH-DAY MEETING with Nenonene was carried on the media in real time on a Sunday afternoon. At the last moment the Baxter administration withdrew their case (the Supreme Court was sure to rule against them, all the analysts said) and permitted the show to go out on American media. Everyone watched. Four o'clock in the afternoon, with three inches of snow on the ground in Dayton. January 20, one week before the Super Bowl.

There had been rumors. Nenonene would dress in African regalia. He'd wear his army dress uniform / fatigues / white priestly robes. He'd wear a business suit and hold a gun. He'd have a saber. The scene would end with Mr. Simpkins's execution by the General. The execution, like the sentence, would have to wait twelve days. The General would/wouldn't do it himself. A beheading / hanging / firing squad / an injection. Or banishment: there was a prison in Nigeria, people said, with rats as big as groundhogs, where prisoners were chained to the walls. President Baxter noted that Cleveland legally, if not practically, was still under federal jurisdiction. Tuuro was an American citizen who'd been cleared (cleared! the genetics were incontrovertible) of Nenonene's charges by the police and prosecutors of Dayton. Perhaps his confession had been obtained by torture. But (the media were all over this) no ambassador or agent of President Baxter's had gone charging north from Washington to Cleveland. Perhaps secretly, everybody said, Baxter was hoping for the sort of gruesome spectacle that would turn public opinion away from Nenonene.

People in Cleveland, people said, were more frightened now of the Gridians than the Alliance. Who knew what the Gridians would do? They drank real blood at their communions, people said; they were training kamikaze soldiers.

The moderator, a former UN secretary general, gave some brief remarks, then Tuuro's confession was replayed on a screen behind Tuuro and Nenonene, both men watching it impassively as somber music played.

"General Nenonene?" said the moderator.

Nenonene turned, still seated. The camera zoomed in surprisingly close. "My fellow world citizens . . ." Nenonene began. Of course this coverage was orchestrated—there was only one media feed from Cleveland, controlled by the Alliance.

He's very smart, Chad thought. A public relations genius. Such simple phrases: *There must be justice, but also kindness.* Nenonene's face filled the screen, his pores visible and sweat beading his brow. *There must be grief, but also hope.*

"What I want to know is, where's the mother?" Sharis said. "All this big drama between the criminal and the grandfather—but where's the boy's mother? He had a mother."

"I hate to say it, but the General is handsome," Abba said. "Beautiful uniform. My boss had a uniform from the Navy like that, with lots of ribbons and . . ."

Chad couldn't stand it. "What, would you think Hitler was good-looking?"

"It's totally different," Abba said, unperturbed. "Hitler was a weasely fellow, and this man . . ."

Nenonene stood. The camera angle changed and took in the whole stage: Nenonene standing, Tuuro sitting in a chair in profile looking up. And it *was* a stage, Chad realized. This whole thing was bogus, scripted, moving toward a predetermined end. Chad looked at Sharis and Abba to see if they recognized the theater of it, but they both looked rapt. Simpkins's arms were pulled behind him in the chair: he was manacled, Chad realized. Nenonene slipped his right hand to his hip.

"Tell me when it's over!" Sharis said, jumping up and running into the kitchen. "I can't stand it." They'd sent the boys to the basement.

"Tuuro Simpkins is a kind-looking man," Abba said. "I don't think a man like that would . . ."

"Shut up," Chad said. "Please."

It wasn't a gun. It was something smooth and round, the size and shine of a silver dollar, that Nenonene took from his pocket. And Nenonene's words, which had droned on like background music, now lengthened, slowed down, stopped. Silently, Nenonene lifted the silver disk and approached Simpkins. He pressed it into Tuuro's forehead and it stuck there.

A target? Chad thought. A new delivery system for poison? He glanced at Abba, astonished at her silence.

"I forgive you," Nenonene said. His voice broke. "I forgive you."

Ridiculous. Tuuro knew it was time to break down and sob, and he wanted to, he yearned to, but the tension in the studio was so great—a charge in the air as if everyone's tiny hairs were standing on end—that he knew if he tried sobbing he'd risk laughing, and laughing would never do. He was worse than a trained monkey. Even though the whole thing was planned down to the placement of his feet, and all twelve people in the studio knew it, in the air was the feeling that they didn't know it, that Nenonene could still surprise them. Tuuro realized that he wasn't raising his face as he was supposed to, and he felt the pressure of Nenonene's two fingers—dry, warm—under his chin, lifting his head into position. The metal on his forehead had lost its reassuring cool.

"Don't be afraid, little man," Nenonene said. "Your life will be your penance. I forgive you."

A uniformed woman stepped behind Tuuro and removed his handcuffs, and Tuuro found himself grabbing at Nenonene like a man pulled from a fire. His ear pressed into Nenonene's belly. The camera moved in for a close-up of his tearstained face.

THAT EVENING TUURO climbed the steps to his porch, the snow already marked with footprints. The tires of the car that had dropped him off spun on the ice, then gripped and drove away. Sitting beside his back door was a paper bag containing a half-eaten box of crackers, a near-empty bag of sugar, and five eggs. Taped to it was a note. *I don't need this from you you scum.*

Why now? he thought. Why now and not after my confession? But then he understood that those around him had been waiting for a punishment, and only now, with no punishment forthcoming, did they feel the sting of being cheated.

Lanita. He would never see his daughter again. He sat at the kitchen table and closed his eyes.

"Should I get a job?" Tuuro had asked when the show was finished. "Do I need to stay in Cleveland?"

Nenonene looked surprised and vaguely irritated. "Akira will help you out."

Tuuro felt not like a man but like the hollow shell of a man, a pumpkin with its innards scooped out. But he had been a great success. When he left the studio, the approval rating for Nenonene in Cleveland (the U.S. numbers would take a day) had risen from 35 to 68 percent. Nenonene was triumphant, shaking hands with Mrs. Calder, with the director, the cameramen, the moderator, everyone in the room. He used Tuuro's back as a surface to sign autographs. "Very, very useful," he said.

I want my daughter, Tuuro thought. I want my life back. "Are you the light man?" the young woman had asked him. It was the night after the Gridding, and she was one of the relocatees, sequestered for an evening in his church. She was lying on a mattress on the floor, her hair fanned on her pillow and her armpit gleaming whitely. For a moment Tuuro had been confused, then he realized what she wanted.

"I am," Tuuro had said, reaching for the switch, "I am the light man." And for years he had been just that, a man who could maintain calm and order, who always left a room improved. An expression of his grandmother's flew into his mind: *No good deed goes unpunished.* He had hated those words, linking them with empty bottles rolling on the floor, his grandmother's scoffing looks when Aunt Stella arrived with books. But now Tuuro remembered his grandmother's sharp eye, the way she said, "Whee, don't we look pretty!" She was right about many things, his grandma. What she said was rarely pretty, but that didn't make it wrong.

CHARLES HAD A confession. The perc stuff Diana caught him at, the stuff he'd tried to hide? He was talking to people about trees.

"Trees?"

He looked excited. His ears were pink and his mustache trembled. "There are a group of us, okay? We communicate. We exchange ideas."

"Tree Lovers of America." Diana laughed awkwardly. "TLA."

"TLW. It's people all over the world. It's a burgeoning field. Trees communicate with each other. They release all sorts of chemicals. There's this guy Moskowitz who followed an olive grove all through the West Bank War. This grove got bombed, it had troops hiding in it, part of it was bulldozed . . . These trees thrived, I'm telling you. They thrived."

"Even the bombed ones?"

"There was some individual loss of life. But as a population, I'm telling you, these trees did great. Moskowitz found out they were releasing this chemical called lepogen into the soil, which seems to be associated with growth and longevity. Moskowitz died of cancer, but his grove is still going strong."

Diana didn't know what to say. Trees. In a way it was unsurprising.

"There's another guy did work in Australia. They had a wind-erosion problem, and they put in rows of trees as windbreaks, but then this guy thought wait a minute, these trees are too linear, it's not like a forest, and he put in wind clumps instead, with a thicker spot at the center, and those trees put out lepogen like crazy."

His lip was actually twitching now, and his hands were trembling. Diana glanced toward his crotch.

"This is a laboratory here, okay? These woods have been untouched for ninety years. There's every reason in the world not to destroy it. They took Brukner, you know." Diana looked at Charles inquiringly. "The nature center outside what used to be Troy. They Gridded it." He talked as if this grievance were still fresh. "Led to a big rodent problem. You can't destroy woodlands without consequences. Can't destroy anything without consequences."

"No," Diana answered, thinking of the screaming woman at the clinic.

"I've been talking to the Grid arborist. He heard about me and he messaged me. The Grid could annex us," Charles said. "We're basically contiguous."

It took a moment for the concept to sink in. "You mean the Grid would take us over?"

"For our protection. For the trees' protection."

"The Audubon Society's going to love that."

"They don't even call me." Diana was startled and moved by the grief in Charles's voice. He had gone to Audubon summer camps, she knew. The Audubon Society had paid for half his college. He had been, at one point, Audubon Intern of the Year.

"So we would become Gridians?" she asked, incredulous. He shouldn't make this decision without her. She was now as much at home in this place as he was.

"Why not? They're farmers: they understand the land like no one else."

"They'd take our dollars?" The Gridian currency situation was reportedly dire: the American government had cut off the Gridians' salaries, and they were bartering among themselves and selling stores of grain to the Alliance in exchange for American dollars. There was a whole black market in currency, apparently, with Cleveland as the usual entry point. Diana had moved her perc next to her side of their bed; she made a habit of keeping up with the news.

"Right," Charles scoffed. "They want us for our money."

"Oh, Charles. I'm not doubting them," she said.

A few days before, on the clear melting day after Nenonene's Great Forgiveness (that was what the Alliance had termed it), Diana had walked across the Englewood Dam to K-Bob's to buy socks. Standing in the store waiting for her debit card to clear, listening to music and watching the few other shoppers, Diana felt as if she had landed on another planet. She realized at that moment how much of her and Charles's isolation was self-imposed. She trudged gratefully back to Aullwood, wondering why no one else ever came here. Were there rumors about this place? Had she and Charles, in people's minds, metamorphosed into murderous hermits? Not even teenagers bothered them.

"It's not like we have to maintain everything; the paths can overgrow," Charles was saying. "These last six months we haven't served any educational function. We don't need the asses' money." *The asses' money?* Diana realized he was referring to the Audubon Society by its initials: *the AS's money*.

A thrill close to fear ran through her. This was a good man. She hadn't been a wonderful person, and now she could redeem herself through a good man. She said, "Have you spoken with them?"

"An intern!" Charles cried. "The Audubon Society had me messaged by an intern who used a translation module for

English! They didn't even send a video feed! Maybe when I message them that we're hooking up with the Grid, they'll let me talk to somebody in membership!" Diana had never seen Charles this agitated. "I can message with everyone on the Grid. I talked to their head agriculturalist for an hour yesterday. They care, Diana."

Diana said, "We could clear out the center accounts. We could pool the money and control it ourselves."

"You can handle that? You can do the money?"

"That's what I do, Charles. I do money."

"I can talk to the Grid president!" he said. "I can get him on my perc in two minutes!"

She worried he was getting too excited. "Are you sure hooking up with them is what you want?" she said. "If the U.S. gets mad, they could bomb us. Where would your trees be then?"

"Bombing a nature center? That would start World War III!"

"Oh, Charles." Tears filled her eyes. "It wouldn't." The pain in his face at these words was unbearable. "Or maybe it would," she said quickly.

"Can I set you up an appointment to talk with the Grid president? Will you do that? Please? I can't go further without you."

"YOU'RE STILL THINKING about that truck?" Sharis said. "You don't know about that truck."

He didn't, really. Yet he did. Abba didn't believe it for one second. Sharis shot him a skeptical look and stirred her eggs a little more fiercely. "Obscene to have another party eight days after that one," Chad said. "What is she trying to prove?"

"Normal life, Chad. Super Bowl parties are normal life."

He had noticed something. Sharis was happier for several days after she'd blown up at him. Releasing her anger seemed to lighten her, bring her a jauntier walk. His own good deed to make her angry. "I think they're immoral," Chad said. "I think George and Gentia are immoral, corrupt people." Then he sat back, waiting for the storm.

Sharis set two plates of eggs in front of him and Ahh? "You may be right," she said

GRADY, THE PILOT, climbed out of his helicopter and looked around him. This was the deepest he'd gotten into the Grid, and it was even flatter here than down by the border. The snow had been swept by the wind into ridges like sand; from the air the white ground seemed almost to be moving. Odd they brought in a purported liaison person by attack helicopter, but Grady supposed that someone had decided to make everything, even the liaison's mode of transport, a threat. Grady was happy that he and his copilot now got to do occasional transport duty. He was weary of border surveillance.

The copilot was reaching back into the helicopter to give a hand to the special envoy. The special envoy was wearing a dark blue skirt and surprising heels. "Those for my benefit?" Grady had asked as she climbed on board.

He never missed with anybody, never. As she flew her legs were crossed in Grady's direction. Her legs were her best feature; other than her witchy eyes, she didn't have much of a face. This was their fourth trip together. They always came to this same place—"The Green House," the special envoy called it, laughing. They were at the center of the Grid, near what used to be Lafayette, Indiana.

There was one of the usual Grid villages about a mile away, but in front of their helicopter, looking more slapdash than the town, was a cluster of aluminum-sided, one-story buildings, the biggest of which was the governor's office. Governor, he was the president now, the president of the Free and Independent Republic of the Heartland Grid, and this glorified prefab was the capital. What a joke. They didn't even have money. All they had was produce and a crop of crazed farmers. Even the name was ridiculous: FIRHG, pronounced like it was spelled; supposedly the Gridians wanted to change it, but there was disagreement at the top. Can't make cash till they have a name to print on it, Grady supposed. He and his copilot, side by side with the special envoy behind them, marched through the three inches of snow to the president's door. There should be a greeting line for her, Grady thought resentfully. There should be a path. Instead there was only the disturbed snow, and a small group of women huddled near the outside door to the offices. One of the group—a young woman with blonde Rapunzel curls—turned in Grady's direction and waved. He winked.

The special envoy was a classy lady. Late thirties and already a big shot, so you knew she had a lot on the ball. She walked with confidence over the snowy ground. A hank of hair whipped over her face; she reached up and tucked it behind her ear.

They were getting a routine. Once inside, the special envoy turned right toward the president's office, and Grady and copilot went left with the Rapunzel blonde to her office, small and wood-paneled and windowless, like a old-time car salesman's office. The blonde then went somewhere to fetch both of them coffee, then the copilot, his needs met ("your tiny needs, your needs the size of a tree frog," Grady said), headed back outside to wait.

"So," Rapunzel said once Kenny had left. She leaned against her desk, chin cradled in her hand. The fall of her hair made her shape a triangle; Grady liked that. Her breasts were small and pointed, triangles also.

"So," Grady said back.

"I think we have a name!"

"Heartlandia?"

"No."

"The United State of Corn?"

"No."

"Oatspeasbeansa?"

"You're terrible."

"No, I'm excellent. Don't you want to try me and see?" By this point he was perched on her lap with his legs spread, facing her. Triangle again

"I'm not a traitor, you know. Don't think you're going to learn any secrets."

"Oh, you don't have any secrets?" He was burrowing. "How 'bout that? Is that my secret?"

"Stop it."

"Cockteaser," he said, slipping his finger into her mouth, letting her taste herself. Women liked that. He loved her mouth, the little peaks at the top of her upper lip. Also, she had especially appealing pubic hair, springy and reddish-gold.

"That it, then?" The copilot asked when Grady climbed back in the Hellion. Three times, that was Grady's rule.

"It's not like I'm going to run into her."

The copilot filled his cheeks with air and blew out. He wasn't particularly expressive with words, but he said a lot with breathing. He'd taped a picture of his wife and two children to the inside of the Hellion door. Grady was tired of him.

There was a movement at the capital's plastic door (capital's! plastic!—didn't that say it all?), and Grady turned over the ignition. "Good session?" Grady shouted as the special envoy climbed in. Until this thing got airborne, it made a heck of a noise.

"Fine. They have a name. Esslandia." She spelled it.

"Asslandia!?" Grady said. The copilot cast him a look, and the special envoy chuckled. Rapunzel was at the capital's plastic door now, but Grady didn't see her. He loved to entertain the special envoy; she stretched her legs and crossed her slender ankles.

CHAD WALKED DOWN Custard Lane from his house to Gentia's, which meant going downhill and over the streambed then up the slope on the other side. The hillside houses were surrounded by groomed woods carpeted in ground-cover, with honeysuckle and seedling trees pulled out. In the snow the effect was elegant and lofty, like some stage set of a woods: trunks rising from a bare white floor. Empty houses, their roofs glistening, were set away from the lane, any yard debris or missing awnings obscured by the snow's conceal-ing blanket. Two squirrels skittered across the snow and up a tree into a hole. Decadent Super Bowl party, Chad thought. Instead of heading to George and Gentia's over the bridge and up the hill, he walked to the bridge and turned around. Up and down the hill he walked, three times, four times.

He had never really understood the transplants that couldn't get over being moved, or why the Gridians insisted they were one with their land, but now he understood on a visceral level the tragedy of the Gridding.

By the time Chad reached George and Gentia's, the sliced ham and Swiss cheese were gone. There was still salami, turkey, and roast beef. I forgive you, Nenonene had said, pressing that coin like a target into Simpkins's forehead. Chad thought: if Nenonene could, with such cold calculation, destroy a single person, why *wouldn't* he destroy a town? Maybe our town.

It must be ego that drove Nenonene, mostly. One World, he liked to say. One World ruled by me.

"You're late," Abba said. "I saved you some food. The boys and Sharis are in the den." Abba had taken to wearing an old tam that had been Chad's father's, which Chad thought made her look like a Jewish leprechaun.

Ernie from across Far Hills Avenue said, "You get lost walk-ing up here?"

All this life around him, all this apparent normalcy, but now it felt to Chad like an old-fashioned movie projection of life, something that—should the light burn out, should the film snap—would simply disappear.

"It's so nice and warm in here," Abba added.

Gentia was talking, George sitting next to her staring at the floor. He was worried about heaven, George had told

Chad. Was he good enough? Would he get there? Chad didn't care about heaven. He wanted his life here.

They walked home in the dark, all five of them close to gether the flashlight beam like a rope pulling them home. Sharts and Abba and the boys kept talking, but Chad didn't say a thing. He couldn't have said if he was better or worse, but he was different. His wife was still his wife, his boys were still his boys, his aunt was—more than he'd realized—his aunt, but other than that there was not much he was sure of. It was a newly mutable world, where the very ground he walked on was provisional. He envisioned, for the first time, tanks rolling down the streets of Dayton.

"human folly is always amusing"

NO ONE RETURNED things to the library any more, Kennedy said. "They laugh at us; they act like we don't matter."

"Well, I matter," Lila said. She tapped her skull. "The only place anyone can find the water map is here."

Kennedy said, "Are you insane? What if they find you out and torture you?"

Lila called the number on Nelson and Solganik's card. "That service you provided for me"—she gripped the phone with her shoulder, twisted a rubber band around her wrist—"could it be undone?" Why hadn't she thought of torture? Incessant screeching noises piped into her brain. Metal instruments tearing at her wound. She hated pain. Their hurting her would make remembering the map impossible, and then they'd hurt her more.

"Undone?" The legend's merry laughter hurtled through the receiver. "Honey, you don't have to worry about a thing. Sue and I are professionals. That stuff's dust now. It's air."

"LANITA'S NOT TALKING to you," Naomi said to Tuuro. "No way."

"Could you hold the receiver in the air when she's talking, let me hear her voice?"

"You listen to me, you erase this number from your mind. Because if you call me back, I'll have to round up my angry friends."

LILA CALLED GERALD Ferrescu, the former city manager. She would never, in her past life, have called someone so eager to be called. But he knew things. They met for lunch at L'Auberge, the most expensive restaurant in town, which appeared to be—oddly or not—thriving. At a table near them sat a woman in lipstick, with painted fingernails, trim buttoned boots, and a purple cap on her head. Unimaginable, looking at that woman, to think that they were in quarantined Dayton. Lila smoothed her skirt—she had only one winter skirt, and it wasn't glamorous—and looked across the table.

Ferrescu smiled. "To what do I owe this pleasure?" Kennedy had told her Ferrescu had a relative who worked in Washington in Homeland Security. Ferrescu never named this relative, or any of his informers; his gossip was customarily preceded by the words "I hear," as if the facts had slipped from the air into his ear.

"Curiosity," Lila said. She'd made it clear that she was paying for his meal.

The Grid had not lost its appeal to her. It struck her that the Gridians might need her water map, that under their umbrella she could be protected. What a crazy irony that would be, working for the Grid after they'd shot her in the leg. People did what they had to. Ferrescu ordered oysters, and Lila thanked God for her savings. She could still afford her lemons, although they cost three times what they had the year before.

Ferrescu was filling her in on Grid history. " . . . and then they enlisted those Lindisfarne people, who were always"—a significant pause—"particularly clannish."

This was no surprise to Lila, but Ferrescu's next statement was a revelation. "They were utopians, you know," he said, the slippery gray of an oyster disappearing into his mouth. "Wanted to be blasted off into outer space."

"Outer space!" This was worth the oysters. There were still a few abandoned space stations circling the earth, but the Mars colony had been shut down during the world recession of 2032, and only schoolchildren and hotheaded scientists talked about space travel now.

"That was why they didn't want babies. You remember that abortion debacle. Their idea was to hold off on reproduction until they had a new world to colonize."

"Bizarre. I thought they had more sense than that."

"Sense? Never Jeff Germantz's strong point, my dear."

"What was his strong point?"

Ferrescu waved his tiny fork. "Intellectually pliable. You figure out something you want, he'll give you the rationale. They didn't have any power, you know. Just those ten thousand acres of Australian scrub one of their members had inherited. That's why they wanted the stars. But they couldn't raise the money for a space mission. So when Babbitt Chromium, who was a friend of Germantz's from Yale, told him that our dear President Brandee Cooper was looking into creating a large dedicated agriculture area, well . . ."

"I heard Germantz was interested in agricultural linguistics," Lila said, hoping to jog Ferrescu back to something interesting.

Ferrescu burst into unpleasant laughter. "The linguistics of exploration, back then. As I said, remarkably pliable."

"Was Allyssa-something part of that first crew? I've met her."

"Ah, Allyssa Banks. Certainly. There were rumors once Germantz had gotten her pregnant. I believed it at the time, but now I doubt it. A child never showed up, and someone like Germantz would never abort his own offspring. You know what they call him on the Grid, don't you? *Father Jeff.* There're a number of baby Jeffs up there, also."

"Not his . . ."

"Who knows? Or maybe just named in his honor. Like baby Vladimirs in the post-Lenin Soviet Union." Ferrescu's voice dropped confidingly. "It was Father Jeff insisted on destroying the towns."

"Really?" Lila had learned this from local government: any outrageous action, good or bad, started as somebody's fantasy. People who thought that one person could do nothing had no idea.

"It was his way of making sure the government got their hands smelly. You know, *Father Jeff* didn't destroy the towns. Listen, my friend: if you can convince someone to do your dirty work, they will be a hundred times more sullied by it than you will. The best they can ever look is stupid."

Jeff Germantz was brilliant, Lila realized. She had never fully grasped this. She shivered in sudden relief that he was dead. And people adored him. One must always be wary. "It's funny we never heard more about Germantz," she said. "All we ever heard about was Brandee Cooper and her cabinet."

"I knew nothing good would come out of a Brandee. A Sherry—okay; but a Brandee? Listen to me, politicians want their idea people in the shadows. If the ideas are good, the politicians look brilliant; if not"—Ferrescu's voice was back to its usual pitch now, gleefully dramatic—"the culprit can be dragged into the light of day."

Lila had never before noticed Ferrescu's hands. They were plump, with tapered fingers, and Lila pictured them bedecked with ornate rings, lifting a tankard of mead, as Ferrescu on a bench in a vast banquet hall regaled the crowd with a story of the king and the noblewoman and the king's best steed. "Don't you get depressed by this?" Lila blurted.

"Human folly is always amusing." Ferrescu raised his wineglass to his lips. Empty oyster shells littered his plate. Ferrescu, Lila saw, did not believe in his own downfall. He was as arrogant as she'd been: they both believed their knowledge would protect them.

"WELL?" CHARLES SAID, sitting up straighter.

"He was very pleasant," Diana said. She was still dazed by the strangeness of it: she, Diana Crupski, alone in a visual feed conversation with the president of FIRHG, newly named

Esslandia. "Reasonable." She considered a moment. "I liked him." It had taken two weeks to reach him; he had not been as eager to talk with Diana as Charles had thought. But once they were looking at each other over the media he was quite gracious. His name was Kyle Beerbower. From just outside the former Hicksville, Ohio, he told her, smiling at its name. He had seen the value of the Grid from the beginning. He believed in work and hope. Red cheeks, little eyes: he reminded Diana of the man who used to come to her parents' house each autumn to check the furnace.

"I don't see where joining up with Grid would upset anyone," Diana said to Charles. "They swear they'll protect us. I mean us like the trees. And us like"—she pointed—"the two of us."

"Did you get into the mechanics?"

She was pleased Charles had trusted her with this, although when she first brought it up President Beerbower had seemed surprised. "We tell them when we want to do it. They'll send people over the barrier to surround the place, and then we inform the Audubon Society and the city of Dayton, and we should notify the federal government, too. We can do all that by perc. And that's it. We have our own generator. President Beerbower said they can guarantee us fresh food. Our media feed may get cut off, but we can hook up to the Grid's. He doesn't think there will be any, you know, violence." She smiled. "It's a big deal for them, having someone want to join them. For the U.S., we're nothing. We're a nature center."

"We're not industry," Charles said, his mouth twisting. "We're not farmland. We're not"—his mouth twisted even more—"money."

"Right," Diana agreed. "Why should we matter?"

He loved her open face, the way she wasn't bitter. He beckoned her to him, wrapped his arms around her slender shoulders. "Are you happy?"

She nodded. "I'm beyond happy. I'm . . ."—it took her a second to find the right word—"thrilled."

"Me too." And both of them thought that what they were doing was worth it, no matter what came next. This moment was worth it.

THREE DAYS LATER the Esslandian troops—about thirty people, wearing camouflage gear and weighted with guns—were on the center grounds by 6 a.m. Charles gave them the coordinates of the center borders, and they fanned out to protect the area. At seven Charles messaged his letter. By 8:30 the media people were arriving—trucks from the networks, local newspeople, even NewsEuropa—and the Esslandians who controlled the road sent them to the place Charles had selected as the media center: an abandoned barn about a mile by foot up the wooded hillside from the center. The Nature Center, in its better days, had incorporated a farm with goats and sheep—Charles walked across the former pasture to reach his sugar bush—but no one had used the barn for years. Now the only signs of habitation were mice droppings in the corners and an abandoned plastic jump rope tossed over a beam in the loft. Charles opened the big front doors of the barn and stood near the barn's back wall. The cameramen glanced warily at the wooden floor. "Come on in," Charles said, pleased when the cameraman obeyed him. "It's perfectly solid."

"I'm going to read this," Charles said once everyone was positioned. He held up a handwritten copy of the letter he'd messaged to the presidents of the U.S. and of Esslandia, the governor of Ohio, and the Audubon Society National headquarters.

"Read it and then we'll ask questions," someone shouted.

"No questions."

"You refuse to answer *questions*?"

Charles's eyes darted to Diana, standing in the corner behind the cameramen. She gave a small nod.

"A few," Charles said. He thought again. "Maybe twenty."

"Twenty questions!" someone exclaimed, and a titter ran through the small crowd. The laughter deflated both the media's nervousness and Charles's authority; when he started reading his voice quivered.

"A NATURE CENTER?" Lila said sharply. She'd been lying in bed telling herself to get up and move. "How the heck can a *nature center* secede?"

"You tell me, lovely Lila," Kennedy said over the perc. "Get on your media feed."

The Aullwood Audubon Nature Center had announced its independence from the U.S. and its alliance with Esslandia. A scruffy-looking male—the label below him read "Charles Hadding, Director of renegade nature center"—was shown reading a prepared statement, which put a lot of emphasis on woodpeckers and the secret emissions of trees and did not strike Lila as totally coherent. The phrase "commitment to the natural world" came up twice, which the U.S., in contrast to the Grid (oops, Esslandia—she'd never get used to that name), was said to lack. Esslandian soldiers (amazing!) were ringing the renegade center; American troops had moved in place to face them. So far, the newsreader intoned, there was a "tense standoff." A statement from President Baxter was expected within the hour.

"Are they crazy?" Lila said, reaching Kennedy on her perc. "They think we'll just let them go?"

IT HAD GONE well, Charles thought. Except for that crack about twenty questions. Let them have their fun. It must get tedious, driving around filming this or that event. A watcher, not a player. Charles had made himself a player. The network trucks had startled him, but the more he considered it the more pleased he was that they had come. The U.S. was taking him seriously! He mattered! Everyone must be talking about lepogen now.

He was almost humming as he made his way along the fence beside the old pasture. A gate ahead, and then the downhill trail through the woods back to the center. Diana had left the barn before the (twenty-seven) questions; she should be home already. In all the morning's excitement they hadn't eaten, so Charles was certain she'd be fixing breakfast now. Charles was surprised he wasn't hungrier. He felt empty, yes, but in an exhilarated way: stripped, light, like one of those beautiful otter skeletons he liked to take out of its drawer and gaze at.

He thought of taking a detour along the ridge to the spring but that would make him late, and he didn't want Diana to worry. He headed downhill. He took the steeper path, to the right, which in spring could become a narrow creek but which now, in the February chill, held water only in the occasional frozen puddle. He saw deer tracks in a patch of leftover snow; heard the cries of a pair of cardinals; stopped to watch a pair of gamboling squirrels who were nesting in a beech tree dead from lightning. He was almost to the junction with the main trail when he noticed the ground ahead of him moving. His first crazy thought was deer.

The men stood. There were six of them, in camouflage gear, faces and lips painted in blotches of winter color: green-gray, dead-leaf brown, twig black. The whites of their eyes were all that revealed them as human. Charles's first thought was to compliment these soldiers on their getups. The Esslandian solders' camouflage, he realized, had been painfully rudimentary. Then he saw the rifles aimed at him.

"Charles Hadding?" The man who spoke stood in front of the others, slouching as only a person in authority would dare.

"Yes." Charles had stopped at his place on the trail. To his right was Aullwood Creek; across it and half a mile down the bank were the nature center building and Diana. How could American troops have gotten here already? It was only a half hour since he'd finished his press conference. And where were the Esslandians? Shouldn't he have heard some shooting as these guys broke in?

"I'm Lieutenant Kiefaber. I wish to inform you that we have taken charge of this nature center and it continues to be, as it has always been, under the jurisdiction of the United States of America."

"No way."

"Under the laws and regulations of the jurisdiction of the United States of America," the lieutenant amended with irritation, as if merely having to say this was insulting. His speaking dissolved his disguise, revealing his small teeth and the pink of his inner lips.

"No," Charles said. The explosive power of that word was almost thrilling; he could see why children said it. "I'm part of the Grid now." A hesitant correction: "Esslandia. There are Esslandian troops all around here. Encircling us."

"They surrendered. You're all alone now, Mr. Hadding."

Charles felt the first fear he'd felt all morning, thinking of Diana back at the center, pouring water into the pancake mix, opening a can of jelly with their antique can opener.

"So?" Charles said, but he had to clear his throat to get out the word. The Esslandians had surrendered without shooting? They had looked pretty tough early this morning.

"So you'll come with us, we take you in. End this stupid little game you're playing."

"No," Charles said, less convincingly this time. In his letter, had he mentioned Diana? He didn't think so. The Gridians knew about her, but the U.S. didn't.

"No?" The lieutenant licked his lip, and some of the brown paint came off. "What should we do, Mr. King of Nature?" One of the other soldiers guffawed.

"You should get out of here! This isn't your country anymore. And leave me alone." He started to walk quickly down the path, but the lieutenant stepped in front to stop him with the point of his rifle.

"You're resisting detainment."

"Why don't you get out of my way so I can go home." It struck Charles belatedly that it was a mistake to say this, that they might follow him to Diana. He took a few steps backward. "Better yet," he said, "I'll go back to the barn."

The lieutenant's eyes narrowed. "Think you'll run to the media, hunh?" he said. "Think you'll get those one-worlders to lick up everything you say?" The lieutenant stood up straighter. "We're a special unit. We know how to deal with traitors."

He's talking too much, Charles thought with a chill.

"Shooting a traitor's pretty standard issue. I don't think anyone's going to go apeshit about us shooting a traitor." The lieutenant reached into a pocket of his camouflage suit and removed a piece of paper and pen. The paper's colors matched his outfit. "You have a last statement?"

"I'm not a traitor." Charles imagined himself collapsing a millisecond before the shots, the bullets blazing harmlessly over him.

"No? You handed over part of our country to the enemy, I'd call that a traitor. What do you think, Sergeant Lipschitz, that sound like a traitor to you?"

One of the men shifted, nodded. "Eh?" the lieutenant said.

"I'd say that's a traitor."

"Private Boyle?"

"Traitor."

"Private Hurtell?"

This one looked, beneath his paint, younger than the others. His eyes had a bruised innocence. Charles heard him mumble a barely audible yes.

Charles stepped back.

"What you scramblin' for, boy?" This was a quote, delivered in a crackling accent, a line from a recent movie about an escaped slave who becomes a cowboy; even Charles recognized it.

My God, Charles thought, I'm going to be killed by a crazy army guy who quotes bad movies. He thought fleetingly of heaven, which as a child had worried him terribly. Were there predators and prey in heaven? How could it be heaven for the prey? On the other hand, without prey, how could it be heaven for a predator?

"Look." The lieutenant pointed to a spot twenty feet away, just up the hill. "You stand by that tree."

It was a maple tree, a lonely sugar maple in a stand of oaks, its catkin carried here on the back of a deer or a raccoon, a misplaced and brave and unlikely tree. It seemed beyond cruel to Charles that in shooting him, they would shoot this particular tree. It was in its prebud phase, thousands of gallons of sap coursing its trunk. You could make syrup for five hundred pancakes from this tree. A bullet hole would bleed it for no reason. Enough bullets would kill it.

Frantically, Charles scanned the group of faces. The young-looking soldier—Private Hurtell—was staring straight ahead, mouth open. Charles aimed his voice at him: "You're going to let them shoot me in cold blood?"

Private Hurtell blinked, but said nothing.

Manna, that was what they ate in heaven. A nonmeat product.

One of the privates—not Hurtell—broke into giggles. "I farted," he said.

"I'm not liking this." The lieutenant's voice changed. "Get by that tree!" He jabbed the point of his rifle into Charles's belly. The pain was terrific; Charles thought for a second he'd been shot, but when he looked there was no blood. He took a step away.

"Just go over there. Get away from us." A new element had entered the lieutenant's voice. "You're too close."

"What," Charles said, emboldened by the lieutenant's discomfort, "you're afraid you'll get my guts on you?"

There was something else pointed at him beside the rifles, a sense, almost an odor, and Charles realized it emanated from the lieutenant's men. They were panicking, he realized.

Panic in nature served no useful purpose. It was one step from death, the panicker's or something else's. Charles's eyes ran over the faces of the lieutenant's men. Their eyes were wide, unfocused, as if they were sitting in front of a visu game controlled by someone else. Only Private Hurtell seemed to really *see* Charles, and Private Hurtell's eyes snapped away.

Were these *soldiers?* Charles thought suddenly. They seemed to be lacking a soldier's resolute hardness, despite their elaborate makeup. And this sort of job—hiding in the woods, intimidation, maybe murder—should be a special ops assignment, not a job for a lieutenant and a gaggle of scared privates.

"I don't think you want to do this," Charles said, aiming his words at Private Hurtell. "You won't forget it. You can't get rid of memory. No matter what drugs you take."

"Traitor!" the lieutenant bawled. "Lowlife traitor!"

"I'm not a lowlife," Charles said. Lowlife: fungus, bacteria, saprophytes. He would end up feeding lowlife, like all highlife in death. "I'm not a traitor to the trees. I'm not a traitor to the birds." He was walking backwards up the hill, repeating these lines like a mantra, aiming his steps away from the big maple. He himself farted. Oh beautiful body, luminous and aching. Oh kingdom of the visible and invisible world.

"Stand right there!" the lieutenant shouted. "*Stand!*"

But he kept walking backwards. No bullets hit the maple.

"LILA, WILL YOU?" Michelle the youngie from Agro repeated, her lips moving after the words. The image feed was slow again today; Lila had heard there'd been damage to cables in southwest Ohio—sabotage, people were saying. Grid sympathizers trying to cut off American communications.

"Today?" Lila said. "With this nature center stuff going on?"

"Why do you think he needs to find a place for her?"

Lila hadn't heard from Michelle in weeks, and then Michelle messaged her at her office asking a favor. A second cousin of hers lived in Dayton with his twelve-year-old daughter. The cousin was a counterintelligence specialist working at the air force base, and the government wanted him to move to on-base quarters. The government had no plans for his daughter, which was where Lila came in.

Michelle said, "I know you love children."

Did she love children? In an abstract sense. She'd certainly always sympathized with their powerlessness. Yet she'd never had to live with one. "I'm not the safest person now, I . . ." Yet Lila was afraid to say more. It was possible that everyone was being monitored. Or maybe not everyone, but her.

"It shouldn't be long. Two weeks? Just till there's some resolution."

"I hate to be responsible for another . . ."

"Her name's Janie," Michelle interrupted. "She won't be any problem. She's a bookworm."

DIANA HEARD THE shots. A whole spatter of shots, then silence. Slightly north of her, toward the barn, along the stream. She knew. It had been madness for them to think their actions wouldn't matter. But she should be, as Charles had wanted her, safe. No one from America—her former country—knew that she was here.

Diana went into the bathroom and stared at her ravaged face. She ended up huddled in the bathroom corner, her back to the cold tiles, and after a while it came to her what she must do.

Her hands were shaking as she punched in the number on her perc. "Is the doctor there? I'm a former employee."

He came to the phone surprisingly quickly. "Hello? You have an emergency?"

She explained in the briefest of terms. Her husband had just been killed, but she wanted his child.

"You don't want his clone?"

"No. I want a mixture, him and me."

"His sperm would be easiest." She nodded. "It isn't difficult, but you'll need a syringe and needle."

"Okay." The taxidermy set in the library.

"What did you say your last name was? (Hipski?" She could picture the specialist frowning. "Can I get a video feed of you?"

"No, not from here. I'm in Dayton."

"Oh, Dayton. When did you say you left my office, '41?" There was the muffled sound of the specialist talking to someone else, then: "Are you the little girl with all the hair? Didn't you write a letter?"

"I was young. I'm sorry."

"Oh, don't be sorry. I even remember what you said. 'Unconscionable immorality.' Rather a nice phrase. I thought you might have some obsessive traits re language."

"It was abstract to me then. Now it's real."

"Oh, that's a good phrase, too. Have you been mapped?"

"How do I get the sperm, doctor? How much time do I have? It may be hard for me to get to him, I . . ."

"Oh, that's right, your young fellow's dead. Well, that's not a problem. You have about eight hours. It's nothing complicated Do you have a freezer? You bring the sperm to Chattanooga and I'll construct and implant the embryo myself. Okay, now: first, you . . ."

baby lettuces

JANIE, MICHELLE'S COUSIN'S daughter, didn't read the sexy sort of books that Lila had. In her hand was a copy of *The Bell Jar*, a book that had been tired back in Lila's youth. This relieved Lila. Lila was also relieved—watching Janie mount the front steps to her condo—that the girl was over five and a half feet tall, with oversized hands and feet, and a body as round and solid as a loaf of bread. Small humps of breasts. As Janie grabbed her suitcase from her father and dragged it alone up the inside stairs, Lila saw her old self in the youth's brash movements. She's only halfway to being a woman, Lila thought. Good. She won't drain me.

In her living room, Lila saw Janie's eyes narrow as her father opened his wallet. "Thanks for doing this," the father said to Lila, handing his daughter a roll of bills. No offer of money for Lila, no magic words to utter if soldiers stopped here, no indication of how long Janie would stay. He seemed to be avoiding Lila's eyes. To Janie he said, "I'll call you when I can. Don't worry." He tapped his daughter once on the top of the head, then left.

Don't worry, Lila scoffed, inwardly shaking her head. Michelle had told her Janie's mother had died of brucellosis—one of Dayton's infamous missed cases, ignored after the state health department announced the disease was wiped out. That silly pat on the head: as if Janie was a once-reliable car being sent to the junkyard.

"Let me show you your room," Lila said, taking the girl to her old office. Then she showed her the rest of the condo.

"What's that?" Janie asked in Lila's bedroom, pointing at the remains of a lemon wedge.

"Lemons," Lila said. "I eat them." She contorted her face, and Janie broke into a delighted, incredulous laugh. The girl had lovely eyes, brown and full. Her hair was unremarkable, almost straggly, but when she smiled her square face broke into radiance.

"Are you really lesbo?" Janie asked. "That's what Daddy said."

"Yup. Always have been."

Janie hesitated, twisting a plastic bracelet around her wrist, and Lila, filled with unease, was both relieved and touched by her next question: "Is it lonely?"

"It didn't used to be."

"Is Aunt Michelle your friend?"

Aunt Michelle. Michelle was enough older than Janie that she must be more like an aunt than like a cousin. "She used to be. Not now, though. She has other friends, and we're so far apart."

"She really likes you," Janie said quietly.

"Good. I like her, too." Lila noted in Janie's face both puzzlement and sadness, as if Janie, glimpsing adult life, was disappointed in what she saw. "I'll make us supper," Lila said.

THE ARMY HAD sent a special ops team to check things out, with helicopters as air support. "What's that down there?" the copilot said, leaning forward.

"Trees are down there."

"I mean the body. See? The guys are gathering around it. They spotted it right off."

"Who is it, you think?"

"Must be the nature center guy."

"The yeti," Grady said. "People've got to shave their necks, man. You can't let hair keep growing down your neck."

"He's dead, okay?" the copilot said. "Grow up a little. No one's making fun of *your* face," he added in a mumble.

THE MAN WHO'D been shot at the nature center was, the media agreed, in many ways an admirable man. Both the U.S. and Esslandia denied responsibility for his death. Nenonene, in Cleveland, had once again been startling in an interview. Who got him? he'd asked, voicing everyone's thoughts. What good is he dead? Was he a threat, or was he target practice?

There were puncture wounds in his scrotum. Torture? Perverse cruelty? A doctor from Cincinnati signed in with a thought: perhaps Charles really was special. Perhaps he had been killed for his genetics.

"HERE," LILA SAID to Janie, flipping off the TV, "try this book." *The Lion, the Witch and the Wardrobe,* by C. S. Lewis.

"What's it about?"

"I don't remember, exactly, but it's better than the news. I read it when I was your age. It's set in a magical kingdom called Narnia. The animals talk."

Janie turned the book over in wonderment. Lila wondered if anyone had ever given her something to read before, or if everything Janie had read she'd had to seek out on her own.

DIANA'S APARTMENT WAS the upstairs left rear quadrant of a two-story brick apartment building. She arrived home at twilight, relieved to find the building intact. She had in a knapsack Charles's sperm in two syringes in a freezer bag, a few of the nature center's cast-off clothes, and feathers she'd plucked from the stuffed owl as mementos. She walked up the building's echoing inside stairs, put her key in the lock, and reentered her past. Her ex-boyfriend's clothes and speakers were gone, but other than that nothing had been moved. Dust. She turned up the thermostat and crawled into her bed with all her clothes on and slept until eleven the next morning.

Quiet, quiet. The downstairs neighbor had an alarm clock and flushed the toilet often, and the one across the hall left the building slamming doors and whistling. But not today. It took her maybe an hour to get suspicious, but by the time she had finished knocking on all the doors she wasn't surprised. She needed groceries, and she set out to the store. The day was cold and cloudy; a frosting of snow had fallen overnight.

The neighboring buildings weren't all empty. Some had parked cars outside and open curtains and potted plants in the windows. As Diana walked she spotted a neighbor leaving the building two doors down from hers. "Excuse me!" Diana called.

Diana's building had been empty for a month, the woman said, since the man from one of the upstairs apartments committed suicide in the lobby. The whistling man, Diana realized, wishing she remembered his name. "Think you'll move out, too?" the woman asked.

A suicide was at least a choice. A suicide in a public space was two choices. Charles had had no choice at all. "No," Diana said, and she walked away very erect, a dreadful spring to her step, although by the time she got to the grocery she felt beaten and sagging, the pears, the bananas, the lettuce all beclouded, the memory of Charles's grievously wounded body floating like a scrim before her eyes. His wounds: the hole below his left nipple; the hole shaped like a teardrop below his right ribcage; the hole just above his belly button, looking like a second navel; the dark hole below his left collarbone that seemed bottomless, as if that bullet had stitched him to the earth. She understood the followers of saints begging for their bodies to clean and kiss and robe; she understood those grieving paintings; she understood everything, it seemed, in those moments when she sat beside him, her hand cradling his cold face and her eyes blessing each wound.

She got through her shopping, not realizing until later how sparse the selections had been. She walked home.

She had in her medicine chest some old ovu-strips she'd used for birth control. She put one on her forehead and it turned immediately red. Perfect. Meant to be.

She'd keep one syringe for the specialist, in case. She put the contents of the other syringe into a turkey baster and carried it to her bedroom.

It was better if the woman enjoyed it. In the old days of sperm donation, she'd been told, the specialist had handed out a dirty movie with each vial. But Diana didn't need a movie. She lay half naked on her bed, a pillow under her hips, thinking of Charles. His mustache with its slightly red cast curling over his top lip. His rough hands moving down her body. The sweat on his shoulders, even in the winter, the way he clutched at her hips, turning her in just the right direction.

"Fuck me, baby," she said to herself, slipping the baster in. An old, old act, that baster: no one did it this simply anymore. And the idea of emptiness—of this room, this building—made the act something thrilling. Into the box inside the box inside the box. The plastic seemed almost human, warming quickly inside of her, and Charles became real again on top of her, with his gripping that was close to pinching, his mouth flying open and his back arched as he pinned her to the bed. Here, here, *here*. She squeezed the baster bulb. She wanted him smeared inside her, every cranny of her cave covered, his sperm released to their frantic swimming. The winner gets the egg!

Make it so, she was praying. *Make it so*.

TUURO TOOK TO messaging. Kelso's wife wouldn't let Kelso talk. Tuuro tried his old landlord, his old neighbors. Not even his former college professor neighbors wanted to hear his side. In the old days, Tuuro thought, people were more forgiving. But he had never been much of a community member, and this time he had sinned again against his own. Or so they thought. Maybe. There was a lot of talk in the media about Nenonene as a master manipulator, about how he'd set up the forgiveness of Tuuro as an elaborate counterpoint to the indelible images of him with the colonel. None of this talk helped Tuuro. The Americans hated Tuuro because he'd let himself be used. Nenonene's supporters hated Tuuro because any suspicion of his innocence tainted their hero.

Akira found Tuuro a job as a restaurant dishwasher. He told himself it didn't matter if the other dishwashers showed up late and didn't care.

Late February under a leaden sky. Tuuro was sitting on his porch with his coat on, trying to look invisible, when a thin old white lady slipped on a patch of ice on the sidewalk in front of his house. She lay on the sidewalk without moving, arms and legs splayed, like someone who'd been dropped from a giant's hand. After a moment Tuuro went up to her. Her cheek lay against the cold pavement. Her eyes were open. Tuuro peeled off his coat and slipped it under her head. "Are you all right?" he said. "I saw you fall."

"I don't know," the woman said in a creaky voice. Tuuro stood hunched over her as she lifted one foot and waved it, then the other. She stretched each arm out in front of her, like a swimmer. "I'm intact," she said. "Help me up?"

Her name was Chelsea, and she lived alone four doors down, in a frame two-story house she'd once shared with her husband and children. Her eyes were bad and she had trouble, chronically, with steps; it helped her to have someone to hold onto. She had always liked a strong young man. "You want to come in for a cookie?" she asked at the door.

"You come by any time," Chelsea told him when he left, "Theodore."

JANIE WAS STANDING in Lila's bedroom door. "Aunt Lila? There's more of them," she said, waving the Narnia book in the air. "This one is really number two in the series." She waggled her eyebrows and grinned hopefully.

Lila lay curled on her side on top of her bed, thinking of nothing. "You want number one? I'll get you number one. How many are there?"

"Seven."

"Seven!" That seemed a little excessive. "Can I see the book, please?"

Janie walked into the room and handed it over. "Oh!" Lila said in surprise as she looked through the list of other books by the author. "*Surprised by Joy*!"

"Pardon?"

"Nothing," Lila said. "I'm just happy you're here. Sure, I'll buy you all seven books."

"That's really generous," Janie said. It struck Lila belatedly that she could have gotten the seven books from Kennedy's library. "You're not even related to me."

Lila shrugged. "That's okay. Relation is overrated."

"I think so, too." Janie smiled, glanced at Lila's bedside table. "Can I try one of your lemons?"

CHAD HAD HAD it all wrong; he'd thought war was pow-pow-pow, fear and excitement, but really, war was waiting. It was possible, with the winter almost broken, that there would be no pow-pow-pow at all, that the doors to Dayton would be opened and the fate of the Grid settled by the peace tribunal that was meeting now in Sweden. Still cold there, reports said. Why Sweden, in the winter? demanded the American delegation, more distressed than the Africans or the South Americans by the snow and wind.

The Alliance would withdraw from Cleveland. The Grid would agree to stay part of the U.S. in a new category of statehood, as a semiautonomous entity a bit like Guam, free to sell its products to any market in the world, with, perhaps (this was a point of contention) favorable rates to its mother country, the U.S. "Empires are like teacups," Nenonene had been quoted as saying. "Too much hot water and they crack."

The Gribble family was talking about returning to their own bedrooms. "Would you mind the guest room, Abba?" Sharis asked. Of course not, Abba said. She was the guest. And—she cast a look at Chad—in her own room she could play her music in peace.

The history department secretary, KayLynn, messaged Chad that she'd been sick in bed all week: would he go check out the department, make sure everything looked okay?

Chad lay on the floor of the living room in the discarded pile of blankets, watching the light through the window play against the wall. *I'm sick in bed, too,* he thought, but he knew that was a lie, and that a refusal to obey KayLynn would mock her doggedness and sense of duty, the very traits he claimed that he admired. She wasn't suffering from soul sickness, not her. If KayLynn said she was sick, then she was on the floor vomiting.

When Chad walked into his department office, he flicked the light switch without thinking, but no lights came on. He'd forgotten the administration had moved to nights-only lighting. He stood a moment and let his eyes adjust to the dimness.

Ramsey's office was empty except for a desk and chair; Montford's office was full of books, lamps, and papers, as if he'd stepped out the moment before, while Hanning's and Chad's offices looked as sad as Prem's did: gutted, stripped down, used. Chad wondered why no one had taken Montford's furnishings as fuel. Montford was in London now, working for an agency that educated Americans abroad.

Suddenly Chad missed—with a keenness that took his breath away—his department: Prem raising and lowering his eyelids in grievous disagreement with something Ramsey had said, Montford shuffling in with a cup of coffee, wearing his shoes that looked like bedroom slippers; Hanning waving her arms and shouting about some illuminated manuscript the university could never afford to buy. And in this room had sat KayLynn, who after twenty years as department secretary still was unable to enunciate Prem's full name: Dr. Sin, she called him for short—a fine name, as Montford pointed out, for a full professor in a Catholic school. "But I am Catholic," Prem would object, his blinking profound.

It wasn't the best department in the school. It wasn't even a very good department, and there were hardly any majors, but still, it had been Chad's place of work. You could imagine, with the quarantine of Dayton, the lights going out in microworld after microworld: a restaurant closed, a veterinarian's, a gas station. The world of brightness, of commerce and communion, slipping away. Everyone scurrying to their dark basements, where they survived alone. This was the destruction of society, Chad realized: the word *society* from the Latin word meaning fellowship, companion.

The Grid had put the lights out, too, on all those little towns.

Chad had a hard time leaving. He stood at the door to the offices and listened to his breathing.

LILA ALMOST HAD the water map back together. Not perfect, but close enough for anyone else to use. She kept this on a sequestered antique computer unattached to phone or cable lines. To get it she had to open her secret closet, pick the right laptop out of the pile of old ones, and type in her special code. Not likely. Still, a backup if she ever needed one. She hardly ever went to the office. Other than the air force base and Consort, water usage had dropped enough that the only problems were related to low flow. Rusty water, low pressure, standing pools. There were two repair crews left, and their supervisors were reliable; Lila contacted them when she needed them, maybe once or twice a week.

"Aren't you supposed to go to school?" Lila asked Janie one day.

"No one does that anymore."

Lila knew that couldn't possibly be true everywhere, but maybe it was true where Janie lived. "Okay," Lila said. "Can you log onto some school sites? Try to learn something?"

"Sure," Janie said. And she seemed to: several times when Lila checked her she was looking at what appeared to be science. "I like biology," Janie said. "I like things that grow."

Lila smiled. "You're growing," she said.

A KNOCK-KNOCK-KNOCKING AT the door.

Sharis froze. She was upstairs editing the Schneiders. No one home but her, thank God: the boys and Chad had walked off to the grocery store. She would leave. She would slip out the back door, just as she'd done years before. Abba—they had planned this—would drop to the floor and roll under the sofa. Sharis would run to the end of Custard Lane and behind the houses and hide in the drainage ditch waiting for the boys and Chad. The Family Escape Plan.

She crept to the window and looked out. On their front stoop stood Cubmaster Terleski.

He had walked over to ask about Webelos. Now that it was getting warmer, he wondered about getting back to their outdoor activities. "You and Chad and the boys been okay?"

"We're fine. Chad's aunt is with us. Your family?"

"Theodosius got pneumonia in December, and I had to finagle some antibiotics out of Cincinnati, but he gets all around the house now without oxygen."

Finagle? Oxygen? Sharis looked at Terleski with fresh respect.

"You think your Howie would be up to it? Our outdoor activity?" He frowned. "Even Leon," he added. "Leon could come." He gave Sharis a chastened look. "What he did wasn't that bad." The wagging penis incident.

"They would love it," Sharis said, adoring Terleski at that moment.

"I've lined up seven kids from my neighborhood."

"Seven! We don't have any kids left here."

"Well, this is a nice neighborhood, Sharis. People here can afford to . . ." He trailed off. They made plans to meet at Terleski's house on Saturday.

"TEA?" CHELSEA SPILLED the hot water in an arc to the teacup. Tuuro was surprised that she could aim so well despite her bad eyesight, but certain gracious gestures must come naturally to her. "Do you miss Dayton, Theodore?" she asked.

"I miss my daughter, but she's moved with her mother to Tennessee. And I miss my apartment. I had a nice place. Near Paul Laurence Dunbar's house."

"The poet."

Tuuro nodded in surprise. "The poet." He loved Chelsea's house. The silence, the clock ticking, the dense floral smell, the polite and slightly stilted conversation. It was the way he'd imagined a house with Aunt Stella, years before. Now he sat in a floral chair in an indentation left by Chelsea's late husband.

"I read about him in college," Chelsea said. "He died at a very young age." Tuuro noticed the elderly slackness around her mouth, the buff makeup embedded in the creases. If she didn't wear the makeup, she would be the same beige as Allyssa.

Tuuro nodded. "TB." But Chelsea must have once been beautiful: those blue eyes.

"I'm sorry, Theodore." Chelsea leaned forward to pat Tuuro's hand. "Would you like to eat dinner with me?"

"PLEASE DON'T BE offended," Michelle the youngie messaged, "but I'm back with my boyfriend." The note went on with apologies and explanations, then ended with a surprise: "Maybe the best thing that happened out of you and me is that Janie has a mother figure now."

Mother figure? Lila stared at the holo-screen. *No way.* It was as if she'd again waked up not knowing where she was. I'm Lila, she told herself. I'm Lila the uto. I'm the Water Queen. But those definitions didn't seem right for her—as if she were using dated equations, keys that no longer fit. Janie had just had her first period, and Lila had gone out with her to buy pads.

What has happened to me? Lila thought. What am I? That thought took her back to the explosion that had come out of nowhere and spared her *(But why?)* and her rape which was not quite a rape ("Are you okay with this?" he'd said, and, yes, in some sense she had understood the question), but if it wasn't a rape *What was it?* and water which was changing but she didn't know how *(What was it?)* and Janie who was not her child or lover but was nudging at Lila in a place Lila was tempted to call her heart. *What was that Janie thing about?* The questions started ricocheting around Lila's brain as noisily as pinballs. She wasn't good with the flippers, the balls kept dropping into the gutter and there was another ball shooting out at her and she had to play it, however poorly, and then there was a ball erupting from a hole she'd never noticed, and why was that other ball skidding down the center like a waterfall? She couldn't find the secret lever, the machine was smoking and the four chords it played as music were repeating faster and faster and . . .

She was sitting at the kitchen table, her left hand supporting her forehead—her thumb on her left temple and her fingers on her right—thinking she was *holding her brain*, a thing no bigger than a grapefruit that could cause such trouble, when a vision appeared to her, a wavery, bowed rectangular vision, and slowly she made out its outline. It was a bottle of brandy sitting atop her cabinets, and, lo! she saw that it was real, and it was good.

CHAD'S FATHER WAS not a good dresser, but he had a friend whose belts coordinated with his outfits. When Chad was a teenager he noticed these details. His dream then was to make enough money to have a belt for each pair of pants. "I bet when you have that much money, belts won't even cross your mind," his mother said.

When Chad hit thirty-five he remembered that comment. He had only two belts then, one brown and one black, and in every one of his outfits he felt fine. That was where things should have stopped. That would have been a normal life.

Now, at fifty, he had no belts. The strips of leather that used to be his belts were wrapped around the logs he carried on Howard's wagon. His pants were getting loose—there was in general less food, although they were nowhere near starving, especially with the two hundred jars of tomato sauce in the basement—and he wore an old scarf of Sharis's threaded through his belt loops and tied in front. He continued to shave, but many days he left rough spots, and he treated his mirrored reflection as a person he was too polite to stare at. His hair, touched with gray, was curling around his neck. Abba had offered to cut it with the kitchen shears, but her work on her own hair had left her with a bowl cut tilted a good inch to the right, and Chad decided that he still had *some* pride. Now his thoughts went to where he'd walk the next day for firewood, how far they could stretch their canned goods, how many sentences Abba directed at someone without a responding word. He wondered if humans could eat tulip bulbs like squirrels did. He thought about what a fool he'd been to insist that he and his family stay through Christmas, how if any of them came to badness (that was the furthest he could think— *came to badness*) it would be no one's fault but his own.

Optimism, persistence: the virtues he'd been stupid enough to fall for.

He didn't talk to anyone. Chad, who had always been so welcoming, whose house people treated like a bar or restaurant, Chad now locked his doors as well as his mind. Even Derk seemed to have forgotten him. Chad had tried drawing more stories for the boys, but they weren't interested, and a week before, in a burst of guilty generosity, he'd penciled a family portrait including Abba, but the boys and Sharis walked away before he'd finished it Only Abba had watched as Chad finished drawing his own hair and shoes, and of course she had had comments.

When did I become the dispossessed? Chad thought, because in a way his moping was ridiculous. He was a man with a family and food and plenty of possessions; the only thing he was missing was an office. Almost every day President Baxter messaged a variant of his message: You are safe; we are working on peace; even if there's a conflict, our first goal is civilian casualty avoidance. It was an election year: he couldn't kill off his voters.

I miss teaching, Chad realized. But that wasn't quite adequate. *I miss my Dayton course.* He missed standing up in front of people and being expansive. He missed talking about life as if he knew it.

"I'M DEFINITELY PREGNANT?"

The ultrasound technician—a beady-eyed woman in her twenties—nodded. Diana felt like she was soaring—out of this room, over this office, above her apartment and back to the Audubon Nature Center.

"I want to be sure I understand this"—the technician's features seemed to bunch at the center of her face—"you want to continue this pregnancy, even knowing the extreme risks? Even knowing that this fetus could have *anything?*"

SHARIS HAD PLANNED to tap their maple tree but didn't think of this until it was too late, in early March, when the daffodils she'd planted started poking up their noses. Somehow she'd thought that sap ran in the spring, not in late winter. But the Internet information she found said she should have been drilling through the bark in late January. Next year.

Her chest filled with a ferocious exultation: she was planning for next year.

Howie and Leon, their teachers settled down, were actually learning things. Long division. Topic sentences. The categories of plants.

Sharis was upstairs in her and Chad's bedroom, finishing her edits for the week. She'd cracked the windows open; that morning she'd pulled up some baby weeds. Chad was lying on his back on top of the bed, hands crossed over his belly.

Lars the Norwegian was next. What affectation. He held his chin up as he spoke. He wore a scarf even at the breakfast table. What had she seen in him? She edited quickly, in something like disgust, using almost three straight minutes of Lars's wife and daughter sitting on the living room floor, the grandchildren romping around them, while Lars slept on the sofa with his mouth open.

She finished Claudia's edit and put on George and Gentia's footage, speeding through hours of their lives. There was Gentia in the kitchen, then George. They sat in chairs in various rooms. Gentia walked across the living room and the transmission cut off. They spoke to each other, briefly. They ate. You couldn't tell one week from the next.

Sharis tried slowing it down. She dropped the speed to three times real, and real time on the words. She got to hear Gentia selling, breathless spiels about ransacked houses and the antibomb guarantee, but George said almost nothing. What kind of soup was for lunch? His elbow still hurt. What good was music? As the moments dripped by, Sharis realized that George was a man in despair. She glanced across the bedroom to Chad. He was still on his back on the bed, eyes aimed toward the window. Sharis quickly returned to her screen.

Chad stirred on the bed. "Sharis, how would you edit your life?"

Astonished, Sharis looked at him and lied. "There'd be a lot of you."

"Good," he said, making a small clap.

"Why don't I record you?" she said. "You do your Dayton course for the boys and Abba and I'll record you."

He sat up. The hopeful astonishment in his face almost broke her heart.

"CAN I LOOK?" Janie's voice behind Lila. "Now that I'm a woman?"

Lila started. But why should she be embarrassed? She wasn't looking at nudes. Michelle certainly wasn't sending her more salacious messages. And, yes, Janie was almost grown now: Lila had taken her shopping for a real bra. The selection wasn't great, but they found something suitable. "See?" Lila grabbed her bottle and pushed her chair out of Janie's way. "Satellite photos of Esslandia."

"We can see those?"

"Why not? It's public knowledge. They block the GPS readings, though. Look." It was too early for planting, except for winter wheat and some exotic lettuces—chervil, escarole, mesclun: the satellite photos had these fields (in the far southwest corner of the Grid, close to the Mississippi River) labeled. Each day more ground was being plowed, grayish rectangles transformed to dark patches with the look of wood. Even the naked fields of Esslandia were gorgeous! Lila clicked to the big picture, then zoomed to fields of different lettuces. She showed Janie several villages, then clicked onto the Alliance troops south of Cleveland, a settlement big as a city, tents ringed by vehicles, with an occasional missile (these were labeled, also) poking out of the flat landscape.

"Why would we want to bomb those places?" Janie said. "Why does there have to be killing?"

Childish questions. But weren't those questions the important ones? Lila heard again the irrigation water trickling at her feet. The cat streaking past her, the rustling of the corn. She batted a bug crawling up her sweaty neck.

"I know what you're saying," she told Janie. She had the bottle of brandy and a squeeze bottle of honey sitting on her desk, as well as slices of lemon on a plate. Lila found something delectable about a sip of brandy followed by a squirt of honey and a suck of lemon; it gave her a near-sexual thrill. "I was on the Grid last summer," she said carelessly. "I spent the night there in a farmhouse."

"Really?" Janie said, squirting from her own bottle of honey and biting down on her own slice of lemon. "You?"

CHAD WORE A tie. They moved all the blankets and sleeping paraphernalia out of viewing range and seated Abba between the two boys on the sofa. Sharis filmed.

"I'm bored," Leon said, before Chad even started.

"Do your holographics in the basement, then," Sharis said, ignoring Chad's hurt look. "Just don't bother us." Leon stayed.

Chad started with the Wright brothers, because they were fun and he knew every sentence by heart. "Name a midwestern virtue!" he said at the appropriate spot.

"Cheerfulness!" Abba cried, and Sharis glanced at Abba's lopsided hair and started laughing.

"Good memory!" said Howard. Chad was off and running. Because Howard enjoyed the Air Force Museum, Chad changed things a bit at the end, finishing with the use of aircraft in World War I and how the people of Dayton, led by John Patterson's son, raised the money to buy five thousand acres that would become Wright Field, the Army Air Corps' original research base. "So while all of us today complain about our taxes, in the 1920s people in Dayton were going in together to buy the government a gift."

"Dupes!" Abba shouted. "Dupes and stupes!" This was an untenable position, because what Wright Field had brought to Dayton in money and talent and publicity was immeasurable, but at the moment Chad felt like scooping up Abba and kissing her.

hubris

"FUNNY TO SEE it without snow!" the copilot shouted. They were taking off from the Esslandian Green House again, the copilot at the controls, the whuppa-whuppa of the helicopter almost drowning his words.

Grady glanced back at the sorry rectangle of a capitol, its flat roof and aluminum siding. He was still stinging a bit from Rapunzel's absence. Or maybe it wasn't absence, maybe she was hiding. Were there really three miles of tunnels hidden under that building? That was the rumor. Where had they put the dirt if they'd dug out tunnels? It was totally flat in the miles around, although there were mounds in the distance.

"Getting kind of routine, flying up here!" the copilot shouted, aiming his words at the special envoy.

But the special envoy wasn't talking. Her jaw was clenched and she was looking out the window. Tentatively, Grady turned and brushed his hand against her calf. He was ready to apologize, but she made no response at all.

"TERLESKI WANTS TO take them up to Taylorsville Dam on Sunday. He can drive."

"Isn't that pretty far north?" Chad knew exactly where Taylorsville Dam was—it was part of his Dayton course—but he didn't want to make an obvious objection.

"It's right near the Grid border, yeah." Sharis said. "It's the dam on the Great Miami." Terleski had become a maniac with Cub Scout activities, although his own son was still too sick to leave the house. He'd taken the boys on a hunt for skunk cabbage, taught them rope-tying, built an obstacle course in his own backyard.

"Are you sure it's safe?"

"Terleski's been up there. He says it's fine." Sharis looked at Chad. "I'd like the boys to go. It's good for them, good for Terleski . . . Good for everyone. And we're still in the middle of Sweden."

"I don't know."

Sharis put her hand over her eyes and sighed. "Speaking of Scandinavians, the Norwegians are falling apart. I'll leave it out, but in six months the wife's going to want me to go back and reedit. I think he's having an affair."

"Tough for you," Chad murmured. He wondered if Sharis would have an affair if the opportunity arose. They certainly weren't having sex anymore, even in the privacy of their own bedroom.

Sharis said, "I worry about their children and grandchildren finding out."

"Isn't there something else you could do? Event editing?"

"How would I make any money off events? You've got to be there for events. And if I tried to get a regular job, they'd want my high school diploma."

Chad was silent a moment. He saw himself pulling Howard's wagon through the snow with his head down, looking like an old and beaten man. "I don't think I've been much good to you lately."

"Don't be silly. You're always good for me." But she knew what he meant. "I liked your talk."

Chad nodded. Sharis filled her cheeks with air, blew it out. "Well, what do you think? What about the dam?" She offered a final lure. "He's taking Leon." Meaning: we'll have some time alone.

"Oh, why not? All their other trips have been just ducky."

"Ducky?" Sharis said. "You're talking way before my time." They both smiled.

MR. TERLESKI WAS doing his stupid hup-two-three-four twenty feet in front of the four Webelos and Leon, and Leon was marching like a goofball, jerking his hips back and forth and throwing up an arm on random beats. "Stop it, Leon," Howard said, shoving in front of him. "Do you want to get us in trouble again?"

Mr. Terleski pointed his right index finger sideways and jerked his arm out, indicating a path uphill through the trees. There were no leaves on the trees yet, it was cloudy and still chilly—"raw," Howard's mother had said—and the path was barely visible and slippery from the morning's rain.

They weren't there and then they were, real men standing around them, with rifles and char camouflage paint on their faces. Mr. Terleski was still marching ahead of them.

"Flippers!" Wilson halted and gazed at the men, and Howard thought this was another of Terleski's surprises, like the puddle at the bottom of the plywood slide in his obstacle course. There was the sound of a shot and a thump up the hill: Terleski fell to the ground.

"You killed him," Wilson said in a high voice. "You killed Mister." Wilson could never get Terleski's name right.

Another figure in camouflage appeared, this one walking down the hill, blending in so well with the background he looked like a waver in Howard's vision. "He's not dead, son, he's paralyzed," this man said. "African poison. Blowgun."

"Really?" Wilson squealed. "Curare?" Wilson started to scamper up the hill to look at Mister but the honorary Webelo,

Bruce the sixth grader, grabbed Wilson's arm and held him back. I'm not dreaming, Howard thought. He felt like he was going to vomit. He reached his hand behind him to grab Leon.

"Why did you shoot our Cubmaster with curare?" said Nolan, the third scout, whose wrists were no bigger than sticks. Howard at the same time was thinking a blowgun shouldn't make noise. Also, curare was from South America, not Africa. He flailed his hand behind him, but Leon wasn't there. "Leon?" he whispered.

"Who's Leon?" Someone jabbed him in the stomach with a rifle, and Howard, doubled over, couldn't think.

"Who's Leon?" someone else said, and Howard as he straightened surprised himself. "I call him Leon," he said, pointing at Wilson. "He's really Wilson but I call him Leon. I didn't see him for a second."

These were not good men. These were bad men.

Could Leon have climbed a tree? He could shinny up one almost like a squirrel, as well as creep through the leaves like an Indian. How had these men not rustled? Howard looked at their feet: their shoes resembled slippers, in shades of brown and gray.

"Come on," said one of the soldiers. "Let's get this over with."

"I should stay here, then?" Under his paint the soldier who spoke looked younger than the others, like a Webelo himself.

"I guess. Which one you want?" And the young soldier, to Howard's horror, pointed at him.

"Rest of you, come with us," the commanding soldier said, and the other Cub Scouts headed behind the soldiers up the hill.

Howard looked at the soldier in front of him. *Be prepared.*

"Guess it's you and me, kid," the solider said in a careless tone. The pairs around them disappeared over the crest of the hill. "I don't have to worry about the killing part," the soldier said. "I've done that; that's no big deal." In that second, Howard understood that he might live. Over the hill, shots rang out. Howard knew better than to close his eyes.

"I don't know why they don't like me," the soldier said. "I'm the best shot." In his voice was a whining ache that made Howard sweaty, because it reminded Howard of himself, "You go stand in front of that big tree now, okay? I'll show you."

Where was Leon? Howard walked to the tree, hoping Leon was miles away, or so high he couldn't see the ground. He resisted the urge to look up, not wanting to give the soldier any ideas.

"I won't hurt you," the soldier said, raising his rifle. "You can tell everyone about me. Don't you move. Right ear." He raised his rifle and Howard closed his eyes.

When he opened them he realized he was indeed alive, untouched, and the soldier was grinning. "See?" The soldier said. "Left ear." Another shot.

"Don't move now!" The soldier shouted. "If you move I can't be responsible!"

"HERE'RE YOUR GROCERIES," Akira said, setting down the bag on Tuuro's kitchen counter. "I don't know why you need two boxes of crackers."

Tuuro said nothing. Akira walked to the wall and checked the thermostat. "Sixty-five is plenty warm," she said, turning the dial.

"I talked to your boss," she said, glancing into Tuuro's living room. "You could work a little less hard; your boss says you're intimidating the other workers."

Live here, eat this, do that. This was not a life with choice; his was the life of a slave. Tuuro understood, for the first time, the anger of the Gridians—every slogan or hoarded cucumber or scrap of rogue liturgy manifesting a sequestered rebellion against the people who had planned their lives. Of course they hated the rest of the U.S. Of course, in their minds, there was only *us* and *them*. In Tuuro's mind there was only *me* and *them*, and the me was getting dull and indistinct. Something in the very air around him was tarnishing his vision of himself. Sometimes his hands when he reached for a paring knife looked like a villain's hands; sometimes his penis, hanging limply, looked as if it had indeed once been a weapon. "I raped him": those were words that he had spoken, and it grew more and more difficult—in this house, this kitchen—to convince himself those words had been a lie.

In Chelsea's house the chairs wrapped their arms around him. In Chelsea's house he took his tea with sugar. In Chelsea's house he was himself, a free and noble human being. Hard to comprehend, much less express, the gratitude he felt in Chelsea's house.

You take away the freedom, you take away the man.

"I'll check on you day after tomorrow," Akira said at the door.

"HOWARD HONEY?" SHARIS said to the figure in the chair, as she and Chad and Leon huddled together on the floor. Abba was lying on her side on the sofa, eyes wide open. "Aren't you going to sleep?"

Howard didn't answer. He was back home but he was different: he was a walking silent room, a room whose door you couldn't find and wouldn't want to. Sharis knew better than to touch him. She and Chad were sure he shouldn't be alone, and they had moved their family bed back to the family room floor.

Howard had only been missing for an hour, until the police, alerted by Leon, found him seated alone on a fallen tree in the woods, the bodies of his four fellow Webelos and Terleski scattered up and over the hill. Leon had jumped behind a tree when the men appeared, and in the furor of the next few minutes scampered back to the parking lot, where he startled a couple by pounding on the window of their car. "He didn't hurt me," the rescued Howard kept saying. He was taken to the hospital, where his body and blood and urine were checked, his story examined by police, military police, and a man described as a "trauma counselor," where everything but his soul was probed. "Retrospective amnesia," the counselor called it, noting that the syndrome had been studied extensively in people who'd been Gridded. "Bring him back to me in a week." A new drug could "unlock" RA, the counselor said, and he would appeal to the Health Service to get it.

"Why don't you make a nest for just yourself, Howard?" Sharis peeled off a blanket from their bed, unfolded another from a pile in the corner. "Here," she said, holding the blankets out to him, "try these. At least lie down," she added in a firmer voice. "You can't sleep sitting up." It was the firmer tone that seemed to do it. Howard took the blankets and lay down not on the rug but the wooden floor, curled up away from them, alone.

Sharis crept to sit on the floor beside him. "It wasn't your fault," she whispered, her voice cracking. "We shouldn't have let you go." *I*, she was thinking. I shouldn't have pushed for you to go.

"Did you see anything, honey?" she had asked Leon.

"I got out of there!" Leon said. "Those men had guns!"

"Howard?" Howard's eyes were closed. The firelight flickered on his thatch of hair. Sharis's hand hovered in the air above him. She finally settled on touching his eyebrow, one quick stroke, and nothing about him flinched. She went back to the family nest, telling herself Howard would be all right. Basically. Like she was all right. She wondered if she remembered everything, if the drug that "unlocked" memory would offer something new to her. What a horrible thought. She had no intention of letting Howard take that medicine.

"Can you sleep?" she whispered to Abba, lying on the sofa. Abba shook her head no, and Sharis wished that she would start her usual babbling. Her silence was hard to take.

In the morning, when he turned on his perc, Chad thanked God for the timing. The dead Webelos could have dominated the media for days, but instead they were a local story overwhelmed by an international one. Esslandia had officially announced its allegiance with the Alliance. The negotiations in Sweden had ended when the Esslandians walked out.

A pill to make Howard remember, Jesus. Where was the compassion in modern medicine, the pill to make you forget? Chad pictured Howard grown up, an empty ache of a man. "You were one of the Webelos, right?" someone would say. "What was it like?"

"Oh, the usual," Howard would answer, knowing how to shut them up. "Murder, rape, depravity." Although he hadn't been raped, the doctor had said. So far as they could tell, he hadn't been touched at all.

The next day Chad went to Terleski's funeral, held in a church downtown. He didn't go to the services for the boys. Terleski's wife had on a lavender outfit, and Terleski's son, wheezy and pale, struggled down the aisle with his corner of the coffin, looking—damn it, Chad thought, damn it to hell—even more the perfect victim than Howard. Why couldn't Terleski's son have been out there walking with the Webelos, why hadn't he been the one terrorized instead of Howard? *My God,* Chad thought, *what am I thinking?* He pictured himself—getting older and frailer, Howard getting larger and lumpier—guiding Howard to seats in public places, shielding him from people's eyes. "My son is damaged," he imagined himself saying, wondering if other people would understand the fate this word implied.

"When Orville had that crash in Virginia, why do you think he didn't die?" Howard had asked him. The crash was in 1908, and Orville's passenger had been killed.

"I don't know, Howard. I guess it wasn't Orville's time."

Howard had nodded.

"Why did that man in Cleveland murder that little boy?"

"I don't think he did it, Howard," Chad had said. "But whoever did was just plain evil."

"I know," Howard had said.

Did he know? *Did* he know? He knew now.

Terleski's wife, heading down the aisle behind her husband's coffin, gave a tiny wave; a woman several rows in front

of Chad waved back. Women. How was it that women managed to keep going? Chad closed his eyes. To keep himself
from crying, he had to twist—hard—the skin between his
thumb and index finger.

You could say that what had happened was simple punishment for pride. Terleski, the dead Webelos, Howard—were
any of their fates surprising, considering they had walked
into that wood? (—*Is it safe?*—*He says it is.*) The minister
talked about Terleski's moral courage—he even used the
word "hero"—but Chad understood that it had been hubris
to believe that in the midst of war and chaos they could live
a normal life. It was like jumping off a boat into the ocean
when you couldn't swim, like walking into a lightning storm
holding a key above your head. It led to tragedy and grief, to
a grave where the dirt tossed over you tasted of tainted water
and machinery, of the barrel of a gun.

In the back of the church Chad might have heard someone say "taco news," but at the time he brushed past everyone, hearing nothing but the roar of his own mind.

"BUT DAYTON SURVIVED," he would say in class. "Dayton
survived."

Remember—he would say—the four investors who bought
the land for Dayton? Remember the surveyors who blazed the
three riverside trees? In 1799, Congress decided that the man
who'd sold to the land to these four investors had never really
held the land's title. The investors, their claim canceled, lost
all interest in the baby settlement. The federal government,
claiming itself the original owner of Dayton's land, demanded
two dollars an acre, an exorbitant sum, from the people who'd
built cabins. People left the settlement of Dayton, other people didn't come. A young man named D. C. Cooper who had
arrived in 1796 and set up several businesses (corn cracker,
sawmill, distillery) bought up all eight hundred disputed acres
and arranged for the other settlers to repay him over time.

Among his many talents, D. C. Cooper was a surveyor. He platted Dayton's streets, making Front Street, First Street, and Second Street parallel to the river, then crossing them with Ludlow, Jefferson, and St. Clair. He raised pigs. As a maid for his wife, he brought a black woman to Dayton, a woman who eventually gave birth to a son who was presumably DC's.

Still, when Dayton was eight years old there were only five men in it, and one of them was a drunk. But it survived. The canal was to come. Mills were to come. The local limestone was waiting to be discovered. And in 1804 D. C. Cooper built, at First and Ludlow, a brick house that reeked of permanence, the nicest house in town.

"Look ahead," Chad would say, almost rising on his toes. "Look ahead." Sharis could tape it.

talking to howard

LILA IMAGINED A cartoon of herself sucking on a lemon (of course), trails of smoke coming out the top of her head. What do you mean there are Alliance troops heading for Dayton? How dare they head for Dayton? Down I-75, the media said, their armored personnel carriers and trucks and tanks greeted by the Gridians with shouts and food and flowers. (No one in America would call those traitors Esslandians.) Suds and Africans were heading straight through the Grid toward the American border and the Consort nuclear power plant beyond it! A brazen show of force! But what could the U.S. do until the Alliance troops crossed into the U.S.? The Gridians, it seemed, had somehow gotten control of the "defensive shield" missile sites protecting the Grid. Yes, but how? *How?* It was a scandal.

Where the hell do the Alliance people think they'll get water for their power plant in Dayton? Lila thought. Out of a goddamn faucet? Out of a giant green hose? She smiled at herself in the mirror. Something funny, sometimes, about an angry person. She started ranting out loud, raising her voice when Janie approached. "Have you purged yourself yet?" Janie would ask, raising her eyebrows. A joke of theirs.

There were almost no cars on the streets; people were moving as far from the Grid as possible within the quarantined area, calling up friends in the south suburbs asking about empty rooms. Lila couldn't take it seriously. She imagined a hundred stick figures running to one side of a raft and sinking it. Pilots riding their planes like wild ponies. Tanks shooting balls of flame that bounced off other tanks and ricocheted back to their throwers. Lila carried her bottle of brandy by its neck and set it down on whatever surface she was next to.

Snap out of it, she'd think. Be adult. You're a threat. You know water.

"Come here, Aunt Lila!" Janie was on Lila's perc. "Look at the chervil. Isn't it char, Aunt Lila? Things are growing like crazy." She grinned. "You can see why people love it."

You can see why people love children, Lila thought. Their clear voices and thoughts. Their shoulders that were happy and unburdened.

Janie moved the bottle from beside Lila's perc to the floor.

"Can we talk to your friend there, Aunt Lila? Please? Can we meet Allyssa?"

FOR A CHANGE, the police had some information. "We're not sure, but we're thinking that the guys who got your Webelos could be Taconoutes." Detective Kettlebaum gnawed at his thumbnail and frowned. "That mean anything to you?" Chad shook his head no.

"Remember that guy from the nature center, declared it part of Esslandia, got himself shot? Taconoute."

"He was Taco-noot? How do you spell that?"

"Taconoute. Not him, the shooters." The detective spelled the word. "They're young, they're male, they're demons. They travel in packs and they kill people. We think they got a woman from Consort out doing a reading at a power station, and a guy from water visiting a monitoring shed. Right up there along the Grid border, that's a hotbed. They've hit around the Grid in Indiana and Illinois, too."

"Are they Gridians?"

Detective Kettlebaum stopped his gnawing. "Yes."

"How'd they get that weird name?"

"Who knows? Thought it sounded scary, maybe." He hesitated. "Ed Meisner—he's retired now—said the name reminded him of Tonton Macoutes, which was the name of the secret police some old dictator had. Rumor has it the Gridians have been keeping their problem children in encampments, and these Taconoutes are kids they've let out to cause trouble."

A MESSAGE ON Sharis's perc from Mrs. Schneider in Texas. *Of course we're reading the news and we're beside ourselves with worry. If you and your family can get out of Dayton and get to Houston you could stay with us. I know that's easy to say but . . .* And the closing: *You're phenomenal. Before we only had our life, but you turned us into a movie.*

Sharis sat for a moment staring at the holo-screen. One of Mrs. Schneider's bursts of attention, this time directed at her. She couldn't say it wasn't flattering. Chad was again at the police station. Leon was downstairs spelling out his name by banging nails into a piece of wood. Abba was asleep with the TV on, old CSI episodes playing in front of her. Howard was sitting in an armchair near Sharis staring at nothing, an open picture book on his lap. Through the open window she could hear the whine of protector planes circling the city. Sharis and Howard both wore sweaters against the chill, but their windows were open. Outside, the daffodils were blooming. I wouldn't want to be a movie, Sharis thought. I wouldn't be better as a movie.

I'm glad you like my work, Sharis typed back. *Thank you for your offer but we're here for the duration. We couldn't get out if we wanted to. We're quarantined.*

NOW, HERE'S THE thing," Sue Nelson, computer genie, said. "We can get through on *our* side, but if you're hoping to communicate with a Gridian, they're going to have to let you in themself. It's one hell of a firewall. You're best off addressing a single person. If you address everyone, no way it'll get through. They're trying to block what they call propaganda." Nelson screwed up her face.

Lila gripped the edge of her desk to keep herself upright. "Here, Aunt Lila," Janie said, hopping up. "Take this chair."

Lila sat. "I have a friend up there."

"I know you have a friend. But that friend is going to have to accept your message."

"She likes me," Lila said, wondering if Allyssa did.

"Good. Then you know she'll want to hear from you."

Nelson used Allyssa's old address, the only one Lila had. She typed in something, and then Solganik, over her shoulder, made a few corrections. Lila remembered her meeting with Allyssa in the high office downtown, the ache Lila had in her chest when Allyssa told her there was no place for her on the Grid. "Okay," Nelson said, standing up. "Lila, put in your message now."

Lila had some trouble shifting chairs. Then she had trouble with her fingers slipping on the keyboard, then some difficulty remembering how to spell. "Want me to type, Aunt Lila?" Janie said. "You can dictate." Lila almost said no, but then she recalled that Allyssa had called her "interesting," and this lifted her spirits. She spoke, and Janie leaned over her to type. She was thinking of the Gridians and Allyssa and wishing everyone there well. She had a young friend who loved watching the lettuces.

"Can you leave for a minute?" Lila asked the genies.

They glanced at each other, affronted. "We'll wait in the hall and you call us. We'll need to go over the entry sequence with you before we leave, though."

"Okay, now type this," Lila said to Janie once they'd gone. "*Are you borrowing our water? I have the means to send you even more.*" She looked at Janie and grinned.

"Oh, Aunt Lila!" Janie said. "This is the charrest. Do you think they'll ask us up there?"

"You can come back now," Lila called to Nelson and Solganik, the message sent on. Janie sat down in Lila's easy chair and rubbed her eyes; she and Lila had been up almost all night talking. Nelson reappeared and crouched at Lila's side. "Okay, you'll need ten commands to get to the U.S. platform, then . . ." She droned on and Lila didn't really listen, knowing Janie would remember this and anyway Nelson would write it down. The brandy was interesting: sometimes it made her sleepy, sometimes it perked her up. Lately she skipped the honey and lemon. She wanted breakfast. She wanted not to deal with Nelson and Solganik, who were talking now about services and payment. But there was Janie's voice, giving Solganik an answer, and Janie could handle it, yes, Janie was competent. Lila's eyelids drooped and for a moment, as she struggled to open them, she thought that she was dreaming, because the holo-screen in front of her was deliquescing into greenness, with words like distant beings streaming towards its surface.

WE ARE ESSLANDIANS. WE NEED NOTHING.

"Wow," Nelson said. "Awesome interface."

"What?" Janie bounded to look. "What?"

Lila had a desperate urge to block the holo-screen with her body, to protect Janie both from Lila's mistake (she had called them Gridians!) and from the message itself, a statement whose fairy-tale arrogance would only—Lila was sure of this—inflame Janie more. But Lila was too late.

HE HAD TO knock ten or twelve times before Chelsea answered, and then she opened the door wearing a nightgown, although it was only seven at night. "Theodore," she said in a peculiarly grateful tone, as though—Tuuro thought this later—she had been getting ready to kill herself and his knock had called her back to life.

"Come in, come in." He had brought her cookies. He held them out wrapped in a napkin. "Did you make these?" she asked.

Tuuro nodded. He had stolen the peanut butter from his restaurant and bought the baking sheet.

"There's a war going on. Did you hear? I couldn't take it. I went to bed." Her eyes sought Tuuro's. "The Grid's hooked up with the Alliance, and the Alliance is sending troops to . . ." She explained the situation, down to the firefights above the Grid's northern border and the American fighters the Alliance had shot down.

It startled Tuuro that Chelsea was presenting this as fresh information. He knew that, because of her bad eyesight, Chelsea didn't watch the media, but wasn't there someone else besides Tuuro that she talked with?. "But this has been happening for a week," he said. "Don't you have at least have a radio to . . . ?"

"People don't understand me, but I don't mind Africans," Chelsea said. "I've always liked Africans. Anyway, I don't need to know about war," she said. "I know war. I was in Uganda when Idi Amin kicked out the white people. I was five, but I remember. I don't tell people. When our neighbor got killed, my mother made me walk around him on the floor to get his food out of the icebox. She didn't think they'd shoot a child."

Tuuro was stunned.

"My parents were missionaries," she went on, her voice bitter. She set down Tuuro's cookies, wadded in their napkin, on a table at the base of the stairs. "The church got us out. They took us to the airport in an ambulance. An African could be bleeding on the road and there wouldn't be an ambulance. But we went to the airport in an ambulance."

"I'm sorry," Tuuro said.

"Dreadful man, Amin." She ran her fingers over the top of her head, pushing her wayward hair even higher. "I had a little African friend named Anna. I never saw her again. That's why I was so happy about Nenonene. A true African leader. A gentleman. Oh, he's not perfect, but . . ." She twirled completely around, as if looking for the way to go. "I've got to get to bed, Theodore. I took a sleeping pill. That thing with Nenonene and the colonel didn't bother me, oh no. He had to do it. I know Africa." With this she hurried up her stairs, leaving Tuuro awkward at the door.

"Goodnight, then," he called, hand on the doorknob, thinking it wasn't even evening, but before he closed the door behind him he heard her call his name. No. What she thought was his name: Theodore.

She wanted him upstairs. He imagined, as he trudged up the steps, that she needed him to reach something. But when he arrived he saw that what she wanted was trickier. She was standing in the center of her bedroom, her big white nightgown twisted and tangled around her, her skinny upper arms quivering and her face deformed by tears. Black streaks from her mascara ran down her cheeks and branched in her skin's crevices. A slick of wetness shone between her nose and her upper lip. Tuuro was stricken by the bald grief of her. "Chelsea," he said, wrapping his arms around her, feeling her face burrow into his shoulder. "Theodore," she kept repeating, "Theodore."

She was gripping him less tightly now, the sleeping pill kicking in. Tuuro wanted to get her into bed, but he wasn't sure how to do this in a dignified way. He tried moving her toward an armchair, thinking he could sit her down. But Chelsea's eyes closed and she became unbendable, and he ended up sitting down and pulling her on top of him, her fluffy hair right under Tuuro's nose. Her body relaxed into him. "Oh, oh, oh," she sobbed, tucking her head under Tuuro's chin, and although he'd pictured himself holding a woman in comfort, this was not how he'd imagined it, but to his surprise this was fine. Her pink scalp smelled clean, her thin hair was surprisingly wiry, and her head on his chest was a human head and an expression, Tuuro realized, of trust. He was right, he could sustain a person.

"You're so strong," Chelsea whispered.

"Now, now." Tuuro freed a hand to stroke her hair. She stayed on his lap until her head lolled and her breaths were deep and even, and Tuuro, barely able to stand, moved her from his body to her bed.

"Goodnight, little lady," Tuuro said, and he reminded himself of the night ages before (could it have only been last summer?) he had put Nenonene's grandson to bed in the earth. Would that this bed for Chelsea turned out better. Tuuro touched his fingers to his lips and kissed them, touched Chelsea's forehead, then headed for the steps, leaving Chelsea's bedroom door ajar. He sat in the living room for an hour or so, checking on Chelsea once before he fell asleep on the sofa. He awoke about midnight, checked her again (she had rolled over, which pleased him), then walked back to his own place, the apartment Nenonene paid for.

—*I DO AND do and do for you, and what thanks do I get?*

—*I might as well sleep with a dog.*

—*Has Georgie called yet?* (Georgie was their son.) *Did you remind him about my birthday?*

—*Didn't you hear me, you fat pig? Not today!*

Sharis, in desperation, had started running George and Gentia's loops with only sound, and in doing so she noticed a strange thing. Their comments often referred to arguments that had started years before. It was enough to make Sharis never want to argue.

George and Gentia exhausted her, but they were income, as well as one of the only households left in their neighborhood. On Custard Lane only two other houses appeared to be occupied. Abba had reported a woman peeking out of one; the other had a shrinking woodpile and a grill Chad and Sharis had seen smoking. But these weren't people they knew.

Sharis tried editing a week of George and Gentia cutting out the images entirely, running only words. She hesitated to send it, thinking it was the spookiest loop she'd ever made, but in the end she pushed the button that messaged it on.

"YOU MUST MISS a woman," Chelsea said, smiling over the rim of her teacup, and then, acknowledging Tuuro's surprise: "Being all alone here in Cleveland, a young and attractive man like you."

"Yes, ma'am," Tuuro said. They were sitting in her living room after dinner, in their customary chairs.

Chelsea smiled. She lifted her chin and turned her head as if she were a modeling a hat. "I'm keeping my eyes open for you," she said.

"Thank you."

"Not that they're very *sharp* eyes."

They sat in silence for a moment before she set down her teacup. "Of course, an old woman gets lonely, too."

"I'm sure she does."

"Not for sex, exactly. For the *holding*."

"I held you last week," Tuuro heard himself blurt, thinking of his putting her to bed.

"Exactly." She looked away. "Maybe I liked it."

Tuuro looked into his lap. "I thought you were asleep."

"Half asleep. Half asleep can be a memorable time."

He couldn't believe he was being seduced by an old lady with blue-white hair and skin the color of a peeled banana. On the other hand, he liked her. He liked holding her. She had made him for that instant—for all instants, really, since he'd met her—a real person.

"You must be very close to Africa," she said. "You have that dignity. You have that beautiful black skin."

"My aunt used to tell me I was Zulu," Tuuro said.

"I thought so."

Chelsea stood up. "Come upstairs with me," she said, her voice almost coquettish, and Tuuro to his shock felt a familiar stirring in his groin. He rose, maybe too eagerly. "For *holding*," she said.

Upstairs, she took off her clothes. She was indeed white, her breasts hanging, her belly round and drooping under a net of veins. Between her legs she was bare as a child. "Now you," she said. Tuuro took off his clothes slowly, meticulously folding each item and laying it on the back of her armchair. He didn't feel shy. When he was fully naked Chelsea looked him up and down. "You make me glad to be alive," she said. Tuuro's penis was a great streaming flag, parallel to the floor. They embraced. "Just *holding*," Chelsea repeated, angling her hips away from his erection, and Tuuro's penis deflated like a popped balloon.

He found, once they were together under the covers, that he was perfectly content to be lying with her, skin to skin, her head tucked on his shoulder, as if she were very small (which she wasn't, she was almost as tall as he was) and he was her protector. He drew his arm around her tighter. He could feel a nerve in it sputtering, a wash of numbness moving up his fingers, but he didn't care, he would never move that arm, he would keep her close to him all night. If someone leaned on you enough to crush a nerve, ah, that was the definition of alive.

How strange this is, he thought when he was half asleep. How strange and what a blessing.

ONE SPRING WHEN Sharis was nine or ten, her grandmother tripped and broke her hip. Sharis remembered visiting her in the hospital, how a weight hung off the bottom of the bed from a cord attached to her grandmother's ankle. "I fell on the green grass!" her grandmother had burst out, and Sharis understood that the adjective made a point, that the greenness of the grass had been astonishing, had contributed in some way to her grandmother's fall.

Sharis noticed the green grass as she walked across her yard. Howard walked beside her, a good foot between her arm and his. Like a silent weight she was dragging beside her. Like a beaten dog that would neither leave her nor return her glance.

Tell me, she wanted to plead. *Something bad happened to me once, and I told Daddy, and you know what? Daddy helped me*. But she was afraid to say that. "What happened to you?" Howard would ask her, a flicker of curiosity or hope in his eyes. She couldn't tell him. She hadn't mentioned it for years, and never in front of her sons. They thought—with everyone else—that her parents and brother had simply died. The Short Time deaths were a cultural phenomenon pervasive enough that no one ever questioned it. "Diphtheria?" someone might ask, wincing—and the shadow on Sharis's face was the only answer they needed.

Of course, that day when she and the boys walked to the troll bridge and ran into the woman with the baby, Sharis had told her sons that her brother had drunk poison. She hoped that they'd forgotten that. Or, more likely, that they were afraid to ask questions about it.

One hundred miles north of Dayton—just west of I-75, the highway their vehicles had taken south—the Alliance troops, fortified by the Gridians, had set up camp and were sitting. Sitting. Every day there were rumors—on the media, on messages, at the grocery store and the police station—and every day nothing happened, apart from the U.S. satellite surveillance and the Alliance troops busying themselves with whatever they were busy with, and President Baxter saying any further movement would be provocative and Baxter's political opponents shouting what was he waiting for?

A terrible time, really. The daffodils had faded and the tulips were starting to bloom—all the fruits of her fall labor—but it was a month too early to plant for the summer (the frost date was May 15) and Sharis felt useless. The parsnips and cabbages she'd buried were gone and she'd used her frozen beans and canned applesauce and they were down to bread she made and occasional ham and endless dinners of pasta with tomato sauce. Basically no fresh food. There was a cluster of May apples in a small wood behind their across-the-street neighbors. Sharis had heard that mushrooms were often found where May apples grow, but when she looked for mushrooms, she found nothing. She sat in the woods at the end of Custard Lane with her rear cold from the wet ground and hair sticking to her sweaty forehead. Harold sat beside her. What was she thinking? She would never cook a mushroom even if she found one, because she didn't know the ones that were safe to eat.

"Come on, Howard," she said, pushing herself up. Howard remained on the ground with his head down, stirring the dirt with a stick. "Howard?" Chad was off making his daily rounds to the grocery story and police station, walking as usual to save on fuel. Abba and Leon were huddled together watching TV.

"Howard," Sharis said again. She hadn't taken him back to the counselor, afraid of what the man might suggest.

"You know what I think, Howard?" Sharis dropped to her knees beside him, and the slight wobble in his poking was the only indication that he'd heard her. "You're perfectly safe now, Howard, because you're with us. Those Taconoutes are crazy, Howard. They're bad people. So whatever they did to you I think you should wall it up. Just get some rocks and mortar and cover it over. It's like . . . burying weeds. You know, when they're too stubborn to pull out. You pile stones and dirt over them. Maybe that's not perfect but it works. I know. That's what I did."

Sort of. Because she'd had Chad to listen to her, to tell her she was Jacob with the coat of many colors, saved for something greater later on. And her mother had been Benjamin, Jacob's relative who had angled to insure Jacob's survival. Even if none of that was true, it had been useful to believe it. Sharis still halfway believed it. She owed Chad, really. For better or worse. Although this morning he'd barely lifted his head off the pillow when she told him she and Howard were going out.

She should push Chad for another recorded episode of his Dayton course.

Howard looked over at her.

"You might as well be practical," she said. "I shouldn't have let you go with the Webelos. I was trying to give you something extra, but no one needs extra right now. Extra's dangerous. George and Gentia could get killed for their extra, not that it even makes them happy. And your father, he's a good man, but he can't get over that these days there's not extra. He feels cheated. Leon's okay because he doesn't expect much. He's like a squirrel, he runs up a tree if there's trouble. But you and me, Howard, we think. And we've got to decide, both of us, to cover up the weeds and keep going. We have a lot of power, you and me. We get to make the choice."

Howard was silent when Sharis had finished, and her head throbbed with worry. "You know I don't have a family," she said. "My parents and my brother killed themselves when the troops came for the Gridding. They would have been fine, but they got scared about what would happen and they drank poison."

Howard's gaze flicked her way. "Did your brother know he was drinking poison?"

Sharis shook her head. "No. He was little."

"Did you drink poison?"

"No. I ran away."

"Good." A brief light appeared in Howard's eye.

"My mother helped me. My mother didn't want me to die. And I'm the same. I want you to live," she said. "Whatever happens."

"Okay." Howard stood up. "Me, too."

Sharis stood up, too, and reached for Howard's hand. He let her take it. They walked back toward their house, Howard's chubby fingers flaccid in her strong ones, and Sharis was afraid to speak or even look at him. After several minutes they reached their driveway. The tulips on each side of the asphalt had opened, their red heads jarring Sharis with their violent brightness. Oh, God, she thought, I should have planted white ones.

"The tulips are pretty," Howard said.

identity, mistaken

"**SHE THINKS YOU'RE** my handyman," Chelsea giggled as they walked down the street. Tuuro, a bucket in one hand and a sack of groceries in the other, had a second of unease. He straightened his back, tried to walk like Nenonene—but perhaps that would remind people of a handyman more.

But that was only one moment—a mere instant, easily erasable—among hours of comfort and happiness, of eating fried chicken and egg pie at Chelsea's kitchen table; of lifting her chipped red teakettle, which didn't whistle so much as moan, off the burner; of sitting in his chair in her living room watching the war on her small TV. Nights she asked him, Tuuro stayed. "Oh," Chelsea might frown, "I hope they don't hurt your Dayton!"—because it looked as if someone might, the Alliance-Gridians in trying to take it or the U.S. in defending it. There was even a rumor—which got a lot of play on the CAVE Network, which they watched only for minutes at a time because of Chelsea's fear of its rude language—that the U.S. was considering evacuating Dayton's citizens and destroying the city, including the Consort plant, so determined were they that the Alliance not seize anything useful.

"It's the Gridians that make the U.S. really crazy," Chelsea said, reaching for one of Tuuro's cookies.

"They feel betrayed," Tuuro said, thinking how, up here in Cleveland, sheltered under the wing of the Alliance, it was easy to refer to his fellow citizens as "they." "Their own creation has turned against them."

"Exactly!" Chelsea beamed. Tuuro felt his face warm. It was so like sitting with Aunt Stella, before she rose up and rejected him, and the only thing missing was that fractured sense, the pull between Aunt Stella and his great-aunt and his grandmother. In this room there were only Tuuro and Chelsea. He had no one to please but her. Many nights she talked of her memories of Uganda, the people walking with bunches of vegetables or jugs of water on their head. "Their balance! The strength of their necks and backs! You don't see that in the descendants here. What do you think happened, Theodore? Do you think there's something toxic in America to an African's genes?"

"You're highly intelligent, Theodore," she said once. "My mother used to say that: In terms of practical thought, no one, no one, no one can beat an African."

Was there something belittling in that repetition? Tuuro played her words back in his mind. No one, no one, no one. Yes. No. Maybe, but Tuuro didn't care.

"HOW WERE SERVICES?" Chad asked George.

"Lovely," Gentia gushed. "But only about fifty people. I don't understand it. There have to be more Catholics left in Kettering." Sharis and Chad and George and Gentia were seated on lawn chairs outside: Gentia had made an Easter egg hunt for Howard and Leon. Abba was in a chair beside the group, asleep.

Leon, plastic eggs dropping from the sides of his basket, was tearing off to a distant tree. Howard was moving more slowly. He picked up, one by one, the eggs that Leon had dropped.

Perhaps George and Gentia, Chad thought, with their distant children, wanted to pretend his family was their own. "How's business?" Chad asked, addressing George.

"Could be better," Gentia said. "We're not getting what we expected from our darker clients." Chad winced. "We billed for a lot of those units. We set up automatic monthly deductions. But people are emptying their bank accounts. I'd be happy with cash, but I'm not going west of I-75 anymore to get it. People are desperate." Gentia made a face. "Not attractive."

I bet not, Chad thought. The luckiest citizens of Dayton were the south suburbanites like them. Even now the sheriff's car made a trip down their lane once a day. Squatters were heading south from northern Dayton, the grocery store manager had warned Chad, but so far no squatters had arrived.

In the back of George and Gentia's yard Howard picked up speed; he swooped and lifted something with both hands. "Is that an egg?" Chad gasped, for a fleeting second thinking it was something terrible, a bomb or a grenade. Abba opened her eyes.

"Esther Price," George said, naming the local chocolate company, and later Chad would realize those were the only words George spoke all afternoon.

"But it's cheaper to live now, don't you think?" Sharis was saying to Gentia. "I mean, there's nothing to buy but food and fuel."

"Our fixed expenses are fixed," Gentia sighed. "But we're looking into other income. That reminds me, dear, your edits are wonderful, but I think we're too boring for every week."

She's firing me, Sharis thought. Because I sent her the loop without images. Because I said we could live more cheaply. "We got one loop without *us* on it," Gentia said. "What happened there?"

"It was an experiment," Sharis said quickly, avoiding looking at Gentia's unhappy face. "You don't have to pay for it. I could do every other week for 50 percent," she suggested, hating herself for being such a suck-up.

"Perfect. And you know that camera in the living room? It's acting up." This was true: lately, Sharis had noticed whole days without input from that station. "I'll pull it down. We're never in there anyway." Gentia frowned, looked across the lawn. "What is wrong with that large son of yours? After the big egg he's not going to look for more? He's going to just sit?"

Sharis didn't answer. Gentia knew perfectly well that Howard had been one of the Webelos.

"I hate those Taconoutes," Gentia said. "They should take people like that and shoot their heads off."

Shoot their heads off? Had Howard seen something like that?

"I hope not," Abba said from her chair. "Not much point."

"They're kids," Sharis said. "The media says they're troubled children their parents shipped away. They're thirteen or fourteen years old." She thought how she'd been that age during the Gridding, but she had never been a youth that anyone would call disturbed.

Leon was standing in front of them. "It's not fair. How come Howard gets the big egg?"

"There's a big egg for everyone, honey," Gentia said. Her voice was unusually harsh, almost glittering; Sharis pictured gemstones spitting from her mouth. "But sometimes you have to look hard."

GRADY WENT RUNNING down the hall, into the locker room, and his copilot was already there, half dressed, reaching to pull up the back of his flight suit. "They found 'em," Grady burst out. "Up in this suburb just south of the Grid. They have this underground bunker that opens out under a tree. It's less than a mile from the air force base, can you believe it? And they'd flown over it fifty times, but this time they were lucky, people had the top of it open for some reason. The FBI's going in. They're Gridians, definitely. They're not Americans."

"What about you?" the copilot said, and Grady, really looking at him for the first time today, was struck by the tension in his copilot's shoulders, by his stare so intense an electrical current seemed to jump between his eyeballs.

"What?"

"I said, what about you?" The copilot straightened. "I mean, aren't you like a grown-up Taconoute, too?"

Grady was stunned. Later, it would seem that all that came after was no more than the comet's tail of this moment. "Me?" he squeaked. "You think I'm that kind of person?"

"WHAT?" JANIE SAID, sitting up suddenly on her bed, pressing the "home" button on her perc.

"Aren't you fixing supper? I got the stuff for pigs in blankets." Janie cooked for them: spaghetti, tuna noodle casserole, soy-meat stroganoff. She had dug out an old cookbook and she loved it.

"I forgot. I'm sorry."

Lila's gaze lingered on the default image on holo-screen. "What were you looking at? Mesclun?"

Janie reddened. "I don't want to tell you." She hesitated, sucked her lips in so they disappeared. "Okay, I'll tell you. Boys."

"Boys?" Lila gripped the doorframe with the both hands, the bottle making a clunk against the wood. It was funny, really. Boys. She knew she should say something, but she couldn't think what. So hard to know what the truth was anymore. Rape. Ugly word, but it had only been that sewing machine needle. Maybe her rapist's penis was tiny, so tiny it fueled him to rape more. She had no idea. Lila's brain seemed overloaded, a warehouse in disarray, essential items tossed in recesses with party favors and plastic flowers. She couldn't find the main thing she was looking for; no, she'd forgotten what the main thing was.

Janie said, "I'm messaging to one. A boy." First Janie used her finger to twist a strand of hair, then, as Lila watched, she was twisting everything: her knees, her elbows, her ankles, her wrists, everything was twisting in.

"What's his name?" Lila said, and Janie's sudden stillness brought back to Lila those days when saying a name was freighted, when uttering "Debbie" or "Serena" or "Linda" seemed like both an incantation and a claim.

Even, not so long ago, "Michelle."

"Alan," Janie said, She stayed still another moment, as if the name were lying on the air. "Alan," she repeated, louder. "He lives in South Carolina." Then the twisting resumed.

"I'll fix dinner tonight," Lila said, swirling away, the brandy in her bottle making its reassuring slosh. She could open up two soup cans and cut up hot dogs. That she could do.

"IT'S OKAY, HOWARD," Chad said. "They're dead. All of the men who attacked you are dead."

The men. The oldest was only twenty—he was called the Havoc Handler, while the younger people were called the Taconoute Havoc Squad. There were many other Havoc Squads, some of whom had not yet been released from their Esslandian home. Chad could only hope that Howard would never have to testify.

"Well, thank God," said Abba. "Don't need those people messing up the world."

Sharis looked toward Howard, who looked ready to cry. "So they were really Gridian kids?" Howard asked.

"The Grid delinquents," Chad said. He gestured to Sharis to lean over, brought his mouth close to her ear. "One was a girl," he whispered.

"They weren't all bad," Howard said, his voice quivering. "Really, they weren't all bad!"

"Are you crazy?" Leon scoffed. "Don't tell me you feel sorry for them!" This only made Howard cry more. Sharis reached for Howard but he shook her off. "Stones," she said. "Wall it up."

"They weren't all bad!" Howard repeated.

GRADY, OF HIS own volition, made an appointment with a psychiatrist. "Why do I seem like something I'm not?" he burst out. "What's wrong with me?" There, he thought, sinking back into his seat. Those are the questions.

"A thinker, eh?" the psychiatrist said.

Grady had always had certain facilities—handling an aircraft was as easy for him as kicking a soccer ball or playing an visu-game—but this was a new sort of challenge, one that required a purposeful concentration. The copilot, who knew him as well as anyone, had believed he could be a crazy, brutal person. The worst shock in Grady's life. The worst pain in Grady's life. His copilot might be checking the indicators, half hidden by his helmet, and Grady would glance at his profile almost shyly, wondering if he had the slightest idea how he'd hurt him. This notion brought the Grady to a deeper grief, that somehow he himself was not quite human, being capable of evoking such suspicion.

FOR THE FIRST day in a month, Chad didn't go to the police station. He did the Wright brothers again, because Howard liked them. Two days later he did Inventions of Dayton, including Freon and the folding ladder and the pop-top can. For Abba's sake he touched on retailing.

"Can a store elevate a community?" he asked. He talked about Rike's Department Store, founded in 1853 as a dry-goods shop and growing through three buildings and three generations of male Rikes into a million-square-foot downtown institution. Escalators, high-speed elevators, the Thanksgiving Day toy parade: what more could a city ask for? The original Rike shocked Dayton by hiring, in the 1870s, a female as a clerk. His son could be found, after the Great Flood, in his store with boots on, cleaning out mud. In 1954 the original Rike's grandson was presented a "Retailer of the Year" award by no less than J. C. Penney. People got dressed up to go to Rike's. Forty years after the store's passing (it became a division of a chain of stores in 1959, and quickly lost its distinction), former salesclerks still straightened their aging bones and lifted their chins when reminiscing about their departments.

Howard's eyelids were sinking. Abba looked tired, too. When Howard's eyes closed Chad decided to go press on with it. "But what does it mean when an institution excludes a whole segment of the community?"

"You mean blacks," Abba said.

"Melanos?" Howard said, his eyes flying open. "They didn't like Melanos?"

Damn, Chad thought.

"OH, BOY," SAID the tech with the pinched face, adjusting the transducer on Diana's belly. They were the only two people in the building; when Diana arrived the waiting room was dark. "It's a goner."

Goner? The tech was allowed to say that in a doctor's office? Even in an empty doctor's office in a dying city? Diana had been bleeding two days and didn't hold out much hope, but the shock of the tech's words sent a squeezing pain through her pelvis. She pictured Charles's sweet dead body, her fingers gently touching its wounds. *My hero.* "Are you sure?"

"Sorry," the tech said. "Wait a minute, you're not attached, are you?" The tech's face lit up. "Doc got in some great sperm last week."

But Diana wasn't listening. Diana wanted, suddenly, only *him*—the specialist, with his cheerful sharp face and uncontrollable eyebrows. He would listen. He would do what she wanted. "I'll probably do it somewhere else," she mumbled. "I have sperm." And then, because it seemed almost dangerous to offend this tech, she added: "I'll get it done somewhere outside Dayton."

"How do you plan to get to somewhere outside Dayton? Have you heard of anyone leaving Dayton?"

"I'll find a way." She pushed herself upright.

"Muchos dolares," the tech said, rubbing her fingers together. "Or maybe . . ." She thrust out her pelvis several times. "But you're in no shape for that."

CHAD WOKE UP. Sunlight pooled on the bedroom floor. Birds were chittering; outside tender leaves unfurled. Beside him the sheet was draped over Sharis's naked shoulder. Some petals of the tulips in the yard were hinged and hanging, giving the blossoms a wanton, iris look. Chad stood up, put his nose to the glass. Every blade of grass stood erect as a soldier. Across the street the roofs and the antennae patched so sharp against the sky they looked as if they'd score his eyeballs. Painfully beautiful, he thought.

The whole human population of Ohio could be wiped out and the state would be none the worse. The highway seams would fill with grasses. Roofs would cave in; rabbits and rats would make their homes in indentations humans had called basements. Poison ivy would vine over foundations. Even the Grid, that apotheosis of man's power over the earth: would it be any less fertile if it weren't plowed? Less green? Maybe it would be more green, the bodies of the fallen Gridians life-cycled into grasses and trees.

"I'll stay down here with the boys," Abba had said an hour before. "You two have some time to yourself." Leon and Howard had fallen asleep on the family room floor as Chad delivered his talk on the birth of the baseball team, the Dayton Dragons.

"She's our marital aid," Sharis had said of Abba when they got upstairs.

"I don't need an aid," Chad answered.

Now, Chad looked down to the hairs sprouting from his belly. He thought of his family: Howard's bad breath, the long scratch on Leon's leg, Abba's whole failing and wrinkled body. Only Sharis was anywhere near physical perfection. Damn humans, Chad thought, smiling.

A timid knock at the bedroom door. Chad pulled his pants on and answered. It was Abba, a strand of her hair poking straight out above one ear. "Chad? The boys are starting to stir down there. And I hate to bother you, but I'm counting out my pills, and it looks like next week I'll need everything."

"Next week?"

"Thursday. Everything. Chad"—a big smile—"I've watched it twice, and your class is wonderful." So far, he'd ended every talk with something upbeat. Even Rike's Department Store: at the end they'd seen the problem, and they'd tried.

Pills were becoming difficult. "No sweat," Chad said.

The next morning he suggested a treat, a family drive to go get Abba's pills. Excited, everyone took their usual seats in the car, but as they drove down the streets of their suburb the adults knew they'd made a mistake. The broken windows and roof tiles were sad enough; worse was the sheer overabundance of the natural world, its encroachment, its *invasion*. As if their city were a plate of food and the plants were swarming over it like ants. In some yards weeds reached up to the windowsills; from the sides of the road grass nipped at the tires. The previous fall the public spaces—the sidewalks and yards in front of the strip malls and office buildings—had been kept up, but now these areas were as overwhelmed as the yards. The honeysuckles, even in late April, were already thick enough to hide snipers or a whole squadron of Alliance soldiers.

Abba's pharmacy was closed. It wasn't clear when or if it would reopen. There were goods on the shelves inside and no message on the door, but at almost noon the place should be open. They drove home.

"That's okay," Abba said. "Those pills just made me sick."

ON A SUNDAY afternoon, on a fresh spring day, Tuuro wrapped a few warm cookies in a napkin and walked the steps to Chelsea's house. He rang the bell his customary three short rings. The door cracked open and a sliver of face appeared. "Get out of here," Chelsea growled.

He thought it was a joke. "Chelsea?" he said. "Is Chelsea in a bad mood today?"

"Get out of here!" she said, opening the door two inches more. "I don't even know you. I don't know you! You took advantage of my eyes."

One of the neighbors? The chubby woman one street over that Chelsea said Tuuro had "supplanted" as her favorite young person?

"Chelsea. It's me. It's Theodore." Maybe she had had a stroke. He reached to touch her arm.

She backed away. "Theodore," she spit, her voice hateful. "That's not even your name. You have a stupid other name. A lying, cheating, ugly, stupid name!" Her lips tightened. "That Akira woman told me."

Akira. Tuuro's fist clenched and the cookies crumbled. "Why do you believe her? You don't even know her. She's just a woman who works for Nenonene . . ."

"*General* Nenonene," Chelsea's eyes narrowed. "She said you didn't treat him with respect. She said you didn't have gratitude. Oh, I saw you on TV! And you know what? I hated that man. And that man was you! I can't help it I can't see. I can't help it all you people look . . ."

Tuuro pushed the door open, grabbed her elbow. "Why do you believe a general who murders instead of me?" He recognized that he sounded like someone frightful. "I loved that boy! I looked after that boy!"

"Let go of me, you're not African! I spit on you, I spit on you." Chelsea's lips closed. She made a weak attempt at a spit.

And there was Dakwon walking upside down, down a stairwell, around a corner, across a driveway slippery with leaves, over small sharp stones that cut his hands. The will it took. The strength it took.

Tuuro, exhausted, let her go. "I'm your friend. I brought you cookies." He gestured at the pile of crumbs on the floor.

"That's what bad man does, makes an innocent person fall for their tricks. And I did that, didn't I? I fell right down into your rabbit hole. Does that make you feel clever?"

He could cry. "I'm me, Chelsea," he pleaded.

"There's nothing about you that's decent!" Chelsea said. "There's nothing about you that's African. You're nothing to me, do you hear me? You're *nothing!*" And then, chokingly (because there were his hands on her neck, and he didn't want to rape her, no, rape was not one brushstroke in this picture), "What are you going to do now, rape me, too?"

Insanity is the fall:

migrations, implantation

"I NEED TO get back to Dayton," Tuuro said when Akira arrived. She came in through the back door, into the kitchen, where Tuuro kept his TV on the table and where he spent most of his day.

"Dayton! Why would anyone want to go to Dayton? I have people there, and you know what? Everybody in Dayton is living in a basement. So much stealing and looting and shooting people moving downstairs like a cave. You don't like Cleveland?"

Tuuro glanced out the window over the sink. "It's cold here."

"What do you mean it's cold here? We keep it sixty-three. You never turned your heat past sixty back in Dayton." Akira gave him a crafty smile. "Yes, I know that. I know all sorts of things. I know you've been consorting with an old blind white woman. What do you expect when you do something like that? Grief and pain." Tuuro turned away, busied himself with the dishes in his sink. "Grief and pain," Akira repeated.

If Akira hadn't told Chelsea who he was, Theodore would be sitting in Chelsea's living room at this instant, reading out loud from one of her English detective books about church bells and dogs. Instead he had strangled Chelsea, then carried her body upstairs into her bedroom and taken off her daytime clothes, including her underwear. He put her in her pale purple nightgown. "Such a cheerful color, lilac, don't you think?" she'd said to him on a better day, and he'd quoted a poem he'd made up in his childhood:

> *Peonies are sure to please*
> *and lilacs are always nice*
> *Spring makes me happy to my bones*
> *when the world breaks out in spice*

"That says it just about all," his great-aunt had said.

"What do you mean, breaks out in spice?" Aunt Stella asked. "That to me is unclear use of language. But the first three lines are lovely."

"Isn't a peony the flower that ants like?" Chelsea had asked.

"Yes, indeed," Tuuro (Theodore) answered. "And the flower needs the ants because they eat the coating around the bud so the flower can open."

"Amazing," Chelsea had said, smiling shyly across her kitchen table. "How one thing helps another."

After she was dead, Tuuro combed Chelsea's hair, touched up her lips with lipstick, laid her on her back in her bed, and pulled up the covers. He touched her cheek, already cool. "Good-bye, little woman," he wanted to say, but the words stuck in his throat. How dare he bid her good-bye? It seemed impossible—inhumane—that he could kill a person and then gaze on that person with tenderness. How could God let Tuuro end up in these terrible situations? He thought of the dog loping down the street dragging the torn scarf. At least Chelsea was inside and protected. It would be days before someone found her. Those bruises on her neck . . . Tuuro was seized with the fluttering thought—doomed? naive?—that they would fade.

"Could you please talk to General Nenonene?" he said, turning to Akira, his mouth dry. "Ask if maybe I could go

through Esslandia"—he made a point of using the new name—
"and get back to Dayton?"

"You are something," Akira said. "You have the conscience
of an insect. Don't you think we know you very well?" She stood
up, wandered to the back door. "Know exactly what you did?"

The door opened, and immediately there were a dozen
uniformed people in the room, men and women of all shades,
with guns out and hard faces. Tuuro put his hands up, knowing that his shock was giving them pleasure.

Wait a minute, he thought, *if I drop my hands they'll
shoot me.* The action was suddenly clear to him, best for
everyone involved.

He dropped his hands. The room was silent. What? He
glanced around wildly, then grabbed for one of the guns.
Contain him! someone shouted, and there were arms around
Tuuro from all sides, a human vise so strong he felt as if his
eyes would pop. But no shots. This was a disciplined crew.

"IT'S NOT CHEAP," Gentia said. They were sitting in a living
room, Janie on the leather sofa and Gentia in a floral upholstered chair. "Do you have resources?"

"You mean money? Not really." Janie had been through
every drawer and closet at Lila's and come up with absolutely
nothing. Janie wouldn't stoop to stealing from Aunt Lila's wallet, although it was unlikely Aunt Lila would notice. In last
week's recycling bin there had been six empty brandy bottles.
If Janie didn't remind her with a written list, Aunt Lila would
go out shopping and come home without food.

"There are some alternative payments." Gentia shrugged
her eyebrows concedingly. "How old are you?"

"Fourteen." Janie was twelve.

"Good enough. Thirteen's kind of my limit, although I
can't say the men care. You on birth control?"

Janie, eyes widening, shook her head no. She had heard
this woman was a sort of travel agent: she found ways to get

people where they wanted to go. A whole network, Janie's perc contract had said. Everyone was in on it: police, the military, judges, politicians.

"That's okay, we'll have him wear protection. Listen, you know what a young girl's got that's better than money?" Gentia tilted her head and looked at Janie sidelong, a nasty glint in her eyes. Janie flushed and looked away. "That's right, *you* know. We got guys like it better than anything. All the stress these days . . . It's a relief to them."

"You want me to have sex with people?" Janie squeaked. She thought of leaving this house and running home. But she had no home. Her father was living on the military base and Aunt Lila slept with a bottle and didn't even know when Janie was awake and on her perc at two in the morning.

"Not people!" Gentia looked shocked. "Just one gentleman. I got an army guy who can really help you. You're lucky, dollface. I couldn't buy my way out of a paper bag with pussy. But you can go anywhere."

"OH, GOD," SHARIS said, resting her forehead in her hand. In front of her on the editon scenes were playing in hypertime.

"George and Gentia?" Chad said. Sharis nodded. "How're the Schneiders?"

"Oh, Kevin had sinusitis, so that was a crisis, but he's better now, and the grandmother's in one of her crying moods, and Lenny has some investments in South America they're nervous about . . ." Sharis sighed, looked at the screen again. George was sitting soddenly in the kitchen; Gentia bustled behind him, heading offscreen toward the living room. "I'm sure Gentia would have fired me on Easter if we weren't her neighbors."

"Sharis?" Chad said softly, patting his knees. Sharis stood and walked to him, sat down, curled up her knees and leaned her head against his chest. A child's pose, she knew, but she never recalled doing this with her father. "What're you going to do next?" she said.

Chad loved her heavy head, the hot smell of her hair. "I think I'll do the park system. I love the park system." The land had been largely donated: generosity, civic-mindedness.

Sharis nodded. "You support us, honey," Chad said. "You do everything. I don't tell you enough how I'm grateful."

She didn't make a sound, and her head was still down, so Chad was at first confused when he felt wetness on his chest. She was crying.

"JANIE!"

Up the condo stairs. A knock on the guestroom door. "Janie, are you awake yet? I've got breakfast, French toast and eggs." A new day. This brandy swilling had to stop. The last thing the world needed was another lesbo lush.

Lila pushed open the door, a shaft of light spilling into the dark cube of the room. Empty.

Later, she would think: how stupid could I be? How did I miss it? But she knew exactly how she missed it. Within the hour she was missing it again.

"SO," GENERAL NENONENE said. "We forgive you, we set you up in a happy life, we feed you, we make everything perfect, and now this."

"I didn't ask for anything."

"She was kind to you, I heard. Kind. Is that how you repay kindness?" Nenonene scratched the back of his scalp with one finger.

Tuuro replayed—again—his last moments with Chelsea. He shook his head. "She said I was nothing to her. And I . . ." he stopped himself. *I wanted to be so much,* he thought.

Nenonene laughed, a low rumble that spread out from his chest like an earthquake. "You don't think I've heard such insults? You don't think such words have been"—*bean,* he said, very British—"aimed at me? But, you! You are nothing." He spoke into an intercom, and a heavyset man appeared in the office, the rawhide-skinned man that had sat with them at Al-lyssa's dining room table, the night Tuuro first met Nenonene.

Nenonene stood to leave. He cast Tuuro a quick look and snapped his middle finger against his thumb, as if he were flicking off a fly.

The functionary sighed. He sat down behind the desk and slipped an unusually thin perc from his pants pocket. He ran through holo-screen after holo-screen, intermittently tapping the perc's face with his finger. He never looked at Tuuro. At some point Tuuro lifted his hand to scratch his nose. "Don't move," the man said.

"Give me your ID card," the man ordered a moment later, holding out his hand.

I made her nothing, Tuuro realized. The irony of it made his scalp twitch. She called me nothing so I made her nothing, while here I am still alive, a general breaking his schedule to talk to me, a man making taps on his perc on my behalf. He saw again the horror of what he'd done. I should kill myself, he thought, and then: no, I should stay alive. Because the alive is the punishment.

"Okay," the man said, feeding Tuuro's ID card into a slot at the side of his perc. "You're erased."

"I should go back to my apartment?" Tuuro asked, confused.

"Oh, no." The man smiled. "We've erased you." He gave Tuuro a chastising look. "And the apartment was never yours."

Tuuro was aware of his heartbeat. "I don't understand. Where do I go now?"

The man shrugged. "Up to you. As far as we're concerned, you're nobody."

THE CAPTAIN CLOSED his office door. "I need you to help me, but I can help you, too." A captain Grady didn't particularly like, lateral in the chain of command, with a rugged face and a soft middle. During the Gridding, it was rumored, he had lost his temper and broken a private's arm.

"Sir?"

"Look here." The captain beckoned Grady to the window in his door that opened to the office lobby, a window Grady knew was mirrored on the other side. "See?"

In the lobby, a female youngie wearing trousers and a pull-over shirt was sitting on a plastic chair. The youngie looked straight ahead, her right foot tucked up under her left thigh. "She's good," the captain said. "Fourteen. Nice and tight." He pointed at her leg. "Flexible, too."

"That's nice." She looked younger than fourteen, Grady thought. A proto-youngie. A smudged look around her eyes and her chin oddly red. Tainted goods, and not her fault.

"You want her?"

Grady shook his head.

"She'll do anything. You just tell her. She's a *baby*."

"I don't want to sleep with her. Not at all."

"What's wrong with you?" The captain kicked the door; in the waiting room the girl jumped. "When'd you get so fucking righteous?" It would have reassured him, Grady realized, for Grady to go along. Maybe a month before he would have. A month before, when his copilot had believed that Grady had the soul of a Taconoute.

"What do you need me for?" Grady asked, remembering there was a favor, tired of his life. He thought—hopelessly, be-latedly—that he had missed his chance to be a hero: he could have agreed to take the youngie for an hour and set her free. But where would that leave him? With reprimands in his file and a captain looking for trouble.

"Transport," the captain growled. "But let me have an-other night first."

"YOU KNOW," THE specialist said, turning to Diana, holding up the vial like a glass of fine wine, "you've got a nice sample of your friend's tissue here. Are you sure you don't want a clone?"

For a moment she hesitated, thinking of Charles's eyes with their downturned corners, the soft curl of his upper lip. But then she caught herself. "I want a mixture of us," she said. "Just stick an egg and sperm together and implant it." That was what Charles would have wanted, she was sure. A random conception to lure a special soul. Diana ached that Charles was already fading on her; the other day she couldn't get a clear picture of his hands.

Money: that was all it had taken to leave Dayton. She had ridden in the back of a beer truck returning to Cincinnati, slipped inside after its last delivery to Dayton. There was a middlewoman she'd talked to via perc but never met, who apparently got a cut of the bills Diana had slipped to the man in the grocery. From Cincinnati she'd taken a bus to Chattanooga, where the specialist had his practice.

"Why don't I do ten sperm-and-eggs, and we'll implant the best one?"

"No. No thank you. No preselects. I want it like the old days. I want an accident."

Oh, I certainly remember you, the specialist had said. *The rebel.*

"There's a reason they're the old days, Diana," the specialist said, kneading his neck with his right hand. "We've made reproduction so much crisper. There's no need these days to risk the random."

"I was random," Diana pointed out. "You were random."

"TRACE IT? THAT'S a little ambitious. You're forgetting about privacy features. You must think we're miracle workers."

Yes, Lila thought. It's no problem, she'd told Janie's father via perc, I know these old computer broads who can do anything. They can find the boy that Janie was talking to.

Janie's father had been surprisingly calm. "You sure she went to South Carolina?"

"That's where the boy was," Lila said. "I don't think she'd lie to me."

"I'm glad she got out," Janie's father said. "Just find her for me so I know." He's military and he knows something, Lila thought.

The afternoon after Janie disappeared, Lila had smashed her last three bottles, using her finger to dab up a final taste. That evening she went out for a new supply. It took Nelson and Solganik almost a week to get to her house—they had a waiting list, they said—and Lila went through at least a bottle of brandy each day. She forgot about the lemons and the honey.

When Nelson and Solganik arrived, Lila wasn't sure what day it was or how long Janie had been gone. The computer broads' matching shirts today were pale blue. "What I can do is cut into your wall and open the broadband, see if it's set up any central circuits," Nelson said. "If you've got those you know a line's been used pretty frequently. It's an automatic function, part of that whole self-healing package they used to talk about. You've heard of that, haven't you, honey?" Lila looked blank. "What's your department again? Waste disposal?"

"Water," Lila said. "A little more elemental than your line of work."

"I'd say communication's pretty elemental."

Lila left the women fiddling with their wires and went and sat on the edge of Janie's bed, looking out the window at the condo parking lot. A few cars were still there, but many of them hadn't been moved in days. Where were the owners? Had everybody really gone? Lila should go, too. She wondered how Nelson and Solganik moved in and out of Dayton. But how could she ask them without feeling even more foolish? And even if she knew, how could she leave? She had the city's water to look after; more importantly, her condo was the place Janie called home.

Solganik appeared in Janie's doorway. "We've got a surprise for you," she said, looking pleased. "You thought that little girl was talking to South Carolina? That little girl was smart. Remember that sequence Nelson gave you when we were here the last time? When you wanted to get a message to your friend on the Grid?"

"I kept it with me," Lila said. "I stuck it in my bra."

Solganik's face cracked into a smile, and Lila had a surge of panic that she didn't have enough bottles. The store would be closed or the shelves would be empty or . . . "That little girl must have memorized that sequence," said Solganik, "because that little girl was talking to the Grid."

THE IMPLANTATION WORKED. Diana was pregnant again. Diana had already been sure.

"You know you're taking a terrible risk," the specialist said. "I can't continue to treat you without a waiver."

Treat her? Why should she need treatment? A woman pregnant by her lover; what could be more natural?

"I CAN'T TALK to you now," Lila said into her perc. She was in her car.

"You've got to talk to me, Lila," Kennedy said. "I'm going crazy here. Have you ever had desires you can't handle? Desires for, you know, terrible things? You know that female agent of havoc, the one who didn't get killed, the one whose photo they keep showing on the media? I can't stop thinking about her. Lila, I dream about her. *Those* dreams. Isn't that sick? It disturbs me so much I can't stand it. I'm afraid to fall asleep."

Lila said: "She's a teenager!"

"I know, that makes it even worse! What's wrong with me? A woman that young, a killer . . . It's not like I'm trying to think about her, I'm trying *not* to think about her. But there she is when I'm dreaming. And I'm a person who feels guilty even setting a mousetrap. Jesus, what is this dark goo bubbling up inside of me, Lila? What is wrong with me?"

Lila had never heard Kennedy sound frantic. "For crying out loud, Kennedy, what does it matter?" Lila said. "It's just dreams, okay? It's nothing you'd act on." In the last four days, Lila had sent twenty messages about Janie to Allyssa, using the pathway she'd tucked in her bra, and still there was no answer. Polite requests, angry requests, threats—still no information. *Just tell me if she's with you,* Lila begged. *I won't come after her. I ask you in the name of all things human.*

All Lila got back from Allyssa's address, over and over, was the interface: WE ARE ESSLANDIA. WE NEED NOTHING.

Lila had reported Janie's absence to the police, but they didn't have much hope.

Lila said, "I don't mean to be harsh, but right now I'm worried about the kid staying with me who's disappeared, and that's not a dream at all, that's real."

"What kid?"

"I told you already! The relative of that Michelle, my friend from Agro."

"Oh, that's right . . ." Kennedy sounded befuddled.

"I don't care about your stupid dreams!" Lila screamed, tossing her perc to the floor of her car. "Stop bothering me about nothing!"

a very clear window

"WHY DO YOU think I'd know, darling?"

"You know everything!" Lila was fine. One drink sharpened her. It was a matter of balance.

"Well," Ferrescu conceded, "I do." Lila felt a sweep of revulsion that her compliment had worked so easily. She thought back to moments before and her confusion when a man who looked like Ferrescu's elderly uncle had opened the door. "Is Ferrescu . . ." she had started, then realized it was him: " . . . ready for the Queen of Water?"

"I'm always ready for royalty," Ferrescu had said, and led her through his cluttered living room to a chair near the window. She had to dodge a birdcage, filled with women's shoes, hanging in the center of the room.

"Tell me about water," Ferrescu had said, sitting across from her, smiling and closing his eyes.

So she did, and then she went on to her water map, its erasure and reimagining, and then she talked about Janie, and Janie and the computer, ending with the girl's disappearance.

"You're fond of this girl."

"Yes, very."

"But not in any . . ." Ferrescu waved his hand.

"She's like"—a daughter, she started to say, but Ferrescu would find this suspect—"a niece."

Ferrescu nodded approvingly. He tented his fingers in front of his face, his characteristic gesture, and Lila noticed a ring slip. He'd lost weight. "You suspect she's on the Grid, and you suspect me of Grid connections."

"I know she's on the Grid. I finally got through to Allyssa Banks, who I'd met up there, and she finally answered. Not much, and she didn't explicitly tell me Janie was there, but she told me not to worry." Lila shifted in her seat, annoyed that Ferrescu's eyes were still closed. "As for your Grid connections, you tell me. You do seem to know a lot about the place. I remember thinking that at L'Auberge."

"What a lovely restaurant," Ferrescu sighed. "I haven't been there for so long."

"I'll take you there," Lila pounced. "You get me into Esslandia and I'll take you there."

Ferrescu's eyes snapped open. "Food first," he said. "After all"—a laugh—"you might never get back!"

TUURO HAD BEEN on his own for two weeks, sleeping under a hyacinth bush in Chelsea's backyard, when he walked into the Euclid police station and said to the male youngie on duty, "I want to confess to a crime."

"What crime?" The clerk almost rolled his eyes; Tuuro realized people must come here routinely with confessions, hoping for shelter and food.

"Murder."

The clerk hesitated, looked up. "Really?"

"The woman is dead."

The clerk seemed annoyed at this response. He had Tuuro sit down in the lobby, where several women were also waiting. Eventually a woman in a uniform led Tuuro into a warren of offices, where she recorded him and spoke into a perc and screened his iris. Then the woman disappeared, and when she came back she said: "No luck fooling us. You can go home now." She started to walk him out.

"But the woman is dead."

"Of course she's dead, she was over seventy."

"I killed her."

They were at the door to the lobby. The woman hesitated, gave him a searing look. "Disappointed her, maybe. Broke her ancient little heart, maybe. But there's nothing to link you to her death."

"What do you mean? I link me."

The woman's look had narrowed into something frightening. "Who are you? If you know what's good for you, you'll go home to Dayton." She pushed the door open, gestured him out.

He hadn't mentioned Dayton. "Did you talk to Nenonene?" he said, almost shouting as he walked through the door. "Is that it?"

"I'm not at that level," the woman said coldly. "If you can talk to him, go to it." The door swung closed, its lock hissing. The women in the lobby drew together, as if they knew Tuuro's sort.

"YOU KNOW WHAT they were trying to do in Sweden at the peace talks? They were trying to do a Dayton."

Sharis and Howard smiled blandly; Abba frowned and wrinkled her forehead.

"The Dayton Peace Accord. Have you ever heard of it? It made Dayton famous all over the world. 1995. There was a country in central Europe called Yugoslavia that was made by bringing all these little countries together, but then it broke apart and all these countries and religions were fighting and the U.S. brought in major figures from the different groups to Dayton and put them together with negotiators until they hammered out an agreement." Chad smiled at Howard.

"Were there bad guys?" Howard asked.

"Well, yes, actually there were bad guys. I mean, there were people who used hate and fear to inspire people."

"Did they get punished?"

"Yes, as a matter of fact they did get punished. Eventually. At least, some of them. But we're talking about Dayton now, and how all the people with all the arguments came together. So many sides you couldn't keep track of them. They stayed at the air force base in the visiting officers' quarters, not very fancy. They went sometimes to a sports lounge called Packy's. They had a gourmet dinner together one night at a restaurant called L'Auberge, just up Far Hills from us. And you know what impressed them? How in Dayton people from all sorts of different backgrounds lived happily together. I remember reading an article about it when I was a kid, and one of the negotiators said that for him Dayton would always mean peace."

A silence. "Does it still mean peace?" Howard asked.

"Absolutely."

"It's still peaceful there? Yugo . . . the place that was fighting?"

Abba looked quickly at Chad. Even Sharis lifted her eyes to him.

"Yes," Chad said. "Absolutely. Peace peace peace."

Sharis clicked the camera off. "You shouldn't dumb it down," she said.

THE GRID'S FARM guesthouse looked exactly the same. Lila watched Allyssa open the door for her into the kitchen. Above Allyssa was the square-hankie light, and behind her, standing on the brick-patterned linoleum, was Janie.

"How did you get here?" Lila burst out. "I was worried sick about you, I thought you'd gone to South Carolina and then the computer genies figured it out and we couldn't believe you'd remembered all the codes and . . ." Lila trailed off, noticing Janie's stiff posture, her unblinking eyes. "Are you okay?"

"You're a very nice person, but I think I'm better off here." Janie's words ran together: verynice, betteroffhere. "I don't want you to take me away."

"How did you get here? I came up hidden in the back of a truck, because my friend Ferrescu does business with . . ."

"Helicopter," Allyssa's voice cut in. She glanced out the window, latched the door, came to stand at Janie's side facing Lila. "She came in two weeks ago by American helicopter. The pilot took a real chance. I didn't know she was coming, but, my God. I couldn't turn her away." Allyssa draped an arm over Janie's shoulder, and Janie sagged into Allyssa. "We all hate what she had to go through, but she got here. She's safe now." Janie and Allyssa exchanged glances. Lila felt suddenly superfluous, excluded from their circle: an outsider looking at the scene would think Allyssa was Janie's mother.

"What did you have to go through, Janie?" Lila asked, her mouth dry. One drink for acuity, but that was hours ago and now she needed more.

Janie looked down. She clasped her hands together and twisted her wrists.

Allyssa's grip tightened on Janie's shoulder. Janie's hands broke apart and she turned her face into Allyssa's shoulder. The movement pierced Lila's heart. I want that, she thought.

"I'll let you two talk on the porch," Allyssa said, pulling back from Janie and stroking the girl's shoulder. "Okay, honey?" Janie nodded. "Coffee, Lila? Cookies? Janie, I'll get you a glass of Grid juice." The girl headed out of the kitchen.

"I don't know why you risked coming here," Allyssa said in a low voice. "Janie has everything she needs."

"Of course," Lila said. "That's what you say: **We need nothing**. Well, you may need nothing but I'm not so lucky. I needed to see Janie was okay." Lila nodded at the refrigerator. "Do you have beer?" An agricultural product. Something an Esslandian would approve.

Allyssa raised an eyebrow. "Yes," she said, leading Janie and Lila through the dining and living rooms, "I have beer."

Lila and Janie sat on high-backed chairs on the front porch facing west, looking out on brown and freshly planted fields carpeting a small hill just across the road, winter wheat green-yellow in the distance coursing over three separate mounds.

"So," Lila said when Allyssa had left them, "how did you really get here?" anticipating the bright and elusive answer—"Helicopter!"—which was all she got.

"Look, I'm responsible for you," Lila said. "Please don't hide things from me."

"The pilot was nice," Janie said. "We had to land three places to find Allyssa."

Lila nodded impatiently—what did she care about the pilot? "I'm hoping you'll come back with me. That's what your father wants, too."

Janie's eyes widened. "I don't want to go back. America is doomed, it's doomed!"

Lila waited a moment before she spoke. "Is that something you heard up here?" Keeping her voice gentle.

"That's something you hear everywhere! Even the lady at the house where I . . ." Janie stopped herself.

Another pause. "Was there sex involved?" Lila hated the taste of beer, but she was stuck with it. She needed alcohol, in any form.

"What do you mean? How could you think that? Why would I even dream of . . ." It was Janie's agitation that gave her away. Her hands again were clasped and twisting. Lila ached to put an arm around her.

"Oh, Janie." The words had a mournful keen to them that caught both of them off guard. "I'm sorry."

Janie bit her lip. "I didn't mean to scare you. I should have left a note but I . . . I was afraid you'd come get me." Her voice quickened, took on a clamorous assurance. She stopped twisting and straightened in her chair. "I love it here. It's perfect for me."

Ah, Janie. So young, trying so hard to sound sure. "Why?"

"It wasn't just your fault!" Janie burst out.

Lila took a long swig to hide her tearing eyes.

"I mean, you're a nice person," Janie went on. "You can't help it that you have alcoholism. It's a spiritual disease. Allyssa's told me all about it. It's a big problem in America. It's not a problem in Esslandia because Esslandia's a healthy place."

Help me, Lord, Lila thought.

"I mean, Esslandia's better than healthy. It's magical, it's complete. Did you know they break down their urine and use it as fertilizer here? Isn't that char? And they use their bath- and dishwater to irrigate the fields. They use leftover corncobs to make soap. America is so profligate!"

Profligate. Surely not Janie's word. Where had she heard it? Conversations and media sessions? Pamphlets and books? Perhaps all of these and more.

"Like I said, I talked to your father," Lila began, wondering why Janie hadn't responded to her mention of him, "and he . . .

"That's another thing," Janie interrupted. "Kids here don't love only their parents. They have a whole community to love. It's like you! If I hadn't come to stay with you, I wouldn't have known how char you are. And there are thousands of adults up here, and all of them are char like you are, and . . ."

Lila sank into her chair, feeling smaller and less necessary with each comment. Janie's two weeks in Esslandia, as Janie told it, might have been her whole life. The storage sheds with their hay-stuffed insulating walls; Esslandian songs; the special church services that ended with the blessing of the seed. "I didn't even know I liked soy loaf!" Janie said. She mentioned friends: Allyssa, of course, and the village planner Peter, the twins Romulus and Remus, Lenora Elkhart, Biddy Shoop. The more she talked, the more Lila's brain ached, a palimpsest worn to near-transparency by Janie's chatter on top of the coordinates of Lila's trip here, on top of Ferrescu's stories, her own stories, the water map. Out of the corner of Lila's eye she saw a flickering in the darkening sky. It frightened her for a second—her own circuits coming unwired—but it was only lightning, far away.

"Let's turn the porch light off and watch." Janie hopped up in excitement. "I love storms."

The storm was coming from the west, the direction they were facing, and they watched it a good ten minutes, the whole sky periodically seizing in light.

"Your father is going to worry," Lila said.

"They're really careful with their children. I mean, no offense, but a lot of time you didn't even know what I . . ."

A jagged line of lightning cleaved the sky directly in front of them. A chill wind hit Lila's calves. "We should go in," Lila said, and they moved to the living room sofa, Lila on the way noticing the pitcher of beer set on top of the TV. Janie sat at one end of the sofa, Lila at the other. Janie twisted herself around so she could still look out on the storm. "I worry about you," Lila said, reaching for the pitcher.

"Oh, Aunt Lila, you have to understand. Aunt Michelle told me about you when you were younger, remember? You had beliefs, didn't you? You had beliefs?"

Lila chugged down her glass of beer and poured a refill. She turned to face the storm, also. A clap of thunder, finally, and a flash of lightning so close that blades of grass were visible atop the hill across the road. What town was that? Lila thought, and then: this is a very clear window. This thought pleased her, seemed particularly profound. "Is this special glass . . . ?" she asked, reaching out to touch it. Before Janie answered Lila knew the answer: this *was* special glass, designed to abolish reflection and bring the outside in.

Everything. They'd planned everything. What a thrill it must be for the Lindisfarne people, to look out on their perfect and self-contained world. No wonder they were willing to link up with the Alliance to keep it. Lila glanced around the living room, and it was no surprise (although she hadn't until now expected it) to spot Allyssa standing silent sentry in the arched opening to the dining room. The rain started, whipping onto the porch.

My God, Lila thought, Janie will never get out of here. She thought of the sentries she'd passed on the road up, their caps and casual guns. Last summer she had passed no such guards. Janie was on her knees on the sofa, nose pressed to the special glass, and Lila's hand as she reached to touch her shoulder had a distinct tremor. "Janie?" she said, glancing toward Allyssa, and to her surprise her next words were hard to form. "I'm going . . ." To. Have. To. Go. Soon. She'd drunk more than she thought. The truck was coming back to pick her up.

"You're not spending the night? Okey-doke." Janie's face turned from the window. "I'm glad you visited." She gave Lila a quick hug. "Isn't it char here?" she whispered. "Doesn't it make you think of Narnia? And Jeff Germantz was like Aslan."

Aslan the lion? He was the God figure, wasn't he? Lila would have to read the books again. In one way, Lila felt absolutely plastered, as if it was risky to stand. In another way she felt totally lucid, old enough to recognize a dream that couldn't last, old enough to know better. "It's something," she said, batting at Janie's tousled hair. She stood cautiously, then turned to Allyssa, the thunder rumbling behind her, and in that moment she had to remind herself this storm wasn't for her, it wasn't apocalyptic, this was no more than a spring thunderstorm in the Midwest.

She eyed the jug, but with Allyssa watching she didn't dare take more. When she got home she'd have one drink for maintenance.

"You'll be fine," Allyssa said in the kitchen. "Our drivers can get through anything." The truck was already idling in the drive; Lila wondered if it had ever left.

"I'll tell her father she's okay." *Her father she's*—was that right? She didn't used to have trouble speaking. "Can I come back here? Can I see her again?" I'm giving you everything, Lila thought, looking into Allyssa's eyes. Give me this shred.

Allyssa glanced back toward the living room. "That depends on her."

"She's twelve!"

"We trust our children."

Lila turned to the window in disgust. "Why does she like you so much?"

"Lila." Allyssa's voice was soothing. "I was only pregnant once, years ago, and that was a boy-child. I lost him. When Janie showed up here I felt like she was everything I'd been missing. I think she feels that, too."

"Forget it," Lila said. "Just get me out of here." She almost took a fall on the wet outside stairs.

AT THE END of April Tuuro got himself onto the Grid, simply walked out into it from the edge of Cleveland, hitched a ride on an Alliance truck with a driver (South American?) who asked no questions, got off within eyeshot of a village, and walked in the twilight to the edge of town. There he stopped beside a one-story building without windows. The air was dark but thick, like a bath of warm milk, and filled with low-pitched interjections like a leaky hinge. A toad? He was aware of a change in the light, like flickering from a TV screen in a darkened room, and then he realized the flickering came from the far sky. There was no thunder, only flashes that made the sky and clouds, for milliseconds, look like the sky filled with angels in those old-time pictures. Tuuro scrunched his back against the building.

God's fireworks, Tuuro thought. As if God was clearing out his warehouse, tossing out the charges left over from previous storms. It had been a turbulent spring.

Tuuro saw Lanita bending over the plate of eggs he'd made her, felt her small hand hanging on the back of his belt. Lately, he'd noticed, he wasn't thinking about her much: his daughter had become unreal to him, as inconsequential as someone else's child. Was this what happened with other absent fathers? Had this happened to Tuuro's own father? Would I even recognize Lanita now? Tuuro wondered. He told himself it didn't matter. He would never get to Chattanooga, and even if he did, Lanita's mother wouldn't let him near her. How could he argue? *I'm not a . . . I didn't . . .* When in his mind the truth would be drumming: I killed Chelsea, I killed Chelsea.

"I see your guilty face," Naomi would spit. "Don't you think I can see your guilty face?"

He was walking to Allyssa. Of anyone, she'd understand.

A man can get so angry when he feels he isn't heard
A man is not a reptile and he's not a little bird
A man can get so angry you might wish he wasn't heard.

He reached Allyssa's house outside Village 42 one morning in the first week of May, on a day that felt more like November than spring. He splashed his face with water from a drainage ditch and ran his fingers along his eyebrows and teeth before he walked up her pebbled driveway to the kitchen door.

"Why are you here?" Allyssa said, astonished, and Tuuro understood immediately she didn't plan to let him in. He saw above her head the same kitchen light, below her feet the patterned linoleum floor.

He was always at the door. Inside or outside, greeted or reviled. But never ensconced somewhere, never permanent, never at home.

"It's me," he said, thinking it could be possible she didn't recognize him. "It's Tuuro."

"I know it's you." Allyssa cast a quick glance back into the kitchen, then stepped outside. "I don't need you here," she whispered urgently. "I have enough going on."

"I thought I could talk to you," Tuuro said. "I thought I could clean."

"Why aren't you in Cleveland?"

Tuuro for a moment couldn't speak. "You saw what he did to me."

"Yes, I saw. Everybody saw. It was useful. Good publicity."

"It was a lie."

"Sometimes we need to lie, Tuuro." For an instant Allyssa seemed to wince, but just as quickly her face returned to its prior hardness. "A revolution is not a dinner party. Didn't I tell you that already?"

She gave him a sandwich, finally, and let him sit on her stoop to eat while she got more information. It was possible, Tuuro thought, that he heard a voice inside that was not Allyssa's, and when the door opened behind him he turned to see not just Allyssa, but a girl—twelve? thirteen? she had the buds of breasts but no visible hips—almost as tall and beige as Allyssa was. "We're getting in the car," Allyssa hissed. She directed Tuuro to the passenger's side and the girl to the back, not introducing them to each other. "I'll drop you off near Dayton," she told Tuuro. "You're not supposed to exist, you know. I had a heck of a time even finding out that much."

They rode without speaking, the fields vast and brown around them. For some minutes the girl in the back wiggled and sighed, but then the car became silent. Allyssa glanced into the backseat, lifted a finger to her lips, and looked at Tuuro.

"What did you expect from Nenonene, Tuuro?" Allyssa whispered. "He had to make you a villain to make himself a hero. This is war. We all make sacrifices. Esslandia is full of people willing to sacrifice even their own children. You don't hear them complaining."

Tuuro cast his eyes toward the backseat. "Is she your daughter?"

Allyssa bit her lip. "Niece." She gave Tuuro a quick look, as if she were daring him to contradict her. *Would you sacrifice her?* Tuuro thought, but he didn't say it, not when the girl had any chance of overhearing. "Talk about sacrifice," Allyssa said. "This young lady gave a lot to make it up here." Allyssa's mouth tightened. "She's still paying."

More silence. The sun was setting to their right, casting an orange light upon the land. "I'm going to drop you off north of

Dayton, near a dam. You can just walk around it and toward town. If anyone on our side questions you, give my name."

Tuuro nodded. He felt like a raft passenger being ferried through dangerous waters, on eddies and currents he had no reason to understand. Lanita, he was thinking: will I ever see Lanita?

"Pretty charmed life you have," Allyssa said, shaking her head. "I thought you'd spend the rest of your life in prison."

For an instant, he felt like killing her. He could do it; killing wasn't hard. Later, he would think it was that moment that changed him—or, more accurately, that gave him the strength to change. He wouldn't kill Allyssa, no. He wouldn't hurt her, or raise his voice, or even speak. Instead he gripped, with both hands, the handle of his door. When they reached his destination Tuuro left the car and walked away, not turning with a thank you or a wave.

lila wakes up (2)

THE TACTICIANS AGREED on water. Bombing was tired. Pestilence or gas—in such a dispersed population—was unreliable. But water had the advantages of ubiquity, of surprise, of historical recall, of metaphor. Patient water, eroding canyons and caves over millions of years. Raging water, which is irresistible. Formless water, which fills up every emptiness. Essential water, which every form of life requires. The Esslandians had come up with the plan. Nenonene, upon first hearing it, agreed totally. He had always understood the Grid to be an aesthetic as well as a practical project. Its timing and his were almost contemporaneous. While he was unifying Africa, the Gridians were creating their own world. He wondered at the time when the Americans, with their blinding self-absorption, would wake up to what they'd done, but they were even slower to recognize danger in their midst than they'd been to see it in the world around them. Something else Nenonene liked about water: its putative—its almost "American"—innocence. Nenonene remembered the meeting when the plan was first mentioned. He remembered picking up his glass and twirling it, the surprising vortex he created with that simple move.

"**YOU LIKED MY** last Wright brothers story, didn't you?" Chad said. "How Dayton itself made attaining flight look easy. How the Wright brothers hid themselves away here, perfecting their plane. Well, I like that story, too, But it's not completely true."

The Wright brothers finished their work on the plane by 1905, and the next three years were spent waiting for their patents and sending out feelers to prospective buyers. The Wright brothers had certain demands. A potential buyer must come to Dayton. The brothers would then present to the inquirer not the plane, not the plans for the plane, not photographs of the plane in flight or on the ground, but a panel of respectable citizens of Dayton to vouch for flights they'd witnessed. Without a contract, this was all the information a potential buyer would get. The brothers saw no reason to reveal more. They were honorable men who had built a machine that could fly. It was an affront and an insult if people chose not to believe them.

There was a family history of righteousness. Steadfast in his belief that Freemasons could not be good Christians, their father had marched a renegade band of parishioners out of the Evangelical Brethren church and started his own denomination, installing himself as its bishop.

"We wanted them perfect, didn't we?" Chad said. "Our idea of perfect. We're midwesterners, we're nice, we want people to conform. But if Wilbur and Orville had conformed, we wouldn't be talking about them now. It's astonishing that two men in a midsized Ohio city even tinkered with flight, much less attained it. Think of the possible missteps, all the various points at which an idea, or a lack of an idea, might have made them go wrong. Imagine a crash killing one of them. You have to take the Wright Brothers as they happened. You have to take it that their stars were exactly right. Take away that zealot father, and you might have different sons. Meeker, maybe friendlier men, men who'd spend their time with customers, not working on a wind tunnel in the back room of their shop."

Because of the Wrights' secretiveness, they were not the darlings of the flight community. Among the audiences viewing their first public flights in 1908 were men, maybe even women, whose joy was not unalloyed, whose thrill was tinged with anger, jealousy, and exasperation.

"Life is complicated," Chad said, smiling at his audience, and all four of them, even Leon, looked back with what he took as understanding.

"WE HAVE A little problem." Allyssa's voice over the perc was brisk. "Janie's pregnant."

"What?"

"It's not a big problem. We deal with pregnancies all the time."

"How did she get pregnant, was it . . . ?"

"Her transaction getting herself up here."

Lila's tongue stuck to the roof of her mouth. "She's twelve," she managed to say, glancing around the kitchen for her bottle.

"You know you're seeing puberty at lower and lower ages, because of the chemicals America has . . ."

"Yes, yes," Lila cut in. My God, a girl had sold her body to get herself to Allyssa's kingdom: didn't Allyssa feel any guilt about the outcome? "But how is she? Does she know?"

"Of course she knows. We're very open-information."

Lila closed her eyes. "How is she taking it?"

"She's fine. We have some very reassuring rituals built into the whole process. We'll do the procedure within the next few days, but technically, technically . . ." Allyssa hesitated. "There's a little pressure here to get the father's consent."

"The father's? When she's twelve years old and he . . ."

"*Janie's* father's," Allyssa said. Lila was startled at the anger in her voice. "Because there are negotiations going on and every procedure like this has paperwork and even in Esslandia there are"—she was almost shrieking—"damn damn bureaucrats!"

Lila felt a pang of sympathy. "I'll call him. I'll get his signature for you."

"Thank you," Allyssa said, and Lila's eyes got teary at the humility in her tone. "But you can't really reach us, Lila."

"I'll use the code words. I'll message you. Allyssa, is Janie really okay?"

"She's fine." Allyssa's tone softened. "I promise you, she's fine. I want her to be fine."

Lila said good-bye and dropped her perc into an armchair.

Fine. Fine, finesse, finish. She took another swallow, sank into the chair next to her perc. What was wrong with those Grid people? Allyssa was a real human being, but the society she'd helped create seemed crazy. Where, between the potluck suppers and this, had things gone so very, very wrong?

WHEN SHARIS OPENED her eyes in the morning, Chad was already awake, facing her from the other side of Howard. Chad raised his eyebrows, pointed at Howard's midsection. "Wet," he whispered.

Sharis was surprised. Howard hadn't wet himself for years, and lately he'd seemed happier. He'd picked irises from the neighbors' and arranged them in glasses around the house.

"I'm soaking," Chad mouthed, extricating himself from the blankets.

Howard stirred next. He burrowed his face into his pillow, rolled over to face Sharis, and wiggled his mouth. One of the joys of being in their family bed again (which they had adopted simply because they didn't want to leave Abba alone) was seeing the boys' faces as they awoke. Almost immediately Howard's face crinkled with puzzlement and his eyes popped open.

"It was a fluke," Sharis whispered. "Don't worry."

Abba sat up on the sofa. "What's wrong?" Her hair was totally flat on one side and stuck straight out on the other, giving her a windswept look. Her swollen ankles were as chubby as a baby's joints.

"Shhh. Nothing's wrong. Howard"—Sharis had an inspiration—"remember the night of the ice? When the ice was falling and we all got scared? Leon went dirty in his pants that night."

A smile crept onto Howard's face. He craned his neck and looked over at his sleeping brother.

"I CAN'T HANDLE it." Janie's father burst out over the phone. "You'll have to handle it." Lila was disappointed in his reaction, but she couldn't say she was surprised. Nothing surprised her. The crazy insularity of the Gridians didn't surprise her. Janie's pregnancy didn't surprise her. Kennedy's being found dead in her living room chair after a heart attack didn't surprise her. Lila supposed she should feel guilty about both Janie and Kennedy, but as long as she kept drinking she felt numb.

—You can't help it that you have alcoholism.

—Kennedy, stop bothering me. I don't care about your stupid dreams!

—It's a spiritual disease. It's not a problem in Esslandia because . . .

What is wrong with you? Lila thought, rolling over in her bed the next morning. Her mouth was parched and her lips cracked, and even the soft skin inside her wrists looked baggy. In the mirror the mole on her cheek was so saggy she looked for the nail scissors to cut it off. No luck. She inspected her face again, and it was her eyes that scared her. She looked worse than an uto: she looked like someone who would just as soon be dead.

Lila, she thought, you used to care. Lila, you saved Dayton.

—Did I really?

—Yes, really.

—That's an exaggeration.

—Well, slightly, but there's truth to it.

She'd saved Dayton. If a person could save an entire city, shouldn't that person be able to save a single girl?

She called Ferrescu and set up another meeting. He made her wait two days. "I'll pick you up," she told him. She gazed at her perc a moment, then turned it off and carried it downstairs into the garage. She hammered shut her bedroom and bathroom windows. She emptied the contents of her medicine cabinet into a bag she put in the kitchen, tossing her razors and scissors in the trash. She filled a pail with water to set beside her bed, and floated a one-cup measure inside it as a ladle. She shut her bedroom door, used her key to lock it from the inside, then slipped the key under the door out into the hall. *Lie down,* she thought, but it was hard to make herself still; inside, she was already shaking.

The night before she had thought today would be an ordinary day, but now she understood that it could not be. *Self-healing,* she was thinking, *that whole self-healing package.*

In several hours she was sweating. Her hands were uncontrollable. She used her hips to push the mattress half off the bed, then crawled under the teetering edge and pulled it on top of her. She was wedged but she could breathe. The weight of the mattress calmed her. By the time she could extricate herself from this room, she would be sober.

She would never be doing this for her own sake. She was doing this for Janie.

"WHY DID YOU tell him?" Leon demanded. "Why?"

"Leon, what are you talking about?" Leon's tears alarmed Sharis in a way Howard's never would. She fluttered around her younger son, making soothing gestures with her hands.

"You told him the *worst* thing," Leon sobbed.

"Oh, sweet potato," she said, understanding. "Howard felt so bad about wetting his pants and I . . ." She stopped herself.

"Why do you always *do* things?" Leon wailed. Sharis was struck by a sudden sensation, a twang as if he'd sounded a note in her that matched exactly a note she'd heard from her own mother. How can you *do* that? little Cheryl's eyes had screamed, watching her mother hold her brother, and Cheryl's mother—Sharis understood this—had had the same horrified recognition that Sharis did now: *This child is right. Dear God, let this child live despite me.*

Astonishing how much lighter Sharis's chest felt, how easily she could breathe, once she realized that Chad was indeed right, that Sharis's mother had indeed been Benjamin, the relative who schemed to save her.

"GET ME THERE tomorrow," Lila said. She was standing behind Ferrescu in his chair in his front room, below the shoe-filled birdcage, feeling ferocious and foolish—but not wobbly, not fuzzy, not as if she couldn't form her words. In Lila's right hand she held a butcher knife she wasn't certain she could use.

Ferrescu was about to cry. "Another day—please, not tomorrow!"

"Tomorrow," Lila repeated, making a jabbing motion. Ferrescu nodded.

HOWARD WAS HAPPIER. Howard set the table for dinner. Howard slept through the night and didn't wet at all.

"What's with Leon?" Chad said. "He's been sulking all day."

"He'll get over it," Sharis said. "He'll be fine, I promise."

In the corner of their garage they stored an American flag in a fabric wrapper. In the past Chad had put it out on holidays, which always made Sharis feel like a foreigner, because after the Gridding an American flag was nothing Sharis could look at without ambivalence. Today when Sharis spotted it, it looked heroic. The media said the Alliance troops were organizing, that ground assaults on Columbus and Dayton and Indianapolis could be expected any day. The Esslandian president made a statement. There was no need for any American citizens to be frightened: the Esslandians would treat them with respect. The Agents of Havoc had all been withdrawn. Like hell I'm cowering, Sharis thought. She brushed away the spiderwebs around the flag and unrolled it and stuck its pole in the holder by the front door. No one but they and the sheriff would see it, but when she walked across the street to look at it, she felt a happiness beyond satisfaction. She felt right.

A WOMAN IN a white uniform called Lila from the waiting room, empty except for her. Another ride in a truck to here, north up an empty I-75 and twenty miles east to this windowless cinder-block building, one story high, that sat in a cluster of similar buildings at the outskirts of a town. A wooden sign outside the door, elegantly painted and carved, read GRID CLINIC, VILLAGE 67; a cardboard addition that read ESS-LANDIAN, printed in marker and covered with clear plastic, had been tacked up under the word GRID.

Through the hall doorway Lila saw Janie, fully dressed, sitting at the end of an exam table with her feet dangling; Allyssa knelt on the floor in front of her, tying the girl's shoes.

"Do we go to the fields now?" Janie asked in a little girl voice, which Lila didn't remember as quite so high and helpless.

"Everything went beautifully," Allyssa said. "You did great."

"She made it," the nurse said, and Allyssa and Janie turned their gazes to the door. The nurse disappeared down the hall.

"Are you done?" Lila asked. "I thought you'd wait for me! Where's the doctor? I brought the consent form."

"Hello, Lila," Allyssa said coolly.

"Hi, Aunt Lila," Janie said, reaching for Allyssa's hand to help her off the table. Lila saw that she'd been crying; the tracks of her tears had left thin strands of salt on her cheeks. "Do we go to the fields now?" Janie repeated to Allyssa. Allyssa responded with a quick and warning glance.

Lila saw Allyssa slip a foil-wrapped item the size of a cigarette pack from the exam table into the pocket of her smock. "What's that?" Lila asked sharply.

"Come on, pudding-face," Allyssa said to Janie, "Let's get you home."

"I'm not drinking now, Janie," Lila said. "I dried myself out."

"Really?" Janie's face lit up. "That's great, Aunt Lila."

"I quit for you, Janie," Lila said. "It was hard, but thinking of you made me do it."

"That's wonderful, Aunt Lila. You should be really proud."

"I am proud. That's why I came to get you. I'm finally ready to take you home."

Allyssa cast Lila a scathing glance. It's a love triangle! Lila thought, astonished, wondering how she'd missed this. She thought of her life of love triangles—she and Kennedy and Leesa, she and Kalana Middleton and Jessica, she and . . . All her other triangles seemed small and misshapen, capable of being mangled, while this one had a solidity to it, this one was iron and equilateral. Mother love was a ferocious thing. What she had missed by not having a child . . .

"Will we go to the fields on the . . . ?" Janie started, but Allyssa gave her shoulder a quick admonitory squeeze.

"You're a true Esslandian, aren't you, Jane-bug?" Allyssa said. Jane-bug. Pudding-face.

Janie smiled and nodded, avoiding Lila's eyes.

Allyssa's grip tightened. "My little Jane-bug."

Lila hugged herself and followed the tight package of Allyssa and Janie down the hall and into the waiting room, hung with Norman Rockwell reproductions, where a woman in a billowing beige shirt and pants full of pockets—worker's pants, Lila thought—sat with her head high, staring. "You don't have to follow," Allyssa said to Lila, pulling her young charge even closer and pushing open the door to outside.

A reassuring ritual. *Do we go to the fields now?* The foil packet in Allyssa's right hand . . . A burial? A sacrifice?

What did Lila used to call Janie? Honey? Little woman? *You're nothing but a dirty old lady,* Allyssa would snap. *How dare you call her your . . . ?*

"Get down from there!" the woman in the waiting room barked. Lila followed the woman's gaze to a boy of about six standing on one of the waiting room chairs. The boy had cropped brown hair and startlingly green eyes; he grinned at Lila. "Jeff!" the woman said again. "Did I say to sit down?"

Jeff? Lila glanced again at his eyes before turning to the woman. "Is he . . . Is he a . . . ?" But she stopped before the word "clone," because the woman would never answer that question, and in the meantime the door to the outside was closing, Allyssa and Janie hidden from her view.

"Where are you taking her?" Lila shouted as she burst outside. "What's this about the fields?" She wondered what the woman in the lobby knew about this, she yearned to catch her reaction, but glancing from the bright parking lot back into the lobby she couldn't make out the woman's face. Allyssa and Janie were almost running, their feet splatting on the parking lot stones, and as Lila pursued them she realized she could never keep up.

"Janie!" Lila shouted. "Janie, do you want this?"

"She's drunk!" Allyssa shrieked. "Ignore her!"

"I'm not drinking!" Lila shouted. "I quit for *you*, Janie. I love *you*."

Janie's face turned then. Still running, she looked back at Lila over her left shoulder, and that lovely face—young, intelligent—had a peculiar trapped and wistful quality, a look that reminded Lila of a girl painted by Vermeer. This was a strange thought for Lila, who never thought about art, but it brought back the elementary school classroom where she'd first seen the painting, where the excitable Picture Lady (somebody's mother who volunteered) pointed at Vermeer's girl and exclaimed that this painting did something only art could do: it *stopped time*. Lila hadn't understood the Picture Lady then, but she did now, at this moment, with Janie's beautiful face still turned and the sky blue and a burial hummock rising in the distance. *Dear God,* Lila thought, *dear God,* and who knows what this meant, curse or prayer, praise or petition, because it was Lila's last thought, just as Janie's face was her last vision, just as every aboveground being, for a radius of two miles,

Janie and Allyssa being almost at the epicenter, experienced at that instant their last thought or vision or tingle, because twenty megatons of power reached its target, an ostensible farm equipment shed which was really (the intelligence reports were accurate, although the tip had come from a dubious character named Ferrescu) a munitions storage depot, *a strategic target,* as President Baxter pointed out, *stricken with surgical precision.* Not that President Baxter meant to dismiss the few civilian casualties, of course, but these were Esslandians, and this was war. And in war, unfortunately, innocent people, at times even children, are called upon to suffer.

the face of war

"WHY DAYTON?" CHAD said. "Why do we live in a suburb of Dayton, instead of Dayton being a suburb of here? After all, Centerville had limestone and the highest elevation in Montgomery County. Centerville had stone sidewalks when Dayton had roads made of mud. Beavertown had a post office."

Abba whispered something to Howard.

"The river?" Howard said.

"Yes, the river!" Chad cried. Ridiculous; no wonder Ramsey laughed at his course. "You're exactly right, Howard: the river is what did it. Think of what you can do with a river"—he was holding out one finger—"you can . . ."

They figured out fishing right away, then transportation and commerce, and last, after a number of hints, the powering of mills. At that moment Chad, to his surprise, was struck with wave of emotion. "But any river has its dark side, doesn't it?" he said. "It gives, it takes away. The first flood was in 1805 and D. C. Cooper wanted to move the town but people said they couldn't afford it, and the second flood . . ." But Chad couldn't go on.

"Life can be bad, Howard," he choked out. "Anything can turn on you. Even faith, even hope, even . . ."

"Good grief," Abba said, "they let you teach this at a Catholic college?"

THE HIT WAS by all reports a great success, taking out not only the munitions warehouse but establishing a pie-shaped wedge of safe airspace, and the pilot and the copilot were sent up on surveillance. They flew low. It was a gorgeous May morning and eighteen hours postevent. In the distance there were green fields and humps and, to the east, a sort of shimmer. "Is that water?" Grady asked.

"Indian Lake," the copilot said. "Been there forever." Grady wondered at this information, because from what he'd heard all the lakes of Ohio—with the exception of Lake Erie, which made up much of the state's northern border and was one of the five Great Lakes—were manmade.

At the center the site looked like the moon, but at the edges you could see, even from the air, clumps of dirt with green on them, cinder blocks and cinder-block fragments, the charred and upended remains of vehicles. "Let's land here," the copilot pointed, and they came down between the remains of the munitions shed (which was pulverized) and another building of some sort, which looking at their coordinates was a possible clinic. All the buildings were possibles: who knew, with the Gridians, what uses they put their buildings to. Grady and his copilot had been asked to land and investigate.

They got out. Hard to imagine this as farmland, as any land worth having. It reminded Grady of the hole gouged out of the ground for his parents' house, but that had been only a gash in a green landscape, and this was the whole landscape. He was glad he'd seen the site first from the air, surrounded by fields and normalcy, and he knew that this was a limited desolation.

The copilot shook his head. "Wild."

It was death, was what it was. Death come from the sky. Grady had heard that bombs hit before the sound of them arrived. You heard the explosion, you knew that you'd survived.

Grady kicked at a wad of soil, knocking it aside. There, lying in the dirt, looking up at him, was a face.

He thought it was a mask at first, because it looked impossible: a woman's face, divorced from any head or body, eyes open and staring, mouth open, forehead furrowed. The most jarring thing about it was that it looked perfectly ordinary, sheared off and unmarked except for a round spot of debris below the right eye. Of all the fluky flung debris, the clod on top of it was the thing Grady had kicked aside.

The face, peculiarly enough, was not terrible to him. All the limbs and body parts he could have come across, and he had found instead a tidy triangle of skin and muscle. He bent over to brush off the piece of debris, then realized it was a mole.

"What?" the copilot said, stumbling toward him. "What're you looking at?"

"The face of war," Grady said, and it struck him that this comment was a profound thing, a new reference point in his life. "The face of war," he repeated, proud of the phrase. Usually the only things he said twice were comments he thought were funny.

The copilot vomited. Grady imagined his stomach torn from his abdomen and erupting out of his mouth, which in this landscape seemed possible. "You okay?" Grady said, patting his copilot's back.

"We've got to bury it," the copilot said eventually, one hand over his eyes. "It's gruesome."

"Okay." Grady hesitated, glancing at the pitted ground around them. A thousand clods of dirt, and he was scared to overturn another one. "It's not very big," he said. At these words the copilot started retching again. "I'm going to bury it right here," Grady said, squatting to dig with his hands. "Nice nose," he added.

"Swear to God, if you start in like this I'm, I'm . . ."

"I was just noticing something, I didn't . . ."

"Stop it!"

"Could you maybe get me the shovel?" Grady asked after several unsuccessful minutes. Must have been a Gridian, he reflected, with this normal, ordinary face. People talked about the Gridians as if they were monsters. He remembered Rapunzel at the Green House, and hoped she stayed alive.

The copilot returned from the helicopter's emergency bay with the shovel. But after Grady had dug the hole—maybe eighteen inches deep and two feet around, too deep for animals to get at—and had the face perched on the end of his shovel, he found himself in a quandary. He didn't want to turn the face over—that *would* be gruesome—but he didn't want to put it in the hole and dump dirt into its mouth and eyes. Let his partner think his sick thoughts about Grady: what Grady felt for this face was respect. He thought of the thin black netting that edged the bottom of his parachute, how from that he could fashion a veil. "Could you grab my parachute?" he asked.

"Look," Grady said when he had the face and its veil arranged in the hole, and he almost said, but he stopped himself: "It's pretty."

The copilot peeked through his fingers. Behind the netting, surrounded by dirt, the wedge of face looked serene and lovely. Queen of the Earth, Grady thought. The mole shone like a dark jewel. *I can leave things better,* Grady thought. *I'm not a monster.*

When Grady had filled the hole, he and the copilot walked to the nearest ruined building. They walked slowly and carefully, eyes down, not wanting to see more.

THE PRESIDENT'S PERC message was more personalized this time: due to the dangers faced by citizens of Dayton, especially with America leaving open the possibility of bombing Alliance military installations just north of their city, Sharis and Chad were being asked to relocate to one of three "SafePlace" camps at the southern end of the quarantine area. The camps were being erected now, with tent space for individual families as well as some trailers; this relocation was purely voluntary, but families arriving at the camp early would get first choice of accommodations. Anyone presenting to the SafePlace camp in the next twenty-four hours was guaranteed an air-conditioned lodging.

Chad studied Sharis's face as she read the message on the holo-screen, the tender skin below her right eye twitching. "It's like the Grid all over the again," she said. "They're moving us out." She stood up. "I'm taking down the flag."

"But it's different. Then they were moving people for their own convenience, now it's for our own . . . President Baxter's always said that his goal is zero American civilian casualties. And now that there's an election next year he has to . . ." The boys, Chad was thinking, we have to protect the boys.

Sharis was heading for the front door.

"Don't take down the flag!" Chad shouted. "I forbid you to take down the flag!"

"Air-conditioning!" she shrieked, already pulling at the fabric. "All we've been through, they think we'll fall for air-conditioning?"

THE CAPTAIN WAS part of the military–Montgomery County liaison team, a hopeless assignment involving monthly meetings he survived largely through sexual fantasies. The Consort rep had had breasts as big and round as cantaloupes, but then she got herself killed and was replaced by a male youngie. The woman from water was a terror, and the captain didn't even look at her for fear of tainting his much-cherished scenarios involving two or three hot women. The other members of the team—representing the air force, Montgomery County government, the City of Dayton, local police, the Metropark system, clergy—were middle-aged men of varying stiffness. The one Melano in the group, the parks representative, scared the captain half to death, but fortunately he missed a lot of meetings. Lately, almost everyone missed meetings.

"Where's the water witch today?" the captain said—a good enough line, but no one even smiled. The air force representative, a holier-than-thou lieutenant colonel, actually winced.

"Do you know something?" the boring youngie from Consort asked eagerly.

"He don't know nothing," the parks man said, and the captain thought, not for the first time, how he hated that affected style of speech.

"What?" the captain said. "She drop out of our council?"

"She's disappeared," the policemen said. "That's not for public consumption."

"She probably just sneaked out of town like everyone else and their sister," the captain said.

The policeman shook his head. "I went over to her house and there was garbage in the sink and a mattress on the floor and water lying around and . . ."—he massaged his forehead—"oh, God. Most people who leave leave things picked up. In my experience." He lifted his eyes wearily to the youngie from Consort. "How you guys doing?"

The youngie shrugged. "We need reliable water."

"That assistant of hers got killed back in December."

"Seymour," the Consort youngie said. "Yeah. We wonder if she got the same treatment."

"The water witch is dead?" The captain leaned forward in surprise.

"Don't jump to conclusions." The policeman's thumb twitched. "We don't have proof of anything. You got your computer people working on the map? It's not in her house, that's for sure. We went through like a hundred laptops." The policeman turned to the captain to explain. "The water map was wiped off all the office computers."

"You need someone with expertise to get rid of that," the clergyman said. And then, as if he'd overstepped his role: "Wouldn't you?"

"Someone tortured her, maybe," the youngie from Consort broke in. "Got into the computer system, got the info they needed, wiped it out for everyone else. Someone's bleeding us somehow. We've got periods of crazy low pressure. Our back-flow preventers are working overtime. If we had the map, we could maybe figure out where the mains are vulnerable."

"You think she's a traitor?" the Captain asked. "Think she's working with the Alliance?"

"Or the Grid," the policeman said. "She went up there for a visit last summer; we found records." The captain felt a surge of irritation. Why were there two enemies to think about? He'd liked it better when there was one. Things were getting very strange, really. Lieutenant Grady had come back from the munitions hit site babbling about burying a face. Absurd. Probably one of those voodoo masks they have up there, hang it on the wall and pray to it.

"Jesus," the captain said. "But our water's fine," he added. "I haven't seen any problems at the Base."

"You're at the other side of the city from us," the Consort youngie pointed out.

The Dayton city manager said, "To be frank with you, we're glad the Feds are pulling people out of Dayton. We can't handle a population right now."

"Speaking of Jesus," the clergyman said, nodding toward the captain, "perhaps we should have a prayer for our missing colleague."

"Speaking of prayer," the parks representative said, "you think we got a prayer of staying alive?"

"MOMMY!" LEON WAS breathless, his face alight; his bangs stuck to his forehead. "Tanks." Sharis cast her eyes inquiringly at Howard, just behind him, who nodded in eager confirmation.

"Where?" The boys had been outside, supposedly in their sphere of six safe lawns. Sharis suspected that they ventured beyond it, although she'd made little effort to know. Like Abba said: better sometimes not to. To Sharis, wanting to know every second where her boys were seemed like giving in to fear.

"Up by Aunt Gentia's. Coming up Far Hills."

"Right in the street?"

Leon's face cracked into a smile. "They waved at me!"

"Someone came out of the top and waved? You saw people in them?"

"No, Mommy." Leon was on his tiptoes in excitement. "They waved their guns at me!"

Sharis couldn't breathe. She backed into the living room and sat herself down. "Leon, this is important. Were these American tanks? Did they have the U.S. flag on them?" Just like the Gridding again. Rounding us up. Her mind was spinning with options and plans. "Which way were they headed?"

Howard made a vague gesture north. "There's a battle up north," Chad said, and she was startled to realize that he was standing behind her. "They're going to meet the Alliance troops."

A barbed understanding flooded her, like swallowing a handful of nettles.

"How many tanks?" Chad was asking. "Were there trucks, too, Howard?" Sharis was grateful for this practicality; she couldn't think anymore. She sank deeper in the chair, feeling paralyzed. It was always like this, she realized. Together she and Chad made a functioning person.

"More tanks than trucks," Howard answered. "Five-to-one ratio, I'd say."

Howard knew ratios? He'd been counting?

"A lot," Leon echoed solemnly. "I'd say a kazillion. Don't you think a kazillion, Howard?"

"Well," Howard smiled, "a kazillion might be an exaggeration."

"Maybe we should check out that camp," Chad said.

LATER ON THAT beautiful spring day, Wednesday, May 13, 2048, kamikaze Alliance planes crashed into and destroyed thirteen bridges over the Great Miami and the Mad Rivers. All the bridges were hit between 2:06 and 2:32 p.m. There was only one recording of any of the crashes, taken by an amateur meteorologist who happened to be filming clouds. Only the four I-75 bridges were left untouched because, as the media pointed out, the Alliance must anticipate a need for them. This was frightening. Until now I-75 south of the Grid border was controlled by the U.S. Soon, the Alliance seemed to be saying, we'll be taking it over.

Enormous wings tilted and rising from the water.

A profile shot of the broken Salem Avenue bridge, its nub ends bristling with cables.

Electrical lines down and sparking.

One of the pilots survived, but before the rescue personnel could reach him he pulled out a pistol and shot himself dead.

An egregious act of war. The routes out of Dayton toward Cincinnati had been left open, as if the Alliance were painting a giant exit arrow heading south. *They're telling us something,* Chad said, his eyes on the TV.

The American tanks rerouted, headed for I-75 to cross north on intact bridges.

The crashed planes were Alliance machines, but the pilots had all been Esslandians. By that evening, videos of the pilots' farewell parties were being run on the media, interspersed with the footage of the broken bridges. Crepe paper, punch bowls, sheet cakes: the celebrations had the look, Chad thought, of the grange hall wedding receptions of his cousins. The youngest pilot was fifteen. They weren't suicides, one of their mothers said. They were patriots, dying for Esslandia.

Chad said. "How can you fight against people who are willing to give up their children?"

Abba said to Sharis, "Thank God you weren't stuck up there after the Gridding."

"Turn down the TV," Sharis said, shutting the door to the basement, where the boys were playing holo-games. "The kids don't need this."

Abba lifted her leg from the soaking pail filled with Epsom salts to rest it on the sofa. Her feet and ankles were red and seeping. "That could have been your son," she said to Sharis, nodding at the face of a pilot on the TV.

"Please," Sharis said. She wanted to tell Abba to shut up, but she couldn't now that Abba was so ill. Abba was too short of breath to sleep flat anymore, and spent her days and nights propped at the end of the sofa.

"Do you think there's medicine at that camp?" Sharis asked.

"Of course there's medicine," Chad said. "How could it be called a SafePlace without medicine?"

FROM THE BEGINNING, the Wright brothers thought their invention could have a military use. They envisioned that airplanes would be useful the way hot-air balloons were, as reconnaissance vehicles gathering information to aid troops on the ground. The first air crash fatality, Lieutenant Thomas O. Selfridge, was riding with Orville as an army observer. The Wrights' first American contract for the sale of a plane (1908) was to the U.S. Army. A German company the next year entered into a licensing agreement with the Wrights to produce their planes in Germany.

Could the brothers have imagined their invention used to destroy the bridges of their hometown? Should they have? Wilbur was dead before World War I, but Orville was around to see fighter pilots and the Red Baron and explosives that dropped on people straight out of the sky. At one point Orville served as a consultant to the military for the development of pilotless bombs.

Orville didn't die until 1948. He saw Dresden, he saw Hiroshima.

Chad had trouble getting to sleep that night, wondering if Orville had cared.

TUURO HAD SETTLED himself in an old barn near the Englewood Dam. Behind the barn was a downsloping wooded hillside he thought it best to avoid, but walking straight out from the barn took him to the road that crossed the dam to a shopping center, where in the parking lot behind K-Bob's he scrounged for food and supplies. He'd found a stash of what were probably old horse blankets in the barn's basement, and he slept curled up in the loft. A plastic jump rope hung over one of the rafters. This reassured him: if things got unbearable, he had rope.

"WE'LL PICK YOU up," said the woman's voice on the phone. "Right away, sir. Two thirteen Custard Lane. Three adults and two children, one family unit."

"What should we look for?" Chad asked. "You won't come in a tank, will you?"

"Oh, no, sir." The woman on the phone chuckled. "Just a regular APC, sir." Armored personnel carrier. The boys would be disappointed. "Remember, one eighteen-by-thirty-inch suitcase maximum per person. And don't worry about sleeping bags. The camp's fully equipped. It's a joint venture with Marriott, sir. We're your place for shelter and more."

Chad felt like he was dreaming. It wasn't yet nine in the morning on Friday, not forty-eight hours after the bridges had been hit, and the afternoon before they hadn't decided what they would do. The president's message had said that the necessary preregistration for the camp could be done on-line. Chad had typed in the necessary data, then hesitated a moment before sending it on. The clock in the kitchen was ticking. Chad was in his usual chair, Sharis was on the family room floor leaning against the sofa, Howard slumped beside her, a reader in front of his nose. Leon was crouched on the other end of the sofa playing a perc game called Conundrum, and Abba was slumped on the sofa sleeping, because lately she slept all the time. A warm afternoon with the windows open and no lights on, an afternoon that felt like summer even though it was only May. No TV on, because of the boys.

The night before Leon had spotted two fireflies, and Chad had been relieved when he couldn't catch them. *Don't hurt the lights of the world,* Chad had thought.

"What do you think?" Chad had asked Sharis about the camp registration. "Should I send it?" Almost impossible, at that moment, to believe anything could hurt them, although less than five miles away there were wrecked planes and sacrificial bodies.

Sharis looked up at him from the floor, and Chad had the feeling—a sort of thrill—that with her fingertip she could reach out and touch, just touch, an enormous metal ball, starting it this way or that, so that later, when it came careening through the woods with all its snapping and heaviness and violence, he would think back to this moment, when she was holding up her finger and deciding.

Sharis said, "When you see tanks, it's serious."

"At the internment camps for the Japanese during World War II everyone ate in the mess tents and they divided themselves into kids' and adults' tables. That was bad, the ages eating separately. It started the breakdown of the nuclear family." One of Prem's favorite points, although Chad wasn't sure why he was mentioning it.

"What if we agree to always eat together?" Sharis had said. "Even if there's a mess tent."

"I want to eat with you, Mommy," Howard said.

"How about you, Leon?" Sharis asked, targeting her voice to the sofa. "Would you always eat with us?"

"Yeah, sure," said Leon, intent on his game.

"What does Abba think?" Sharis asked.

Chad shrugged. "I'm sure she'll agree with whatever we decide."

Abba's easier than a child, Sharis had thought, and then it hit her that that might be something Abba worked on. She was different since the day Howard and Leon had been through their trauma with the Webelos. She'd stopped 90 percent of her talking, and what she did say seemed to matter.

Sharis said, "I think we should go to the camp because of Abba. I bet they'll have her medicines."

Chad was already drifting away, his mind flying out that green rectangle of window—wishing, more than anything, that his neighborhood in late spring wasn't beautiful, that he couldn't hear its call to him to stay.

GRADY'S FATHER'S VOICE was hardy over the perc, his face red. "Great opportunities! Durable goods are at a ten-year low. Everybody's rushing for Marriott, but that's too creamy for me these days. But the market for beds and sleeping bags! Did you know Duradown puts out a . . . ?"

Grady wasn't listening. He was watching his father's lips move, thinking that single-mindedness like his father's, in one way, kept the country going, but in another way it was insane. He had buried someone's face. Three whole cities—Columbus and Dayton and Indianapolis—were being evacuated, while half of his army colleagues had been ordered to move from the air force base into downtown Dayton to defend it.

"Have you thought about moving that money you got from Aunt Laura? Make a move when you can, son. Time waits for no man. Seize the day."

"I'm getting married when this is over," Grady said, and then, when his father's eyebrows raised: "No particular person."

Marriage sounded good to Grady now. He wanted something solid, something stable.

"ALL ABOARD!" THE army driver said, and the five of them clambered into his Ford APC, his cheerful cry making it seem as if this was an adventure, a trip to a prank-filled camp that might be featured in a summer movie. Leon and Chad sat next to the driver; Sharis, Howard, and Abba took the back, the editon in Sharis's lap. The driver had signed on for four years, then reupped. Wait'll they saw the pool and the playgrounds. And the cafeteria tent, huge. With a special food line and seating section just for kids. The driver twisted his head and winked at Howard.

The relocation camps for the city of Dayton and its suburbs were all south. Far enough south? the media asked, but there had been political considerations, with the counties below Montgomery unwilling to give up land. Dayton's population west of I-75, largely Melano, had been stranded by the destruction of the bridges, and was being bused an hour west to an abandoned church camp being managed by Elderkind, the nursing home giant.

The driver took them south on Far Hills for five miles, up and over the midpoint of Centerville, which was the highest elevation in the county, then turned left and drove two miles to the Schoolhouse Haven SafePlace. In the foreground of the SafePlace lay a vast expanse of enormous tents and portable toilets, punctuated by an occasional tree, and it took Chad a moment to get his bearings. Schoolhouse Haven had once been Schoolhouse Park. Chad had played baseball several times here as a boy, when his team traveled to compete with a Centerville team. Across Nutt Road from the SafePlace entrance was an army reserve encampment, with modular buildings that looked much more substantial that the Safe-Place tents. "Where are the trailers?" Chad asked.

"Wait a minute, here's a joke for you boys," their driver said. "If you're dying in the dining room, what do you do?"

Leon wasn't listening, but Sharis knew the word "dying" was too much for Howard. "I give up," she answered quickly.

"Go to the living room!"

"Where are the trailers?" Chad repeated.

The gaze of the lackey (Chad suddenly saw this was what he was) turned vague. "I'm not sure they're here yet. You'll have to talk to the concierge." He pronounced this "consy-URGE." "She'll be right with you." He stopped the truck where it was and hurried unceremoniously off, disappearing into a shed forty feet away that appeared to be an office, with blinds and an air conditioner in its single window.

"I don't want to stay if we don't get a trailer," Chad said in a low voice. There were a number of uniformed soldiers milling around them, and he didn't want to be overheard.

"But if Dayton's going to be bombed . . ." Sharis said. "And if Abba can get *medicine* . . ."

"We're not in Dayton, we're in Centerville."

"I don't think bombs recognize borders."

"Are you kidding? Bombs recognize nothing but borders."

Abba was staring out the small APC window. There were times she didn't seem to hear them.

"Not local borders." Sharis snapped. "Not borders between cities and suburbs."

"Stop fighting!" Howard cried out. There was a moment of silence.

"Howard, do you see any trailers?" Sharis asked, craning her head.

"Is that a trailer, Mommy? Over there?" But it was not.

"Mommy, I'm bored," Leon announced.

"You'll just have to be bored, Leon," Sharis said, and Chad, hearing the tension in her voice, erupted: "You shut up, Leon! How can you say you're bored when at this moment we . . ." He stopped talking at the sight of a young woman in camouflage shorts and a white shirt walking toward them, waving an iris scanner and smiling.

"It's the 'urge," Chad said, sitting up straighter, smiling back.

"You must be the Gribbles," the concierge enthused, sticking her hand through the open window. "I'm Julie." She spotted Abba and her voice rose. "Oh, and you brought your own elder!" Sharis looked at Chad, her flat gaze filled with misgiving.

IN CHATTANOOGA, DIANA found a job doing administrative work for the Red Cross. The first few weeks she did little more than relay messages, but then the news of the camps outside the various cities erupted. The Red Cross people were distressed about the camps; they couldn't believe the Feds had partnered with Marriott and not them. And getting Elder-kind involved was just a joke. Eventually, many more camps might be needed, outside other Grid border cities, and Diana's new job was to monitor media transmissions from the evacuated cities and compile daily reports using notable moments. If Marriott made itself look terrible, so be it. "They have no idea what they're getting into," Diana's boss said of Marriott. "They're recreation, not rescue."

Diana had been sitting at her monitors when the planes crashed into the bridges in Dayton. Since she had the biggest monitors in the room, within minutes she was the center of the uproar.

"Jesus H. Christ."

"It's like the World Trade Center."

"And another beautiful day."

"It has to be the Gridians. Don't you think it's Gridians?"

"God, those Esslandians aren't even human!"

"They're human," Diana said, remembering the Esslandian president's little eyes. He had talked to her by videophone for close to an hour. What did she mean to him? The girlfriend of the nature center's director. He was desperate for an ally, she thought. He wanted someone outside the Grid to understand him. It comforted her to remember that time, because already her days in the nature center didn't seem real. If it weren't for the infant growing in her belly, Charles could be a person she'd dreamed up.

"How can they be human? Life means nothing to them."

"They take a long view," Diana heard herself saying. "They're more interested in the survival of a population than a single individual."

She'd had no more spotting. Her pregnancy was fine. Meant to be.

"Species survival." Someone was muttering. "Bullshit."

"But it's not," Diana said. "Species survival is important. Look at groves of trees!"

She didn't stop. By the time she finished people were backing away from her. No one asked her where she'd gotten such ideas. At the end of the day she packed up her purse and went home, knowing that she'd used up all the goodwill engendered by her pregnancy, that tomorrow she would need to start explaining.

the safeplace camp

"THEY'RE SPLITTING UP nuclear families," Sharis said, following Chad through the door and inside. "You can't deny that."

Chad was trying to stress the positive. He was very impressed, for example, with the door of their apartment (their "dwelling," to use the Marriott term), which had a frame and locked and opened and was tall enough that Chad didn't bump his head. Those Marriott people knew their stuff. Chad said, "Howard and Leon are with us a ton. You don't mind them making friends, do you?" The kickball games, the crafts, the children's activity center with its hologram hall. The cheerful and ubiquitous concierge—"the 'urge," as everyone called her.

Chad kept his voice down, because despite the sound-muffling fabric you could often make out your neighbors' words through the partitions. They were staying in what appeared to be a former catering tent now divided into eight dwellings. Because Abba made their group larger than the average family of three to four, they had been given a corner area. Sharis and Chad and the boys slept in bunk beds against the adjoining inner walls. Abba had been given a fold-up cot topped by an air mattress, although she was more comfortable sleeping sitting up in the inflatable armchair. There were indeed medicines here for Abba, but not precisely the ones she had been taking. Also, the camp doctor was covering all three Dayton camps, and Abba so far had only seen a physician extender.

Sharis hated the camp. No, that was inaccurate. The camp itself was pleasant enough, and all the inmates (ha!) seemed reasonably happy, but simply having all these powerless people lumped together took Sharis back to the Gridding. It seemed impossible that people who asked her which street she was from and what did she think of the remaining school year being canceled couldn't tell that she was different, didn't see her as a shredded being. Get me out of here! she thought. Save me from this unrelenting niceness. The nighttime noises of crying or snuffling or the occasional imprecation were a comfort to her, proof that other people here could be unhappy. There were times she hated Chad's optimism, the beautiful weather, the hundreds of people around her, and, perhaps most oppressively, the enforced good cheer. There seemed to be a secret pact that people wouldn't talk about the future. On the other side of their tent a group of families whose sons had played football together gathered each evening for a songfest, and the music and shouts from the campfire were almost more than Sharis could bear.

Most nights, Sharis stayed up past midnight editing. The whole family, even Abba, complained about the light from the editon, and Sharis ended up hanging a sheet from the top bunk as a screen, doing her work in what became a hot little cave. "Do you have to keep working?" Chad said. "No one else here is working."

"I don't want the boys to think it's normal for adults sit around all day and do nothing," Sharis said. "Do you?"

Even Chad admitted there was something eerie about the place, with the breakfast buffets and the sloppy joes and the fried chicken with mashed potatoes and the freshly poured concrete slabs topped by tents with names like "The Dragon's Den" or "Orville's House." It was as if the few remaining citizens of south Dayton (there were three thousand Daytonians and suburbanites in this camp, a little under four thousand in each of the two others) were being seduced to think their days here were a vacation. The Elderkind camp west of Dayton, Chad heard, was much more rustic; already some of its residents were threatening antidiscrimination lawsuits.

Abba had made a new friend, Betty, a woman who had been, of all things, an acquaintance of Abba's deceased little brother in Cleveland. Betty and Abba sat in the dining room and talked all day, a running commentary. *What if you had a husband looked like that? You remember Demi Moore? I can't stand too much salt in deviled eggs. That granddaughter of mine, I don't know.* It was a relief to both Chad and Sharis to have Abba talking.

On a warm afternoon when Sharis was working inside and the boys were playing volleyball under a sub-'urge's supervision and Abba was chatting with Betty, Chad wandered down to the edge of the tent near the musicians. He almost envied the families there for their nightly singing, although he knew it drove Sharis crazy. Surprising how territorial they'd become: Chad was careful not to walk too close to the tent, for fear of disturbing anyone's private yard. The Marriott people had supplied outside chairs, two per dwelling, and no one ever sat in another family's chairs.

A bombing campaign had been attempted against the Grid (un-American to call it Esslandia; President Baxter referred to its "illegitimate government" and "de facto leader"), the goal being to soften its defenses in preparation for an American ground invasion. But things had gone wrong. The Grid's surface-to-air missiles were very effective, and earlier in the week three American bombers had been shot down in one morning. Since then the bombing had been desultory, and rumors of dissent in the air force ranks had reached as far as the SafePlace cafeteria.

No one was at home at the singing end of the tent. There was a fire circle forty feet away, and a female youngie was hunched on a rock there with her shoes off, skirt bunched between her legs, using a Swiss Army knife on her toenails. "Hello," Chad said, recognizing the girl as the granddaughter of Abba's friend, Betty. "What's your name again? I'm Chad.

The girl looked up warily. "I know you're Chad. I'm Flower." Chad smiled at the name, because this girl looked more like a Thistle. Flower said, "Aren't you going to sit down?"

Flower had ideas. Flower wasn't happy about being stuck in some god-awful camp, but hey, what did America expect? "You think about this," Flower said. "We were the top dogs in the world for years. And it didn't make the rest of the world happy."

"True," Chad said agreeably, wondering if Flower was over twenty.

"And we weren't the only country that suffered through the Short Times. And then we got the Grid, and then we hoarded." Her face became severe, reminding Chad of Sharis's face when she was planting bulbs. "You can't eat all the apples off the tree. You've got to share your apples." She hacked off a piece of toenail, flicked it into the ashes of the fire circle.

Where were Flower's parents? Betty said they had left Dayton for Iowa months before. Betty and Flower and Flower's football player brother had been living in a house by themselves. Flower reminded Chad of certain angry peace-niks who'd showed up in his parents' kitchen. His mother had mollified them with food and conversation, like feeding a wild animal honey from the tip of a spoon.

"It all comes from thinking you're special," Flower said.

Chad thought of the strip mall of his childhood in 2006 or so, the nut and candy shop owned by Pakistanis and the gay florist with the talking bird and the crazy Jews wearing big felt hats—like Jews from old Prague—hidden behind blinds in their Jewish Information Center and the video shop with its flashing sign advertising 1000 Adult DVDs and kids hopping around in white pajamas in the tae kwon do academy (academy!) and the photo shop where the Easter Bunny arrived each year in a pink furry suit. Wasn't that special? All that divergent life, all those various dreams, under one long L-shaped roof?

"We were special," Chad said. "We had a special way of life."

"You think it's right to have everything?" Flower waved her knife. "Everything while the rest of the world has nothing?"

What had happened to those Jews? "They drove to Cincinnati to bring back kosher plates and silverware for a banquet!" Chad heard his mother say, her voice a mixture of awe and exasperation. What kind of plate did a man like that eat off now? Chad saw a bearded behatted man in a long overcoat running down the sidewalk past rows of broken windows, past teenage looters grabbing up the 1000 DVDs and suburban mothers turned scavengers poring over picture frames, picking ones to keep not for aesthetic qualities or size but because they looked like good burners. Anything for a fire, a bit of warmth. The detritus of civilization turned to fuel. But it hadn't been like that. Some of the businesses had closed during the Great Recession, but others of them had struggled on. Later, during New Dawn Dayton, when Consort built its nuclear plant and the center-city industrial park filled with factories, the strip mall once again got busy and new strip malls were built. The Short Times hurt everyone, of course, but Dayton, because of its industrial base, less than other cities. Even in the last two years, as the city was slowly abandoned, there were occasional break-ins but no looters. Some vestige of politeness and gentility, like a man on his deathbed reaching out to shake a hand.

"One world!" Flower was saying, and Chad realized she'd been talking all along. "Don't you think that's a reasonable thing to hope for?"

"No," Chad said. "Not at all."

She didn't hear him. She wasn't the sort of person to listen, except to people she'd decided ahead of time were right. Chad considered arguing with her, but it seemed like too much work. He might not be able to explain the strip mall without fading into tears.

TUURO WAS WALKING back from K-Bob's across the levee. He walked on the north side of the road, on the steep grass of the earthen dam's side. No one could spot him except someone watching from the Grid.

Today, Tuuro was happy. He liked being outside and living alone. He liked the weather, the smell of the morning, the baby weeds sprouting all over the farm. When things had settled down he'd take a bus to Chattanooga and demand to see Lanita. If Naomi didn't agree, he'd get a lawyer. He'd find another job in maintenance. What did they have on him? Nothing. The genetics had cleared him about Cubby, and no one in Dayton had ever heard of Chelsea. Forward, onward and upward. No more cringing.

The fireball came from behind him. Tuuro was aware of light before he felt the heat, and then he realized—this was the strangest thing—that the orb was rolling with an almost stately pace. Tuuro had time, actual time, to consider what to do and how to do it. All his life, circumstances and people and his own self had contrived to make him less. Even Aunt Stella, by leaving him, had made him less. He was sick of being less. If he survived, he would fight to be more.

DIANA WAS SITTING at her desk at the Red Cross with her monitors split into four screens, thinking about making a baby quilt incorporating some of the clothes she'd taken from the Center. A male voice spewed out from one of the feeds into her earphone. "How the hell did it happen? How the piss-ass hell do I know how it happened? All I know is there were Grid troops camped there and apparently they'd been walking across the fucking dam for supplies. Walking across the fucking dam! Going shopping at K-Bob's! You tell me this isn't army incompetence."

Levee? K-Bob's? It sounded like the angry man was talking about the dam by Diana's old nature center. The voice was coming from monitor 4. Diana turned the sound off on the other monitors. Monitor 4, broadcasting from a media outlet in Dayton, was displaying its usual default image of a live view of some SafePlace tents.

"Unbelievable." A woman's voice now.

"Damn straight it's unbelievable. That's why I believe it. We secured that area! We got rid of the Taconoutes and we turned it over to the army and . . ."

"Can we get you on camera?"

"Wait a minute," the male voice said, "let me settle down. If those Gridians had troops holed up there since that nature center debacle . . ."

"Don't calm down," the woman said. "We love that anger." A new image appeared on the screen: a tall uniformed man and a short blond woman in front of a white wall emblazoned with the words WAR FOR UNITY. "We're already on?" The woman lifted a finger to her ear. "Colonel, we're on camera now."

I should turn this off, Diana thought. I don't want to miscarry. But she had her job to do.

"I'm here with U.S. Air Force colonel Herman Weatherby, and . . ." There was a button Diana had to push to save things, and she'd pushed it a hundred times, but now she couldn't remember where it was. " . . . we have just received reports that the Englewood Dam northwest of Dayton has been destroyed, I repeat, a dam northwest of Dayton . . ."

Diana found the button. She dropped her right hand to her lower abdomen and cradled little Charles.

" . . . and our sources believe that this was not a bomb, this is not believed to be a bombing attack, but the destruction was apparently secondary to explosive devices placed throughout the . . ."

Why would anyone want to blow up the Englewood Dam? Diana used to walk across it to go shopping, and she remembered looking down from it north to the Stillwater River, which in March had swollen up enough from rain that the shoreline trees looked like sticks poking out from a puddle. A dam over a hundred years old, she recalled, part of the system built after Dayton's Great Flood.

"Of course we are treating this as a hostile"—the colonel sounded determined and almost cheerful, all traces of his earlier rage gone—"Gridian action."

Diana in her mind saw Charles quickly turning off his perc when she walked into the room; she saw the Esslandian president beaming at her on the holo-screen; she saw the paper in Charles's hand tremble as he headed up the hill toward the barn for his news conference. "They care about us!" Charles had cried, in his euphoria twirling her like a square dancer. "They want to protect nature!"

My God, Diana thought. We were dupes. They never cared about our trees. They were after the dam.

GRADY AND HIS copilot got into their helicopter and awaited orders. "You have to admit," Grady said, "those Esslandians sticking around to blow up the dam was pretty smart. And did you hear how the Grid's been selling corn to the Alliance for years?"

"Of course they're smart!" The copilot barked. "They started out American!"

CHAD WAS CUTTING across the football field toward the bathroom when he got the news. "They blew another one!" A man shouted. "They blew Taylorsville!" Taylorsville was the concrete dam across the upper Great Miami. Chad ran to the nearest TV monitor, mounted on a pole at the edge of the football field.

But why? There was no significant water behind either dam, only two meandering rivers. "What the heck are they doing?" Chad said to no one in particular. "They going to wait till next spring and flood us out?" A crowd was gathering, and with it a crowd of opinions.

"They're trying to goad us into doing something."

"It's got to be psychological, right? What else could it be except psychology?"

"They're goading the Chinese. They know how the Chinese feel about dams."

"It's just to show that they can penetrate. It's like a fuck you, USA."

Chad pushed through the people and headed for his tent. "Where is everybody?" he said, flinging open the door.

Sharis, sitting in the inflatable armchair, looked up quickly from her editon. If Chad had been more observant, he would have heard the flatness in her voice. "They're at laser tag. Abba's with Betty."

Chad sat down heavily on the edge of his bunk. His breathing was fast. "The Gridians or the Alliance or whoever it is blew another dam." He took several slower breaths, then told her all he knew.

"But why . . . ?" When the Englewood Dam was blown up, Sharis had said she wasn't watching any more news.

"Scaring us. Frightening us." His speech was ragged and not quite coherent, and he seemed angry at her question. "Showing off their power." They are scaring you, Sharis thought, looking at her husband. Something clicked inside her, like a knob turning off the possibility of fear.

"I have some news, too," Sharis told Chad. "I streamed George and Gentia's week today, and George shot himself on Tuesday."

Chad looked at her uncomprehendingly. Sharis took her index finger and pointed it at her head. "I don't know how I'm going to edit it. Or even if I should. I don't know where Gentia is."

"George is dead?" Chad's voice was like a child's, high and curling.

Sharis nodded.

"He shot himself on camera?"

"In the kitchen." Sharis turned off the editon and folded down the screen. "No last words."

"Does Gentia know?"

"You see her arm and back come in on Friday, and then the camera gets turned off."

Chad said, "He talked to me. He worried about going to heaven." In front of his eyes he saw both Sharis sitting in front of him and George with the gun looking at the camera, but wavy lines overlaid both these images, as if he were looking through glass brick. "You watched this just now?"

"Five times. I wanted to be sure it was real. Why would he do that?" Sharis said. "Why would any person not want to stay alive? I mean, life is scary and menacing and you never know, but, a lot of the time, it's glorious." She looked at Chad, gestured toward her editon. "I do these lives, and I see people getting caught up in the stupidest things, and they don't, they don't . . ."

When Sharis was a child named Cheryl Mae, her father had a joke effect he called Making Himself Big. He started walking toward her normally, but then he hunched his shoulders and lifted his arms and pushed himself onto his tiptoes, and this, coupled with his drawing closer, made him indeed look huge, made him look like a monster. Chad at this moment was making himself big. "You are insane!" He yelled. "You are sick! You have no human feelings at all!"

Sharis looked up at Chad in wonder, amazed the trick still worked. "Of course I do," she said. Her voice sounded child-like now.

"Five times?" he shouted. "You watched George shoot himself five times? I don't even know you!"

"Of course you do," she said, her voice even smaller, and really, now she was afraid, not of herself or broken dams but of her husband.

"You don't even care!" Chad bellowed. "You watch someone die and the world falls apart and you don't even . . ."

"Why are you like this?" Sharis said, squirming. "Didn't you hear me?" She wanted this to end, for Chad to return to his normal self, for there to be exhaustion and remorse and a tender groping that would make them wish for their old big bed.

Instead the door to their room flew open, and there was Abba, hunched over, mouth open, her forehead slick with sweat. "I can't breathe," she gasped, heading for Sharis's chair, and Sharis leapt up so Abba didn't sit on her.

"Are you sick?" Chad asked. "What's wrong?"—and those question made Sharis start crying, because Abba was beyond sick: her skin was gray and her knuckles white and her eyes glittered with fear.

"Get help, Chad," Sharis said, pushing Abba upright in the chair.

"How?"

"Get the 'urge." Sharis placed herself directly in front of Abba, held her shoulders, looked her in the eye. "We're getting help for you, " Sharis said. "We'll do everything we can."

For once Abba wasn't talking, even though her eyes were open.

Don't die, Sharis was thinking. *If you die, we die.*

memorial day

"THIS IS THE first time I really feel threatened," Sharis muttered to Chad as they ate supper, Abba-less, the four of them clustered around the table in their dwelling. They'd carried out their loaded plates from the dining tent, dodging the 'urge and her minions. "I'm glad we brought dinner home."

Home, Chad thought with a flash of bitterness. Two and a half weeks here and we call it home. That's what the government and Marriott wanted, right? He burrowed in his mashed potatoes. But he would have used the same word.

They'd just gotten word that the Huffman Dam, an earthen dam across the Mad River, had also been exploded, but incompletely and not irreparably. "The Alliance can't be happy about this one," one of the newscasters said.

"Is Abba going to die?" Leon asked.

"No," Chad and Sharis said at once.

"EVERYTHING OKAY?" THE 'urge chirped at breakfast. Saturday, two days before Memorial Day.

The bridges were out, the dams were destroyed, they were sitting in a refugee camp awaiting the attack on their own city. Abba was in a hospital south of them, in Middletown. "Fine," Sharis said.

For the past weeks Sharis had been living in a perpetual present—she had lost control of her own life—and in an instant another moment would be propelled at her, as sudden and mysterious as a bird (she'd been watching them all week: the way they hurled through the air like packages, their feet uselessly dangling). I want to go home, she thought, remembering lying on the family room floor and gazing out the rectangle of window, the pillow's indentation cradling her head. "I miss my fuzzy afghan," Abba had said. "I miss the cushion on your toilet." Oh, Abba.

"Filled with water up to her eyeballs," the cheerful nurse on duty had said over the perc-feed. Heart failure, she explained. *Pulling through beautifully,* she said. Of course, Abba wouldn't be coming back to the Schoolhouse SafePlace. They'd find a bed for her in Cincinnati, in an Elderkind facility.

Only three weeks before, when they were still in their house, Sharis had been able to plan. Cabbage and tofu for supper. Dig out the last carrots from their root cellar. Finish the Schneiders by dinner. Make Howard explain long division. But now the future had been removed from her: the distant future by uncertainty, the daily future by Marriott, Inc. She heard people around them coping. They told fantastical stories, they gossiped, they entered into casual friendships and romances that blossomed into need. She supposed she could have escaped into the worlds of her editees, but their normal lives disgusted her. Lars was especially odious, prancing around his kitchen like the King of Norway. If she'd had more energy she would have edited them angrily, but as it was she did them in the simplest way possible, trusting they'd never work up the cruelty to fire her. Any money she earned now could sit and grow, she thought, buy them a new and bigger house in some new and distant city. It struck her that her mind was in a sort of hibernation, storing up for the burst of will and intelligence it would take, someday, to push her family back to normal life.

SUNDAY CHAD WAS sitting by himself after breakfast at one of the long tables of the dining tent, sipping on a cup of coffee, when the 'urge lifted a corner of the tent and came inside. All the camp inhabitants used the doors, but the staffers treated the tents quite casually. This morning the 'urge looked excited, as if, Chad thought bitterly, she'd just received a commendation. When she saw Chad she waved; for some reason, maybe Abba's illness, the 'urge seemed to take a special interest in the Gribbles. As she walked past Chad's table she hesitated, looked both ways, then sat down. "Wait till you hear this," she said. "Nenonene's dead."

"Dead? How can he be dead?"

The 'urge flashed Chad a look both quizzical and patient, as if she thought he understood life better. "He was flying from Cleveland to the Green House and his plane went down," she said. "They don't know what happened. We're not claiming responsibility. They're even thinking it could have been a missile shot from the Grid." The 'urge glanced at Chad's face to see if he understood this. "Like a coup," she said. "Don't tell anyone. It's not on the media yet. Well, it's on the media that a plane's down, but they're not saying it's Nenonene. But I got a message from a friend in Defense"—she tapped her wrist phone—"and he's definitely dead."

"But what will happen?" Chad said, and the instant he spoke this he regretted it, not for the question but for the way it was directed, because why the hell would the 'urge know, and why had he spoken as if she did?

"You know he's not their only leader. There's Colon, and Simon Pumphrey, and Chinua Digges. I've heard that Digges is the real brains. So it's not going to stop their war effort. But in terms of their morale . . ."

One man. Here they were living as refugees, with Cleveland for almost two years an occupied city, their country fighting for its very existence and way of life, and all this was because of one man. Chad was struck with a pang for the paltriness of his own life, where he reacted to events more than he made them, where even the country of his family had two rulers, where so little, so very little, depended on him. Even the 'urge (look at her)—silly, female, not much older than Sharis—had enough authority that Chad cringed at her approach. What was he? Where was his own dignity? He finished his conversation with the 'urge, thanked her for her information, walked back to Dwelling 12D and opened the door, and all eyes—this was unusual, every member of his nuclear family present—were upon him, their eyebrows raised as if they were asking *Now what?* Chad knew before she said them that the next words out of Sharis's mouth would be *Did you hear?* He knew that it was time for authority, reassurance, a single speaker speaking to a crowd.

Chad went to a bunk and sat down facing them. "I heard the news," he said, "and I heard from the 'urge that it's definite that Nenonene's dead, but what we need to remember is . . ." He said more, his chest filling with love for them and his mind awash with satisfaction, because he, one man, was saying the right things.

THE ESSLANDIANS HAD shot the plane down.

A difference in tactics. With the exception of Cleveland, everywhere Nenonene had conquered, he had gone first for the locals' hearts and minds. He followed this with ground troops. The resistance was always less than the existing government expected. The citizens were always happy (or at least relieved) to have the old government gone.

But Dayton hadn't been prepared well. Nenonene didn't have good people in the city. The Historical Society there, which he relied on, was less interested in the future than the past. So while Nenonene wanted to wait and watch before taking over the city, the Esslandians were hungry for action. Their sending their pilots in Alliance planes to knock out the bridges had been an independent action designed to force the Alliance's hand. The Alliance had believed that the pilots, at an airfield near the Green House, were trainees and not combatants. But after the pilots successfully knocked out the bridges, the Gridians had an upper hand. "We've got Dayton ready for you," the Gridians were saying to Nenonene. "Just come in from the north and the whole city's heading south. You'll have the nuclear plant. You'll have momentum." There had already been a massive exodus from the city; much of the populace, even before the SafePlace camps were up and running, was gone. "What more do you want?" the Esslandian president, Kyle Beerbower, demanded of Nenonene. "This dog's got its tongue out and it's showing you its belly."

Nenonene had no desire to destroy Dayton. He had agreed to the Esslandians' ideas about taking over the city, but largely as a means of convincing the Americans that God was on his side. He had hoped, once the flood subsided, to enter downtown Dayton in a Mustang car. He wanted people to greet him, to cheer.

The Esslandians wanted destruction. It was the only way, they said, to balance out what America had done to them. This was absurd, Nenonene pointed out: the land they loved, Esslandia itself, would never have become what it was without the demolition of its towns. To be frank, Nenonene said, the Esslandians should be grateful for the Gridding.

Reactionary, they called Nenonene. Deficient in will. Not interested in anything but retaining his own power. Africanist.

On top of that the Esslandians loved their plan, an idea they'd been working on for years. Germantz himself, before his death, had said that the concept was as elegant as a wheat stalk, one of his highest compliments. It wasn't particular to Dayton, but certain of Dayton's features made the city a perfect first target. The plan appealed to the Esslandians' sense of nature, to their very essness, in a way: the element that had made Dayton possible would be the thing to take it down.

So it wasn't really a missile, the Esslandian president told his advisors, that shot down Nenonene. It was something much more dangerous, a dream.

IT WAS AFTER 3 p.m. that Sunday when the 'urge walked out to meet the last group of arrivals. Above her crows and raptors were circling. The trees were tossing with a heady turbulence, as if a giant hand were batting them back and forth. The day, which had started out beautiful, was changing. The air was heavier, the wind warmer. Weather was coming in.

The arriving APCs crossed a grass field to stop in front of the central hospitality tent. The new entrance procedure—in place for the last week—was to acclimate the new guests with food and movies, then take them to their dwellings. The first guests had arrived sporadically and been basically tossed into their spaces, but the 'urge had seen right away that this led to guest insecurity, and it was she who thought up and implemented the new procedure. She liked the order of it. She liked standing in front of a crowd of a hundred and making each person feel at home. But today was different. A memorandum from the Feds said to expect as many as a thousand people in this "final evacuation." They recommended erecting all available tents, and canceling any staff days off for a week. They recommended disuse of the phrase "back home."

They don't think they can hold Dayton, the 'urge realized. They're worried that the city will be destroyed. Maybe it was the wind that made her see this, maybe it was the tossing trees. She was startled by the clarity of her vision: she wasn't accustomed to seeing things on a grand scale. Dayton was doomed. No one else realized, she thought. Not the large woman with the odd name (Ginja? Geranium?) destined for Dwelling 123F, raving about how she shouldn't be here because she was a widow who needed special protection and WHERE WAS THE PERSON IN CHARGE?; not the man quarreling with a sub-'urge about going back to get his car; not the girl who walked around cradling a disturbingly thin cat. These people each thought their tiny concerns mattered. Silly people, the 'urge thought, you're lucky to be here.

"Come on, folks!" the 'urge shouted. "Let's look happy! This is the best place you could be!" Several older men turned her way and smiled. People needed encouragement, the 'urge thought. They needed someone to show them how to behave. We'll sing while we're waiting for housekeeping, she thought, but the only song she could think of was "The Farmer in the Dell," which she hesitated to launch into because in the end the cheese stood alone. Instead she tried "God Bless America," which didn't get a big response. My God, the 'urge thought, wait until tomorrow. She would have to order extra ice cream in from Cincinnati, be sure every recreational venue was fully staffed.

They were eight miles due south of Dayton, over the Centerville hill. When the Alliance hit the city, the 'urge expected the drone of planes and the thunder of bombs. But all night long it was quiet except for rain. At one point the 'urge was half awakened by a series of muffled thuds, no louder than the sound of a fistfight in the dwelling next door. Still, when the 'urge got up a couple hours later and turned on her perc, she couldn't say she was astonished at the news.

CHAD ROLLED FROM his bunk and padded over to Sharis's. "Get up." He nudged her. A smell of bodies in the room. Amazing how adaptable humans are, Chad thought. "It's after ten." The breakfast buffet closed at 10:30, and if the boys didn't get a bite for breakfast they were miserable by lunch. Leon and Howard, at the top of the two bunks, moaned and buried their heads in their pillows. They slept in their clothes, so it was easy to get them ready for breakfast. Since they'd gotten here everyone slept in separate beds. The thought of sleeping in a heap here seemed impossible. Their scanty living space made each bed seem deliciously private and huge.

"Get up, get up, get up," Chad said. He unlocked and opened their door as the boys slid from their bunks.

"I'll check on Abba," Sharis said, reaching for her perc.

A crowd outside. The air was scrubbed and pleasant, the grass wet, and everyone seemed to be up and wandering. In the near distance Chad noticed a big group around the soccer field monitor, and beyond that a field filled with APCs. Usually the APCs were off on runs in the mornings, but today they were all parked. "What's going on?" he said to a large young man hurrying past him.

The man turned. "Flood's going to hit downtown Dayton," he grinned. He had a long brown beard, one gold front tooth and another tooth that was sickly gray. "They got real-time satellite photos. Everybody's watching it come it."

"A flood? Water?" Chad's mind halted, as if he'd opened and shut a door on an astonishing sight and was standing in the hallway making sense of it. *One of the most admired flood control systems in the world. Delegations traveled from as far away as China to see it.* "Wait a minute," Chad said, already knowing the answer, "there was that much rain?"

"Nope, not rain. Guess the Grid's sending all its water down their rivers."

Chad's mind halted again. Something familiar about this young man's voice. "Derk?" he said.

"Professor Gribble?" Derk's eyes widened. "You got . . . you look . . ."

"I know. I got old. Sharis looks the same, though. You got hairy."

Derk dropped his eyes in embarrassment. "My wife likes a beard. I'm sorry I never stopped by, we just got . . ."

"It's okay. Did you have your baby?"

"Yeah, Enola. She's great. What dwelling you guys in? I'll bring her by . . ."

Chad told him, then returned to the troubles at hand. "So Dayton's really flooding? That's terrible." Part of Chad was truly appalled; another part was thinking how the river was downtown, at least five miles from their house and much, much lower. Their house should be fine.

"Well"—Derk was still grinning—"at least no one's around. I mean, they got some troops there, but they're moving them back. And things dry out, you know? Even after a flood, things dry out."

If the streambed on Custard Lane overflowed, their house was at the top of the hill. Downtown could be inundated, there could be water up to the inner suburb of Oakwood, but Chad and Sharis's basement would stay dry.

Is this how people think? Chad thought. Is everyone else as selfish as I am?

"We're in Kettering, we're high," Derk said. "I think our place is fine, thank God."

WATER. EVERY FAUCET and hose in Esslandia turned on, every drain taking water to a pipe that ran into a bigger pipe that took it to a ditch along a road. Wells pumped almost dry. The floodgates of the big reservoirs by Village 49 and Village 131 opened to the south; the southern banks of Indian Lake and Lake St. Mary's blasted. The drainage ditches filled first, then the streams, and last the rivers. The water headed downstream toward Dayton, Dayton where the rivers meet, Dayton with its watery history.

Around three the next morning the first boatloads of Alliance and Esslandian troops arrived in Dayton, special forces troops armed with rifles and knives. They steered their crafts to the southern shores of the Greater Miami River and landed at Third Street (First and Second Streets were already underwater) and began moving through the night, carrying inflatable dinghies that proved quite useful. The troops slit the throats of two army guards at the old Salem Street Bridge site, overpowered and shot a group of marines holed up in a balcony of the Schuster Center (the lobby and theater were underwater), then rowed and walked up Main Street inspecting buildings. What little defense Dayton had—sentries stationed in and around buildings—fled. The water scared them more than the troops did. In twenty-four hours the Miami River had gone from a brown ribbon they hardly noticed to the dominant force in their lives, and it was still rising. The baby grand piano in the Women's Club banged against the first-floor ceiling. Squirrels and rats were paddling furiously, and dogs barked from window ledges and rooftops. Forever unclear if an American commander gave an order to withdraw. It didn't matter: a voice told these soldiers to leave.

The muffled thuds the 'urge had heard the night before were Alliance B-52s—ancient machines, obtained via Chinese middlemen—bombing either side of the Greater Miami River two miles downstream from downtown Dayton. The riverbanks collapsed into the riverbed, making central Dayton a clogged basin with its faucets still running.

The fall of Dayton took sixteen hours. By nightfall on Memorial Day, in a cruel finale, a singing troop of Esslandian women rode in on an old army Duck that had once been owned by Dayton Metroparks. The Duck was a World War II vehicle, designed to be a bus on the road and a motorboat on the river. The swollen waters of the Greater Miami were a bit much for the Duck, and its time in the river was short. By then the remains of the airplanes that had hit the bridges were washed downstream, the debris for the most part lodging at the impromptu dam that the B-52s had created, although one wing was carried south through Cincinnati and into the Ohio River to be found a week later jammed against a lock in Lawrenceburg, Indiana, a turtle basking on an aileron.

"OUR HOUSE SHOULD be fine," Chad told his family. "I hate to say it, but that's kind of the important thing."

"But, Daddy . . ." Howard started.

Chad said, "Our house should be fine."

don't shoot me

MEMORIAL DAY NIGHT, Chad and Sharis were awake until 2 a.m., sitting outside in their chairs watching the media on the giant screen over the soccer field.

A funny thing: all mornings were the same. As Chad unlocked and opened the door, the boys were moving in their bunks.

"I'll check on Abba," Sharis said, reaching for her perc.

A crowd outside. It was warmer today, and humid, the sort of morning that made Chad's mother announce that it was going to be a scorcher. Everyone seemed to be up and wandering. Chad headed for the soccer field monitor, and to his surprise found himself in step again with Derk. "Morning, Professor Gribble," Derk said cheerfully. Today he was carrying a can of paint and several brushes.

"We seem to have the same schedule," Chad said. "When did you get here?"

Derk, grinning maniacally, seemed oblivious to Chad's question. "You hear the news?" he said. Before Chad could shake his head, Derk burst out with what he knew. "We got back Dayton! We bombed the Alliance out of downtown and now we got troops heading north into the Grid and they're just rolling down the highway. Manganero on MediaOne thinks the Alliance and the Grid are gonna surrender in the next twenty-four hours. They'll have to." He winked. "We're burning their fields."

Chad thought he was dreaming. "I went to bed at 2 a.m.," he said. "They kept showing all those Grid women in that boat floating around Dayton."

"Yeah," Derk chortled. "On the Duck. Listen, those women are dead ducks now! You didn't hear the bombing? Lot of people didn't. They finished about eight. They had the fans on full blast all night, if you noticed." He nodded toward the monitor. "President Baxter's supposed to make a speech any minute." He lifted his paint can. "The 'urge wants me to do up some graffiti. She's got a special place for me to put it. I thought "God Bless America," what do you think?"

Before Chad could answer, the PA system crackled, and President Baxter's voice boomed through the camp. Derk set down his equipment and stood with his hand on his heart. My student, Chad thought. He hoped his other students had more intelligence that Derk did.

Some people kept their percs on twenty-four hours a day and had themselves beeped for significant news. Chad wondered if he should have done that. On the other hand, he and his family were rested.

" . . . a stunning success . . . We have met our objectives . . . while the loss of property is heavy, we are blessed with no loss of civilian American lives . . ."

Chad was suddenly aware of noises that sounded like gunshots. "What's that?" he said.

Derk burst into an even bigger grin, gold tooth flashing. "Guys at the reserve camp. Celebrating. You know. Cleaning out their firearms. The 'urge cleared it." The reserve camp was south of the SafePlace Camp, on the opposite side from the arriving trucks.

My God, Chad thought. It's almost over. We'll get back home. It seemed almost too easy. President Baxter was talking about strategic objectives and the healing of the country. The Gridians were valued members of the American family, President Baxter said; treatment of the insurrectionist Gridian leaders would be harsh, but the Gridian people would see justice tempered by mercy. Fourth of July, Chad was thinking. Independence Day, we'll be back home. My family should hear this, he thought, turning back toward his dwelling.

One of the boys was cringing, huddled beneath his cot, but the other was whizzing around the room like a bottle rocket, screaming. It took an instant for Chad to grasp that the hysterical boy was Leon.

"Leon," Chad said, "they're shooting into the air."

"Don't shoot me!" Leon was shouting, the fear in his voice so raw it infected Chad.

"Leon," Sharis said, "it's nothing. They're celebrating. Getting back Dayton is a big victory. You don't want to go back to our house and be ruled by the crazy Grid people, do you?" Her perc was on, and Chad realized she'd been listening to the president, too.

Odd that Chad didn't feel happier. They'd go back to their house, yes, but what else would they do? Would he still have a job? Would UD students from New Jersey or Florida make their return to Dayton? Nothing would be the same. Their grass would be too high to use the mower, the Hofmeisters would be mad about their awnings. Maybe the Hofmeisters wouldn't come back.

Chad told himself that none of this mattered. They were still a family, including Abba, whom they'd rescue from the Elderkind facility and take back to their house. He and Sharis had held out for normal life, and, in the most personal of senses, they had won.

But he couldn't really think about that now, with Leon screeching and scrambling on his hands and knees under the bunk. "Could you grab him for me, please?" Sharis said and Chad bent over and scooped Leon up, pried his fingers off the corner of the bed, and deposited him in Sharis's lap.

"I agree with you, Leon. I hate shooting," Sharis said, stroking his hair. Leon's residue of that day with the Webelos, she was thinking. She should give him a talk the way she'd talked to Howard.

"The soldiers are young bucks and buckettes," Chad said, nodding toward the noise. "It's a release. What the heck."

Sharis made a huff of disgust. "What about discipline? Isn't the military supposed to believe in discipline?" Ah, Sharis, Chad thought. My passionate girl.

"The 'urge cleared it," Chad said.

"I hate that stupid 'urge," Sharis said, gripping Leon tighter to her, but Chad didn't really hear his wife, being so caught up in the moment: the palpably quiet air now that Leon had stopped screaming; Baxter's winding up his speech with a statement that sounded like a prayer; Howard lying on his cot with his head tilted back, looking at the world upside down. A baby was crying somewhere on the far side of the tent, but outside their door people were intently listening, their heads bowed or tilted to one side. The speech ended, and after a moment their fellow SafePlace guests (Chad still recoiled at that term) erupted in laughter and conversation. Everything outside their rectangle of door was a glowing green; the smell of wet grass wafted through the doorway, and the shots, Chad realized, were almost finished, ammunition giving out or discipline kicking in.

"Come on," he said, feeling himself, his wife, their whole existence soften. "Let's go outside and see the great big world."

Leon shook his head ferociously.

"Come on."

"I can't carry him," Sharis said.

"I'll take him." Chad lifted Leon off Sharis's lap, his son's stiffening only momentary before he collapsed, spent, with his cheek on his father's shoulder. "Come on, Howard." Chad waggled his free hand.

"Is it safe?" Since they arrived here, Howard had spent 90 percent of his waking hours outside.

"Sure, it's safe. Everything's over. It's never been safer."

The whole camp seemed to be outside. Outside and milling, their clothes looking brighter and cleaner, their faces lit up the dark circles beneath their eyes somehow faded. Sharis walked beside Chad and Leon through the door of their dwelling, Howard scrambling to his feet behind them. Outside the sky was like a picture, blue with puffy clouds. Chad put his arm around Sharis and squeezed her ribs, the bones caving slightly beneath his fingers, and his first thought when she went limp was that he had hurt her, he didn't know his own strength, what kind of brute was he? Then he saw the hole in the top of her head and how it filled up like a magic thimble. The sight mesmerized him, and it took him an instant to realize the liquid in the hole was blood. The blood spilled into Sharis's dark hair. Leon shouldn't see this, Chad thought, loosening his grip so his son would slide to the ground. "Go inside!" he said, meaning to warn Leon and Howard, but other people outside—and they weren't really happy, he could see that now, the clusters of children and adults and adolescents (they break down the nuclear family in here, they do)—were turning toward him, their faces changing as they took in the limp wife and the blood running down her head and face, and within seconds it was a panic, no other word for it, people were diving into the tents, and Chad, when he thought back on it, remembered no particular person beyond his family, just the hurtling bodies and the screaming.

A stray bullet, fired in celebration. Infinitesimal, the media would say later of the odds. Tragic. Interviews with the offending reservists, the commanding officers, physicists who explained the trajectory of the bullet.

Chad lifted Sharis back through the doorway and put her on the ground. "Get further inside!" he said to Howard, who backed into the canvas wall. Leon was sobbing and clinging to his brother's leg. Sharis's face was very white, her eyes open. Chad was not sure she still existed. "I'm glad I married you," he said. She blinked. Oh, God, he thought, I haven't shaved for days. She had never liked his beard. He hoped desperately that he didn't look like Derk.

"Me too," she said. And then, as if her words might not be clear to him: "You." Her pupils got big and round, like drains forced open. He dropped himself on top of her, gently, and he lifted her and cradled her in his arms, but there was never an instant—despite what people thought—that he didn't understand that she was dead. He knew she was dead as soon as he saw her pupils widen, but accepting it took time. *I'm an adaptable person,* he was thinking, *I can cope, I will cope.* At the same time this new reality was too much for him. He saw that it would take days, weeks, months before he truly understood it. *My brain can only do so much.* Sharis's body was a comfort to him, the last bit of her he had. He wanted to cradle it. He didn't want to let it go. Later, the 'urge told him he'd been scary. Even the commands of the medical personnel and the stares of the gathering crowd and his own children and the blood spreading over his chest and arms and pants had not been enough to make him assent to have his wife taken away from him. Scary? he felt like shouting at the 'urge. Good! I wanted to be scary!

DIANA SAT IN front of her bank of monitors, mouth agape. Every station, it seemed, was showing the same footage, people screaming and running, a field clearing, and, in the distance, one man lifting something and carrying it into a tent. "Did you get that?" Her boss was yelling. "Did you see that? That would never have happened in a Red Cross camp!"

CHAD HAD HEARD once from Prem that the Gridians didn't bury their dead, but instead chopped them up and distributed them on the fields. "Gem of the day, huh, Prem?" Chad had responded, because Prem delighted in being a fount of gruesome knowledge. "It is true!" Prem squealed. "Absolute truth! Think of that when you eat your next potato"—aiming this dig at Ramsey, the ancient history specialist, who practiced a particularly righteous vegetarianism.

Chad wanted to do that for Sharis. He wanted to take her back to their old yard and let her feed her bulbs. She would love that. She would want that. Chad tried to explain this to the 'urge and the other officials, but everyone thought he was crazy. Someone appeared with an injection. "What is this?" Chad shouted, twisting to get free. "Is this Calmadol?" Thinking of Sharis and the night she had escaped the Gridding, how without a molecule of medication she'd been strong enough to watch. "I don't want—" he yelled, but by then the shot had taken hold.

"**WHAT DO YOU** think? They were bleeding the water system, and then the head of water disappears, and with her every bit of information. Of course she's alive. She's up there on the Grid eating corn fritters with maple syrup." The general licked his lips. "Wait till they catch her. She was friendly with that Ferrescu, who everyone knows . . ." The general bit off his words. "I can't believe the level of corruption in this town! You almost think: no wonder it got destroyed. Like Gomorrah or something. You familiar with Gomorrah?"

"No, sir." Twenty-eight hours after the final bombing, Grady had brought the general to a piece of remaining high land, a hill just south of town. Around them the ravaged landscape looked like a swamp of unthinkable size, the smoking remains of buildings dotting the water like rotted stumps. South, in the distance, was a broken line of fuzzy green. North there was nothing but brown and, above it, brown smoke from the Grid fires. Somewhere northeast the air force base remained intact, but the pilot couldn't make it out from here.

"Town that got destroyed by God in the Bible. Old Testament. Bad town."

Dayton wasn't Gomorrah, Grady thought. He wondered if victors always blamed a place's destruction on the place itself.

Probably even Gomorrah wasn't Gomorrah. The ground beneath their feet was littered with plastic bags and pieces of wood: Grady suspected this hill had started out as a landfill.

"You know what my father used to say?" The general said. "Sometimes you've got to spend money to save money. And sometimes you've got to destroy a place to save it." He brought a hand to his forehead. "Oh, God, do I have a headache. I think it's the smell. You notice that god-awful smell?"

Acrid and something else, something rotted and organic. Dead Alliance solders? Animals? Collapsed sewer lines? The dump beneath their feet? Everyone kept saying they had gotten all the natives out. *Casualty-averse.* That thing with the mother named after the movie star had been a freak accident, not a war casualty at all. Of course, President Baxter had said that no Americans had been killed during the munitions raid, either, but that was where Grady had seen the Face of War.

"What happened to your face, by the way?" the general said, turning, and for a second Grady thought he'd read his mind. "You didn't crash a Hellion, did you?"

"No, I . . ." but before Grady could finish the general was singing: "Putre-, putre-, putre-, putreFACtion. Putre-, putre- . . ."

He's a sick human being, Grady thought. The realization made him feel jostled and confused, as if he were trying to stand upright on a swaying train. Life was easier if you didn't think things. He remembered Rapunzel at the Green House, her blonde, soft bush and its sweet, clean smell. Impossible that the world could contain both this and that, and yet it did.

"WHERE ARE MY boys?" Chad said when he woke up. By then it was Saturday. "Where's Abba?"

Everyone was soothing. *They're fine, they're fine . . .*

"I want to go home," he said. "When do I get back to my house?"

They're fine, they're fine . . .

Sharis was slated for burial in Woodland Cemetery, Cincinnati's oldest and most historic graveyard. They'd been lucky to find a space there for her; Abba had consented.

"Cincinnati? What about Dayton? What about Davids Cemetery near our house?"

A mental health tech stepped in. "No one's going to be going back to Dayton for a while." Something about chemicals in the water, about the aquifer being contaminated. The Gridians had sent them tainted water.

The world could be terrible, Chad thought. Things happened that were random and vicious, and no virtue in the world could ever stand up to them. No virtue in the world except, perhaps, persistence.

I should have taught that, Chad thought. I should have had that in my course. He'd add it to the presentation, he thought—but then he realized Sharis would not be there to film him.

"We'd better get him on meds," the mental health tech was saying. "I don't see this guy handling the funeral bare."

AFTER THE DAM explosion, Tuuro was picked up by an army medic truck and taken to a hospital in Dayton. When he woke up they asked him his name. Theodore Simpkins, he said. In the last rush out of Dayton before the flooding Tuuro was placed in an ambulance and driven south through Cincinnati into Lexington, Kentucky. "I'm going the wrong way," he thought when the nurse told him they were crossing the Ohio River. But he had no choice.

In Lexington he managed to heal. The artificial skin took hold. It left him a slightly paler color on his back and face. He thought to himself that he no longer looked African.

He was released from the hospital to a convalescent center, and it was there, sitting in a flock of people in wheelchairs in the intake room, that he had his great opportunity.

"How many people today?" the doctor was saying. She was young, with long red hair and a face that veered between sympathy and impassivity, as if it were incompletely hardened. With the war over, a huge influx of refugees, some of them injured or sick, was swamping any outpost of the health care system within two hundred miles of the old Grid border. "You look simple, what's your name?" the doctor asked, pointing her finger at Tuuro.

"Bob White," Tuuro said.

"Bob White like the bird? You look pretty good, Mr. White. You don't look like you're drowning in medical complications. You basically healthy?" Tuuro nodded. "Cathy, grab his vitals and let's get him to a room."

"I don't see him on the list," Cathy said.

"What happened to you?" the doctor asked. "Where'd you come from?"

Tuuro told her in two sentences.

The doctor raised her eyebrows. "You lived through one of the dam explosions? Wowsa."

Tuuro nodded. "Lucky Bob," he said, and he did seem impossibly lucky, because his old kind self—*Tuuro, two u's*, and *I will bury you, my son*, and *Yes, General, I will help you*—had been hopelessly stupid and trusting, an embarrassment, and it amazed him that such a person had survived.

The doctor looked over Cathy's shoulder. "They may have forgotten him. Or mis-ID'ed him, like that woman yesterday."

Tuuro decided to push it. "They were calling me something like . . . Simpson? But I'm not Simpson."

Cathy said, "Here's a Simpkins."

"You're not Theodore Simpkins?" The doctor asked. "Hold on a minute." She pulled out her perc and typed something in. "It's not an absolute ID," she said. "He's got eye damage from the burn."

Craftiness would help him. That and anger, real or feigned, and the strength to keep resisting and *demand*.

"I am not Theodore Simpson!" Tuuro bellowed. "My name is Bob White!"

"Okay, Mr. White, calm down," the doctor said. "These things happen. You have to remember, lately there's been lots of confusion." She keyed the new name into her perc. "Get Mr. White to a room, Cathy." She patted Tauro on the shoulder. "Good luck to you. Be brave."

AFTER THE BOMBING of Dayton, the U.S. ground troops in trucks and tanks crossed the I-75 bridges and headed north, spreading out along the southernmost Grid roads and then fanning north in parallel. The fires they set behind them were methodical and limited, the Grid roads themselves being fire barriers. Their instructions were to evacuate the villages, and there were actually buses for that purpose, but in many villages there was resistance, and in Village 57, home to the former environmental engineer from Lindisfarne who had become the unofficial Grid (Esslandian) theologian, the troops discovered the entire population, including women and children, lying dead in a vast circle in a field.

You could try all you wanted, President Baxter said in his daily message, but you couldn't save people who were bent on their own destruction.

The army kept moving. The projection was that only 20 percent of the Grid would require alighting, but it was closer to 40 percent before the Esslandian president, in his bunker under the Green House, shot himself and his family, leaving the remaining Esslandian officials scrambling to ascertain the mechanism of surrender. Two more villages were destroyed before the Esslandians resorted to white sheets and pillowcases hung out of windows. With the Grid back in American hands and troops heading north, the Alliance pulled quickly out of Cleveland, and eventually all parties signed the Malmö (Sweden) Accord.

The ash from the Grid fires spread over the entire Midwest, the satellite photo of smoke and flames displacing in everyone's mind the previous image of green.

2071

not the end of the world

HOWARD AND LEON grew up and got married, Howard
to a woman who was fascinated by his story. Chad worried
that Howard was a sullen husband, but as the years passed
it became clear that Mella wouldn't leave him, that the adhe-
sive glamour of his tragedies stuck Mella to him too firmly to
pick off. Chad overheard Mella once at a picnic when Howard
stayed in the car. "I don't push him, I would never push him
after what's he's been through." As Mella spoke she had the
baby (Janeth) in one arm, and the bigger children (Howard
Jr., called How, and Katherine) clutching at her legs. She was
the household's wage earner, working as a repair crew super-
visor for Consort. Howard stayed home with the children,
grilling sandwiches for lunch and stringing cranberries and
popcorn for Christmas and making flash cards to use with
How, who was a slow reader. "You're a very active parent,"
Chad had told him once.

"Like you and Mom were," Howard said.

Like you and Mom were. A comment Chad remembered
as he lay in bed, wondering what his life had been good for.

Leon, in contrast, couldn't seem to keep a family. His first
wife was a beautiful woman of East Indian background with

whom he had a son. After she and Leon divorced she married another Indian, and Chad often wondered if her parents resented her lavish first wedding, involving imported foods and costumes and much strained goodwill. Leon's second wife had a stroke and six months later Leon left her, telling everyone he was planning to leave her anyway. His third wife, another beauty, abandoned Leon for a fireman after bearing Leon's second son.

Leon was witty and always seemed to have a crowd around him. He worked in global investments and made enormous amounts of money. He had gotten a corrective plate to fill the gap between his front teeth. To most people he appeared much more successful than his brother. Chad wasn't sure. He wondered if Leon was capable of living in peace. Chad worried that something in Leon's motor was broken and intrinsically dangerous. Leon gambled; he was always looking for a new vehicle or a more remote vacation spot or a better place to live. Howard's motor was slow to start and sputtered, but basically intact. It wouldn't rev up and fly off the boat like Leon's might.

Chad was thinking of boats because he, his wife, Howard and Mella and their children, along with Leon and both his sons were vacationing beside a lake in Tennessee, a TVA lake that had been created in the 1930s by flooding a valley and its two towns. This was the first group vacation they'd managed since Leon's adulthood; in the past, Leon's custody quarrels and travels had kept them incomplete. Chad and most of the crew were sitting on the porch of their cottage at a table overlooking the water when Leon mentioned, as he often did, his mother. "She planted all those bulbs, remember? She was a maniac for bulbs." Leon's glass of beer, like his forehead, was sweating. He lifted his head and squinted at something far out on the water—probably a female water-skier, Chad thought.

"Is he talking about Mrs. Sharis?" Janeth asked her mother. How they came up with that appellation Chad never knew.

"Yes, baby," Mella said, wrapping her arm around her youngest. "You should have seen her. She was really, really pretty." Of course she knew this from Howard, but also from old media images, still available on the Internet, that had popped up when Sharis was killed.

"She's with Jesus," Janeth said. Chad was always startled to hear his grandchildren talk about Jesus—that was Mella's influence—but life, he'd realized, was full of such surprises. Still, he was relieved to see his granddaughter Katherine's quick frown. Chad suspected that Katherine, like himself, didn't want a God to snuggle into. She and Chad both preferred a God that was grander.

Sharis *was* beautiful, Chad wanted to say. Beautiful and intelligent and tough. He ached to say this as a tribute, but he couldn't, because KayLynn, his former department secretary and new wife (not so new anymore; they'd been married over twenty-two years), might overhear him from inside the cottage. KayLynn had treated Chad's boys like her own and cooked and saved and steered Chad through faculty politics at three separate colleges; she was undoubtedly a woman of many virtues, but tolerance of Sharis was not among them. One day Chad's old photo chip, the one he'd brought from their house in the suburbs to the SafePlace camp, had simply disappeared. Chad was certain that KayLynn had disposed of it. At the time, Howard was having problems with school, Leon was flirting with dubious friends, Chad's department chair was being replaced, and perhaps all that stood between the family and chaos was KayLynn's tenacious grip on order. To KayLynn, Chad realized, his and KayLynn's marriage was the only marriage. If it was to continue, he must pretend he felt the same. So Chad did the husbandly thing. He pretended.

Persistence. That might indeed be, Chad thought, the only useful virtue. That and a certain generosity of spirit he always associated with Abba. "Think about it," she told Chad before she died. "That shot could easily have hit one of the boys. So Sharis saved them. I know you miss her, but it's not the end of the world."

It wasn't the end of the country, either. It was a new America now, a country that no longer cowed its neighbors. But still multiracial, still aggressive, still (the rest of the world laughed at this) optimistic. Old America, waving its plastic sword. Yet an American type of democracy had taken hold throughout South America and much of Africa, and other countries, especially China, found the American military game and often useful. The Chinese had even implemented, on the Yangtze, the water defense barrier plan the U.S. had been planning for the Mississippi.

Dayton itself had become famous in its destruction. Old issues of the *Dayton Daily News* were collector's items. A relative who'd lived there was, if not a status symbol, at least a reliable topic of conversation. And if he cared to mention Sharis in a public place, Chad would never have to buy a drink again.

"Mrs. Sharis was a pretty woman," Chad agreed, touching Janeth on the nose. "Like you." KayLynn could stand to hear that, he decided.

"She was glorious," Mella sighed.

Chad reached to touch his other granddaughter's nose, but Katherine predictably dodged his finger. Sharis, Chad thought, would have been more graceful with the grandchildren than he was. He winced to see his scrawny arm reaching over the table. He'd been a big man, once.

ONE MORNING WHEN Chris was twelve, Diana asked him to set out his piano books for his afternoon lesson. "I'll put them in my car," she said, because she would be picking him up from school. But once Chris left on the school bus, Diana couldn't find his music books anywhere. This was odd because Chris, for all his awkwardness and dubious grooming, was generally reliable. She got in her car and found the books placed on the passenger seat. At that moment she knew she had made the right decision.

No preselects. Just a random child.

Sometimes she would listen to other parents and worry that she rarely worried. The scrapes Chris (his full name was Charles Christopher) got into were always minor. He was working in a restaurant now as an apprentice chef and living by himself; a year before, after finishing college, he'd gotten himself a factory job and a room in a house full of youngies. She suspected he was a person who would keep testing life like this, randomly yet somehow methodically, until one day the world caught fire for him. She thought of Charles then, crouched over, eyes up, creeping his way toward a bit of bird-song. She couldn't identify any bird sounds anymore. Pity. Or not a pity: enough else in her mind.

Except to her son, Diana never mentioned Charles. And she'd spoken to no one, not even Chris, about her experiences during the war. She had her stock phrases. "It was a chaotic time." "People went through all sorts of things." She had trav-eled once to what used to be Dayton and tried to find the area that had been the nature center, but the bombing had destroyed the Stillwater riverbed, and a new and straighter channel had been laid down. Like me, Diana had thought. I'm flowing in a new channel, too.

Sometimes she wondered if Charles's death could have been prevented. Her and his hopeful stupidity was painful to recall, but there were worse flaws than being young and fool-ish. They weren't greedy. They cared about things bigger than themselves. They had tried to improve the world.

Diana worked as a counselor at a center for damaged women. She had started as an office person, then gotten training for client services. Clients could tell her anything. Scaldings re-ceived and given. What they really felt about their stepdads. Lusts. She didn't ask a lot of questions, didn't exhort people, didn't tell them they were better than they were. She simply heard them.

One peculiar comfort was that as she saw more and more preselects—and also, in smaller numbers, clones—she realized that they were normal people. They were only in the most limited ways distinct from other people. They were humans. They could still fall in love with the wrong person or wake up at night with dreams of drowning. It was madness—Diana had come to believe—to think that human beings were created equal, and yet they must be treated as if they were.

Once a woman who'd been the mother of one of the infamous Jeff clones came to Diana as a client. "I don't think I raised him right," the mother said of her son. "He was like a baby god to me. The real Jeff's parents didn't treat him like that." This woman's Jeff had been killed during the Grid takeover; the garage that he'd been hiding in collapsed. "You think the real Jeff would've let himself get killed?"

The Grid survivors, this woman told Diana, had yearly picnics. Many of them still ate in outside structures in the fall. A lot of them didn't like talking to non-Gridians. "You can tell right off if someone was part of it," the woman said. "Those summer nights up there? That was paradise." At that time there was a lot of media interest in a Jeff clone who had started up a church in Nebraska. "They watch him all the time, you know," the woman said. "Why's a country do that unless they're scared? And why are they scared if they're so right?"

"I talked to your president up there once," Diana offered as the woman left. "President Beerbower. He was very nice." The woman shot Diana a wide-eyed look and headed straight out the door. She never returned.

SO IS THERE any Dayton now, Zadie? "Zadie" was the Yiddish term for "grandpa," and what Chad had called his mother's father. "There's a plaque," Chad said, answering his granddaughter's question, "where the Mad River and the Miami River come together, and there's a museum nearby."

It was like the dying out of a family, the last heirs not reproducing, but still: the species lived on. "There are houses and parks and stores," Chad went on. "It's a town and it's where

Dayton was, but it's not Dayton." The name had been too freighted to be reused. "It's basically a town for people starting out. The developer was a man named Casey Bloom, so he called it Bloomville, but people like to call it Boom City."

The suburbs were still there, Chad could have told her. The Gribbles' old house was still there, although for ten years no one lived in it because of the time needed for decontamination. Chad left this out to make the story less confusing.

Years before, when Bloomville was first being constructed, Chad had paid a visit to the Dayton Memorial. In the museum were two early NCR cash registers and a replica of the Wright brothers' bicycle shop. The mementos struck Chad as an insult to the thriving hive that had been Dayton. He thought with a pang of the fake Indian villages he had visited in his youth.

Wilbur and Orville, honoring a promise they'd made to their father, flew together only once, in 1910. Two years later, sick with typhoid fever, Wilbur, the big brother, died. The brothers' father, the bishop, died in 1917. Orville stayed on in Dayton with his sister, Katharine, making his living as what biographers call an "aeronautical consultant," but his heady days were done. When Katharine at age fifty-four married an old college friend and moved to Kansas, Orville came perilously close to never forgiving her, although he did travel to be at her bedside when she died. Battles over patents, arguments with potential biographers, grouchy letters to the Smithsonian—these were the actions of a man protecting, not building, a legacy. Orville Wright was often spotted walking around Dayton, but he was proper and private and many people were afraid to say hello. In October of 1947 he collapsed running up the steps of the NCR main building. Employees at other buildings in the complex gathered at their windows for a bird's-eye view. That heart attack didn't kill him, but another one three months later did. In his will he left a large bequest to Oberlin College, his sister's alma mater.

Is it possible, Chad used to ask in his Dayton course, that to invent the airplane one person was not enough? Did Orville and Wilbur, by some mysterious combustion, together made a whole inventor? By 1901 they signed their checks "The Wright Brothers," with each of their initials by the name.

"Boom City," Janeth repeated, grinning. "Boom-Boom City." Chad wished that he were young again, standing at a mirror preparing for the bars of Boom-Boom City. As people aged, Chad thought, their words carried the past. A single sentence had its own long hall behind it, doors opening and closing, ghost people walking forward or away, a flickering vista out the window at the end. That was another way his grandchildren comforted him: the brilliant surfaceness of their speech, their sentences saying no more than they meant to say.

"I want to live in Boom-Boom City," Janeth said. "I want to live where Mrs. Sharis lived."

Glorious, Mella had said. Where had Chad heard that word?

A WOMAN CAME in, picked up a candy bar, tossed it on the counter with some bills. A splatter in the neatness of his shop. "Sorry, I don't take cash," Bob White said. His shop was in Newport, Kentucky, just across the river from Cincinnati.

The woman bit her lip and picked up her money. "All the Crescent Hill shops take cash," she said. Bob White sighed. He knew this woman's type. He'd had protestors in front of his shop less than a year before. He shouldn't sell beer. He shouldn't sell tobacco. He shouldn't sell those magazines. *SHAME, SHAME* read one of the signs.

"They don't have the clientele I'm dealing with," Bob White said, meeting her eyes. A fine, curvy, dark-skinned woman of medium height, her hair straightened and pulled back from her face.

The woman started to cry. "I'm your daughter, Daddy."

It took him a moment to form the words. "Lanita? You're Lanita?"

She nodded, sniffed, gave a little smile.

"Well, well," Tuuro said, and there was an echo in those words, an old man's voice, maybe a grandfather's. He wanted to walk around the counter and grab her, but such a move might frighten her away. "What brings you here?" he asked.

"My husband and I want to have a baby, and there's diabetes on his side, and the new research says the grandparents' genetics matter, too, so . . . I want your genetics. That's the reason."

"Is your mother well?"

"She's fine. She's got her house in Chattanooga, got her job."

Bob White felt as if a huge soap bubble had filled itself between them, iridescent and lovely but so fragile a hug or a touch or even a heavy breath could break it. He wanted desperately for that bubble to stay whole. Lanita. Never had he dreamed that she would walk into the store.

"What do you know about me?" he asked.

"I know everything," she said. "I know you changed your name." He waited with an aching hope, because that was not the thing he'd prayed for. "I know you didn't hurt that boy. I know that Nenonene used you. I know something happened up in Cleveland." Lanita's mouth twisted in a way Bob White recalled from years before. "I know you lived through that dam explosion."

"All that's true," he said. She knew a lot. If she could find out those things then the authorities could surely learn them, too, which must mean that the authorities didn't care. Had never cared.

"You look different," Lanita said.

"They didn't have skin quite my color."

"That's not what I mean. You look harder."

He made a helpless shrug.

She pulled a card out of her handbag. "If you'll call this number, they'll come and get the specimen. It won't cost you anything."

Do you work? He wanted to ask her. What is your husband like? Do you remember me from real life, or photos? Do you hate me? But there was that bubble, and he must not break it.

He nodded at the candy bar. "It's yours."

"You'll call that number?"

"I'll call today. What's your last name, now? So I can tell them?"

"Simpkins. Lanita Simpkins."

Bob White lifted his hand toward the candy bar. "Take it. Take it, honey."

He was not perfect, he was in many ways broken, and yet he had survived. In certain ways (his shelves of merchandise, his sparkling floor, the display in his front window) he had flourished.

Lanita turned without picking up the candy bar. Maybe she hadn't heard him. She said, "I told them if you call, you'll be Bob White." As she pushed open the door she looked back at him. "Remember three-minute eggs?" With that the bubble floated outside with her, luminous, intact.

THERE WAS A fan of the Boom City Bombers who sat alone above the dugout tunnel every home game, wrapped in a nimbus of silence. Julie had heard he'd been a Hopi Hellion pilot. She supposed she could have asked him about the war—her experience as 'an urge would have been an entree—but she doubted it was worth the effort. A divorce, bad kids, bad job: she could predict the stories. All blamed on the war somehow, the world's biggest excuse. Every game she said hello to him—being the Bombers promotion chief, she always greeted people—and moved on.

Julie was running for a seat on the Bloomville City Commission. She had fantasized about running for water commissioner, but then she learned that this wasn't an elected job. On top of this, Julie's original inspiration, the water commissioner her father liked so much, had ended up being a traitor.

Channel 7 had recently run a feature, "Secrets of Lila de B." It turned out that Lila de B. had been having an affair with one of the Grid leaders, a woman named Allyssa Banks. Channel

7 had found records of Lila visiting—twice—Allyssa's farm-house, and Internet usage records showed the two in regular contact. *The city of Dayton was destroyed not for money,* Channel 7 said, *but for love.* The clincher: new testing had found evidence of Allyssa's and Lila's bodies within feet of each other on what used to be the Grid. They'd been killed together during a strike on a munitions warehouse a few weeks before the flood. *The destruction of Dayton, plotted by these lovers, would take place in their absence.*

The Channel 7 special had a postscript: genetic material from a third person had been found near Lila's and Allyssa's. This material had been linked to a twelve-year-old girl Lila had been looking after while the girl's air force father worked in military intelligence. When Lila had fled to the Grid and Allyssa, she'd taken this girl with her. She and Allyssa were planning a life together including the stolen child. On camera, Channel 7 delivered this news to the girl's father, now almost seventy. He cried. For years he'd blamed himself, wondering what had happened to his daughter.

Julie felt a little sorry for Lila de B. Love could really mess up a good person. What troubled Julie was the twelve-year-old girl. What made Lila de B. think the Grid was any place for a child? Julie shivered at the thought of the Forces of Havoc and their handlers.

Julie was standing in the dugout tunnel when she heard two men talking above her. She glanced up. To her surprise, the ex-pilot was speaking. His copilot, he was saying, met a girl from Australia and moved there. The copilot now owned a chain of hair-coloring salons; any elegant woman in Australia, the man said, had a head of hair topped with a Grady-shade. And another Gradyshade for the lady area.

"What?" the listener answered. "How . . . ?"

"Bedroom Gradyshades, he calls it." Julie knew about Bedroom Gradyshades. A salon in Bloomville did them, and one of the umps had had hers done for her honeymoon. She loved it, but it cost too much to keep up. "All sorts of colors, too. Green, pink, rainbow. Want to hear the slogan? *Have some fun Down Under.*"

The listener was laughing. "Who thinks up these things?" he said.

"I flew with that guy three years," the pilot said. "I thought he was loco. But turns out he was brilliant."

A voice erupted over Julie's walkie-talkie. "There's a faucet dripping in women's restroom B. I got an elder going crazy here."

"Oh, God," Julie said. "Call maintenance and I'll get up there." Every elder in this town was a certified hydrophobe.

"WHERE'S KATHERINE?" CHAD asked, the lake at his feet in front of him.

He was a trial to them, he knew. Their Zadie who worried about everything, who was not nearly as much fun as Grandpa Max or Papa Kyle or Grandy Raj. But they took him seriously. For a moment the three children hesitated, turning their backs from Chad to look around. "There she is," Hemant said, pointing at his cousin.

Oh, you wonderful children. You children who will find what an old man needs.

"I see her now," Chad assured them. Katherine was standing behind a honeysuckle, rooting with a stick in the edge of the water.

She ees heeden behind the leafs, Chad thought, remembering his father at the bus stop. He started to say it: "She ees heeden . . ." But he couldn't keep going. Protect them, he prayed. But what generation is promised protection?

Little Janeth looked up at him, her face stricken. "Baba, are you all right?"

"I'm fine," Chad said, touching her cheek. Glorious. Sharis had said life was scary and awful but glorious, on the day that the Taylorsville Dam was blown and Abba got sick and

Sharis ran George's suicide on her editon. Glorious. In all his days since that one, Chad had forgotten that word.

He let his eyes move over his grandchildren, Hemant's grimy hands and Joe Mateus baseball jersey, the ragged part in Janelli's hair. Through the leaves, Katherine threw him a defiant glance. Protect them, he started again, but then he stopped himself. That was a coward's prayer. Better to wish for them the surprising virtues that he'd taught about in his Dayton course: skepticism, audacity, ambition, the sharp and dangerous virtues, the virtues that can change a world.

acknowledgments

THE FIRST NOTION of *Sharp and Dangerous Virtues* came to me one morning as I was driving home from the grocery store and had a vision of tanks moving down Whipp Road past the elementary school. This was in 1998. I'm not prone to seeing things, so I paid attention.

My primary resources for the "factual" parts of this book are *Ohio Water Firsts*, by Sherman L. Frost and Wayne S. Nichols, and *Grand Eccentrics*, by Mark Bernstein. I also, many years ago, had a helpful talk with Dayton historian Curt Dalton. Most recently I heard a few new Wright brothers stories unearthed by Nick Engler, head of the Wright Brothers Aeroplane Company (website: www.wright-brothers.org). I apologize for any inaccuracies in the book. I'm sure there are many, both in its portrayal of the past and (I hope!) in its imagining of the future.

I'm a native Ohioan. My husband and I moved to Dayton in 1988. I like this city very much. Certain people in Dayton have inspired me to enjoy life as it happens and to appreciate the place I live in. I often think with gratitude about Jack Kinsey (cookies and stories), Phyllis Heck (companionship, vitality, and stories), and the late Glenn Thompson (former editor of the *Dayton Journal-Herald* and a man who was instrumental in founding the county park district).

I send special thanks to my friend Jill Herman, who through many years and revisions encouraged to keep gnawing on this book.

Mostly I want to thank my family, whom I love.